Martyr

Martyr

RORY CLEMENTS

JOHN MURRAY

First published in Great Britain in 2009 by John Murray (Publishers)
An Hachette UK Company

2

© Rory Clements 2009

A CIP catalogue record for this title is available from the British Library

Hardback ISBN 978-1-84854-077-4
Trade paperback ISBN 978-1-84854-082-8

Typeset in Adobe Garamond by Servis Filmsetting Ltd, Stockport, Cheshire

Printed and bound by Clays Ltd, St Ives plc

John Murray policy is to use papers that are natural, renewable and recyclable products and made from wood grown in sustainable forests. The logging and manufacturing processes are expected to conform to the environmental regulations of the country of origin.

John Murray (Publishers)
338 Euston Road
London NW1 3BH

www.johnmurray.co.uk

To the memory of my father
who knew more than most about overcoming adversity

Chapter 1

ROSE DOWNIE SAT on the cold cobbles, cradling a swaddled baby that was not hers.

She leant her aching back against the wall of the imposing stone house, close to its arched oak door. Under any other circumstance nothing could have brought her near this building where baleful apprehension hung heavy in the air like the stink of tallow, but the man who lived here, Richard Topcliffe, was her last hope. She had been to the court of law but the justice had merely shaken his head dismissively and said that even had he believed her – which, he said, with a scowl, was as unlikely as apple blossom in November – there was nothing he could do for her.

The constable had been no more helpful. 'Mistress Downie,' he said, 'put the baby in a bag like a kitten and throw it in the Thames. What use is it alive? I promise you, in God's name, that I will not consider the killing a crime, but an act of mercy, and you shall never hear another word of the matter.'

Now, outside Topcliffe's house in the snow-flecked street, close by St Margaret's churchyard in Westminster, Rose sat and waited. She had knocked at the door once already, and it had been answered by a sturdy youth with a thin beard who had looked her up and down with distaste and told her to go away. She had refused and he closed the door in her face. The intense cold would have driven anyone else home to sit at the fireside wrapped in blankets, but Rose would not go until she had seen Topcliffe and begged him to help.

The bitter embers of sunlight dipped behind the edifices of St Margaret's and the Abbey and the cold grew deeper. Rose was fair, young, no more than seventeen, with a face that, in other times, sparkled with smiles. She shivered uncontrollably in her heavy gown and clutched the baby close to share what little warmth she had. Occasionally, she lifted out her large, well-formed breast to feed the infant; the milk was free-flowing and rich, and her need of relief was almost as insistent as the child's hunger. Steam rose in the icy winter air as the child sucked with ferocity, and she was thankful for it. Monstrous as she considered the baby, some instinct made her keep it and feed it. The day moved on into darkness, but she was as immovable as stone.

Chapter 2

JOHN SHAKESPEARE STAYED up late into the night and when, finally, he crept into bed he slept fitfully. Like all Englishmen in these terrible days he was fearful for the safety of his queen and country. At night these anxieties spilled out in dreams and he woke bathed in sweat.

Before dawn, he was out of bed, breakfasting alone at his long table. He was a tall man, six foot, but not powerfully built. His eyes were hooded and dark and carried the cares of the world in their depths. Only when he smiled, and that had been rare enough in these past few months, did he appear to shake off the worries that permanently clouded his face.

His maidservant, Jane, was bleary-eyed in her lawn coif and linen nightdress as she lit the fire. He liked to see her like that, unkempt, buxom and still warm from her bed, her breasts loose and swaying beneath the thin material. He guessed from the way she looked at him that she would receive him with warmth, energy and generosity, should he ever climb the stairs to her attic room and slip under the covers with her. But there would be a reckoning. Such nectar always came at a price, be it the parson's knock at the door demanding the banns be called or the wail of a babe no one wanted. And Shakespeare was too cautious a fox to be so snared.

Jane served him three small hen's eggs, boiled hard the way

he liked them, good manchet bread and salt butter, some Dutch cheese, common saffron cakes, which she had bought from the seller the day before, slices of spiced rump beef and a beaker of small beer. The room was lit by beeswax candles that guttered in the draught through the leaded window. This winter of early 1587 was cold and Shakespeare ate well to fill his belly and stir life into his limbs.

While Jane cleared away the remnants of the meal, he knelt briefly and said the Lord's Prayer. As always, he spoke the words by rote, but today he laid emphasis on 'Lead us not into temptation'. He was twenty-eight; time to be married. These feelings – urges – were too powerful and needed an outlet other than those to be found in the comfort of a single man's bed.

At first light his man, Boltfoot, was waiting for him in the panelled ante-room of the ancient house. He was talking with Jane but she scurried away to the kitchen as soon as Shakespeare entered. Shakespeare frowned; surely there was nothing between them? He shook his head dismissively. A young woman like Jane would never see anything in a grizzled former mariner with a club foot.

The building John Shakespeare called home was a handsome four-storey wood-frame house, which had creaked and moved and bent sideways with the passing of the years. At times he wondered whether it might fall about his ears, but it had lasted two hundred years so far and was conveniently close to Mr Secretary Walsingham's fine city house in Seething Lane. Though not large, it served as office and home.

'Is Slide here?'

'Two men, Mr Shakespeare,' Boltfoot said, in his habitual perfunctory manner. 'Slide and a constable.'

'I'll see Slide.'

Boltfoot Cooper was like an old oak, thought Shakespeare,

the sinews and raised veins of his face weathered and rutted like bark. He watched his servant as he turned towards the door, his body short and squat, the left foot heavy and dragging, as it had been since birth. He was in his early thirties, or so he believed: his mother had died of childbed fever and his father could not recall the year or month of his son's birth. Somewhere around 1554 seemed most likely.

'Wait. What does the constable want?'

Boltfoot stopped. 'Says there's been a murder.' His brusque voice, deepened by years of salt air in his time as a ship's cooper, revealed him to be from Devon.

'Just that? A murder? Why come to me? Why not fetch the justice or the tipstaff?' There was an unmistakable edge of irritation in Shakespeare's words. At times, these days, he felt as if he would seize up like rusted iron, that the pressure of responsibility laid on him by Walsingham was simply too great for one man.

'Says the woman killed looks high-born,' Boltfoot said. 'Soft hands. Says there are papers and strange letters, and the house where she was found was burnt down. He's scared.'

Shakespeare sighed in resignation. 'Tell him to wait while I see Slide.'

Harry Slide bowed low as he entered the ante-room, sweeping aside his sable-edged cape with extravagance and, as he rose, extending his fingers like the neck of a swan.

'All right, Slide. You're not at court now.'

'But I *am* in the presence of greatness, am I not? The magnificent Mr John Shakespeare. I have a hundred marks says you will be a minister of the crown before too long.'

'If you had a hundred marks, Harry, I doubt you would be here.'

Shakespeare eyed Slide's glittering clothes, his taut collar and stiff doublet with gold and black slashes in the Spanish style.

With such expensive tastes, it was hardly surprising he was always impoverished. 'So, what can you offer me?'

'I hear *everything*, as you know, Mr Shakespeare. Today I heard that the Archbishop of Canterbury was caught in the vestry on Sunday last with his cassock round his waist swiving a member of his flock.'

Shakespeare raised a disapproving eyebrow. Such irreverence could cost a man his life or, at the very least, his ears.

'Nothing very strange about that, you might think,' Slide continued, 'but the next day he had her for dinner with carrots and some garden mint.'

Shakespeare couldn't help laughing.

'At least she was a ewe, not a ram, so I suppose that's all right. Isn't it?' Slide said. 'I'm afraid I'm not sure of the teaching on such matters in the new church.'

Shakespeare laughed again. He was grateful to Slide for lightening his mood. There had been much darkness lately: plots against Her Majesty, a pending death sentence hanging over Mary, the Queen of Scots. 'You will get yourself hanged if you don't take care, Harry Slide.'

'Perhaps. But, for the present, could I interest you in the whereabouts of two priests of the Society of Jesus?'

Shakespeare suddenly paid attention. 'Two Jesuits? Garnet and Southwell?'

'The same.'

'Well, yes, of course, that would be a big catch. You have them?'

'As good as in the net, Mr Shakespeare.'

'Tell me more.'

Slide was a slender man with open features beneath fair locks. It was said he could charm eels out of rivers or bees from their hives. Even those he betrayed, and there were many, found it difficult to dislike him. 'I want a hundred marks for my information.'

Shakespeare knew he was dissembling, that he did not know as yet where the notorious Jesuits were hiding, but if anyone could find them it was Slide. He claimed to know what was going on everywhere in the capital and said he had at least one informer in every prison in London and Southwark. Shakespeare didn't doubt it. Slide had played a major part in exposing the recently foiled plot to murder Elizabeth and replace her on the throne with the Scots Queen. It was the Scots Queen who now seemed likely to have the shorter life, for she had shown herself to be up to her slender royal neck in the conspiracy against her cousin. Tried and condemned to death, Mary now awaited her fate in the bleak confines of Fotheringhay Castle in Northamptonshire. All that was needed was a stroke of Elizabeth's quill on the death warrant.

Mary's plight was in no small part thanks to Harry Slide for he had infiltrated the conspirators and followed their every move on behalf of Walsingham and Shakespeare. The guilty men – Babington, Ballard and the rest – never stood a chance. Their short lives had ended in torment and butchery at Lincoln's Inn Fields, hanged by the neck but not allowed to die, their bodies sliced open, entrails drawn from them, beating hearts tossed carelessly into the cauldron, then their carcasses quartered and spread about the capital. Finally, their heads were thrust on pikes and raised above London Bridge to warn other would-be traitors.

If Slide felt anything for these hapless, tragic men, whom he had come to know so well and whose friendship he had encouraged, he did not show it. He was an expert in the art of projection, feigning sympathy with a cause to draw its adherents to their doom. It might be impossible to trust Slide but, like a sharp kitchen knife that could slip and cut you, he was necessary. And, as far as Shakespeare was concerned, he was good company.

'You will have to tell me more before I can even *think* of parting with such a sum for a couple of Jesuits.'

'Well, I have sound knowledge that Southwell is living close by the city.'

'Where exactly?'

'I will know within forty-eight hours.'

'And Garnet?'

Slide grinned disarmingly and shrugged his well-padded shoulders. 'Garnet is not here, I think. Gone travelling among his flock of traitors in Norfolk, I believe.'

'Well, that halves the price to start with.'

'Mr Shakespeare, I have expenses . . .'

Shakespeare took his purse from his belt and removed two coins. 'You mean you have tailors, vintners and whores to keep happy. Gaming debts, too, I don't doubt. Three marks now and twenty-seven more if you bring me to the Jesuit.'

Slide took the coins and jingled them jauntily in his hand. 'You are a hard man, Mr Shakespeare.'

'Luckily for you, I'm not as hard as I might be, Harry, or you'd spend half your life in the pillory. But keep alert as always. We need intelligence.'

'Your will be done, O master . . .' Slide departed with another sweep of his expensive cape.

The constable could not have been more of a contrast as he bent low beneath the oak lintel of the door. He was big, with longbowman's arms that bulged through the woollen smock beneath his oxhide jerkin, yet he was shaking with something akin to terror. He smelt of fire.

Shakespeare called Jane to bring ale to calm the man's nerves and then the officer blurted out his story of a woman found murdered. Shakespeare listened intently. It was a grim tale and one that Walsingham would expect him to investigate without delay.

The three of them – Shakespeare, Boltfoot and the constable – took horse and rode through the busy morning streets up through the Bishop's Gate, beneath the piked heads of thieves and murderers.

Ten minutes later they arrived at Hog Lane, close to Shoreditch and just north of the theatres where the old Holywell Priory had stood before Great Henry pulled it down. Their horses stood in the cold winter air, steam rising from their flanks and hot breath shooting from their nostrils. In front of them was a burnt-out house. The depressing stench of soot and scorched straw hung round them. Blackened debris lay at the horses' hooves on the hard, icy earth.

Shakespeare huddled into his black bear cloak, a welcome gift from the New World presented to him by Walsingham at Christmas last. It was a generous gesture and typical of Walsingham in his dealings with those he loved or for whom he felt responsible. He had taken Shakespeare into his employment nine years earlier, when he was a young lawyer newly arrived in London from the Midlands. Shakespeare's master at Gray's Inn, Paul Ballater, was a friend of Walsingham and had recommended his pupil for the post, thinking him more suited to practical work than endless dry books. 'I see you looking out of the window when your mind should be on precedent law, John,' Ballater had said. 'Take my advice and go with Walsingham. You will find no better patron in all of England.' Shakespeare had seen the truth in this and had not hesitated in accepting the post. He had suffered few pangs of regret, though Walsingham – the world called him Mr Secretary – was an unbending driver of men.

The constable brought him back to the present. 'I believe the fire was set deliberate, Mr Shakespeare,' he said. 'When it caught, at midnight, the house and thatching suddenly went up into flames. I am told it was as if a taper had been put to powder, sir. George Stocker, the bellman, was here very quickly.'

'Where is he now?'

'At home not far away, sir, abed. He sleeps by day.'

'Fetch him.'

The burnt house stood on a row of a dozen or more frames that had clearly been thrown up quickly on three or four acres of uncultivated land. Shakespeare recognised it as part of the expansion outwards from London into what had been until recently open country to the north of the wall, past Spital Fields towards Ellyngton Ponds. The encroachment was everywhere. The ruined house had not been well built, but hastily erected by the landowner. Shakespeare guessed its purpose was to accommodate incomers from the shire counties; there was good money to be made providing lodging for skilled men who had any sort of work. London was growing fast, with men moving from all parts of the country and from over the water, either seeking wealth or escaping persecution in France or the never-ending war in the Spanish Netherlands. The city could no longer contain all those who would live there.

Under the eaves of the stabling near the house, four vagabonds, all men and sturdy beggars by the look of them, lay beneath woollen rags on the bitter ground, sleeping off a night of strong ale. They looked the sort of people no one wanted, the sort who could not get a bed without thieving the wherewithal, and then, most likely, swinging on the fatal tree at Tyburn for their trouble.

'Wake them, Boltfoot. But keep them here. I want to question them.'

Boltfoot dismounted from his horse and approached the gang. With his good foot he kicked them one by one in the ribs and pulled them to their feet, ordering them not to move on pain of a flogging. They stood stiffly in the cold but made little protest; the sight of Boltfoot's short-muzzled caliver slung round his back and the cutlass hanging loosely from his right hand was enough incentive to keep them standing obediently in their tatters, shivering.

The bellman, George Stocker, arrived with the constable from the direction of Shoreditch. He was still adjusting his smock, having been raised from his slumber, and his bell clanked as he walked. He was a well-fed man with a belly like a pig ready for the shambles.

'Tell Mr Shakespeare what happened, George,' the constable ordered.

Stocker removed his hat. His beard was thick and full of goose grease, and his brain was clearly as slow as only a bell-man's could be. He grunted some indecipherable greeting, then began his story. 'I did ring my bell hard and loud, sir, and called out. Folk came from their beds in the houses around, sir, and drew water from the well in pails. We did douse it quite quickly, sir.'

Stocker glanced at the constable, who nodded. 'Go on, George. Tell the master what you told me.'

'I did find . . . Sir, I do not know whether I should say this for it feels like a sin to talk of it.'

'I believe you found a body. Is that right?'

Stocker tensed and looked down at the rough earth beneath his paltry-shod feet. 'There was the body of a young woman, sir. Unclothed, sir. And most terrible dealt with.'

'And what else, bellman?'

'Papers, sir, with writing on, I know not what.'

'You can't read?' Shakespeare asked.

'No, sir.'

'And you, Constable? Can you read?'

'No, sir. Though my wife's brother knows some reading. Should I fetch him?'

Shakespeare ignored the question, slid from his grey mare and handed the reins to the constable. 'I shall go inside. Hold my horse and stay out here with them.' He nodded towards the beggars.

The neighbours had done a good job of dousing the fire; London was built largely of wood, and fires were frequent, so every husbandman had to be proficient at fetching and carrying pails to douse them. The walls of this house were still standing, though blackened. Shakespeare allowed the bellman to lead the way through the gaping hole where the door had been kicked in. He was conscious of the time. One of Walsingham's post riders had arrived late the previous evening saying Shakespeare was wanted at Barn Elms by midday on a matter of urgency. The Principal Secretary would not wait.

Shakespeare looked around the gloomy shell of the house. It was remarkably intact, given the ferocity of the fire described by the constable. Something caught his eye on the sodden floor. He picked it up. It was a paper, wet and unreadable. Then he saw that there were more papers lying around among the burnt stubble of thatching. Some bore distinguishable words and all were unfolded, which meant almost certainly they were new printed. He signalled to Boltfoot. 'Gather them all up.'

There were other things, too: type sorts for printing. But no sign of a press. 'All of it, Boltfoot, the type sorts, too. I will examine it later. Perhaps we can discover the letter foundry where it was made. Now, Mr Stocker, where is the body?'

Above them the roof was burnt away and the sky hung a brilliant grey where the ceiling should have been. A few flutterings of snow began to drift down.

The staircase was intact, though charred, and they ascended it to the first floor where, in a jettied chamber at the front, they found a woman's body, naked and bloody, stretched obscenely on a large oaken and canopied bed. A kite was pecking at her eyes but flew up through the skeleton of purlins and rafters as they approached. The bellman gripped his hat in his hands as if he would wring it dry, and averted his gaze. Shakespeare understood why he would wish to do so and why the constable had seemed so shaken.

Her throat had been slit until her head was almost separated from her body. The pink of the woman's skin had turned a ghastly blue and the blood a coagulated red, like dark rusted iron. Her head hung limply with a gaping wound like a second mouth, but that wasn't what caught the eye. It was her splayed legs and her woman's organs that commanded attention.

Her belly had been torn open and her womb exposed. A foetus, perhaps three inches long, had been pulled from her and lay above the wound, still attached by its cord. Shakespeare shuddered; its little head seemed perfectly formed. Pulling his eyes away from the tiny body, he approached the bed and examined the woman's face. Though twisted and contorted by her death agonies, he knew her features. He turned to the bellman. 'Leave us, Mr Stocker. Wait outside with the constable.'

The bellman needed no second bidding to leave this charnel house; he was gone like a hare from a hound.

'What do you make of it, Boltfoot?'

'Most profane, master.'

'Do you recognise her? She's a Howard. Lady Blanche Howard.' She was, in fact, as he knew well, a close cousin of the new Lord High Admiral and commander of the English Navy, Howard of Effingham. She had been brought up in his household when the plague took her parents. The Lord High Admiral was known to treat her as his own daughter.

'Yes, sir.'

For a few moments Shakespeare was silent. He looked closely at the body, then took in the surroundings. What had a woman like Blanche Howard, a cousin of the Queen, been doing in such a place? Though far from the worst sort of tenement, this house was a long way from the palaces and great country houses to which she had been born.

'This is a bad business, Boltfoot.'

Shakespeare had seen Blanche at court from time to time, and thought her to be about eighteen or nineteen. She had seemed typical of the younger women of the nobility who made their way to court and fluttered about like butterflies or attended the Queen's chamber until their parents made a match for them and they were consigned to their husbands' country estates. Were there rumours about her? Was she married or betrothed yet, and if not, why not? He thought he recalled hearing that she had fallen in with some of the more loose-living, wanton elements, but there was nothing unusual in that. The young ladies of the court were not known for their purity. Suddenly Shakespeare felt the cold of the morning through the thickness of his long fur cloak and doublet. He held out his gloved hand to Boltfoot, who passed him the papers he had gathered.

'Is that all of them?'

'I believe so, master.'

'Check again. And start a fire outside.'

Shakespeare shuffled through the papers. They were all the same, new printed. The scattering of type sorts seemed to suggest this had been the site of an unlicensed 'wagonback' press, an illegal printing works that could be transported relatively easily from hiding-place to hiding-place. It also seemed certain that whoever had been printing here had left in too much of a rush to gather up the remaining papers and type sorts. What kind of infamy had Blanche Howard found herself involved in? And, more importantly now, with *whom* had she been involved, and who had killed her?

He took the best preserved of the papers and held it away from his eyes under the snowy light. It was headed, 'God's

Vengeance on the Bastard Usurper'. After a short preamble it read:

> Whereas previously we have discussed the deceits, dissembling, lying, flattering, complots and secret practices of the said monstrous Earl of Leicester and his designs for the Crown of England, let us not neglect the wretched sins and wickedness of that same Virgin by which he would have succeeded in his foul and corrupt aims. Withal she had the pox, this great sovereign lady, daughter of the harlot Boleyn and murderer in heart of her father's true-born daughter, yet it was not God's visiting on her but a base man, with the aid of his complice, the self-same Mother Davis, of whom we have heard, that brought her abed. And a strange pox it was that swelled her belly and brought forth another bastard of her abominable line, wet-nursed by the sorceress Davis and brought to her majority in great secrecy . . .

Shakespeare shook his head dourly. 'That same virgin' was clearly the Queen. The curiously phrased tract seemed to suggest that she and Leicester, her favourite courtier, had had a child together. And that it had been suckled by the notorious – almost certainly fanciful – sorceress known as Mother Davis. It was a preposterous accusation, but certainly not the first time that such a publication had suggested the Queen had given birth secretly to Leicester's baby. The problem was, the more often such allegations appeared, the more they came to be believed by the gullible among the Queen's subjects. That was why it was necessary to stamp down so hard on these libels.

This was turning out to be a very bad day indeed. Shakespeare read on. There was more of the usual diatribe against Leicester with additional accusations against Walsingham and Archbishop Whitgift. Finally, it came to the Scots Queen, Mary. The threat in the paper was clear: should sentence of death be carried out on her, then the 'bastard usurper' – Elizabeth herself – would die, too. Shakespeare's jaw tightened.

Outside, Boltfoot had a fire going. The band of beggars shuffled closer under the watch of the constable to get some of its heat. Shakespeare emerged from the house and gazed at the bleak scene with a dispassionate eye. Those vagabonds were a sorry lot, but he couldn't take chances: they must be held until he had time to question them. One put up his hand and tried to say something. He was a tall, rangy man with bird's nest hair and a bright red jerkin that had seen better days.

'You will have your chance to speak later,' Shakespeare said curtly. He turned away to toss the libellous pamphlets on to the fire. He kept one, the least damaged by water, and thrust it into his doublet, along with a corner of a damaged one that was printed with a good sample of typefaces.

'Boltfoot, make sure all these burn so that nothing survives. Ensure no one reads any of it. Then go through the house again, every nook and cranny. If you find more of these papers, burn them. If you find anything else, hold it for me. Then enlist the constable, the bellman and any other respectable neighbours you might need. Get the body to the searcher of the dead at St Paul's and inform the coroner. Take the vagabonds under guard to Bridewell where you will have them put to work. It will do them good. Leave sixpence for their food. Also, enquire who owns this house. We will meet in Seething Lane at dusk.'

Boltfoot motioned towards the group of beggars, singling out the tallest, in the frayed red jerkin. 'Mr Shakespeare, that one says he would speak with you.'

'I know, Boltfoot, but he will have to wait. I must hasten to Barn Elms.'

Shakespeare remounted and was about to spur his horse towards Bishop's Gate when he heard the clump of hooves on hard earth. He turned and saw four horsemen approaching. He stopped. They came on fast, halting in a fury of stamping hooves, rearing, twisting necks and flying manes. Shakespeare recognised their leader instantly: Richard Topcliffe, the Queen's servant. He was appalled.

'What is here, Mr Shakespeare?' Topcliffe drew his horse alongside, so he and Shakespeare were face to face.

'A murder,' Shakespeare said slowly and deliberately. He fixed his eyes on Topcliffe's and held his gaze. 'It need not concern you.'

Topcliffe's brow clouded, like an approaching storm. 'I decide what concerns me, Shakespeare. The Queen's life and the security of her realm concern me, and anything pertaining to these matters. Answer me: who has been killed here?'

'You will find out in due course.'

Topcliffe was silent a moment, as if considering his response. Then he said slowly, 'Would you *cross* me, Shakespeare?' When Topcliffe spoke, in his distinct Lincolnshire tone, it was more like the growl of a wildcat from the menagerie at the Tower than a human voice.

Shakespeare breathed deeply. He and Topcliffe had clashed over the recent Babington conspiracy to murder the Queen. Some of the accused had ended up in Topcliffe's hands at the Tower. He had brought torture to bear and muddied the waters. Shakespeare, who had been deeply involved in breaking the plot, had wanted to interrogate them. He was convinced that more could have been elicited from the plotters by gentler means, including the names of other conspirators; Topcliffe, who had done his grisly work with the full authority of the Queen, had simply broken their bodies on the rack. When Shakespeare had protested, he and Topcliffe almost came to blows. Only the intercession of Walsingham had kept them apart. Now Shakespeare could smell Topcliffe's brutish animosity. It was a stench beyond sweat. Shakespeare held his ground. 'Speak with the Principal Secretary. I report to him, not to you.'

Topcliffe jumped from his horse. He was a man in his mid-fifties with the raw physical power of a fighting ban-dog. In his hand he carried a silver-tipped blackthorn stick, heavily weighted at the silver end like a cudgel. He strode two steps to Shakespeare's horse and casually wrenched him from the saddle.

Shakespeare sprawled on the ground and was dragged by his prized bear cloak like a sack of beet. He scrabbled with his feet against the hard ground as Topcliffe pulled him towards the house. Shakespeare gained a foothold and stumbled upright. Undeterred, Topcliffe reached out, took the nape of his neck and pulled him like a reluctant schoolboy, then stopped in his tracks.

Boltfoot had the slender, octagonal muzzle of his ornate caliver full in Topcliffe's face, primed and ready to fire.

Topcliffe weighed up the position for no more than two seconds, then laughed and let go of Shakespeare. He smacked the silver end of his blackthorn in the palm of his hand menacingly. 'I'll have you, John Shakespeare. I'll sup on your blood. And you, Boltfoot Cooper.' He left them and marched into the house.

Shakespeare was shaken. He dusted down his clothes. They were muddy and damaged, and he was angry. He followed Topcliffe through the doorway. Boltfoot stayed outside, his caliver levelled at the remainder of Topcliffe's band, all still mounted and looking very little concerned.

In the first-floor chamber, Topcliffe stared down at the corpse of Blanche Howard for a moment, then grasped her hair and lifted her head to get a closer look at her dead face.

'Who is she?'

'You'll find out when Mr Secretary or the Council sees fit to tell you.'

'The Council!' Topcliffe snorted with disdain and flung the near-severed head back on the bed. He turned to Shakespeare and rested his broad hands on his hips. 'If we waited on the Council, we would have a Spaniard for our sovereign.'

'I know what I must do, Topcliffe.'

'Do you? You are a boy trying to do a man's job, Shakespeare. And do you really think I don't know who she is? She's a Howard. Now, where are the papers?'

'Papers?'

'I am told there are papers here. Give them to me.'

'There were papers here, but not now. I have had them burnt.'

'All of them?'

'Yes, *all* of them, Topcliffe.' Shakespeare had to restrain himself from folding his arms tight round his chest where the paper was secreted.

'If I find you lie to me, I'll have your head, Shakespeare. I know your father's little secret. And are you any different? You say so – but so do many.'

Shakespeare's skin rose in bumps. 'You know nothing of my family, Topcliffe.' But clearly he did, and the words worried him.

He had entered the service of Walsingham believing that the new religion, this Church of England, was the *true* religion, that the Roman way, with its sale of relics, its superstition, its cruel Inquisition and burning of flesh, was the corruption. In his soul, he could only fight for this English version of Christianity if he believed in it utterly. And yet family loyalties tore at him: his father still clung to the old religion in private, breaking the recusancy laws by not attending the parish church on Sundays. Such knowledge, in the hands of Topcliffe, was like a charge of gunpowder in the hands of a child playing with flint and steel. It could go off at any moment, ruin his father and do little for his own prospects in the service of the Crown.

Topcliffe spat at Shakespeare's feet. 'I know what I know and you know that I know it. And I'll tell you this. The Howard business is Queen's business and I'll deal with it. I know what's happened here. Southwell, the Romish girl-boy, has done this. It's all his ilk know to do with a woman. I will find the Jesuit Robert Southwell, and then you shall see the murderer. I will hang, geld and bowel him myself. I will wash my face in the blood from his heart and there will be much merriment.'

Chapter 3

THE TIDE WAS still rising when Shakespeare reached the
steps just upstream of London Bridge. As he waited for a
tiltboat, taking precedence ahead of the bustling throng with
his cry of 'Queen's business', he thought of what Topcliffe had
said of his father and was unnerved again. Yes, his father had
been fined for recusancy and, yes, the old man did still hold to
the old ways; it had caused endless arguments between father
and eldest son and, finally, a rift that might now be irreparable.
Shakespeare felt an immense sadness. He still loved his father,
but thought him wrong-headed in his stubbornness and the
cause of unnecessary misery to his family.

Now Topcliffe was suggesting that the father's recusancy
might somehow reflect on the son. It was obvious to Shakespeare
how dangerous such words could be, when the merest hint of
popery could result in a midnight call from the pursuivants,
the feared band of heavily armed men who did the bidding of
government officers such as Topcliffe.

And what of Topcliffe's belief that the Jesuit Robert Southwell
was the killer? Yes, Southwell was a wanted man, probably the
most hunted in England, but did that make him a murderer?
Perhaps Topcliffe had information of which Shakespeare knew
nothing.

As he stepped into the tiltboat, the smell of the river was

rank: the incoming currents pushed up shit and rotting animal bodies from Deptford, Greenwich and beyond. But it was a good strong tide and it carried the boat speedily upriver on its swell towards Surrey and Barn Elms, country home of Sir Francis Walsingham.

Dismissed in characteristic fashion by Walsingham as 'my poor cottage', Barn Elms was in fact a fine manor house on a bend of the river, with extensive acreage, both gardens and farmland. In summer the soaring hundred-foot elms that had given the estate its name shadowed the house in fair dappled light, but now they were leafless and dark and hung like black crows over the land. The stabling was remarkable; almost seventy good-quality horses boxed in fine brick-built quarters that a working man would not have been ashamed to call home. Keeping the stables running smoothly was a full-time operation, with a master smithy and his apprentices working all hours to keep them shod, while servants fed, worked and groomed them. There were ten or more permanent post riders, cantering day and night with messages to and from Westminster, London, Greenwich and farther afield. This was the hub of Walsingham's intelligence network, which stretched to every capital of Europe and even to the bazaars and seraglios of the Turk.

By the time Walsingham received John Shakespeare in his office he had already heard of the death of Lady Blanche Howard and had sent word by messenger to court so that her family, the Privy Council and the Queen might know of the crime.

Walsingham's room was simple, with little furniture or ornamental plasterwork, reflecting his own austerity. This was a room for work and planning, full of books, letters and vellum parchments in piles and on shelves. In these papers, he stored information from all corners of the world, even the Indies and the heart of the Spanish colonies. Walsingham was privy to it all; he knew what each piece of correspondence and document contained and where it was amid the seeming chaos. He had two large oak tables, one of which was covered with maps and charts, some plundered from Spanish ships, others made by his own cartographers. The second table was clear, apart from his writing materials and quills.

Walsingham, dressed as always in dark, sober clothing and the most modest of ruffs, sat stiffly, plagued by his back and kidneys. He had a small silver cup at his side. He nodded at his chief intelligencer. 'This is bad, John.'

Shakespeare bowed low to him. He knew better than to ask after his master's health or indulge in other pleasantries. Instead he removed the paper from his doublet. 'There is worse, Mr Secretary.' He handed him the paper.

Walsingham read it quickly. 'Does anyone else know of this?'

'Not what it says, I think. The constable and bellman could not read. Topcliffe turned up. He had heard of it, but by then I had burnt the others and did not tell him of it.'

'Why not, John?'

'I considered it to be for you alone.'

Walsingham looked gravely at Shakespeare. His dark, molten eyes could see into men's secret corners. 'Your cloak is muddy and your clothes are torn. If you are not careful, you will be dressed as dully as I.'

Shakespeare laughed at Walsingham's typically self-deprecating humour. It was pointless dissembling: Mr Secretary always knew everything. 'I was pulled from my horse.'

'By Topcliffe?'

Shakespeare nodded.

'There is bad blood between you, John, and I will not tolerate it. The farm that is riven will fall into disarray, its crops will fail, its beasts sicken and die. We fight a common enemy. With the Spaniard beating at our door, threatening us with her ships out of Lisbon and Parma's armies out of the Low Countries, we have no time to fight one another.'

'I know that . . .'

'But you don't like each other's ways. Topcliffe thinks you weak. He doubts your commitment to the cause of Christ and England. You think him cruel. Well, I know he is wrong. I know that you are not weak, merely . . . *earnest*. But I say this to you, John: needs must in these times when we face a cruel enemy. Topcliffe is effective and the Queen honours and admires him and he *will* be allowed to go about his business in his own way. If you cross him it will be at your peril. As for your man with the caliver, I think he has made an enemy for life.'

Shakespeare smiled almost imperceptibly. 'I don't think that will cause Boltfoot Cooper many sleepless nights. A man who has gone round the world entire with Francis Drake and has fought and bested hunger, tempest and the Spaniard is unlikely to fear Richard Topcliffe.'

Walsingham's voice did not rise, but the tone stiffened. 'Perhaps not. But you will take care to obey my wishes. Answer me this, John. Why do you think I chose you as my assistant secretary and chief intelligencer?'

'Sometimes, I confess, I wonder.'

'I chose you, John, because I saw something of myself in you. Not that we are the same. You have less . . . *rigour* in religious matters. But you are diligent, John, you are loyal. And, most importantly, you worry. It is your anxiety – *our* anxiety – that leads us to take care of the detail of the work we do. And it is the detail that will achieve results. This is not a task for those who think to solve matters of state with an impassioned speech and a grand gesture. We must toil in the dark, like moles. Each inch of the way through the tunnel will be torment to you,

John. If it is not, then I have misjudged you. And remember this always: what we fight for is *worth* fighting for. The enemy would destroy everything we both believe in.'

Shakespeare was left in no doubt as to the serious purpose of what Walsingham said. He bowed low once more to the Principal Secretary of State in acknowledgement. 'I understand, Mr Secretary. But I must protest that I have never disagreed with *your* methods. I realise that when the security of our sovereign and realm are at stake then extreme measures are necessary. And if that includes torment of the body to obtain information, then so be it. But I cannot stomach a man who breaks men – and women, at times – for pleasure.'

Walsingham silenced him with an angry wave. 'Enough. I will hear no more of your feelings on the subject of Mr Topcliffe.' He signalled for Shakespeare to sit and his voice eased. 'There is more, John. I wish I had endless funds to hire an army of true Englishmen to fight this war of secrets, but these are straitened times and we must live within our means. You will continue your enquiries into the affair of Blanche Howard. I fear that far more is at stake here than the death of one woman. Discover her familiars. Had she turned Papist? Who has done this to her and why? What is the meaning of the text and who was behind it? Jesuits? Involve Slide more. Use his network. He owes his neck to me and he'll likely know who's behind this. Find Robert Southwell, too. He is dangerous. Is he responsible for the death of Blanche Howard? I hear Topcliffe thinks so. It would not be the first time a Southwell helped do away with a Howard. Did not this Southwell's father, Sir Richard, come forward as chief accuser against Henry Howard, Earl of Surrey, and bring him to his death? There is no love between these families, John.'

'But this is different.'

'Is it? Let us find out, shall we. Within weeks, God willing, the Scots devil will lose her head and then we shall see a reaction.

Then the powder will ignite. We must be prepared. Every scrap of intelligence, every disloyal word in the ordinaries and inns of London and beyond must be scrutinised. There must be no more attempts on the life of our sovereign majesty.'

Shakespeare felt his stomach knotting like cable round a capstan. At times it felt as if the whole future of Elizabeth and her subjects rested on his shoulders alone. How could he, one man, stand against the threat of the so-called Enterprise of England – Philip of Spain's growing armada of ships now being assembled to invade the country and destroy the Queen?

The enemy was everywhere: London and the counties seemed to be awash with priests sent from the seminaries and colleges of Rome, Rheims and Douai. Their aim? Sedition, insurrection and the perversion of men's souls. The common-or-garden priests were a poor lot. It was the Jesuits, disciplined and determined though few in number, who threatened the stability of the realm: the devil's army of the counter-reformation.

'There is another matter, John,' Walsingham continued, his voice quiet, as if the walls would hear him. 'That of Sir Francis Drake.'

'What of him?'

Walsingham sipped sweet Rhenish from his small silver cup. His face was half in shadow in the weak, wintry light. There was a fire in the hearth, a single small log glowing without enthusiasm; it did little to dispel the chill. He rose and fetched a paper from a pile near one of the tables, and handed it to Shakespeare, who saw instantly that it was encrypted in a Spanish code.

'Berden waylaid that in Paris. It was on its way from Mendoza to the Spanish King.'

Shakespeare was aware that any communication between Mendoza, the Spanish ambassador to Paris, and King Philip was of extreme importance. No one had done more to undermine Elizabeth and the English state than Don Bernardino de Mendoza; he had been expelled from England three years earlier for his endless conspiracies, and even as he left under armed guard, he had turned to one of the Council and told him he would return as a conqueror. As for Berden, Shakespeare knew of him as one of Walsingham's top intelligencers in the field. There would be no reason to doubt the authenticity of this intercept.

'I assume you have had it deciphered?'

'It is a subject close to your own heart, John. Phelippes has broken the code and finds this message: "The dragon slayer has been despatched to England." It goes on to ask for funds of seventy thousand ducats to be made available in the event of a successful outcome. This note is a warrant for murder, John. It tells us an assassin has been sent to England to kill Drake. We have no way of knowing when he was sent, how long he has been here or how far his plans are advanced. But there is no question as to the import of the message and the seriousness of the position.'

Shakespeare nodded assent. He knew that Thomas Phelippes, Walsingham's cipher expert, would not have made an error in discovering the meaning of such a paper. It was his breaking of the Queen of Scots's intricate code that had convicted her of treason. And now, if this encoded message was to be believed, a killer had been contracted to murder Sir Francis Drake. All Spaniards feared Drake and called him 'El Draque', meaning Dragon. His title was Vice-Admiral of England and yet his repute far exceeded mere titles. In a country of superb mariners – Walter Ralegh, Martin Frobisher, Thomas Cavendish, Humphrey Gilbert, Richard Grenville, John Hawkins and Howard of Effingham – Drake was peerless. And he was driven by hatred of the Spanish. It was a loathing born of the cruelties meted out to his friends and comrades-at-arms long ago, in 1568, when they were taken by the Inquisition at the débâcle of San Juan d'Ulúa in the New World. The names of those men still gnawed at Drake's soul and he thought of them often: fellow Devonian Robert Barrett, burnt to death in the *auto-da-fé* at Seville; William Orlando, dead in the same town while festering in a dungeon; Michael Morgan, tortured, whipped almost to death, then put to the oars as a galley slave; George Ribley of Gravesend, garrotted and his body burnt at the stake. This was what infused Drake with feral courage and kept hot his bitter enmity for the Spaniard. It was a hatred that had been fuelled by every Spanish outrage that occurred: the 1572 massacre of men, women and children in the Dutch town of Naarden; the slaughter, rape and sacking of Antwerp. These events had seared themselves into Drake's memory and kept his rage burning like molten iron. His enmity was returned in kind by King Philip II, who had long since decided that Drake must die.

As a junior intelligencer in Walsingham's service five years earlier, Shakespeare had helped to break another Spanish plot against Drake. The money offered to kill him then was twenty thousand ducats. Shakespeare had worked to identify the con-spirators. It was a simple and amateurish plot: Pedro de Zubiaur, the Spanish agent in London, had recruited a merchant named Patrick Mason to persuade an old enemy of Drake's to kill him. This enemy was named John Doughty, the vengeful half-brother of Thomas Doughty who had been executed before his very eyes by Drake on his round-world voyage. A little judicial torture and Mason had named names. As far as Shakespeare knew, Doughty was still rotting in the Marshalsea prison.

And now King Philip was raising the stakes. Seventy thou-sand ducats would tempt desperate men.

Walsingham continued: 'Philip plods with feet of lead across the world's great stage. It is easy to make merry at his expense when he complains like a girl-child about Drake, Hawkins and the rest plundering his treasure. But though he plods, he has weight behind him, thanks to his riches from the New World. And he can crush. I would say that, at sea, my good friend Drake is more likely to die of scurvy than fall to the sword or pistol of a hired killer, but now that he is on land, fitting and supplying the fleets in the reaches of the Thames, he is an easy target. In the shipyards by day he is vulnerable, John, and at court by night with his wife, he can scarcely be safer. He's in danger, just when we need him most. Santa Cruz, King Philip's admiral, is like to sail with his fleet this spring or summer. My spies tell me he conspires to meet the Duke of Parma's armies in the lowlands and protect them as they cross the sea to England. With Drake out of the way, their passage would be a thousand times easier.'

Shakespeare hesitated. Everything he knew of Drake suggested he would not need anyone's help to survive. 'Surely Drake will look after himself,' he said at last.

'Will he, John? At sea, yes, of course. But on land, in the teeming shipyards, full of foreigners of every hue and creed? Who will spot one man with an arquebus or crossbow among the hundreds at work? Drake needs protection – and you will provide it.'

Shakespeare ran a finger around his ruff. He felt hot, despite the lack of warmth in this cheerless room. 'And Lady Blanche Howard?'

'And Lady Blanche. And all your other duties. We are all stretched like bowstrings. Anyway, it seems to me you have the perfect servant to assign to Drake in your former sailor, Mr Boltfoot Cooper. I believe he already knows Sir Francis well.'

Shakespeare almost laughed. There was nothing to be gained from arguing. Walsingham must know that Boltfoot had parted on bad terms with Drake, having protested that he had been cheated of his fair share of the colossal plunder taken aboard the *Golden Hind* from the Spanish treasure ship *Cacafuego*. He had also said that after three years at sea in Drake's company he would never board a ship again, and certainly not one of Drake's. No, Boltfoot would not be happy to be in the Dragon's company once more.

Chapter 4

Night had come and gone when Rose Downie was startled awake. Topcliffe was standing over her, prodding at her with his blackthorn. She scrabbled to her feet, heart pounding. Her hands were stiff with cold, clutching the baby. The child chose that moment to wail. Its piercing, monotonous cry, like the howl of a cat, sent shivers down her spine, but Topcliffe merely smiled.

'Is it baptised in our church?' he asked, and touched the strange face with its curious, unhuman eyes.

Rose felt fear in her heart but she needed this man. Her friend had told her that he knew everything about everyone in the city, that he would help her as he had helped others, but that he would demand much in return. 'My own child was baptised, sir, by the Bishop of London himself, but this is not my baby.'

'Then you have stolen this one.'

'No, sir, mine has been stolen. This . . . *creature* was left in its place.'

'Let me see its face by the light.' Topcliffe bent towards the face of the child in the gloom. He pulled back the swaddling bands from its head and gazed intently at it. Its face was small and round, its eyes spaced widely. Too widely. There seemed to be no chin to speak of and the ears were curiously low. Any mother, Topcliffe thought, would want to disown such a thing.

'Come in with me. My boy Nicholas tells me you have had a long vigil here. I'll beat his arse raw for leaving you out in weather like this.' He pushed back the oak door to his home. Rose hesitated, fearing to enter. The hallway was lit by the flame from a candle that cast strange shadows in the breeze from the open door. She stepped forward into the unholy gloom.

On a dark-stained coffer lay a large, gilt-bound book, which, though she could not read, she recognised as a Bible. Topcliffe took her right hand from the baby and held it down hard on the book, as if to ensure solid contact. 'Do you swear by Almighty God that the baby you are holding is not yours?'

Rose felt colder inside the house than she had outside in the winter wind. There were strange smells in this place, the chill and smell of a slaughterhouse. It brought to mind the shambles of Newgate Street where she would go to buy meat for the household. 'I do swear, sir, it is not my baby. My baby, William Edmund Downie, has been taken from me. Please help me, sir. I believe that only you can.'

'Where is your husband, Mistress Downie?'

'He died, sir. He was out with the train-band at Mile End Green by Clement's Inn after church a month past and his hagbut did explode.'

Topcliffe touched her arm with seeming compassion. His hand remained there, keeping her close to him. 'I am sorry to hear that, Mistress Downie. England has need of such men. Such a thing should not befall a pretty wife.'

Tears welled in Rose's eyes at the memory but she refused to weep. She had been heavy with child and he was late home from practising with his arquebus and wielding his pike. He, like thousands of other good men, had been doing his duty, she knew, training week after week in the open countryside or within the brick walls of Artillery Yard. He had volunteered for service in the Carpenters Company contingent. It was men like her husband who would stop the Spaniard. That day she had waited for him on the road, but instead of his jaunty step and broad smile coming towards her, she saw six other members of the train-band approaching, pulling a handcart with what, at first, she took to be a dead animal. Then she saw it was her husband's bloody remains and collapsed in a faint. Later, they told her his arquebus had misfired and exploded in pieces, ripping open his throat. They had been wed less than a year, by the Bishop who would later baptise their child. Her husband's name was Edmund and she called him Mund. He was such a fine man, a yeoman carpenter with shoulders as wide as his smile. On the day of their wedding, they had scarcely been able to wait for the Bishop to give his blessing before retiring to their room to tear the clothes from each other's backs. When he died, she had felt her life was over. She hungered each night for his body over hers. But instead of the joy of him she had nothing but tears. And then the baby came a week later and she began to find a little life again. He was a boy and he was perfect in every way. His name was William Edmund, but she called him Mund, like his father. He would be the new man in her life.

'Come further into my home,' Topcliffe said, his arm moving round her shoulders, 'and have a draught of beer, for you must have a thirst to slake.'

If she had been asked to tread through the portals of hell, she could not have been more scared, yet she could not say no to this man. She knew his repute as a brute, but she also knew he had power. Her friend Ellie May from the market had told her she must go to him, for he could see into souls and was privy to dark secrets that no one else could know.

In his teeth, stained mottled amber, Topcliffe clenched a long wooden stick, which he drew on every now and then and blew out smoke. She looked at it, astonished, as if he were breathing sulfur from the fires of Satan, for she had never seen such a thing. He laughed at her bewilderment. 'It is a pipe of sotweed, from the New World.' He called in a servant to bring drink, then another to stoke the fire in the hearth and – as the man crouched to the grate with bellows and logs – cursed him for letting it go so low.

He asked her questions. How she survived, where she lived. She told him she was a malkin, a kitchen drudge, in the buttery of a great lady. She had left her service when she married Edmund, but on his death she had been received back into the household in her old serving post.

As she talked, Topcliffe smiled at her with his hard, dark teeth. Eventually he put down the sotweed pipe. 'Well, Rose, I should like to help you if I can. We must find the mother of this changeling.'

He drew her to him. 'We must look after Her Majesty's subjects, must we not? Especially the widow of a fine young man who died for his sovereign. Tell me, Rose, where was your baby stolen?'

She recalled the day precisely. It was a week past, when the child was just twelve days old. She had gone to the market for cheese and salt pork. The baby was swaddled and she held him in her arms. But there was a disagreement with the stallholder and she had put him down for just a moment because her arms were full of groceries and she was counting out the farthings to pay for them. The argument became heated and the short moment of leaving little Mund in a basket by the stall became a minute or two. She was still angry when she went to pick him up, but then her anger turned to horror, for her baby was no longer there. In his place was this monster, this creature, this devil's spawn.

'Well, we must find little William Edmund,' Topcliffe said at last. 'But, first, let us become better acquainted, Rose.'

His arm was strong round her now, and he pulled her down.

She did not resist, as if she had half expected this as part of the price. In one movement, he lifted her kirtle and smock, turned her with a strength she could not defy and, without a word, entered her with the casual indifference that a bull takes a cow.

Chapter 5

IN THE CRYPT of St Paul's, the Searcher of the Dead stood in his bloodstained apron over the unclothed carcass of Lady Blanche Howard. For a long while he was silent. With his strong hands he moved her poor head this way and that with practised gentleness, examining her wounds; he did the same with her paps and with her woman's parts; he held up the scarce-formed baby, still attached to her womb by its cord, and looked at it from all sides. He ran his fingers through the woman's flaxen hair and he explored the pits of her arms, the backs of her legs and the soles of her feet.

The stone walls of the crypt glistened with trickles of water. The Searcher parted the legs of the cold body and examined further. He removed objects and put them to one side dispassionately. He moved his face near the fair V of her womanhood and sniffed.

Shakespeare stood back and watched. The Searcher, Joshua Peace, was so intent on his work that he seemed unaware of his presence. He liked Peace: he was a man of knowledge, like himself, the type of man to shape the new England now they were almost rid of the superstitions of the Roman church. Above them, in the nave of the great cathedral, the throngs of people went about their business, dealing, conspiring, laughing, fighting, robbing each other or simply passing the time of day. But down here the only sound was the shuffling of soft leather soles on stone and the occasional drip of water from the walls and ceiling.

Peace was of indeterminate age, perhaps late thirties, but he seemed younger. He was slim but strong and his head was bald on top, like a monk's tonsure. He sniffed some more, around her mouth and nostrils, then stood back from his work and met the eye of John Shakespeare. 'There is the smell of fire on her, and also the lust of a man,' he said. 'And not just that, Mr Shakespeare. There is the three-day smell of death.'

'Three days?'

'Yes. Three days at this time of year, the same as a day and a half in summer. Where did you find her?'

'In a house that had been burnt out, towards Shoreditch.'

'Well, that explains the scent of fire. From the smell of her skin and mouth, I can detect no poison. I take the cause of death to be the slash of a butcher's blade or some such to the throat. Tell me, was there a great deal of blood around the body?'

Shakespeare thought back to the horror of the scene he had encountered, then shook his head, surprised. 'No. She was on a bed and there was staining on the sheets, but very little.'

'Then she was killed somewhere else, or in another part of the house, and taken there. She would have lost much blood with these injuries.' The Searcher held up the objects he had taken from the body: a piece of bone and a silver crucifix. 'These were inside her, thrust in most unkindly. I think the bone is a relic, a monkey's bone passed off as the finger of a saint for all I know.'

'What was it doing there?'

'You will have to ask her killer that, Mr Shakespeare. All I can tell you is that the girl was about eighteen, certainly no older, and in good health. As for the child, it was twelve weeks gone, a boy. From the spread of blood about her person, I feel certain that the wound which ripped it from her belly was inflicted after death, which may be some small comfort to her family.'

Peace pushed his arms underneath the body and lifted it so that the bare back was visible. 'Look at this, Mr Shakespeare.'

Shakespeare moved closer. Her slender back, from nape to hip, had two red raw lines in the shape of a cross. He had not seen this at the house in Shoreditch where she had lain with her face exposed to the sky.

'What is it? What has caused this?'

Peace ran a finger down the bloody stripes. 'It seems to be a crucifix, crudely cut after death.'

Shakespeare stared at the wounds as if he would go back in time to when they were inflicted. 'Is there some religious meaning?'

'That is for *you* to answer, Mr Shakespeare. There is something else, too . . .'

As Peace spoke, carefully laying the body back on the slab so that the wounded back was no longer visible, the ancient door to the crypt was flung open. Two pikemen marched in, taking up positions at either side of the doorway. They were followed by a man of later years, probably in his fifties. His hair and beard were as white as the snow outside and his eyes were keen. He was tall and lean with the languid air and fine clothes of the nobility. Shakespeare recognised him immediately as Charles Howard, second Baron of Effingham and Lord High Admiral of England. Howard looked first at Shakespeare, then at Peace, without a word. He walked forward to the body of his beloved adopted daughter, Blanche, lying on the searcher's stone slab, for all the world like a carving on a sarcophagus. For two minutes he stared at her face, then nodded slowly before turning on his heel. In a moment he was gone, closely attended by his pikemen.

Shakespeare caught Peace's eye. 'I suppose there was nothing to say.'

'No. Nothing. Now let me show you this one other thing.' Peace lifted her hands and showed Shakespeare the wrists. They were marked with a raised weal. 'That is a rope mark, Mr Shakespeare. The brute who did this to her tied her up most cruelly.'

Shakespeare looked closely at the marks, then winced at the thought of the suffering the poor girl had endured before death. He shook Joshua Peace's hand. 'Thank you, my friend. Consign her body to the coroner. In quieter times it would be a fine thing to pass an hour or two with you and a flagon of Gascon wine at The Three Tuns.'

'Yes,' said Peace. 'And let us drink heartily to quieter times.'

Outside, in the daylight, Shakespeare was surprised to find the Lord Admiral and his pikemen waiting for him. It was snowing properly now, dropping a carpet of white round St Paul's, but if Howard of Effingham felt the cold he did not show it. He stood stock still, like a soldier, his colourless face set and hard.

'My lord . . .'

'She was with child?'

Shakespeare said nothing. There was sadness in the older man's voice that needed no response.

'Who did this thing to her?'

'I intend to discover that, my lord. May I ask you about the people she knew? The identity, perhaps, of the father of her child?'

Howard breathed deeply. 'You are Shakespeare, Mr Secretary's man, I believe.'

'I am.'

'This is a tragic business. I loved Blanche as if she were

my own child. She was part of me. But it is also delicate, Mr Shakespeare. There is the family to think about.'

'I understand. But you must wish to find her killer.'

'I do, I do.' He hesitated again. 'Let me just say that of late there had been people in her life of whom I did not approve . . .' He stopped.

Shakespeare needed to probe deeper. He needed every piece of information this man could provide, but he began to realise it was not going to be forthcoming. 'These people . . .'

The Admiral looked distraught. Briefly, he reminded Shakespeare of a lost puppy he had chanced upon in his schooldays and taken in, much to his mother's disapproval. 'I can say no more.'

'Do you, at least, know anything of the house in Hog Lane by Shoreditch where her body was found?'

'I am sorry. I know nothing of such things.'

'My man Boltfoot Cooper has made enquiries but he failed to discover the landlord or tenant of the building.'

Howard said nothing. He stood like a rock.

'Perchance in a day or two you might speak with me, my lord?'

'Perchance, Mr Shakespeare. I can promise no more.'

'One last question. Was she of the Roman church?'

It seemed to Shakespeare that Howard of Effingham clenched his teeth. He did not answer but nodded to his pikemen, then turned and walked to his horse, which was tethered nearby. To Shakespeare, his reaction spoke more than a printed volume could have done.

As Howard rode away eastwards, some apprentices threw snowballs at Shakespeare and one hit him. He laughed and gathered up some snow, crunching it together in his gloved hands before flinging it back at the boy.

It was Friday, a fish day. Many days were fish days, as a means of boosting the fortunes of the fishing fleets, but that was no hardship for Shakespeare, who enjoyed fish in all its forms. Soon it would be Lent and every day would be a fish day. Jane had given him smoked pike instead of meat for his breakfast that morning and he would have eel and oyster pie before bed.

The trees were decorated white as Shakespeare walked through the streets of high houses, their shutters thrown back to let in the air. Thick woodsmoke belched from the chimneys, adding to the permanent city stench of ordure until the mixture clogged the nostrils and the lungs. Summer was the worst, particularly here, near the confluence of the rivers Fleet and Thames and close to the Fleet and Newgate prisons, where the rotting flesh of dead convicts might be left uncollected for weeks; at this time of year, thankfully, the stink retreated to a background whiff.

An endless procession of carts, drays and wagons, laden with farm produce, barrels and building materials, trundled nose to tail in both directions, their horses' iron-clad hooves turning the new snow to slush, slipping and stumbling in the endless potholes. There was barely room for them to pass on the narrow streets and they often ground to a halt, setting the carters to shouting and swearing. At times, blows were exchanged before a beadle interposed and brought some order.

In a few minutes, Shakespeare had followed the road out of the city, over the Fleet river (if such a putrid ditch was deserving of the name), soon turning left towards the high, forbidding walls of Bridewell. Every time he came here, he found it difficult to believe that such a dark fortress could ever have been a royal palace, yet barely sixty years ago, Henry – Great Henry – had entertained his Spanish queen to dinner behind these walls. His son, Edward VI, had handed over the dreary place to the corporation for the housing of the poor. And now it was little more than a prison for the city's harlots, gypsies and vagrants.

A squadron of eight armed men, pursuivants, marched past him with a prisoner, their boots stamping through the snow. They came to a halt, throwing their prisoner to the ground, and their sergeant, whom Shakespeare recognised as one of Topcliffe's men, hammered on the huge door. Almost instantly it was opened by the gaoler, clutching his clanking keys.

'A priest of Rome for you, gaoler,' the sergeant said.

The man grinned, revealing a couple of brown, broken teeth. 'And very welcome he is too, Mr Newall, for his friends will pay well to feed him and keep him alive. They are all welcome here, all your Popish priests.'

'Well, don't forget our agreement.'

'A mark for each, catchpole. Bring them in! Never have I fared so well. Last month they brought me a vicar of the English church. He starved because no one brought him a crust of bread, and why should *I* feed him? They are like vermin here. Bring me Romans, catchpole, for they do garnish my table.'

Newall pulled the priest to his feet and handed him, man-acled and shackled, to the gaoler. 'Mind you work him hard, making nails or stripping oakum to caulk Her Majesty's ships. And flog him soundly, or I shall take him off to the Marshalsea or The Clink, where he should be by rights.' The sergeant spotted Shakespeare and grinned. 'I'm sure Mr Topcliffe wishes you good cheer, Mr Shakespeare.'

Shakespeare ignored Newall, whom he knew to be of small wit and too close-coupled to Topcliffe for comfort, and walked past the squadron. He nodded to the gaoler, who knew him well, and went through the doorway. He was immediately knocked back by the stink of human dung and sweat. Before him in the first large courtyard and the cloisters was a swarming mass of the lowliest of humankind. Here were hundreds of beggars, whores, doxies and orphans. Many had come to London in search of a better life and had been brought here by way of punishment and hoped-for redemption. In vain. Shakespeare saw their dull eyes as they toiled on the treadmill or performed one or other of a dozen unpleasant tasks set them by the gaoler to pay for whatever food he might consent to give them. The gaoler pushed the newly acquired priest forward into the crowd where he was seized by a taskmaster.

'Some vagabonds were brought here yesterday by Boltfoot Cooper,' Shakespeare said at last, when the sergeant and his squadron had gone. 'I will see them.'

The gaoler's brow creased in puzzlement. 'Of course, I do remember them, Mr Shakespeare. They were Irish beggars or some such, I believe. But they were taken away this morning on your orders, sir.'

'I gave no such orders, turnkey.'

'But, Mr Shakespeare, I saw the warrant that the two men brought. It had your mark on it.'

'My mark? Can you read, turnkey?'

'Why, yes, sir, enough. Your men said the vagabonds were to be taken to some other gaol as criminals, as I do recall. They had your mittimus from the justice. I have seen many such warrants.'

'You say my men took them?'

'Aye, sir, and did leave me a shilling for my trouble.'

Shakespeare's blood rose. How dare Topcliffe cloy away his witnesses? He felt a sudden overpowering rage and hatred for the man.

The gaoler grinned, his mouth hanging open like a Bedlam loon. 'But tarry a while, Mr Shakespeare. You be just in time for the Friday floggings. If you'd care to stay and take some wine with me, we can observe them together.'

Shakespeare did not dignify the offer with a reply.

Chapter 6

TRAMPING THROUGH THE slush in his fine leather boots, with a winter cloak of crimson worsted and white fur, the man called Cotton could not fail to catch the eye of the goodwives, procurers and water-bearers crowding the muddy, cart-thronged thoroughfare of Long Southwark. Though he was slight and lean, he was striking. Beneath his black velvet hat, embroidered with crimson beads, his hair and beard were golden-red and trimmed short. His grey eyes were at once intense, good-humoured and watchful. He walked briskly, with the confident air of a gentleman who knew his place in the world. For a man who might have wished to go unremarked, he was brazen and conspicuous, but that was the very quality that made him invisible to searchers and pursuivants: they were looking for men in hoods and dark cloaks, loitering in shadows and doorways, and they failed to see what their eyes alighted on so easily.

The weak afternoon light was fading fast as he made his way with purpose southwards, past Winchester House, St Mary Overies, the inns and bawdy-houses, towards the high walls of the Marshalsea prison, where he was immediately given entrance in exchange for a coin.

The gaoler clapped him on the back in welcome. 'Mr Cotton, sir, it's good to see you again.'

'And you, gaoler.'

The gaoler, a big, long-bearded man with a heavy woollen smock and wide leather key-belt strapped tight round his great belly, grinned broadly at Cotton as if waiting for a reaction. 'Well?' he said at last. 'Do you not notice something about the place, Mr Cotton?'

The man called Cotton looked around the dark walls of the entrance chamber. It seemed as bleak and cold as ever.

'The smell, Mr Cotton, the smell. I have reduced the stench of the prisoners' dung.'

Cotton sniffed the air politely. It was still putrid, but perhaps slightly less so than usual. 'And how have you effected this, gaoler?'

The gaoler once again clapped his shovel-sized hand on Cotton's back. 'Pails with lids, sir, pails with lids. Hogsden Trent, the brewer of Gully Hole, sells me his old and cast-off kegs. I cuts them in half and fashions a lid for them, then sells them on to the prisoners, Mr Cotton. No more shitting in the straw, sir. No more pissing against the wall.'

For a moment, Cotton envied the gaoler his simple pragmatism; it stood in sharp contrast to his own other-worldliness where the day-to-day functions of eating, sleeping, drinking and defecation were but furniture to God's great purpose. He and the gaoler walked through the echoing, tallow-lit passages, past cells where, occasionally, prisoners moaned and shouted, until they arrived at a solid wooden door, strengthened with thick iron straps, on which the gaoler was about to bang his enormous fist. Cotton shook his head, almost imperceptibly. 'Leave me now.'

The gaoler lowered his hand, bowed and backed away. Cotton was waiting for him to go when he heard the man's faint whisper from the shadows: 'Bless me, Father. Please . . .'

Cotton hesitated only a moment, then made the sign of the

cross and spoke the words the gaoler wanted to hear: '*Benedictio Dei omnipotentis, Patris, et Filii, et Spiritus Sancti, descendat super vos et maneat simper . . .*' There were many like him in England in these days, men and women who pledged loyalty to the new church in public, fearing persecution and a fine if they failed to attend Sunday service, yet who hungered in their souls for the old Roman ways.

Cotton watched until the gaoler, warmed by his benediction, slid away down the passage, then opened the door a few inches, revealing a large, low-ceilinged cell with bare brick walls. In a building rich in human misery and squalor, it was surprisingly clean and well-kept. More surprisingly, there was a table in the middle of the room, with six chairs, two on each of the long sides and one at each end. It was laid with platters of cold food and a flagon of wine. Cotton stepped in and clanged the door shut behind him. Three women and two men stood at the far end of the table, the women's faces drawn in fear and anticipation. Cotton smiled at them. He made the sign of the cross again. '*Dominus vobiscum,*' he intoned.

The five who faced him, all dressed in fine clothes, crossed themselves and replied, '*Et cum spiritu tuo.*' The strain fell from their faces. They moved apart to reveal a small covered altar, complete with the sacred vessels – a silver chalice and paten – and good candles, which were already lit and cast a warm, flickering glow over the cell.

Cotton moved forwards and was welcomed by the five in turn; he held each one by the hands, kissed their cheeks and blessed them. One held his eyes longer than the others: the one with the secret to pass on. As the man greeted Cotton, he clasped him and held his arms tight so that he stayed in his embrace. Cotton tensed, disgusted by the stink of the young captive priest, whom he knew to be called Father Piggott. He and the other man, Plummer, were priests sent covertly from

France by the English college at Rheims where they had studied. They were held here as prisoners, though their movements were not greatly restricted. Piggott and Plummer had been caught by the magistrate Young and sent here untried, but they were fed well by their friends and not ill-treated by the gaoler.

'So fine to meet you, Mr Cotton,' Piggott said, his voice thick and unctuous. 'I have a message for you to pass on, an important one.'

Cotton felt sick. He unclasped Piggott's talon-like fingers from his arm and found that he was shaking. Stepping back, out of Piggott's reach, he nodded tersely, took a deep breath, steadied himself and prepared to say mass.

With an extravagant sweep, Harry Slide slapped a broadsheet down on the ale-soaked table. 'You owe me a penny for this, Mr Shakespeare, and more.'

They were in a partitioned booth in the Bell tavern in Gracechurch Street. A good fire was blazing in the hearth and the windows were steamed over. From beyond the panelling came a din as a group of city merchants celebrated the arrival of a carrack from the Indies. It was clear from their loud and drunken voices that the vessel had come laden with spices and silver, having been away more than a year and feared lost. They had ventured a large amount of money and now their faith had paid off, their wealth increased many times over. This evening they were happily drinking away a small part of their profits while being entertained – if that was the correct word. A shabbily dressed young troubadour, plucking at his lute in a corner by the kegs, was singing a mournful ballad with feeling but little joy. Outside, the sky was cloudless at last and sharp with cold, turning the slush of day to a thin sheet of ice.

'Don't worry, Harry, you'll get more. A lot more.'

'Well, *there's* a change of tune, Mr Shakespeare. Yet I would be more content if the minstrel would change *his* tune, too.' He cupped his hand to his mouth and shouted, 'Something cheery, minstrel, for pity's sake!'

John Shakespeare tugged at his short-cropped beard and sighed. 'The truth is that I need you, Harry.' He reached over and touched his arm by way of emphasis. 'I need you to assist me as an employed man. There is much to be done, not just the Jesuits. My hands are full. Will you help?'

Slide took a long sip of Gascon wine, dark red and sweetened with sugar, and considered the proposition. It was one thing bringing intelligence to Mr Shakespeare and Walsingham when he had a juicy morsel to sell, but it would be quite another to be a hired hand, a journeyman intelligencer. He was not, however, in the least surprised that he was needed. 'Would this have something to do with Lady Blanche Howard?

'So you know about that.'

Slide threw up his hands, palms exposed, to the ancient beamed ceiling. 'The whole of London knows about Blanche Howard.' He nodded at the broadsheet lying on the tavern table.

Shakespeare picked it up and felt the prickles rise on his neck.

The broadsheet was titled *The London Informer*. Printed on one side, under the heading 'Horrible Tragedy of Lady Blanche Howard', and the secondary heading 'Murdered by Foul Priest', it proceeded to give intimate details of her injuries and the manner in which she had been found. It went on with a rambling discourse, referring mischievously to Howard of Effingham's sisters, Lady Douglass and Lady Frances, suggesting they might not have been so enamoured of Blanche as their brother. The tract concluded,

Friendly reader, we must tell you, though it pains us so to do, that they may well have just cause for their reluctance to don the drear weeds of mourning. How else could it be, when we know that the Lady Blanche had already hazarded her place in God's Kingdom by her monstrous associations with lewd Popish beasts, one of which, the notorious Southwell, late of Horsham St Faith in Norfolk and the traitors' colleges of France and Rome, had brought her with child and, fearing for his own mortal life, has taken hers with a cruel dagger. This Southwell is thought abroad in London, given solace, food and lodging by those who wish harm to our Sovereign Lady Elizabeth. He is the foul murderer, with cross and relic and blade, and we beg you all, our fellow English men, if ever you happen upon him or his confederates, to spare no mercy but to bring him to the hangman's righteous rope.

'Where did you get this, Harry?'

'It's Walstan Glebe's. He had a bundle of them by Fishmongers' Hall, selling them at a penny each.'

So this was Glebe's work. Shakespeare knew of him. He was a rat from the sewers, a pedlar of dirt and dissimulation. Before taking up his profession as broadsheet writer, printer and seller, he had scratched a living stealing the odes of others to sell as his own. Swooning lovers had paid him money for poems to woo their fair ladies, yet he had merely copied the work of other scribes and poets and handed it over as his. His crime had come to light when a red-faced swain had gone to the magistrate complaining that his intended had laughed at him for reciting to her an ode that was already common currency. For his pains, Glebe had been branded with a hot iron on the forehead: L for Liar. Now he wore his fringe low and had acquired a reputation for printing the most seditious and salacious broadsheet in the city.

'What do you make of it, Harry?'

Slide's mouth turned down uncertainly. 'I don't know, Mr Shakespeare. You tell me. Does the paper speak the truth? I thought you should see it.'

Shakespeare gave it consideration. He had to concede that it was generally accurate, surprisingly so, given Walstan Glebe's history, though he had no way of knowing what Lord Admiral Howard's sisters, Lady Douglass and Lady Frances, thought of their adoptive sister. Was there bad blood between them? What was interesting was the suggestion that Lady Blanche had been associating with Jesuits. Was this Topcliffe's voice? Most of the other information could certainly have come from him or, indeed, from the constable or the bellman.

But one thing puzzled Shakespeare, the line that read, 'He is the foul murderer, with cross and relic and blade . . .' The cross and relic had not been discovered until the Searcher of the Dead, Joshua Peace, had drawn them out. Peace would have told no one, of that Shakespeare was certain. So how had Glebe known about them?

At last the mournful minstrel took a break from singing and playing. Harry Slide cheered and clapped with painful irony. Shakespeare found himself laughing. He knew a little about Slide's past or, at least, the story he chose to tell: his father had been a lawyer who lost a fortune gambling at cards, cock-fights and horse races. When he ended up in The Clink for debt, he hanged himself, leaving nine-year-old Harry and his mother destitute. She had scratched a living working for a tailor and bought Harry an education. It had not been the easiest of childhoods, but plenty fared worse. So why did Harry Slide seem so . . . half formed? It was as if some of his soul were missing, that he could draw men in with his seeming good character only to betray them. Shakespeare downed the last of his wine and felt its warm sweetness course down to his belly. 'We need to talk to Mr Glebe, Harry. Can you find him?'

'I can find anyone, given time.'

'We don't have time. Find him quickly. And what are your thoughts about the connection with Southwell? Might he be involved?'

'It is possible, of course . . .'

'But you have doubts?'

Slide nodded.

'Well, make enquiries about him and bring him in. He can't be allowed to remain at large any longer. Mr Secretary wants him in custody – as, I know, does the Queen. Let us lock him away as safe as the Crown Jewels. And use your best connections to discover the truth about this murder. Three marks a day, Harry, with twenty-five more for bringing me Southwell and a further twenty-five for finding the killer of Blanche Howard.'

Slide was silent a moment as he thought it through. What it came down to was that he needed the money to see him through this chill winter. He smiled that winning smile. 'Of course, Mr Shakespeare. A most generous offer. Consider me your man.'

Chapter 7

A T SEVEN, LONG after dark, the Marshalsea gaoler lumbered along to the cell for Cotton and the three ladies. 'I must lock up now, Mr Cotton,' he said apologetically.

The six dinner guests had almost finished feasting and were sipping wine, discussing the dark plight of England. All were fearful that Mary, Queen of Scots, the great hope of their Catholic cause, might soon suffer a martyr's death. Even now they prayed for a miracle to save her and raise her to her rightful place as anointed queen of England.

They had, for a short while, been able to forget their anxieties: the Latin mass said by Cotton had suffused them with a fleeting joy, especially the three women, the Lady Tanahill, Lady Frances Browne and Mistress Anne Bellamy. They were from three of London's leading Church of Rome families and all were suffering harshly in these times when the iron-clad gauntlet of the state could beat down their door at any hour of day or night. Lady Tanahill's husband Philip, a one-time favourite of the Queen, was now in the Tower, having been arrested while attempting to leave the country to meet Church of Rome leaders abroad. The Countess had been left at home with their small child, who had never yet seen his father. Her heart was heavy, yet the still, loving presence of this man Cotton brought comfort.

As Lady Tanahill watched Cotton talking animatedly of his

belief that the true church would rise again in England, she made a decision: she would invite him to be her private chaplain, to live in her home and bring the sacraments to her daily. But she would not mention it here in front of these others. The arrest of her husband, betrayed by a priest they had befriended, had taught her a bitter lesson in trust.

Piggott and Plummer wiped the last hunks of bread round their trenchers and ate greedily. The food, though necessarily modest in that it had had to be served cold, having been brought in boxes by Anne Bellamy, had been hearty, with good joints of mutton and fowl even though it was a fish day. 'May as well be hanged for a sheep as a fish,' said Plummer, laughing. And the wine was sweet.

Cotton, with Plummer and Piggott, remained in the cell while the three women left together. After they had gone, Plummer said farewell to Cotton, holding his hands and urging him to be strong in the faith. Then Piggott again embraced him, holding him in a screw-like grip. Cotton flinched. Piggott's breath rasped and his coarse black beard, ill-covering his pox-pitted face, scoured Cotton's cheek as he spoke low into his ear so that Plummer could not hear him, only Cotton.

'Tell our friend this, Father Cotton. Tell him Cogg. Cogg of Cow Lane outside the city wall by Smith Field. Cogg has what he desires, Father Cotton.'

Again the proximity of this man made revulsion well up within Cotton and he wrenched himself free. For a few moments the two men stood eye to eye, until Cotton looked away. He took his leave of Plummer, who seemed to smile sympathetically, then left the cell and slammed the door without looking again at Piggott. A family of fat rats scuttled ahead as he followed the gaoler back through the dank corridors to the great door. He was still shaking from his encounter with Piggott as the gaoler clapped him yet again with his giant's hand

and whispered conspiratorially, 'Pails with lids, Mr Cotton. Pails with lids.'

The crisp night air eased his tension and he walked over the bridge into London, slipping and sliding through the icy, deserted streets. The evening was moonlit and he had accomplished his task, yet by the time he arrived at the riverside house where he lodged, he felt uneasy. Piggott had worried him, and he did not like his message.

For a few moments he waited at the end of Dowgate, near the Tower, peering back down the streets of tall houses, their leaded windows heavily curtained or shuttered and only the merest flickerings of candlelight visible. He was looking for movement and shadows, listening for footfalls. When he was sure he had not been followed he went to a side door of the house and banged twice. The door was opened to him almost immediately and shut again the instant he stepped in.

It was a large and very new wood-frame house, a work in progress but already part-occupied by its owner, Thomas Woode, a widower in his thirties, and his two young children. His wife had died of consumption when Grace was little more than a year old and Andrew was three. Now they were four and six and the building of this house was his way of forgetting the past and forging a new future for the family.

The children's governess, Catherine Marvell, stood at the door. She was a slender creature with remarkable blue eyes, unblemished skin and long dark hair pulled back from her face, which was now fixed with a look of horror.

'*Pax vobiscum*, dear Catherine,' Cotton said, and held her hands between his own. She was shivering. 'What is it?'

'Have you not heard?'

'Heard what, Catherine?'

She spoke low, though there was no one to hear. 'Blanche is dead, Father. Murdered.'

'What?'

Catherine closed her eyes, as if she would blot out the imagined vision of Blanche that would not leave her mind. 'By Shoreditch. Her body was found most horribly wounded in a burnt-out house.' And then she whispered even lower, with urgency, 'They say she was with child, Father.'

He tried to hold her in his arms, to comfort her as a father would a daughter, but she backed away from him. Cotton understood. The touch of another human being is not always the best remedy for grief and horror. Lady Blanche? Who could or would have done such a thing to so beautiful and loving a woman? Cotton had brought her to the holy Roman church. Was this a cause of her death? She had never, as far as he knew, harmed a soul.

Cotton wanted to stroke Catherine's long dark hair, but he feared his touch would be unwelcome. They stood awkwardly in the passage, neither knowing how to deal with such news.

He tried saying words to console her, but they sounded trite and unworthy. He tried to soothe her, though he wondered whether it was he who needed soothing more. The Jesuit colleges had removed him from the physical world of human contact and oft times he missed it, the touch of a hand or the brush of a cheek.

She led him through to the hall, where logs were burning and crackling in a wide stone hearth and a man was waiting for them. The room was large and high-walled, hung with rich tapestries of blue and gold, displaying the wealth of the owner. Everything seemed new, the green oak beams vibrant with colour in the brilliant light of dozens of candles.

The man who waited was lean and tall. He stood close to the fire, soaking up its heat. Unlike the fine dress of Cotton, he wore simple clothes in dark colours, the livery of a senior household valet or butler, though he was nothing of the sort: he had a modest ruff, a black doublet over a white shirt, knee-length black breeches in the Venetian style and white hose. His hair was cut short and he was clean-shaven.

He bowed his head. He did not smile. 'Good evening, Father Cotton,' he said slowly and deliberately, his voice faintly accented.

'Good evening to you, Father Herrick.'

'What news of your day?'

'A fair day, Father.'

There was a stiffness between the men. They were not friends. Cotton had been ordered to help Herrick and he would do so; that was as far as the relationship went. It had started with a letter from Rome, signed by Claudius Aquaviva, general of the Society of Jesus, requiring Cotton to welcome Herrick to England, to help him find lodging and put him in contact with important Roman Catholics so that he could begin his mission in safety. Cotton had bowed to Aquaviva's command, but felt uneasy.

At first he had asked Thomas Woode, the owner of this house, if Herrick could stay for a night or two. Woode had not objected, though Cotton could see he was unsure about having another priest in the house. Two doubled the risk, and if he was caught harbouring priests, particularly Jesuits, his life might be at stake.

Cotton had intended to find somewhere else for Herrick to stay almost immediately, but somehow he hadn't so Herrick had remained there, posing as a serving man and going about his spiritual mission in his own way. It was a situation that, Cotton realised, both Thomas Woode and the governess Catherine Marvell wished to end, and soon.

Catherine stepped back into the doorway. With her master at a livery-company banquet, the house creaked between these three disparate people. Upstairs, the children of Thomas Woode slept in their little beds.

At last Catherine spoke. 'Can I bring you refreshment, Father?' Her words were directed at Cotton, and pointedly to him alone.

He shook his head and smiled. 'No, thank you, child. I have supped well. And you, Father Herrick?'

'Perhaps a little food before bed . . .'

Catherine caught his eye. She had no wish to prepare anything for Father Herrick. 'And do you have word for me, Father Cotton?' Herrick said, when they were alone.

Cotton hesitated. Something was very wrong here. During his eight years of training for this mission, Cotton had met many curious men, not all of them holy. There had been ambitious men, fearful men, angry men, spies sent by Walsingham and, of course, many devoted men. But this Herrick – Cotton realised that was not his real name – was different in a worrying way. How, exactly, did he fit into the Society of Jesus and its cause? He was not forthcoming about the work he had undertaken, though he intimated he had served the cause in the Netherlands and hinted at time spent in the New World saving heathens for Christ. 'Let us sit down, Father Herrick, and take a little wine together while we wait for Catherine to bring your supper. It has been a long, cold day.'

'I think you know I do not take wine, Father Cotton. I know, too, that you would wish I was not here in this house. Yet we both work for the same great cause . . .' He spoke perfect English but for that faint accent. Only the trained ear could tell its origin as Dutch Flemish, for he was the product of a Dutch father, who had been a musician at the court of Queen Mary, and an English mother.

'Do we?' Cotton asked, and regretted the question as soon as it was asked. 'I am sorry, Father.'

Herrick's expression betrayed nothing, but he chose his words precisely. 'Whatever you think you know, Father Cotton, I can assure you I know more about you than you do of me. Most vitally, I know you have the information I need, the meaning of which is not for you to think on. This is required of you by our superiors in Rome and you will obey their wishes.'

Cotton was surprised by the harshness of Herrick's words. For a minute he did not speak. A voice inside told him to say nothing, to refuse, for no good could come of it. But his Jesuit training had taught him total obedience, even at the risk of torture and death, and it was quite clear that Aquaviva wanted him to give Herrick everything he required. In this case, that was the name and address of the man Cogg. Who Cogg was or what he did, Cotton did not know, but he feared that it had little or nothing to do with the holy Roman church.

At the doorway Catherine Marvell had reappeared and was about to enter with a tray of cold food for Herrick. Briefly, she shrank back, watching the two men.

Cotton spoke quietly to Herrick: 'Cogg. Cow Lane.'

The ghost of a smile crossed Herrick's face. His lips moved. 'Thank you, Father Cotton. *Pax vobiscum.*' Then he turned to the doorway where Catherine stood rooted to the spot. He made the sign of the cross. 'Bless you, too, child.'

Chapter 8

THEY MADE SPEEDY headway towards Deptford. The watermen had an easy job maintaining four or five knots downstream with the receding tide. Shakespeare sat in the back of the tiltboat beneath the canopy. A salt wind billowed from the side and blew the hat from his head. It caught the edge of the boat, but Boltfoot Cooper grabbed it just before it bounced into the choppy grey waters.

Boltfoot grinned into the spray as he handed back the hat. 'Paying your respects to our sovereign nonpareil, Mr Shakespeare? I believe she is in residence.'

Shakespeare ignored him. The Queen was indeed at Greenwich Palace beyond Deptford. With its sweeping lawns and its views of the river, crowded with the towering sails of great galleons, it was the loveliest of her homes, a palace of dreams divorced from the commotion and dirt of nearby London. Yet in these noisome days, the palace was, thought Shakespeare, probably the least pleasant place in the realm, No one would wish to be in the presence of the Queen as she wrestled with her conscience over the death warrant awaiting her signature. Shakespeare had no intention of going there if he could avoid it and he did not envy the courtiers and Privy Councillors who were with her day by day.

Having met her on several occasions, he felt fortunate that

she had not taken a greater interest in him. Though he revered her as his sovereign, he liked to keep his distance. Those who caught her eye lived a life between heaven and hell depending on her moods, which were as changeable as the weather: one moment sunshine and balm, the next thunder and rage. Now, her sunny spells were not in evidence; nothing but black clouds and the boom of cannon fire. He understood why Walsingham was protesting illness and staying at Barn Elms – anything to keep away from her in these gloomy times when she was consumed by indecision, torn on the one hand between her desire to be rid of her treacherous, scheming cousin and, on the other, her reluctance to do away with a fellow prince and bring down the wrath of the Roman Catholic world on England.

The rowers held a steady course, battling the current as they passed the dangerous West Ferry at the tip of a thumb of land where Kent bulged into the river, then turned southwards. The waters eased and they ran smooth towards their destination, Deptford, where Drake was said to be overseeing work on the ships of war of which he hoped to win command. Give him the vessels, he said, and he was confident he could take on the Spanish King and conquer him anywhere.

The dockside at Deptford was a madness of shipping. You could scarcely see the shore for the forest of tall masts and their web-like rigging. The gaunt spars of the berthed vessels were as bare of sails as the trees on land were now leafless. Dozens of large ships, galleons and barks, were moored there, their great oak bulwarks and castles towering over the houses onshore. There were also pinnaces and dozens of smaller craft. From the river it was a stirring sight. As they came closer, it seemed thousands of men were at work among the long line of shops, riotous inns, ship-chandlers, cooperages, sailmakers, spirit-sellers, caulkers, pitchmen, timber merchants, joiners and carpenters that lined this stretch of river.

As the tiltboat pulled up at the stairs by the naval yard, it was immediately clear from the shouting and commotion that something was afoot. On the shore, a throng of men was grouped around something prone on the pebbles. Disembarking, Shakespeare told the watermen to wait for him. Though they knew he was on the Queen's business, they began to argue with him, saying they were due to wind up their day's work, but Boltfoot silenced them by producing his razor-sharp dagger and drawing it lightly across his throat in warning.

On the shore, the crowd was growing larger. Shakespeare crunched down from Deptford Strand across the gravel and mud to see what was at the water's edge. Through a gap in the crowd he thought he saw a giant man in black lying there, twitching.

Shakespeare pushed his way through the jostling crowd, receiving angry elbows for his pains. As he got closer, he saw that it was not a man but a huge black fish or sea monster, twenty-five feet or more from nose to tail. It seemed to be alive for it was moving slowly, its fins flapping gently against the ground. A couple of apprentices were laughing and kicking it.

'That'll make a few fish suppers,' said one young journeyman with the work apron of a joiner round his waist.

Shakespeare felt a curious pity for the beast. Its grey-black skin shimmered in the cloudy light. It was encrusted with barnacles. Seaweed growths straggled from its great belly. He moved forwards and tried to stop the apprentices kicking it. They laughed at him and carried on, their fellows joining in.

'It's an omen,' someone said. 'A sign of evil tidings.'

'I think it's a Spaniard,' said the journeyman joiner.

'It's Phil himself,' said another, standing beside him. 'Big fucker, isn't he?'

Shakespeare turned to Boltfoot Cooper. 'Put the fish out of its misery.'

Boltfoot still had his dagger in his hand. He moved forward and knelt beside the crippled animal, stroking its huge forehead. He seemed to whisper something to it, then thrust upwards through its exposed, white underside. As he withdrew the long blade, a rush of blood poured out. The animal thrashed for barely a minute, with Boltfoot cradling its enormous head, then died.

''Ere, he's killed the King of Spain!'

'Good riddance to him, Romish bastard. Now let's get the Scotch whore topped.'

'It was a leviathan,' Boltfoot said quietly to Shakespeare, as he stood up, wiping his blade on his kerchief. 'I saw many of them in the southern seas. Sometimes they'd follow us in our wake. Twice the size of that one there, some of them. Fifty foot or more.'

Shakespeare felt a hand on his shoulder and turned sharply.

'Hello, John. I thought it was you.'

Shakespeare found himself staring into a face he knew well. 'Harper!'

'At your service. I was told to expect you.'

Captain Harper Stanley was a proud man with a high ruff that looked preposterously uncomfortable to Shakespeare. He had a broad brown moustache that tapered horizontally into points above an equally pointed beard. He was just a little too tall for a naval man; he'd have to stoop below decks, for there was little headroom even for the most dwarfish man.

Shakespeare smiled warmly as they shook hands. He had always liked Stanley. 'We're looking for the Vice-Admiral.'

'He's at Greenwich. Let me take you to him.' Stanley turned to the two mariners who accompanied him and ordered: 'Impound that whale. Have it rendered to lantern oil and set aside the jawbone for carving.'

Captain Stanley led the way. As they passed the weatherworn carcass of the *Golden Hind*, the ship that had encompassed the globe, now laid up forlorn behind the Royal Dock for all the world to come and gawp at, tread upon and carve keepsake pieces of wood from, Shakespeare cast a glance at Boltfoot. His eyes were fixed determinedly ahead as though he could not bear to look upon it. Stanley, also, spotted Boltfoot's aversion to the sight of his old ship.

'Seen a ghost, Mr Cooper?' Captain Stanley enquired, with a light chuckle. 'Flogged on the fo'c'sle, perhaps? I'll wager there are some bad memories for you there, sir.'

Boltfoot grunted a denial and walked on, dragging his club foot forwards as fast as it would go.

Stanley took them to a ship's boat and ordered the coxswain to take them to the palace. As they settled on the benches, he said at last, 'What is your concern here, John? Sir Francis received your message yesterday afternoon that you wished a meeting.'

Shakespeare tried to reconcile this confident fellow with the callow young ship's officer he had met five years earlier while investigating the plot by Zubiaur, Mason and John Doughty against Drake's life. Harper Stanley had not been on the *Golden Hind* but had entered Drake's service in 1581, the year after the ship's return. He had arrived from the north-east of England with letters of recommendation, which Drake had studied dubiously. He was not keen on gentleman sailors but liked Harper Stanley's persistence and had taken him on. Nor was he disappointed. Stanley quickly proved himself an able mariner and won rapid promotion.

When the John Doughty plot was revealed, Drake was as unconcerned as ever. He had nothing but scorn for the King of Spain and any attempt he might make on his life. Grudgingly, he assigned Stanley to help Walsingham and Shakespeare with the inquiry into the conspiracy, but wanted nothing more to do with it himself.

Shakespeare had wished to know more about the events behind the plot. Why had John Doughty been so set on revenge for his brother? It was then that Harper Stanley had produced Boltfoot Cooper to give Shakespeare a description of the trial and execution of John Doughty's brother, Thomas.

Boltfoot had already left the sea and had his own reasons for disliking Drake, but he was a fair witness. Though taciturn at the best of times, he had spoken freely of the unhappy events of July 1578 at Port St Julian, as if he had something to get off his chest.

Those were the days before Shakespeare had had his own home and office and he had interviewed Boltfoot Cooper in the ante-chamber of Walsingham's house in Seething Lane. Boltfoot, who had settled to work away from the sea in a large London cooperage, was ill at ease in the high-chambered room with its great leaded windows. He had spoken quietly at first to explain how he had entered Drake's service. 'I had been pressed by John Hawkins when I was an apprentice cooper, about twelve or thirteen, I'd reckon. It was an illegal act because I was bound to another man. He assigned me to the *Judith*, under the command of Captain Drake, and I stayed with him thirteen years in all.'

'And your main role was cooper, making barrels?'

'Yes, but he would often have me help the carpenters with mast repairs and careening. And when there was action I fought alongside the rest of the men. I know that he did like me and trust me and I suppose I looked up to him as a father. He was always a fair man . . . in those days.'

'And latterly, Mr Cooper, you were with Sir Francis – or Captain-General Drake as he then was – on his venture to the Magellan Strait and through to the Pacific Ocean?'

'Yes, sir.'

'And so you knew Thomas Doughty and his brother, John?'

'Yes, sir. For myself, sir, I did not like Thomas Doughty. He thought he was the Captain-General's equal, yet he was not – by no means. He and the other gentlemen aboard the *Pelican* were nothing but idlers. They had no respect for the men below decks and we had none for them.'

'And Doughty?'

'Thomas Doughty and his brother John were the worst, lording it over us, taking our plunder, then trying to bribe us to betray the Captain-General. The Doughtys were like wasps in a nest, whispering together. Before entering the Plate river, I refused an order from Thomas Doughty to climb the rigging to spy out the coast because it wasn't his place to give me such an order when the ship's master and the Captain-General were both aboard. Captain Drake would never have given me such an order because he knew about my foot and the difficulty I would have in climbing. But Thomas and John were pigs. They must have known that I could not climb, but when I refused Thomas Doughty's order, John Doughty took a length of cable and started to whip my head, sir.'

'I'm very sorry to hear that, Mr Cooper.'

'He was laughing, sir, as if it were a jest.'

'Finally, as we now know, Captain Drake had had enough of being undermined by Thomas Doughty and put him on trial before a jury of forty men at Port St Julian, some hundred miles north of the Magellan Strait, and sentenced him to death.'

'We called it Blood Island, Mr Shakespeare. It was where the Portuguese sea-captain Magellan had put down a mutiny and hanged a man some sixty years ago or more, before he went through the strait that now bears his name. I am not a superstitious man, but there were some believed that place was haunted. We did find the gibbet where Magellan hanged the mutineer, with black bones and shreds of clothing beneath it still.'

'And the execution of Thomas Doughty?'

'That was strange. I seen men go to their deaths before, but never so well as Mr Doughty. His death was the making of him. He chose the axe ahead of the rope, which was his right, and Drake gave him two days to prepare himself. In those last days, he made peace with Drake, and they did dine together in Drake's tent.'

'And where was the brother, John Doughty?'

'He held himsself apart, went down to the rocks at the water's edge and sat there. He wasn't laughing then. When the execution was taking place, the Captain-General made the whole fleet's company assemble to witness it, and John Doughty was brought forcibly to watch. His arms were held on either side as the axe fell on his brother's neck. John Doughty didn't blink, sir. I was watching him to see what he would do or say, but he did nothing and so I knew . . .'

'You knew what, Mr Cooper?'

'I knew that one day he would seek retribution.'

'Thank you, Mr Cooper. You have been a great help.'

Cooper's hand had gone into a pocket in his workman's jerkin.

'Before you go, Mr Cooper,' Shakespeare had said, 'I believe you are no longer on terms with Sir Francis Drake. Is that right?'

Boltfoot had grunted. 'There's many as won't talk to Drake now. For he is a rich man from the spoils we took. And do I look a rich man? Yet we braved the same storms and endured the same scurvy. He is a great man, a fair man at sea, but on land . . . I will say no more on the matter, if it please you, sir. But take this, Mr Shakespeare.' He had held out a piece of aged wood, shaped like a small tankard, which he had just removed from his pocket. 'I did pull down Magellan's black and rotted gibbet and carved out many such cups on the long way home for my shipmates as remembrances. I tell you this, though, I never gave one to John Doughty.'

Five years later, Shakespeare had the cup still, though he never drank from it. He also had the services of Boltfoot Cooper, for Shakespeare had seen that he was not happy in his new life building barrels for brewers. He had also seen some quality in Boltfoot, a steadfastness that would repay loyalty a hundredfold. So they had made a contract, and Boltfoot had worked for Shakespeare ever since.

Now Boltfoot sat with the coxswain while Shakespeare spoke with Captain Stanley at the back of the ship's boat. 'It seems there is another plot to do for Drake,' Shakespeare said quietly. 'I want Boltfoot to guard him.'

Stanley laughed. 'Boltfoot? Are you moon mad, John? Drake won't let Cooper shadow him.'

'That is my fear. It was Mr Secretary who suggested it. You're close to Drake, Harper. How *can* we protect him?'

'Does he really *need* protection?'

'Mr Secretary believes he does. I admit I am worried, too. The Spanish were serious about it before and it was chance alone that foiled their plot. There is evidence that they mean to get the job done this time. I fear they have found someone more adept in the bloody arts than John Doughty.'

'Well, they won't have an easy time of it. Drake is always with people who would hazard their own lives for him.'

'Where does he lodge?'

'At court, usually, with his pretty young wife. Sometimes he will stretch the hours by staying aboard ship at Gravesend when he journeys there. When he is here at Deptford he spends much time in meetings with the Lord Admiral who, you must know, has a house here on the green. But if you ask me how we can protect Drake, I would say just this. Send him to sea as quickly as possible.'

Chapter 9

O N THE FIRST floor of a broad tenement house in Cow Lane near Smith Field, Gilbert Cogg was sweating profusely, which had less to do with the heat from the fire and more to do with his three-hundredweight girth and his exertions with a girl named Starling Day.

She had come to the door of his workshop asking for employment in his bawdy-house. He told her he would not employ her without sampling what she had to offer, and said she could have sixpence and a tankard of ale. She asked for a shilling. After a brief bout of bargaining, they had agreed on tenpence. She had earned her money well, half crushed to death beneath his prodigious weight. As he pounded greedily into her body, his enormous bed threatened to break its boards and joists and collapse through to the ground floor.

But it survived, as did Starling Day. Now they lay together on the dirt-grey sheet. Cogg was panting as if he would soon breathe his last. His belly and chest heaved and sank like a ducking stool. Starling rolled over and slid out of the bed. She was thin from lack of nourishment: she had walked nearly from Nottingham to escape a marriage in which she had been beaten once too many times. Though her ribs looked like a washboard, her bruises had faded and she was still womanly. She would have been pretty, had she had the opportunity to take more care of her hair. She dressed quickly, watching Cogg as his breathing subsided. At last she held out a hand to him.

'What would that be, then, my pretty bird? Sixpence, I do believe?'

'Tenpence, Mr Cogg. You did agree tenpence.'

'Did I now? Did I so?'

'You did, sir.'

With difficulty he shifted himself upright off the bed. Standing naked in front of her, his member was now flaccid and barely visible beneath a belly that hung low like a sack of turnips. He pushed his stomach forward with evident satisfaction and grinned as he gave it a hearty slap. 'You don't get a belly like that without some hard eating and drinking, my girl.'

'No, Mr Cogg.'

'It's living so near the shambles, little Starling, that's what does it. The slaughtermen and butchers bring me offal and offcuts and I helps them with little things in return. Money for the rentman, pretty favours from friends like you. You name it, Cogg provides it. I provides fine favours for gentlemen, too, so those as works for me never knows who they might meet. You want fine sotweed? Cogg can get it. You want a prime view of a hanging, drawing and quartering? Cogg provides.'

'I had heard you were a generous man, Mr Cogg. I was told you might be able to give me work.'

'Well, we'll see, won't we? You're new to Romeville, my girl, but you've already got some nice Boleynish tricks there. I reckon you could do with some feeding up, though. So, I tell you what, I'll give you a whole shilling this time so you can buy yourself some pies and perhaps you'll come to me again on the morrow and we'll see what we can do.'

'I'd like that, Mr Cogg. Thank you, sir.'

He handed her a coin and squeezed her paps, then clasped her face to his in a fetid kiss. She knew better than to pull away.

'And do you have a lodging, my pretty bird?'

She shook her head. There was a time when she would have cried in her misery, but those days were long past. Nights in the open, or huddled beside the other poor and dispossessed in barns and byres, had hardened her.

'Well, get yourself to the vaulting-house by the Bel Savage, my girl, and tell them Cogg sent you. Talk to Parsimony Field. She's my best girl. She'll look after you and find you a comb to pretty yourself a little. A cot, too.' He slapped her behind as she left, knowing that the shilling was a fine investment. It would pay him many times over.

Cogg was still naked when Miles Herrick arrived, soon after the girl had gone. Swiving gave him a strong appetite and he had just sat down to devour the remains of a fat and fresh turkey cock that a farmer's son from Suffolk had given him in exchange for a night with Parsimony. Most customers banged on his workshop door, but Herrick appeared in the chamber while Cogg was licking his fingers and chewing some crisp, fatty skin from the wishbone.

The man stood there, watching him, a dark shadow in black clothes. Cogg recoiled in shock, then jumped up from his three-legged stool, knocking it backwards into the hearth.

'Who are you?' he demanded, trying to regain his composure as he scrabbled for his breeches and shirt.

'I was given your name.'

'So you just walk into a man's chamber when he's at his repast?'

Herrick smiled. 'I think I watched your repast leave by the front door. A fine but skinny wench, Mr Cogg. It is Mr Cogg . . . isn't it?'

'It is, sir, yes, but who are you?' Cogg was half dressed now and trying to impose his authority on the situation.

'I bring you gold, Mr Cogg. and I believe you can supply a certain item in return.'

Cogg pulled the stool from the fire. 'That depends on who I am talking to.'

'My name is Herrick. Miles Herrick.'

As if a taper had been lit behind them, Cogg's eyes brightened. 'Ah, yes, Mr Herrick. I had been expecting you.' Suddenly all was clear. Cogg's manner changed: here was the prospect of good money. He had been considering how to squeeze this orange ever since the commission had been agreed. 'Let us go down to my workshop, if it please you. It is more of a place to strike deals.'

He led the way through the doorway, his bulk barely managing to negotiate the narrow frame, then down a flight of thirteen wooden and ominously creaking steps to a large shop-like area that took up the front half of the ground floor of the wide building. He opened a door to the rear and showed Herrick through.

The back room was a cluttered heap of boxes and barrels. A layer of dust covered many trunks and crates. The ceiling and corners of the room were clothed in cobwebs. 'Whatever you desire, Mr Herrick, I guarantee you'll find it here.'

Herrick's eyes flicked round the dimly lit room. He looked at Cogg, who was panting like a dog in summer.

'I tell you, Mr Herrick,' Cogg continued, 'as a boy I used to dig marl. From the age of eight until I was twenty, day after day after day, I dug the same thick white-grey clay in the depths of a dark pit in the shire of Northampton. Back-breaking work that left me strong as a bull. The farmer treated his kine better than he treated me. But one day I left and walked to London where I got work slitting pigs' throats in the shambles. I had my eyes on a better life, though, so I'd find things for people, like the fore-man, who had a taste for chewing Moorish hemp. I'd go down to the docks and buy things from the mariners, then sell them, strange foods and odd carvings, knives taken from Indians and Mussulmans, medicines from the ends of the earth to cure the ague, wenches of every hue, not all of them Christian, wild beasts such as you'd never find even at the Tower menagerie. I can find you liquids that flame to burn down a house and perfumes that will poison with a sweet smell. Whatever a man could desire, Mr Herrick, Cogg gets it for him.'

Herrick's voice was cold. 'You know what I want, Mr Cogg. The question is, do you have it?'

Cogg waddled ducklike among the crates and barrels. 'Oh, yes, you had a very special request, as I recall. Not one of Cogg's easier undertakings. A long-muzzled gun with a barrel of exactly two feet eight inches, using a strange firing mechanism: a snaphaunce lock. Is that a Hollandish word, sir? You do sound a little Hollandish, if I may say so. I believe there is a bit of common flint in the gun's cock, which sounds strange to me, but if that is what you want . . . Most clients want wheel-lock pistols, sir, gold-damascened and small as you like to proudly display at the waist . . . or conceal up a sleeve.'

'So you have it?'

'Cogg doesn't fail, sir. You said you wanted the barrel rifled, fine rifled. And provision of a fine powder, using good willow coals, the best I could discover in all of England. There were to be twenty-four balls so crafted that they would be a perfect fit for the barrel. Would that be the sum of your requirements, Mr Herrick?'

'Let me see it.'

Cogg raised a hand, a bulbous white thing with five protuberances like outsized maggots. 'Mr Herrick, I have, indeed, had the gun made. By a gentleman called Mr Opel, a Germanic living here in England. He told me he had never produced such a fine weapon. Reckoned it could kill at a hundred and fifty yards. Said he had never heard of a gun that could find its target at more than fifty yards. So this gun, Mr Herrick, what would it be for killing? A deer? A man? It is a very curious shape, to be sure, and sadly lacking in ornament.'

Herrick's eyes pierced Cogg's. His voice lowered but did not soften. 'I was told you didn't ask questions.'

Cogg raised his right hand defensively. 'My apologies, Mr Herrick. I meant no offence. The use of the gun is your concern. But it is such a remarkable piece, sir, that I would like to know about it. Perhaps there is a market for such articles. Would gentlemen want such a weapon for hunting? Tarry, Mr Herrick, sir, take some Spanish wine so we can talk a while and drink to the Spanish King's death.'

In a movement of elegance and speed, Herrick went forward and his hand was at Cogg's fat neck, crushing his windpipe. Cogg writhed but the grip was like an iron vice. Then, as suddenly as the assault began, Herrick released him.

'I do not want your wine. I do not want to talk with you. Bring me the gun, for which a price has been agreed.'

Cogg sat down heavily on a low crate and fought to regain his breath. His hand went to his throat and rubbed it. For a moment he had thought he would die, so powerful was the hand that held him. Gilbert Cogg retained much of the strength he had had as a young man, but this man's power was of a different order. His common sense told him that Herrick could kill him with casual ease and that he would do well to hand over the gun at the price agreed, but instinct told him never to pass up an opportunity to make ready money. And now in this game of cards with Herrick he held the kings because he had the gun still, and Herrick would be pressed to find it without him.

'Remind me, Mr Herrick,' he said, his voice rasping from the assault on his throat, 'what was the agreed price?'

'Nine marks, Cogg, as well you know.'

'In gold?'

'In gold. Four sovereign coins.'

Cogg knew he should stop now, take the money offered. There was a good profit in it already, three marks for him, six for Opel, and yet he could not because he knew the weapon was worth far more to Herrick than nine marks. It was one of a kind.

'Mr Herrick, this weapon has cost me far more than I had thought. My man Opel has worked long hours to a standard never before seen in the gunmaker's art, using new methods to meet your requirements. I have had to pay him more than double the fee we did agree.'

Herrick smiled then. 'How much, Cogg? How much will it take for you to be silent and for me to walk out of this room with no more cheapening?'

Cogg's mouth pursed, his shoulders wobbled. At last he spoke, in his most reasonable voice. 'Can we say thirty marks, sir?'

'And that is your last demand?'

Cogg rubbed his pudgy hands together. 'My *very* last.'

Without another word, Herrick took the purse from his belt and counted out thirteen gold sovereigns and two crowns. Cogg took the coins. The gold glinted at him from his white palm. He looked up at Herrick. 'And now, if you will excuse me, sir, I require privacy while I retrieve your piece for you.'

Herrick shook his head. 'Get it now.'

Cogg hesitated a moment too long. Herrick slammed his head down hard on to the top of a large cask, then, with his right hand clasped on the nape of his neck, he pulled his left arm up by the wrist. 'Where is it?'

Cogg grunted as if he were trying to speak. But the words, if there were any, were too indistinct for Herrick to make out. In a single motion, Herrick snapped back Cogg's wrist and there was an audible crack as the bone shattered. Cogg screamed.

Herrick pulled his head off the cask and rammed his gloved

fist into the screaming mouth to silence it. Blood spattered from Cogg's loosened teeth down his unkempt beard. Herrick had his dagger out now, clasped in his left hand. Blood from Cogg's mouth dripped over its black bone handle. The dagger was thin with a point like a needle. He held it to Cogg's right eye, the tip touching the black centre. 'Another sound, except for the words I want to hear, and I will prick out this eye, Mr Cogg.'

Cogg knew now that he was going to die but the thought of his eye being pricked and the fluids therein bursting forth was too much to bear. 'I'll fetch it, right away, Mr Herrick.'

Herrick released him. Cogg's hand hung loose from his arm, the bone protruding at an unspeakable angle through the skin and flesh at the wrist. Like a bullock at the slaughter, he stumbled through the boxes and barrels, falling over them in his haste.

The weapon was concealed beneath floorboards near the back of the house by a door that gave out on to a small court-yard where chickens clucked and pecked. With his one working hand and a jemmy, he prised up the loose boards and brought out the weapon. It was in two parts, a plain thing, wrapped in jute sackcloth that did no credit to its fine craftsmanship. His fingers trembled as he lifted the gun. It was heavy and difficult to balance with just one hand. He turned. Herrick was in front of him, the thin dagger loose in his right hand. He slid it into its sheath and gently took the gun from Cogg. The sacking was tied at both ends with coarse string, which he quickly slipped off.

The gun did not look much like a gun. One part was a bare wooden stock, triangular but curved on the shortest of the three sides. It had two joiners' hooks to attach it to the front of the weapon, a dark-metal barrel and the snaphaunce mechanism. Herrick clicked the two pieces together, then examined it closely, turning it this way and that, peering down the muzzle, testing the lock and pan cover, cocking the hammer and letting it fall against the frizzen. The action was smooth. At last he looked up. 'Where are the balls and powder?'

Cogg saw his last chance. 'I kept them separate, Mr Herrick. They are at the front in an old cabinet where I keep smaller things.'

'Remember your eyes. Nor will I stop with the pricking out of your eyes. I will slice off your pizzle and stones and you will go to your death a girl if you make just one little error.'

Cogg shuddered, but there was one thing he had to try. Herrick dismantled the gun and replaced it in its sacking. He followed Cogg to the front room. It had a ware-bench, like a shop, and behind it a tall wooden dresser with cupboard doors at the top and little drawers below. The pain in Cogg's broken left wrist was almost beyond enduring. As he pulled open one of the cabinet doors with his good hand, the packages were revealed on a shelf: the black powder wrapped in a large purse of leather, the balls in a bag of jute cloth. As he picked up the balls and powder he turned and threw them into Herrick's face, then launched himself at him in a last desperate effort to survive, as hopeless as a chicken running from the farmwife's blade.

Starling Day stopped halfway down Cow Lane. She knew now that Cogg would take her on, so why did she have to wait another night to hear it? Why couldn't she do a deal with him today and start work immediately? She needed the money badly for she wanted clothes and food. She also had debts, for which she would suffer if she did not repay them by the week's end. She had learnt about Cogg from her cousin Alice, who was already whoring at his bawdy-house by the Bel Savage.

At first Alice had not been pleased to see Starling; she was less than a year older and they had played together as children, swimming in the stream in the summer and sifting coal from the slack tip when winter froze the land. Perhaps she was ashamed of what she had become. But when she realised Starling intended to enter the same line of work, she had warmed to her. 'I never understood what you saw in him,' she said, when Starling told her about her husband's viciousness. 'I wouldn't have married any of the men in that village. I'd rather die of the French pox in London Town than live as a beaten goodwife with a drunken coal hewer for a husbandman in Strelley.' They had had some drinks together in the Bel Savage and then she had told Starling where to find Cogg.

'This is how things are with him, Starling, so listen well. He's as fat as six men stuck together, but never laugh at him or shy away from him. He likes Paris tricks, so use your tongue like this.' Alice rolled and curled hers to show just what Cogg wanted. 'His terms are half and half, but you'll have to pay him for food and lodging, too. Not the best bargain this side of Cheapside, but he always gets us a good price. Keeps us free of the pox, mostly, which is what the men want. You'll learn how to look at them, see if they're diseased – and tell them to piss off if they are. He's got ointments of herbs from the apothecary to keep us clean. Told me he paid for them with the eyes and tongue of a hanged woman. But remember this: if you do get the pox, it's the lowest stews in Southwark for you or back to Strelley.'

Starling was about to knock at Cogg's front door when she heard a noise from inside. Voices. It seemed he had another visitor – but this was a man's voice, not a girl's. She turned the handle and found the door was open, the lock sheared away from the wood. Whoever was in there with Cogg had done this; she was sure the lock had been secure when she left. Starling slipped into the front room. She heard footfalls at the top of the steps and hid herself, crouching behind a workbench and boxes to the right of the room.

The man she saw with Cogg was tall, dressed darkly, clean-shaven. She felt a chill of unease and wished she had not entered. As she watched him follow Cogg through to the back room, then heard a whump and Cogg's shrill scream, she drew back in fear.

She knew too well the smell of violence. It stank of the sleeping room at the cottage she had once called home. When her husband, Edward, had returned from the coal mine, his face and hands and clothes all black, he would eat whatever food she had scavenged or grown, drink strong ale and hit her. Every night of the year, without fail. Some nights he would make her lie flat on the straw, her wrists tied to the rough-hewn bedleg with his leather belt as he beat her with the broken haft of an old hayfork. And then, inevitably, he would occupy her, brutally but briefly, as if only her pain could bring him pleasure. Every daybreak when he went off to be wound down the well into the pit of the earth with his little tallow lamp and coal pick, she would pray for the walls to cave in and bury him. And when that didn't happen she stopped believing in God and took the road for London.

Huddled small behind the workbench, Starling could hear her heart. Did that mean the man in dark clothes could hear it too? She saw them return to the front room. Cogg's left arm hung limp at the wrist, broken, blood dripping where the bone protruded through the skin. She felt no pity for him. She felt no pity for any man. The other was carrying something. It looked like a tool, but she had never seen its like before.

Cogg took something from the cabinet behind the ware-bench and threw it at the other man's face. It was a pathetic effort, evaded easily, and as Cogg lunged towards him, the dark-clothed one easily sidestepped and pushed Cogg forward so that he fell to the ground, flat on his face. He sat on him, his legs straddling the huge back, and pulled back Cogg's straggly hair. Then, with a thin, black-handled dagger, he stabbed twice at his face, the blade descending each time into the eyes and through to the brain. To the hilt. Cogg didn't scream, but gurgled and thrashed and grunted with the urgency of an animal that suddenly finds itself prey.

The dark-clothed man stood up and left Cogg to die. He wiped the blood and brain from his blade and sheathed it before putting some gold coins into his leather purse. Then he picked up the objects that had been thrown at him, slung the unidentified tool over his shoulder and left quietly.

Starling waited five minutes behind the workbench. Cogg's feet were twitching but she knew he was dead. At last she came out from her hiding-place and went over to him. He was no use to her now. She spat on him. Then she spat on him again. Somewhere in this house, she realised, there must be a goodly pile of gold. Cogg had been a wealthy man.

Chapter 10

THEY FOUND DRAKE pacing a wood-panelled ante-chamber at Greenwich Palace like a man demented. Boltfoot had seen him pace like this many times on the quarterdeck when the wind wouldn't rise.

He was a short, thick-set man of forty-six. His sharp little beard was still fair and golden but now with flecks of grey. His hair was more red, greying also, curled and combed back off his broad, deep forehead. His eyes retained the vital blue of his youth. He wore court clothes, a brilliant green velvet cape over a green and silver-wrought doublet, all tailored at great cost by Gaston de Volpère of Candlewick Street, along with an outrageous ruff, as wide as a serving platter. His blue eyes could twinkle with amusement but now they were angry, like the dark blue of the stormy sea that was his home.

He was angry, very angry, and nothing the two people with him in the small official room could do or say would calm him. His young wife, Elizabeth Sydenham, had tried to soothe him without success and now sat on some cushions with a book of poems, trying to shut out the raging torrent that foamed from her husband. His constant companion, Diego, the slave he had freed in the Spanish Indies and who had since circumnavigated the world with him, stood at a window, gazing idly out at a bark drifting slowly downstream towards the estuary. He had seen these rages so many times before that they had long since ceased to frighten him. Drake looked at the new arrivals – Shakespeare, Stanley and Boltfoot – and stopped his pacing. He glared at them.

'In God's Faith, this is a sorry affair, Stanley. She won't see me. There was a time when I would be admitted to her presence eight times a day. Now, when we need her most, she closets herself with lady's maid poltroons like Davison and Burghley. This realm will be a Spanish colony before summer's end if she continues so.'

Captain Stanley bowed briskly, then rose to his full, proud height. 'Sir Francis,' he said, 'may I introduce Mr John Shakespeare, an assistant secretary to Mr Secretary Walsingham?'

The brutal cloud lifted momentarily from Drake's brow. 'Ah, yes, Mr Shakespeare, I have been expecting you.'

'It is an honour to meet you, Sir Francis.'

'Likewise, likewise. A good man, Walsingham. England would be lost without him. I love him like a brother. Now, what is his concern?'

Shakespeare viewed the tableau before him with fascination. The great, heroic mariner, in a rage because the Queen refused to see him, his wife so busy in her poems that she scarce looked up at the new arrivals, and a blackamoor dressed like a fine English gentleman and affecting disinterest in the proceedings. What glue held these three creatures together?

Catching the direction of Shakespeare's eye, Drake broke in before he could speak: 'Forgive me, Mr Shakespeare, I have not introduced you to my wife, Elizabeth.'

Elizabeth's delicate, heart-shaped face lit up in a guileless smile that seemed to cast sparkles in the sapphires, rubies and pearls that adorned her neck and fingers. Shakespeare bowed to her and she held out her delicate white hand for him to kiss. Drake, meanwhile, was moving swiftly on: 'And my very good friend Diego, who probably hates the Spanish even more than I do.'

Boltfoot Cooper had been hanging back, behind Shakespeare and Stanley, but now Diego caught sight of him and strode forward to shake his hand. 'Boltfoot, it is good to see you.' He clapped him on the shoulder.

'And you, Diego.'

'I saved Diego from the Spanish in Nombre de Dios,' Drake continued, addressing Shakespeare and Stanley but ignoring Boltfoot. 'I think they had an idea that a hanging would make their saints look favourably on them, and Diego was to be the day's entertainment. Luckily he has a strong neck because he was already dancing the hempen jig when we cut him down. He's been my fine companion ever since. He is a master of tongues who has helped me many times talk to my captives when we have boarded a ship or taken a town. How many languages do you speak now, Diego?'

'Four.'

'Four! English, Spanish, Portuguese . . .'

'And Mandingo, my own tongue.'

'Tell me again, Diego, what would you like to do to the Spanish King?'

Diego laughed too, as if he had heard it all before a thousand times. 'Chain him up, brand him, sling him and two hundred other Spaniards into the stinking hold of a slow carrack across the western sea, set him to work on a Caribbean plantation for ten years, then hang him.'

Drake clapped his hands. 'And may he burn an eternity in hell, as he has burnt so many others.' At last he turned to Boltfoot. They were both short, squat men and they stood toe to toe, neither man blinking. 'And you, Cooper, what in God's name are you doing here? Why aren't you shaping your staves, bending your hoops and fashioning your faucets?'

'He is in my employ,' Shakespeare said.

Drake put an arm round Boltfoot's shoulders. Boltfoot stood sullenly and stiffly, as if in the grip of a tropic snake. 'I know, I know. He works for you and Mr Secretary. You're a shipwreck of a man, Cooper. You should be building casks, which is what God put you on earth to do, not promenading round London with your caliver and cutlass like some landbound pirate.'

'And you're a common thief, Mr Drake.'

Drake took his arm from Boltfoot's shoulders and pushed him in the chest. 'I've killed men for less, Cooper.'

Boltfoot stood his ground. 'You were not the only man to journey round the world, Mr Drake. I was there with you near death from ship's fever, hunger and the bloody flux. Where is *my* share of the treasure?'

'Why, you have had gold.'

'Enough to keep me from starving, perhaps. You feed us a pension in dribs and drabs as it pleases you, and you turn us into beggars for what is rightfully ours. Where are the riches you promised us?'

'I will hear none of this. Mr Shakespeare, please remove your man.'

Boltfoot was not so easily silenced. Rarely had Shakespeare heard him say more than a dozen words together at a time and now he was in full flow. 'Do you not recall the gold Will Legge and I found in the chest of the master's cabin aboard the *Capitana* and gave to you? Six and a half pounds that you had not seen. You cut us a wedge of twenty-nine ounces, marked it with our names and pledged it to us when we reached England. Where, then, is that gold now, Mr Drake? For Will and I have seen none of it.'

Drake was near foaming with anger. 'God's faith! You are the vilest knave that ever lived, Boltfoot Cooper. I tell you, you and all the men have had your share and more. Did I not write your names in glory?'

Shakespeare decided it was time to intervene. 'Sir Francis, if I may speak with you a while in private—'

'I'll run you through, Cooper, you base scoundrel!'

'Sir Francis?'

Drake snapped out of his tirade and turned to Shakespeare. 'Get me away from the company of this monstrous, dissembling, perfidious, lame, bilge-scum of a man. Come, Mr Shakespeare, Mr Stanley, let us adjourn and take some wine. Diego, stay with Cooper.' He nodded briefly to his wife. 'M'lady . . .'

Drake strode ahead of them into the adjoining room, the slight limp from a leg wound sustained in his raid on a Spanish mule train at Nombre de Dios still evident fourteen years later. The three men sat at a table and Drake hammered on it with his fist. 'The Queen will not hear me. She affects to despise me for the lack of pearls, gold and emeralds brought her from the Spanish Main this last year, but she knows I wreaked terrible harm on the Spanish King. And if she gives me now the commission of ships I need, I will go and sink him and his Enterprise for ever.'

'Sir Francis—'

'I know, I know, Mr Shakespeare, you have something to say. But hear me out. I am the one man who can save this Queen and this realm from the foul anti-Christ of Rome and his Spanish toy dog.'

'That, Sir Francis, is why I am here.' Shakespeare knew as well as any the boastfulness of Drake. It was common knowledge in England and throughout Europe, and those who did not fear or admire him sneered at him for it. And yet he had much to be boastful about. The plunder taken on his three-year round-the-world voyage amounted to five hundred thousand pounds. Much went to the Queen, yet Drake himself was left one of the wealthiest men in the realm. He had won it through cunning and courage and attention to detail. Never did he shy away from a fight – yet his belligerence was tempered with mercy.

'Tell me, then, sir. Why *are* you here? Some threat to my life, I am told.'

'A threat that Mr Secretary takes exceeding serious, Admiral, coming as it does from a ciphered message between Mendoza and the Spanish King.'

Drake laughed, a long, crashing wave of a laugh. 'The Spanish King kill me? I will nail his ears to the flummery altar in his Escorial Palace before he kills me, Mr Shakespeare.'

'We believe Mendoza has found a seasoned mercenary, a paid assassin, to do his work for him, and the price on your head has increased considerably.'

'Well, well, and what are they offering now? Twenty thousand ducats last time, I do believe.'

'It is now seventy thousand.'

Drake clapped his hands, like a river fisherman who has just landed a twenty-pound pike. 'They will be offering ten times seventy thousand before I am in my grave, Mr Shakespeare. What say you, Captain Stanley?'

'I agree, Sir Francis. But perhaps it would be prudent to hear Mr Shakespeare out. The world knows you are invincible at sea, but now you are ashore, you are not so safe.'

'Indeed, sir. And do I seem afraid? Is John Doughty at large again with his wooden sword to scare me into my mother's bed?'

This was going to be difficult. Shakespeare understood that it was vital to play to Drake's vanity. 'No, Sir Francis, you seem anything but afraid. And that, we believe, is the card Mendoza and his hireling will play. Because you are so very visible at Deptford, at Gravesend and at court, you are a tempting target ... dare I say an easy target for a determined killer. I understand that you do not fear for your life and never have, but we must all fear for the life of Her Majesty and the future of England. If you should fall to a Spanish ball, bolt or blade, we will all be lost.'

Drake stood up and started pacing again. His face was florid now, a hot red. He was silent a while, then turned sharply to Shakespeare and Stanley, who were sitting side by side on the other side of the table. 'So, then, what does my friend Mr Secretary propose?'

Shakespeare sighed. 'He wants me to protect you.'

'And how would you do that?'

'First, by asking you to curtail your movements. Make yourself less visible, surround yourself at all times with trusted lieutenants. When you board a ship to inspect its caulking and provisioning, spend as little time on deck as possible. When you are at court, avoid the public areas. When you are in the dock-yards or chandleries, keep a watchful eye and do not tarry in one place. Take no chances, Admiral. Your apparel,' he nodded towards Drake's brilliant velvet attire, 'is too noticeable.'

Drake's brows knitted in amusement. 'You cannot imagine I would wear a cape and doublet like this outside court? I'm a mariner, Mr Shakespeare, I dress in sea clothes. How else would you protect me if God wills it otherwise?'

This was the difficult bit. Shakespeare took a deep breath. 'I would assign Mr Boltfoot Cooper as your personal guardian, Sir Francis.'

Drake exploded with laughter. 'Cooper! My personal guardian!'

'He is very handy with his caliver and cutlass, Sir Francis. He knows your ways—'

'Never. In God's faith, never.'

Shakespeare played his final card. 'Mr Secretary Walsingham, your friend, requests this of you. He understands your reluctance and the bad blood between you, caused I am sure by Mr Cooper's avarice, but he begs this one indulgence.'

Drake was pacing again. His right hand gripped the hilt of his sword, but it stayed firmly in its scabbard. 'Boltfoot Cooper protect my life? I have sailed tempests and seen strange sea monsters and been at one with God on the empty ocean, but never have I heard such a thing. What say you, Stanley?'

'He has courage, sir.'

'Aye, I'll give you that. He has courage. He was always a fine man in a fight with the Spaniard. Never did he hold back when the powder was burning hot.'

'I vouch he is indeed a fine man, Sir Francis. I would swear before God that he is loyal, true and strong.'

'Well, then, be done with it and give me the knave. I'll remind him what it is to be Drake's man. But he is under *my* command, Mr Shakespeare.'

'I understand.'

Drake's eyes twinkled suddenly. 'I will set him to making casks for the fleet. That is a far more useful occupation. It is well-barrelled water, ale and salt pork that keeps a man alive at sea.'

Shakespeare had to intervene. 'Forgive me, Sir Francis, but not in this instance. Your own life is what will keep your men alive at sea.'

Drake gave Shakespeare a hard look, thought a moment, then changed the subject. 'And, tell me, what has happened to John Doughty? Is he hanged yet?'

'I fear I do not know, Admiral. The last I heard he had been consigned to the Marshalsea, but that was four or five years ago. God willing, he has died of the plague . . . but I mean to find out.'

Chapter 11

STARLING DAY COULD scarce contain her fear and excitement. What could she do with all these riches? Where could she hide them? And what of the body?

She sat on a trunk, staring at Gilbert Cogg's corpse. In the palms of her open, spread hands was a bar of gold, which, though she had never seen its like before, she knew to be worth riches beyond her imagining. Upstairs, in a coffer, hidden behind a barely visible door in a low cupboard to the side of the hearth, there was yet more gold, much more, with silver and stones set as jewellery. Much more than she could reckon.

She clenched her fingers into talons over the gold as she tried to concentrate. Unless she moved Cogg's body it would soon be found. She had to get the treasure out of this house quickly. But there was too much of it, and too heavy. Her mind kept drifting. How would she use such wealth? Fine clothes, a great house, good wine and food. But how could she buy all this and ensure her sudden wealth went unnoticed? Her dearest wish would be to return to her home village, Strelley, and parade in finery in front of her cruel husband and his witch of a mother to show them what she had become, but that would never be possible.

Alice. She would have to bring in Alice as her confederate. She could not manage it alone. And, anyway, there was more than enough to share. She looked again at the body. It was the size of a two-month heifer, more than three times her own weight. She would never be able to move it alone. Perhaps, together, she and Alice could shift it. In the meantime she would have to cover it. She knew that Cogg had many visitors and he could be discovered at any moment.

The body was uncomfortably close to the front door. There was a bolt on the inside, which she had slid into place. Two people had already knocked on the door since she had been there, eventually leaving disappointed. How long before someone broke in? She feared, too, that if someone looked closely through the window they would make out the body.

Starling went back upstairs and took the covers from the bed where she had endured Cogg's grunting, slathering weight. There was a carpet bag there, into which she put the gold bar she already held with another. Then, concealing the rest of the hoard as well as she could, she brought the bag and the bed-covers downstairs. She covered Cogg and moved the table so that the huge mound of his body was less visible from the window.

She waited, listening with trepidation for footsteps. Finally, she slid back the bolt and wrenched open the door. Her heart thumped in her chest. She looked right, left, then shut the door behind her and went quickly down Cow Lane, clutching the heavy bag to her breast, hunched forward into the cold wind.

It was a brisk ten-minute walk through the mud and slush to the Bel Savage by the Fleet prison, hemmed in between the ditch and the western wall of London. The tavern was one of London's most famed, attracting a fine crowd of lawyers, merchants, market traders, whores and those who merely wanted to get knockdown drunk. There was always merriment to be had, with lively minstrels and players staging entertainments. The tenement next to it was well maintained, considering its purpose as a bawdy-house for the sale of women's bodies.

Downstairs there was an ante-room, where customers – many of whom had spilled straight out of the Bel Savage with a belly-ful of ale or brandy befuddling their better judgement and keeping them from their wives and homes – could consider their purchase. Upstairs there were a dozen rooms, each with a bed and a fire and each shared by two whores for sleeping but interchangeable when customers were to be entertained.

Alice had just finished with one of her regulars, a balding, half-blind old retainer from the Earl of Leicester's great mansion just along the Strand. He was so decrepit it had taken him an hour to get started and another to finish. Starling pushed past him into Alice's first-floor room and slammed the door with her shoulder. She dropped the bag with the gold bars on the far side of the bed in case anyone entered unannounced, then clenched her fists and let out a silent scream of joy. 'Alice, something has happened that I must tell you. We must be quick.'

Alice finished washing and began to dress. 'That bastardly gullion! He took two hours and paid me for one. He's getting worse.' She pulled her blouse about her breasts. She was more rounded than Starling, her skin clearer and more luminous, her hair fairer. Cogg had made sure she was properly fed with meat from the market at Smith Field and had plenty of ale.

'Alice, forget about him. You must listen to me.'

'What, cousin, have you won at the cock-fights?'

'Better. Oh, Alice, riches beyond your imagining.' She clasped her cousin in a hug. 'Look in the bag, but hurry. I'll stay by the door.'

Alice went beside the bed and opened the bag. As she looked at the gold bars she could not at first decide what they were. Then she thrust in her hands and pulled one out.

'Keep it low, Alice. Someone might come in.'

'Starling, where did you get this?'

'It was Cogg's but now he's backed.'

'Cogg? Dead?'

Starling nodded furiously. 'Dead, Alice, murdered . . .' She saw the horror in Alice's face. 'No, no, no – not by me!' Quickly, she gabbled out the sequence of events as they had unfolded at the house in Cow Lane. Alice listened, still unbuttoned, her clothing forgotten.

'I need you,' Starling said at last. 'We've got to hide Cogg and take the gold to somewhere safe. I'll give you half of everything.'

'Starling, this is dangerous. You'll have us both strung up at Tyburn.'

'It's our one chance, Alice. You've got to help me.'

Walking from the river stairs by London Bridge to Seething Lane, John Shakespeare felt uneasy. He kept turning, certain he was being followed, but he could make out no one suspicious among the rowdy throngs of merchants, clerks and apprentices who crowded the streets, or among those driving the slow, ox-drawn wagons laden with produce from Kent.

He had left Boltfoot at Greenwich with Drake. Boltfoot had been discomfited, and Shakespeare felt bad, realising he was in for a hard time, staying close to his former captain twenty-four hours a day.

As Shakespeare left the palace, there had been great excitement along the royal jetty. He saw Robert Beale, among a group of courtiers, about to get into a state barge. Beale was clerk to the Privy Council and brother-in-law to Walsingham. Shakespeare knew him well.

He greeted him with a wave. 'What news, Robert?' And then he saw that Beale was white, drained and distracted.

'The best and the worst, John. I would say more but cannot.'

'Has she signed?'

'I can say no more.' With that Beale stepped into the barge and disappeared from view.

Shakespeare's heart pounded. It sounded as though the Queen had signed the warrant for the execution of Mary Stuart. But Elizabeth changed her mind a dozen times within a day. If it were to be done, it would have to be done quickly before she thought better of it. And if the head fell? The reaction from the Catholic world could be bloody and swift. This sobering thought occupied him on the long journey back upriver against the tide. He reclined beneath the canopy on cushions and pulled a blanket round him, closing his eyes as the watermen strained their sinews to the oars. He thought, too, of his father and his refusal to attend church, and worried again. Did Topcliffe really have influence in the Midlands?

At his door, Jane was waiting anxiously. 'Someone has been here, master, while I was at the market.'

'Did they leave a message?'

'No, master. I fear they have robbed us.'

It was then that Shakespeare saw the door was broken at the lock. He went into his ante-room. It looked undisturbed.

'Your solar, master. They have been among your papers and books.'

Shakespeare went upstairs to his solar, the light-filled room he used for working. His papers were strewn across the floor; cabinets and tables were turned over. There was damage to the wall panelling, and boards had been ripped from the floor as if someone had searched for something. Topcliffe. Shakespeare slammed his fist against the wall in frustration and anger.

He turned and saw Jane. 'Forgive me. A cup of wine, I think.' She was standing in the doorway and he could see the shock and incomprehension in her face. 'And one for yourself, if you wish it.' He liked Jane. He liked her openness, the generous proportion of her breasts, her moon face framed by auburn hair, which always crept untidily from beneath a lawn coif, the way she carried herself. She had come to London from the county of Essex, the eldest daughter of a family of twelve girls and no boys, and had been with him two years now. She was easy to live with, but he knew this was not the perfect position for her: she was hungry for a husband but would find none in this house, unless she took a liking to Boltfoot, which was as probable as a man growing wings and flying. She was used to a big noisy peasant farm household, full of shouting and tears; this house was quiet and contemplative, with just the three of them.

There were times when Shakespeare wondered whether she entertained hopes that she might be his one day. Yes, he liked to gaze upon her body. What man would not? But marriage had to be based on more than common lust. He would tire of her and they would resent each other.

He started to pick up his papers. He wondered if Topcliffe had been looking for the one he had found near Blanche Howard's body. He might have suspected that a sample was kept.

Later, as Shakespeare sat with his wine, having cleared up the papers and righted the furniture – the damage to the panelling and boards would have to be repaired by a joiner on the morrow – Harry Slide arrived. He was dishevelled and slipped in quietly with none of his characteristic fanfare.

'Well, Harry?'

'Not at all well, Mr Shakespeare. I have not felt so bad in all my life.'

'Are you ill, Harry? Sit with me by the fire and take some warming hippocras.' As Slide seated himself awkwardly on a bench by the fire, shivering, Shakespeare saw that his face was bruised and bloody. He looked like the loser in a Bartholomew Fair bout of the heavyweights. His nose was cut and his eye blackened, while his expensively barbered fair hair, normally swept back to good effect, was ragged. His neat beard was rusty with caked blood. 'Harry, by the Lord, what has happened to you?'

'I was set upon, Mr Shakespeare. My purse was cut from me. He came at me from behind. Before I could draw my sword I was flat down on the ice, being kicked in the face. Look at my clothes.' Slide pulled off his cape, which was relatively unscathed, to reveal his fine yellow doublet, torn and muddy.

Shakespeare called Jane to bring warm water and towels to wash his wounds. 'Where were you, Harry?'

'Holborn. I'd been in a few ordinaries and taverns, asking the gossip. It was gullish of me to be caught like that.'

Jane came in and began to attend to Slide's face. Shakespeare poured him a large goblet of spiced wine.

'At least I discovered where to find Walstan Glebe,' Slide said. 'It seems he has a press in Fleet Lane. I'm told he's not always there – the fox has many lairs – but he might be about tomorrow morning, early.'

'Are you much hurt, Harry?'

Slide sipped the wine. 'Well, my head feels as if the headsman had taken an axe to it and caught it a glancing blow, but I'll live.'

'Yes, Harry, please survive. Stay here tonight. Jane will make you up a bed.'

'I shall, Mr Shakespeare, but first I have other things to tell you.'

'Yes?'

'It may be nothing, but I was told of a curious dinner at the Marshalsea two nights past. Two priests had four visitors. Together they broke bread and took fine wine and one of the priests said mass.'

Shakespeare had heard of such things happening before. The Marshalsea and The Clink seemed easy-going with their captive priests. It was not something that concerned him greatly. 'And do you know who any of these people were?'

Slide smiled and immediately regretted it: too painful. 'Well,' he said, 'the priests were not important. Piggott and Plummer. Piggott is a poor creature who deserves hanging. Plummer is my source. He long since discarded Romish ways, but it pays him to stay there. The Romans give him money for food and I give him more for information.'

'What of the others?'

'Three gentlewomen, all of known Romish families – Lady Frances Browne, a young girl called Anne Bellamy and the Lady Tanahill.'

Shakespeare was surprised. 'Lady Tanahill? She is living dangerously, considering her husband is in the Tower. And the Bellamy girl has already lost two brothers to the rope for association with the Babington plotters.'

Slide nodded. 'But it is the sixth and last member of this band who most interests me. His name is Cotton and he is a Jesuit priest.'

Shakespeare's brow creased. 'Another Jesuit?'

'Yes, Mr Shakespeare. Another Jesuit. Most assuredly, from what Plummer says.'

How, Shakespeare wondered, had a Jesuit slipped in without Walsingham's knowledge? His spies in Rome and the other English colleges abroad knew the names and movements of all the English Jesuits, or so it was believed. Walsingham had known Southwell and Garnet were coming to England even before they set sail from France. This was grim news if it meant there were now three at large in England. Walsingham would not be happy to hear that. And the Queen would be even less so. She did not like Jesuit priests abroad in her realm.

'There is, of course, one other possibility,' Slide said through the corner of his split lip. 'It occurred to me that Cotton is unlikely to be his real name. He may, perhaps, be the man we are searching for. Robert Southwell.'

'What did he look like?'

'I am told he was well dressed. Golden hair, lively grey eyes, a confident air. And Southwell is said to be a handsome man. A priest told me that when he was at Douai everyone called him the "Beautiful English Youth".'

'Well, Harry, we must find out the truth of this.'

Slide rose painfully to his feet and rubbed his neck. 'There was one other thing, Mr Shakespeare.'

'Yes?'

'The man who kicked me. As he was leaving, he turned and said something.'

'What was it?'

'It was difficult to make out. My ears were ringing, but I thought he said, "There's more where that came from, Slide." How did he know my name, if he was only a cutpurse?'

Chapter 12

SHAKESPEARE AND SLIDE took horse and were across London and through the city wall by the New Gate just before first light. Their destination was Fleet Lane where they hoped to catch Walstan Glebe off guard.

'Over there,' Slide said at last. 'That's the place.'

Snow was falling. The horses' hooves were silent on the empty road. As they stopped, Shakespeare jumped down nimbly from his grey mare. He handed the reins to Slide, who had woken feeling stiff and battered. He looked haggard but had insisted on accompanying him. 'Wait here with the horses. I'll go in alone.'

'Call if you need me.'

'I will.'

It was a tall wood-frame house with an exaggerated over-hanging first floor that blocked out much of the rising eastern light. There was no lock so Shakespeare went straight in. The entrance hall was empty. He went through to another, larger room, where he found a printing press, surrounded by boxes of type sorts. The press was a rickety device that stood against one wall to the height of a man. Shakespeare had a good idea of how it worked; the lead type would be set letter by letter, along with woodcut pictures, into formes propped on an easel, like an A-shaped two-sided lectern. It would then be tightened into each forme with quoins – wedges – and inked before it was inserted into the bottom of the press, where paper would be placed above it. The press would be screwed down a sheet at a time for printing. Nearby lay a pile of broadsheets entitled *The London Informer*, already printed, the ink dried, and waiting to be distributed. Shakespeare looked at the papers and found himself stifling a laugh.

'Amazing Sea Monster in Thames' said the first line. Underneath, it said, 'Behemoth is evil omen, avows soothsayer.'

Clearly Walstan Glebe had a refined knowledge of his customers' reading requirements, but he had missed what Shakespeare believed to be the tastiest news of the day: that Mary, Queen of Scots, was about to be relieved of her head.

Shakespeare climbed the steps to the first floor, where he found a door. From outside it he heard a chorus of snoring. He raised the latch and went in to find a large, canopied bed with what looked like a solid mass of bodies in it. Stepping further into the shuttered room he could tell that there were three people: two female and one male. The man was in the middle and most of the snoring was his, although his friends were contributing to the noise. Shakespeare leant over one of the females, a buxom doxy lying on her back with her mouth wide open and her hair splayed out in a dark frame to her face, and shook the man.

He opened an eye groggily. 'What is it?'

'Get up. Queen's business.'

'Queen who?'

'Queen Elizabeth, and if you don't like the idea of a day in the pillory, I suggest you move. Now!'

The man sat up sharply and tried to get his bearings. 'What is this?'

'My name is John Shakespeare and I am here on Queen's business. Get out of bed, Glebe.'

The man yawned and scratched his head. 'You've got the wrong man. My name's Felbrigg.'

Shakespeare leant across the bed again and grabbed the man's fringe of thick, tousled hair, wrenching it upwards. An angry red L was revealed on his forehead. 'L for Liar, Glebe. You were branded for stealing the work of other men.' Shakespeare let go his hair.

Glebe shrugged his bare shoulders and grinned like a grammar-school boy found copying his fellow scholar's work. 'Very well. Give me time to cover myself.'

The two women were stirring. 'What's going on?' one asked.

'Nothing. Go back to sleep.'

'You've woken me now, sweeting.'

'Well, then, put on your clothes and piss off. Take your sister with you.' Glebe turned to Shakespeare. 'I'm sorry, sir. A rough night and strong ale.' He was out of bed and had started pulling on a shirt and breeches. He nodded back towards the two women. 'Not bad for a cold night in February. I can fix you up if you're interested.'

Shakespeare was in no mood for frivolity. 'Come downstairs, Glebe. You're in trouble.'

In the press room, Glebe stood with his shoulders drooping, scratching his balls.

'A case of the French welcome, Glebe?'

'Me and everyone else I know, Mr Shakespeare.'

'That might say a lot about the sort of people you know.' Shakespeare gestured towards the press. 'Has that been licensed by the Council through Stationers' Hall?'

'Of course, Mr Shakespeare.'

'You have been branded a liar, Glebe, and you are still a liar. If you don't answer me truthfully, your press will be closed down and your broadsheets destroyed. Not only that, but I will bring down the full weight of the law on your head for sedition. Which, to my mind, is another word for treason.'

'Mr Shakespeare, this is a gossip sheet, harmless news for the people of London. There is nothing treasonable here. Look, sir.' Glebe held up a copy of his pamphlet. 'The whole world wants to know about this great fish. It is the talk of the city. What harm is there here?'

Shakespeare tore the broadsheet from his hand, crumpled it into a ball and threw it to the floor. 'I'm not interested in that, Glebe. It is the murder of Lady Blanche Howard that interests me. Where did you find your information for that pamphlet?' He pulled it from his doublet.

Suddenly Glebe looked worried. He spread his hands beseechingly. He was about thirty, short, with a pinched face, sharp teeth, clever eyes and a knowing smile, almost a grin, hovering permanently on his lips. But now his brow furrowed. 'It's the gossip, Mr Shakespeare. Every tavern, inn and ordinary from Westminster to Whitechapel is alive with word about the Lady Blanche. A tragic tale, to be certain, sir. I simply listened and wrote down what I heard.'

'There is a line in the broadsheet blaming the Jesuit Southwell for the murder with what you describe as "cross, relic and blade". What does that mean and where did you hear that?'

Glebe looked past Shakespeare as if he could not meet his eyes. 'Why, sir, again it is the talk of the town that this lewd Popish beast is the killer. Surely you have heard it yourself.'

Shakespeare was losing his temper. 'I may have heard the suggestion, but I know of no evidence. That is beside the point. What do the words "cross, relic and blade" mean?'

Glebe hesitated, as if he did not understand the question. He seemed to be sweating, despite the cold of the morning. 'Mr Shakespeare?'

'The cross, man. The relic. What information do you have about these things?'

'Why, sir, none. I meant them only as a metaphor. That is, they are symbols of the devilish Roman practices at work here. What could you have thought I meant, Mr Shakespeare?'

Shakespeare was becoming increasingly irritated. He did not believe a word Glebe said. The man was as slippery as a pan of slow-worms. 'And what of this imputation against Lady Douglass and Lady Frances, that they do not mourn their cousin's death?'

'That is what I heard.'

'It is tittle-tattle, Glebe. You have already been branded. For listening to such idle talk, you may expect to lose your ears. And for repeating it, I could easily recommend you have your tongue pulled out by its root and fed to the kites. I have heard enough from you, Glebe. We will continue these inquiries at Her Majesty's pleasure. You are under arrest. Come with me.'

Glebe put up his hands, palms facing Shakespeare as if he would push him away. 'Mr Shakespeare, what do you wish to know? I will tell you the truth, I swear.'

'You know it already, Glebe. I wish to know who mentioned a relic and a cross to you. I wish to know who mentioned the name Robert Southwell to you. Furnish me now with this information or tonight you will sleep with thieves and murderers and may be questioned under duress.'

Glebe's narrow eyes were flickering. Shakespeare knew he had him where he wanted him: desperate and afraid.

'Mr Shakespeare, I heard it all in a tavern, talk among apprentices and merchants, sir. The lifeblood of London. Everyone wants the news. I could sell *The London Informer* twice over, sir.'

'Glebe, I don't believe you. You will come with me.'

'Let me dress properly first. It's bitter out there.'

'Just fetch your cloak and boots.'

Shakespeare heard a low whistle behind him and spun round. The two wenches from Glebe's bed, sisters if he were to be believed, were standing at the bottom of the stairs not three feet from him. They did look alike, as sisters would. They were healthy, plump girls, both naked from head to toe, thrusting their goodly-sized chests towards him.

Shakespeare stared at them a moment too long. They were alluring, in a base way, and he was stirred, as any man might be. He turned back in time to see Glebe making off through the back room. Shakespeare stepped forward to pursue him but found the two women at either side of him, rubbing themselves against him, trying to kiss him, holding his arms, restraining him, tickling his stones through his breeches. Angrily he pushed them aside and forged ahead after Glebe. But he was gone.

The two women cackled.

'There will be a price to pay for this,' Shakespeare told them in a fury, and immediately felt foolish.

'A price, love? We're free. Whenever you like.' Again, they fell about laughing and Shakespeare saw it was a lost cause. He would send men later to break up the press, but there was little else to do here. The women disappeared upstairs with much hilarity, presumably to get dressed, while Shakespeare searched the room. He found a print of the poems of Aretino and some woodcuts illustrating the bawdy verses. There was also a pile of almanacs containing the preposterous predictions of the French fraud Nostradamus and an account of Sir Walter Ralegh's recent venture in the New World. Shakespeare took copies of each, with the most recent *London Informer* broadsheet, and carried them outside to where Slide was waiting with the mounts.

'Was he there, Mr Shakespeare?'

'Don't ask, Harry. Don't ask.'

Chapter 13

JOB MALLINSON SAT in the court room at Stationers' Hall by St Paul's and looked out of the tall window on to the company's bleak winter gardens. He held his hand to his bandaged jaw as if that might relieve his toothache – it had afflicted him all night. In other times, when his head did not throb like a smithy's hammer beating an anvil, he was known for his good humour and amusing tales. Now he sat, shivered and wished the day away. He had decided to come here because he could no longer bear his wife's ministrations. She had given him salves for his tooth, but they had done little to help and her talking doubled the pain. A walk to Stationers' Hall through the brisk air seemed the best way to take his mind off his pain.

A liveried manservant came in and spoke to him. He hesitated a few moments, then nodded and the servant vanished, only to reappear a minute later with John Shakespeare.

Mallinson rose to greet him and the two men shook hands. They had met before, first at a Guildhall banquet celebrating the setting sail of John Davis's expedition in quest of the north-west passage, then two or three times since on state business when seditious materials had been found.

'I am sorry to see you have some ague about the face, Mr Mallinson,' Shakespeare said, indicating the bandage.

'Tooth,' Mallinson said, as well as he could.

Shakespeare, knowing that Mallinson would find conversation difficult, came straight to the point of his visit. 'Mr Mallinson, I need information about some prints that have been discovered.' He held up the scrap of paper. 'Is it possible to identify which press was responsible for this?' He held out a copy of Walstan Glebe's broadsheet. 'And might it have been printed by the same press that produced this?'

Mallinson examined the papers. As warden of the assistants with the Stationers' Company, he was steeped in printing, yet he knew his limitations. In a faint voice, he said, 'Yes, it is possible, but I am not the man to help you. You need one with more expertise in such matters.' He winced as he spoke and a trickle of blood seeped from the corner of his mouth.

'Is there someone here who might be able to help me?'

Mallinson shook his head, then closed his eyes. He breathed deeply, steadying himself to speak once more. 'No, sir, not here. But there is a man who might be of assistance. His name is Thomas Woode. He is a book merchant and an agent of Christophe Plantin's printworks of Antwerp. He has made much money by his printing of playbills, for which he possesses the monopoly. He has a house close by the Thames at Dowgate. You cannot miss it, sir, because it is scaffolded. If anyone can help you, Thomas can. He is a good man.'

'Thank you, Mr Mallinson. And I wish you well of your tooth. One more thing. Tell your men to break up an illegal press in Fleet Lane. It is run by a scurrilous fellow called Glebe.'

Mallinson attempted to smile, but it was more like a grimace. 'Oh, yes, Mr Shakespeare. I know of Walstan Glebe. We have been looking for him for quite some time. It will be a pleasure for our men to break his press into a thousand pieces.'

Starling Day and her cousin Alice were drinking and singing in the Bel Savage. They were certain they had covered their tracks. Half an hour earlier, in Cogg's bawdy-house, they had given a piece of their mind to Parsimony Field and sauntered out, laughing and jeering. Now they were buying drinks for any girl who wasn't at work – and anyone else who happened to be in the tavern.

Parsimony, who was not only Cogg's best girl but also ran the whorehouse on his behalf, had been struck dumb by the audacity of Starling and Alice. No girl had ever dared tell her to fuck off before and if any had she would have been beaten senseless for her pains; Parsimony was tall and strong enough to hold her own against a lot of men, let alone women, and she had the backing of Cogg. But she had been caught off guard by Starling and Alice. After she had calmed herself she followed them into the long bar of the Bel Savage and watched them getting more and more drunk by the minute.

Alice caught sight of her. 'Come on, Arsey-Parsey, come and have a drink with us. I'll buy you a beaker of nightshade cordial, ducks.' And she thrust two fingers in the air as a salute.

For a moment, Parsimony considered dragging them by the hair back to the stew. But she wasn't sure she could manage both of them and she didn't want to humiliate herself in front of the other girls. Cogg would expect her to act, though, so she must do something. He wouldn't want to lose two girls.

As she watched, the taproom became more and more raucous. In unison, Starling and Alice turned their backs on her, lifted their skirts, bent forwards, exposing themselves, then farted at her in unison and collapsed on to the sawdust-strewn floor, laughing. When they got up again, Parsimony noticed something she hadn't seen before: they were wearing jewellery, necklaces and bracelets, which looked very much like gold, not the gaudy trinkets whores usually wore. Parsimony knew then that she had to get to Cogg straight away. He would want to know of this. Something smelt bad here, as rank as a basket of six-day-dead mackerel. Slipping out of the tavern, she gathered up her skirts and, though not dressed for the cold weather, ran to Cogg's house in Cow Lane.

He wasn't there and he hadn't locked up. Parsimony was puzzled. Cogg never went out; couldn't move with his great girth. She went up to his bedchamber. There was a platter of almost-finished food, chicken bones or something, and the bedsheet was awry. She sat on the bed and tried to gather her thoughts. He should be here. She couldn't remember the last time he had gone out. He couldn't even walk to the whorehouse by the Bel Savage these days, which was why the girls came to him. He had slowed this past year. Something must have happened to him.

Parsimony twiddled the ends of her pretty hair in her fingers. She had been with Cogg since her bricklayer husband ran off to be a player and writer of plays when she was sixteen. That was seven years ago. She had liked the life of a whore from the start; swiving for a living was easy money and, at times, enjoyable. She liked the mariners best, the ones back from long voyages: they were free with their pay, liked to laugh and had strong, weather-hardened bodies. More to the point, she and Cogg had a good understanding. He let her keep twice as much as the other girls in return for managing the stew. She reckoned that by working for him she would have enough set by to start her own trugging-house before she was twenty-five.

She stood up and began to look for him in earnest and soon found his body downstairs, packed into a large barrel that had contained hides and furs from the Baltic lands. The skins had been pulled out and shoved into a pile that looked, at first sight, like a great sleeping bear. The barrel had been tipped on its side so that Cogg's vast corpse could be pushed in. It didn't fit. It was only because the opening was turned to the wall that she had not spotted his blubbery naked feet immediately. It was clearly not a method of concealment that had been intended to last long.

So, they had killed him. The dirty, cross-biting, light-heeled trugs. She guessed they had probably robbed him, too. Well, she'd do for them. And she knew how.

But where was Cogg's fortune? Had they found it all and taken it, or was some still here? She spent a few minutes searching, but found nothing, and hurried back to the Bel Savage for fear they would have skipped away.

She threw open the door to the taproom. It was thick with woodsmoke and the fumes of ale. Starling Day and Alice were insensible with drink, snoring on the taproom floor, their dress awry and their limbs splayed. The other girls stood around drinking with their money and making merry with some traders.

For a moment, Parsimony stood there unnoticed. Then one of the girls spotted her and nudged her neighbour. There was a sudden silence as they ceased carousing and looked at Parsimony fearfully, seeing the anger in her eyes. She strode over and slapped one girl hard across the face, then told them all to deal with Starling and Alice. 'Get them back to the vaulting-house and stand over them,' she said, in a cold voice that she knew would be obeyed. 'Don't let them out of your sight. I want a word with them two foul cozeners when they wake. Break the ice on the cask in the yard and throw a pail of water over them. It'll be nicely chilled.'

Chapter 14

'HAVE YOU SEEN that play yet?' Denis Picket asked, over a gage of booze in The Falcon post inn at Fotheringhay.

'No,' Simon Bull replied. 'What was it called?'

'*Tamburlaine*. A good lark, Bully. Lots of fighting. Lots of laughs.'

'Where's it on, then?'

'The Curtain, Bully.'

'Oh. And it's *Mr* Bull to you, Denis.'

'Sorry, Mr Bull.'

'What's it about?'

'Turks, I think. Lots of battles and killing.'

'Not for me, Denis. I don't like the bloodshed they put in the plays, these days.' Bull glanced round the room and noticed the eyes of the regulars turning away quickly, as if they had been caught staring at him. He was used to that and didn't give it a second thought, but he was worried about his assistant. Picket was young, good at his job at the shambles by all accounts and he'd done his share of rope tricks, but he'd never had a job as big as this one. He didn't want to make him any more jumpy than he already was.

'Where's Digby staying, Mr Bull?'

'Up at Apthorpe, with the gentry. Mr Secretary wanted us to go there, but old Mildmay wasn't having it. Thinks we're too low-born. But I can tell you, Denis,' and here he reduced his voice to a whisper, 'I've lopped men every bit as noble as him. We're all one when our heads are on the block.'

'So what you done with the axe, then, Bully?' Picket asked at last.

Bull put the index finger of his very large right hand to his lips. 'It's in my trunk, Denis, but keep it down. Don't want to worry the locals. And it's Mr Bull. I won't remind you again.'

'Sorry, Mr Bull.'

Less than a day earlier, Simon Bull had been at his house outside Bishops Gate when Walsingham's man Anthony Hall arrived with news of the commission. There had been some haggling over the price, but in the end they had agreed on ten pounds in gold, travel costs, and good board and lodging for him and his assistant. There had been some dispute over the usual access to clothes and jewellery removed from the body, but Bull had stood firm and Hall had said they could decide such things when the time came. There was no point in upsetting the headsman before he had done his hideous work.

'Now, Denis, how about one more quart while I gets some food inside me? Then it's bed and a good night's sleep. We've to be up early.'

'Yes, Mr Bull.'

'Good lad. I fancy a couple of pigeons and a bit of beef. See if they can do something like that for us, will you?'

'Yes, Mr Bull.'

'And some fresh bread with butter to mop up the juice would go down well.'

'Yes, Mr Bull. I'll see to it.'

Starling Day was woken by the sting of Parsimony Field's hand across her face. Slap, slap, back and forth from side to side, hard.

She recoiled from the blows. 'Please, Parsey, lay off,' she begged, her voice weak but desperate.

'I will when you tell me where the gold is, Starling Day.' Parsimony hit her again. 'You're in trouble up to your scrawny chicken neck.'

Starling was bound to the four corners of a wooden bedstead. Her head was spinning from the drink. Her backbone against the unforgiving wood was causing her agony. She felt the bile rising, turned her head away from Parsimony and vomited.

'If that'd gone over me, I'd have killed you.'

Starling closed her eyes. In her boozy delusion, she was back in Strelley, tied to the bedpost being beaten by Edward. She had thought that was behind her. Gradually the events of the night before came back into focus. They had hidden the gold and jewels, except for a few necklaces and bracelets to pretty themselves up, and then went back to the bawdy-house to collect Alice's few pitiful things. Something in them, some rash boldness, had made them give Parsimony Field a piece of their mind and then go to the Bel Savage for one last drink before disappearing for ever. And why not? Arsey-Parsey had no idea what had gone on at Cow Lane, and she couldn't restrain both of them. But the drink had taken hold and now they were paying for it.

Starling wanted to clutch her pounding head, but she couldn't because her wrists were tied to the bedposts. Half a day ago the world was looking good; now it was a blocked-up jakes of a place again. They had to get out of there quickly.

Parsimony's fist came down hard towards the centre of her face. Starling just managed to turn her head sideways before the blow struck or her nose would have been broken. But it hurt. Parsimony hit like a man.

'I'll show you where the gold is,' she screamed.

'And what gold would that be?'

'You know what gold. Cogg's gold. We'll split it three ways. You, me and Alice.'

Parsimony sat at the end of the hard bed. 'By my reckoning you'll be lucky if I don't turn you in because if I did your chicken neck would be in the halter at Tyburn scaffold before morning and I'd be there cheering the hangman on. As I see it, you owe me, Starling Day. You owe me your life. So it's three-quarters for me. You and Alice can share the rest.'

'But I never killed Cogg!'

'No? Looks like it to me and I reckon the Justice might agree. Dead body found in barrel, deceased's worldly wealth found in possession of Starling Day. How will that sound to a jury?'

'Half to you, then. But you won't get nothing if you turn me in or if you do for me. Now untie me. Please, Parsimony. And I *didn't* kill Cogg. But I saw who done it.'

'I'll think about that, Starling Day. I will. I'll give it thought. But first I'm going to get myself some breakfast.' Parsimony stood and turned towards the door.

Starling panicked. 'Wait. Why don't we go and collect the treasure now, eh? There's so much of it, Parsey, plenty for all of us. It's like he plundered a Spanish galleon.'

'Let me think about it.'

Starling wanted to be sick again. She writhed on the bed.

'I know,' said Parsimony. 'I've a better idea. Why don't you tell me where the gold is and I'll fetch it? Then, when I've got it, I can untie you.'

'Parsimony, I'm begging you! I'll be fit for Bedlam if you leave me like this.'

'Simple then, isn't it, dove? The sooner you tell me where to look, the sooner you'll be free.'

Starling was at the end of her tether, but she knew that if she told Parsimony how to find Cogg's jewels, she'd never let her go. She'd either kill her or lay information with the constable to set her on the road to the gallows.

'You got to let me free first, Parsey. I can't tell you nothing tied up like this. And where's my cousin?'

'Oh, don't worry about her, my dove. She's asleep upstairs.'

The words chilled Starling. 'You haven't done nothing to her, have you?'

Parsimony's mouth was set hard. 'What if I had? It'd mean more for you and me, wouldn't it?'

'Do you know what, Bully—'

'Mr Bull, please, Denis.'

'Do you know what, Mr Bull? Last summer I worked killing dogs when the weather got hot.'

'I didn't know that, Denis.'

'I hated that line of work, Mr Bull. We rounded 'em up every day by order of the city corporation and did away with them any way we could, drowning, strangling, cutting their throats, smacking their heads between stones. I understand it's necessary because they carries the plague, but I didn't like it.'

'A job's a job, Denis.'

'You're right, of course, but I was brought up with dogs. I trained 'em to get rabbits and hares for the pot.'

Simon Bull looked at the boy and shook his head. They were dressed the part now, standing in black with butcher's aprons and masks, strong like proper headsmen, their muscles rippling. Bull's enormous hands rested on the haft of the long-handled axe. He knew he was a terrifying sight; he had stood long hours in front of the glass perfecting the pose. Best that way: if the intended wasn't intimidated all sorts of trouble might ensue. Once he'd had to chase a young noble all round the scaffold, trying to catch him, like a farmwife after a fowl. A nasty business, that, bits of body all over the place, blood everywhere. Today would be easier.

They were at the side of the black-velvet-draped platform. It had been hastily erected, the hammering reverberating around the hall these past two days in preparation for the blood-drenched ritual.

'We've been here more than three hours now, Mr Bull. I'd have had more breakfast if I'd known I'd still be here at ten o'clock.'

'We'll sup soon enough.'

There was a murmur and they turned. Mary, the Scots devil herself, walked in, dressed in black velvet, head held high. Behind her, weeping, walked six chosen attendants in pairs, three men and three women.

'One of the dogs, a mastiff it was, looked at me with these sad eyes, Mr Bull . . .'

'Ssh, Denis, not now,' Bull said, in a low voice, as the murmur of the two hundred people in the hall subsided. They were a strange, solemn bunch, some shuffling awkwardly, others standing stock still. Steam rose from their rain-drenched riding clothes as the fire in the hearth roared out its scorching heat. Their eyes were fixed to the front, straining to make out the features of the black-clad woman against the black backdrop of the stage as she climbed the steps. Armour-clad halberdiers guarded her and supported her at each elbow. She took her place in the black-draped chair that had been placed there for her. Bull's eyes followed her. He didn't look at her face but, rather, her apparel and the things she carried. There would be good money there. She held an ivory cross, and at her throat a chain of beads was attached to a cross of gold. At her waist, she wore a rosary. Her clothes were dark and sombre, but they had quality and would fetch him a good price. The black velvet gown could be cut into small fragments, squares of an inch or two, to be sold as relics. On her head she wore a cap of white cambric, trailing a white linen veil. Such things would sell very well. Even her kerchief, a burnished yellow that seemed to glint in the firelight, would fetch a pound or two. His man in Cheapside would pay him a pretty penny; the Papists would give well over the true value to get their hands on such items.

Mr Beale, the clerk to the Council, who had travelled up to Northamptonshire with Bull, Picket and Walsingham's servant, George Digby, read out the warrant citing the condemned's conviction for high treason and conspiracy against the person of Her Majesty. Then the Earl of Shrewsbury took over the proceedings. 'Madam, you hear what we are commanded to do?'

'Do your duty,' Mary said, in a quiet voice that quavered only slightly. 'I die for my religion.'

Picket's nose itched and he scratched it. His back ached from all the standing around and his stomach was a hollow pit that needed filling. He wished they could get on with it and cease the chatter, but then some vicar or bishop got up and started to speak, while the condemned droned on in Latin.

At last, Mary fell from her chair on to her knees and her rising voice cut the Dean of Peterborough short. 'I shall die as I have lived, in the true and holy Catholic faith. All your prayers can avail me but little.' She held her ivory cross above her head and called on God to convert England to the true faith and for Catholics to stand firm.

She seemed disinclined to cease her ramblings, praying for England, for Elizabeth, for the Church of Rome. Bull nudged Picket and spoke quietly in his ear. 'This is it, lad. Let's speed things up a bit.'

Together they stepped forward and knelt in front of Mary, in the time-honoured tradition, then asked forgiveness for what they were about to do. She readily gave them absolution. 'I forgive you with all my heart,' she said firmly. 'For I hope this death shall give me an end to all my troubles.'

Bull rose from his knees and started to remove her gown. She shied away from him, then seemed to laugh, maiden-like, saying, 'Let me do this. I understand this business better than you. I never had such a groom in my chamber.'

Bull backed away. No matter. If the lady wanted to be coy with him that was her choice. The clothes would all come to him anyway. Two of her three ladies took over, fluttering and weeping as their dainty hands undid her stays and removed her black gown to reveal her satin underbodice and kirtle, all crimson like a wound. There seemed to be a gasp from the witnesses in the hall but perhaps it was the soughing of the wind in the chimney.

Removing the gold cross and beads from about her neck she asked Bull whether she might be allowed to give it to her maid and that he would be paid more than their value in gold. He shook his head, and prised the crucifix from her fingers, placing it in his shoe for safe-keeping. Then he took her ivory cross, and the rosary, and handed them to Picket.

Unbidden, as if suddenly deciding she wanted no more delay to the proceedings, Mary gestured to her ladies and one of them bound her eyes with her kerchief, with a knot at her neck, a target for the axe. She stretched forward and rested her chin on her hands, over the edge of the block. Bull nodded to Picket, who stepped forward and pulled away her hands so that her arms stretched out in front of her, held gently in his.

She was speaking now, Latin once more, first a psalm and then, over and over, she commended her soul to God's hands: '*In manus tuas, Domine, commendo spiritum meum.*'

Bull raised the heavy double-edged axe high above his head. It hovered there, at the top of its swing, for an eternity, then fell in a great arc into the back of her skull. The sound of sharp steel cracking bone, like the thud of the butcher's cleaver, shattered the silence. Bull looked down through the slits in his mask at the gory mess below. Shit, he'd missed her neck. Quickly, the blood rising to his face, he raised the axe again and brought it down once more. This time his aim was true and the blood spurted forth in a fountain.

He knelt down beside her to reach into the gore to pick up her severed head but saw that it still wasn't severed. Gristly tendons still attached it to the body. With the edge of his axe he sawed through them, then clasped his blood-greasy left hand in her hair and held it up high for all to see.

'This is the head of Mary Stuart,' he bellowed. Only it wasn't. It was her auburn wig. Her head, grey and shaven, had rolled across the platform. Luckily, no one could see behind his mask, for now he closed his eyes in the closest thing Simon Bull ever came to shame. At last he remembered his lines and took a deep breath. 'God save the Queen,' he said, with conviction.

It had been a bad day for Bull and it got worse. As they were clearing up and stripping the body, the clothes were taken from him to be burnt. He was deprived, too, of the crosses and beads he had taken from her. Walsingham would decide what happened to them in due course. When Bull, feeling cheated, protested that the effects were his right to keep, someone muttered about 'not having any relics left to make a martyr of that bloody woman'.

Finally, there was the dog, a little terrier, all covered with gore, that scuttled out from the dead woman's clothes as they were cut from her body to be taken outside and burnt in the courtyard. Picket's eyes lighted on it first and his masked face broke into a smile. 'Hello,' he said, lifting it up.

'Put it down,' Bull said sullenly. 'If we can't keep a cross, they won't let us keep a dog, will they?'

Reluctantly, Denis Picket put the dog down and it ran,

whimpering, to the now naked corpse of its mistress. Picket eyed it with something akin to yearning. 'You know that mastiff I was telling you about, Mr Bull? I couldn't kill it. Still got him at home and a fine creature he is. I call him Bully after you.'

'Well, then, boy, you should have called him *Mr* Bull, shouldn't you?'

'You're right, Mr Bull, I'll do that. From now on, I'll call him Mr Bull.'

Chapter 15

BONFIRES LIT THE damp night sky. On every street corner and in every tavern, minstrels played merry tunes and people braved the rain to dance, drink and rejoice. The murdering, adulterous witch of Scotland was dead. After nineteen long years, England was free of her malign presence. By midnight, the pitch black sky was howling, and the flames of the bonfires fanned into a firestorm, before finally dying down to sodden embers in the early hours when the revellers sank, drunk, into their beds.

Thomas Woode was shaking. While others sang and danced and drank, he sat alone at his table. And when the rest of London was snoring, he stayed awake. He had bitten the last of his nails to the quick and was now nicking pieces of the hard, stubby flesh at the end of each finger. In the grey rain of dawn, his white teeth glimmered in the light of three good beeswax candles, each burnt down to an inch. Their flames flickered and leapt briskly in the draughts that rushed up from the river and in through the gaps at the edge of the leaded lights in his private office in Dowgate. Rain slapped at the window in squally gusts.

This night past he had done without a fire: it would have been improper for him to have warmth when the butchered body of Mary Stuart lay cold in a box. He tore off his ruff and hurled it across the room, then picked up a quill, sliced the tip with his desk knife and dipped it in the ink horn. Hurriedly, he wrote on a scrap of parchment, then scratched out the words. He needed to compose a business letter to Christophe Plantin in the Gulden Passer, the great Antwerp printers and bookworks whence so much of his wealth emanated. The words would not come. He was tired; this was not a time for mundane business dealings.

He heard a scurry, a knock at the oak door. 'Come in.'

It was the governess, Catherine Marvell. Woode was wealthy, a merchant of the class that now owned London, but he did not keep a large household. It wasn't safe, not with his secrets. Maidservants came in during the day to see to the housework and cooking, as did carpenters and masons for the building, but at night it was just himself, Catherine, the children and their two guests, the Jesuit priests Cotton and Herrick, who wore the clothes of serving men in case anyone should call on the house. It was their presence that endangered the family.

Thomas Woode knew that everyone in the house was in mortal danger, and it troubled him. Harbouring priests sent from abroad amounted to treason in the eyes of the law. London was full of spies and betrayers who might track the priests here at any time and inform the heavy-booted pursuivants of their whereabouts. But Thomas Woode was obligated to accommodate these men; it had been his wife Margaret's dying wish that he bring up their children in the true faith. They needed instruction and they must hear the mass regularly. Margaret also wished him to support the persecuted church in whatever way he could. He had agreed to her requests because he loved her and because she was dying. Yet he regretted it every day. He would never have taken this path of his own accord. There were times, if truth be told, when he doubted his own belief in God.

There were practicalities to be observed. Yes, Cotton and Herrick could come and go as they pleased; when they went out they wore the garb of tradesmen or gentlemen. When they were at home, they remained hidden by day. Only by night, when the household staff had left, did they venture out of the room they shared to eat and converse with the family, dressing as servants.

'Catherine, it is good to see you.'

'Master.'

'A sad day.'

'Yes, master.'

'We must take comfort in the certain knowledge that she is in a better place.'

Thomas Woode had never met Mary Stuart, yet he had revered her. Yes, his faith sometimes faltered, but he was certain that if there was to be a religion, Mary's Roman church was the only possible way; he saw the Anglican church of Elizabeth and her ministers as a sacrilegious imposter, a manifestation of power rather than spirituality. When he imagined Mary of Scots, he pictured her with the face of his late beloved wife. He smiled wanly at Catherine. 'These are bad days. The people sing and dance, but the ports have all been closed down and the prisons shut to all but official visitors. Pursuivants march the streets, searching and questioning anyone they don't like the look of. Even the ordinary people play their role, pelting stones at anyone they take to be foreign.'

Catherine's dark hair hung in soft waves. The shrug of her shoulders was almost imperceptible. 'Well, then, let us stay strong.'

Woode found her a strange creature; the fire in her belly was most uncommon in a young woman. While he was mourning a queen others reviled, and grieving for the future of this and every Catholic family in the land, she spoke of strength. And he had to concede that she was strong. She had brought new life to this family since the dark days following Margaret's death. The children had grown to love her.

'How is the boy?'

'Making mischief as ever,' Catherine said. 'The fever has subsided. It was naught but a winter sweat.'

'That is good.'

She looked up, and he saw that her startling blue eyes were still bright. In her hands she held a cup of fine Gascon wine, unsweetened. She put it on his worktable, close to his right hand.

'Thank you, Catherine.'

She breathed deeply, composing herself. 'May I speak plain with you, Mr Woode?'

'Why, yes, Catherine. My door is always open to you. Please, sit down. What do you wish to speak of?'

Suddenly she laughed. It was a laugh of release not of humour. 'You will think me a fishwife or a gossip, Mr Woode, coming to you with tittle-tattle.'

Thomas Woode was in his mid-thirties, his sandy hair greying at the temples. He felt himself ageing; his eyes and brow were lined. Yet he was still a well-formed, handsome man. He drank some reviving wine.

'I do not know how to say this without causing offence or showing myself cowardly and lacking in fortitude,' she said. 'I would say nothing for my own sake, but I fear the danger to Andrew and Grace.'

Woode rose and went to sit beside her. He held her hands and squeezed them gently. 'Speak out, Catherine. You are like a mother to my children. Nothing you say can seem out of place to me.'

She was silent a few moments. 'It is Father Herrick,' she said at last. 'I have . . . doubts. In plain speaking, I do not like him and I do not trust him, Mr Woode. I fear he is not what he purports to be.'

Woode felt the prickles rise on his neck. The sudden thought that a traitor, a spy, was in his house was terrifying. 'You think he is one of Walsingham's men?'

She shook her head. 'That is *not* what I think – not necessarily, though it is possible.' She wrung her hands. 'I think he may be something else.'

Thomas Woode smelt her warmth, the salt scent stirring him, something he had not felt with any girl or woman since Margaret's death. 'You must speak openly, Catherine. What you say will not go beyond these walls.'

How could she explain her doubts about Herrick? It seemed to her that when the priest had first met her friend Lady Blanche Howard at the Bellamys' house, Uxendon Manor, where they both worshipped, he had looked at her not as a man of chastity should. Blanche had liked him, that was clear. His feelings for her were not so obvious.

There were Herrick's strange comings and goings, the calculating looks Catherine sometimes caught when he thought she wasn't aware of him at a meal or during mass. His eyes had followed Blanche in an unseemly fashion: had he been thinking of her carnally? She suspected that Father Cotton might share her doubts, although he had not said as much. Now she needed to convey her misgivings to Mr Woode.

'I know it is sinful to speak ill of the Reverend Father but . . . let me start at the beginning. When he came into our lives, we welcomed him. You, Father Cotton and I went out of our way to bring him to the attention of our fellow Catholics and many welcomed him into their homes to say mass, or visited him here. We did no more than our duty. One of those he became close to was Lady Blanche, who had been brought to the true faith by Father Cotton and subsequently became my friend. It is the

nature of that closeness that came to concern me. He was very
. . . familiar with her. I noted it more than once in the way that
he touched her. You may think me too free with my opinions,
and I will confess that is true. You may even think me lacking
in Christian charity, but it seemed to me that Father Herrick's
great interest in Blanche coincided with his learning of her
connection to Lord Howard of Effingham.'

'He was sent by the Society of Jesus, Catherine. There can
surely be no doubt about their motives.'

Catherine smiled. 'Of course not. But when I heard how
Blanche had died, the face of Father Herrick came immediately
to my mind, as in a dreadful dream. I sensed darkness in him,
Mr Woode. Now, that must make me seem even more the village idiot and you may wish to send me to Bethlehem hospital.
I set no store by dreams, yet this vision haunts me. Even in
waking moments, it is an image I cannot dismiss. Why does it
trouble me so?'

'A dream, Catherine?' Thomas Woode raised a quizzical
eyebrow. He stood up and walked the room, slowly. Her
imaginings disturbed and bewildered him. He was exhausted
from his night without sleep and he could not think clearly.
He needed to rest his head on the pillows and sink beneath the
covering of his bed.

'Yes, master. But not just a dream.' She had not wanted to
speak of it, as if somehow it were her shameful secret, but now it
was necessary. She took a deep breath. 'Last week, as you know,
the children and I went to the menagerie at the Tower. Andrew
was complaining of a stomach pain, so we came home. As we
arrived back at Dowgate, he was asleep in my arms and Grace
was quiet and subdued. I could hear noises from upstairs. I
thought it was one of the maidservants, but then I recalled it was
a holy day and they were not at work. As I opened the upper-floor
gallery, I saw two people, Father Herrick and a woman. I turned

away quickly, trying to shield Grace's eyes, but she had already seen what I had seen. "What are they doing, Mistress Marvell?" she asked me, in her innocence. I knew not what to say. They were without clothes. Father Herrick was stretched out, face down on the floor, and his back was red with weals. The woman's right arm was raised. In her hand was a knotted scourge, about to come down on Father Herrick's back. She turned and saw us, her hand hovering, not completing its stroke. She smiled at me. I pulled the children away and ran to my room with them. Later, Father Herrick came to me. "Mistress Marvell," he said, "I had not expected you so soon." I asked him what, in God's name, he had been doing. He looked at me as if I were slow-witted. "*Pax vobiscum*, child", he said. "I am sorry you have witnessed this. As you must understand, I was exorcising my sins through the offices of that poor sinner." I fear I laughed. "Father Herrick," I said, "I am afraid I do not believe a word you say." Darkness crossed his eyes and I thought for a moment he might kill me, so I went on, "Of course, I understand it is a private matter and none of my concern." Father Herrick hesitated, as if weighing up what he should do. In the end he bowed. "Thank you, Catherine. I will trust you not to mention this to Mr Woode. He may not understand the severity of our Jesuit ways." I did not argue. I just wanted him to go away. I told him I would say nothing. But now I think you need to hear this.'

Thomas Woode spoke firmly. 'I am shocked, Catherine, shocked and deeply sorry that you have been exposed to such abomination under my roof. I will ask Father Herrick to depart this very day. There is a safe-house for priests of which Father Cotton has knowledge. I will ask Father Cotton to take him there. As for Father Cotton himself, he will be leaving us in the next forty-eight hours. He has been offered sanctuary elsewhere. It will be more convenient for him, and safer for us. It has become too dangerous for either of them to remain here. I must confess,

Catherine, it will be a great relief to me too. I can scarce sleep for worry.'

Catherine rose from the settle. 'Thank you, master.' She lifted the latch to let herself out of the room. But she did not feel completely reassured. It wasn't enough for Father Herrick to leave. A dangerous man was dangerous anywhere.

Chapter 16

Four men sat at the long table in the library of Walsingham's mansion house in Seething Lane. Mr Secretary had at last recovered enough from his long-standing and debilitating illness and was in London from his country retreat of Barn Elms where he had stayed these past weeks.

'I think it is the falling of the Queen of Scots's head that has taken the weight off Mr Secretary's sh-sh-shoulders,' Arthur Gregory, an assistant secretary, whispered in John Shakespeare's ear as they waited for Walsingham to appear. 'It was a very convenient malady.'

'Not so good for my Lord Burghley,' said Francis Mills, another of Walsingham's secretaries, who had heard the remark. 'I am told the Queen has quite cut him dead. He implores and whimpers like a puppy to be allowed back into her presence, but she won't see him and won't read his letters. He has never known its like.'

Shakespeare sat silent, as did the fourth man, Thomas Phelippes. All four had been summoned urgently but had now been waiting an hour for Walsingham to appear. All were aware that the Queen was in a thunderstorm rage over the death of Mary Stuart. She blamed everyone but herself for it, as though it were not her own name scratched on the death warrant. William Davison, one of her two secretaries of state and the man who had brought the signed warrant before the Privy Council to act upon, had been taken to the Tower and was threatened with the rope. The Lord Treasurer, Burghley, looked likely never to be spoken to again. Of her senior councillors, only Walsingham had escaped the worst of the censure, because he had been ill at the time of the decision to proceed with the execution. 'And yet it was his hand behind the deed,' said Mills, laughing. 'He was the one who brought this thing to pass with his machinations. Signor Machiavelli would have been proud.'

The room descended once more into silence. The tension was palpable. Each man at the table was racked by the demands made on him in these difficult days, for they were at the heart of Walsingham's intelligence operation.

Mills was a tall man, slender, of middle years, with small, sharp eyes and a short white beard. He was of equal rank to Shakespeare, though, unlike Shakespeare, he was not active in the field. His talent was interrogation, particularly of the many priests sent over from Europe and captured.

Gregory had brown hair and a pinkish tinge to his skin and eyes. He spoke slowly and deliberately and sometimes stammered. He had been brought to Walsingham's attention because of his remarkable ability to reveal invisible writing on a supposedly blank paper and to open a sealed letter and reseal it without anyone being the wiser. This had enabled Walsingham to monitor letters going in and out of the French embassy, the conduit for Mary Stuart's intimate correspondence.

Phelippes was, in many ways, the most important member of the team. Proficient in at least six languages, he was short and physically ill-favoured. He wore thick glass spectacles on his pox-holed nose and his lank hair hung yellow and wispy about his sallow face. But whatever the deficiencies of his features, the inner workings of his mind were a thing to dazzle. He was the cipher expert who had broken the Spanish codes and the coded letters between Mary, Queen of Scots, and the Babington plotters. Phelippes was methodical and dedicated to his work. He would spend hours and days poring over a new cipher, analysing the frequency of symbols to discover which were 'nulls' – meaningless additions to deceive the code-breaker – and which were likely to be the most common words and letters used by those involved in the correspondence. So far, no code had eluded the alchemy of his extraordinary mind. He had another skill too: the ability to forge any writing style. It was this that had eventually won for Walsingham the names of Anthony Babington's fellow plotters, for Phelippes had forged Mary Stuart's hand to ask Babington for those names. The result had been bloody retribution meted out at Tyburn for Babington and thirteen other young men in front of a cheering crowd.

The door opened. Walsingham stood a moment, looking at his assembled officials, then walked unsteadily to the head of the table. He was pale, and Shakespeare thought he seemed less well than when he had last seen him at Barn Elms. Mr Secretary smiled little at the best of times, but now his face was set and drawn. His dark eyes were fixed ahead as he took his seat. He would not engage in small-talk.

'I have brought you here today on matters that concern the very future of our Queen and the realm of England.' He held up a letter. 'Mr Phelippes already knows the contents of this missive. It contains powerful and incontrovertible evidence that the Spanish fleet will sail on England by summer. Our information is that sixteen new galleys of more than a hundred tons are being readied in Santander. Fourteen more of similar tonnage in the Passage of Gibraltar. In Laredo, there are eight new *pataches*, which I believe are what we call pinnaces, and in San Sebastian, six galleons of three hundred tons and four of two hundred. In Bilbao there are six more *pataches*, in Figuera four new barks of a hundred tons. More are being built on the river at Fuenterrabia. In the estuary at Seville, there are eight great galleons of three hundred tons and four *pataches*, in St Mary Port, two more galleys and four *pataches*. Tally it, gentlemen, then add to the total the possibly two hundred ships already at the Spaniards' disposal: carracks, galleons, galleasses, galleys, hulks, pinnaces, zabras, armed merchant vessels. I do not wish to weary you with naval detail, but the picture is clear. Philip is amassing the greatest fleet the world has seen and its intent is plain: the invasion of England and the death of Her Majesty.'

The room remained silent. No one doubted the stark figures. All present knew the extent of Walsingham's network throughout Europe and Asia Minor. He had at least four permanent spy bases in Spain itself. Nor was he one to exaggerate or become excitable; if he was worried, so should they be.

'What this means is we must have Drake afloat and sinking Spanish shipping as soon as possible. We must delay Philip for as long as we can while we strengthen our own fleets and land defences.' He looked pointedly at Shakespeare. 'I trust I make myself clear.'

Shakespeare nodded. 'Yes, Mr Secretary.'

'So Drake's safety is paramount, but it is no longer enough simply to protect him, although I am sure Mr Cooper will do a workmanlike job in that wise. You all know there is an assassin sent by Mendoza to kill Sir Francis. It is now vital that this man be hunted down like a rabid fox and disposed of before he can do harm. He must not be allowed to come close to the Vice-Admiral. And if he has associates, they must be rendered harmless, too.'

Shakespeare ran a hand through his hair. Easier said than done, Mr Secretary, was his immediate thought. Easier said than done. London was full of gossip and intrigue, but one man sent alone, with no known connections, was every intelligencer's worst nightmare.

'I know what you are thinking, Mr Shakespeare, but if you have doubts about the serious nature of the threat we face, there is more.' Walsingham turned to the man to Shakespeare's left. 'Mr Mills, your report on the Dutch connection.'

All eyes turned to Mills. He bowed, like a player taking centre stage, then cleared his throat. 'For this,' he said, 'we must go back almost three years, to July the tenth in the year 1584, when William the Silent, Prince of Orange, was murdered in Delft. His death was the most outrageous act of political violence of our age. He was killed with three shots from a pistol fired by a Roman Catholic named Balthasar Gerard, in the pay of Philip of Spain. Gerard was captured almost immediately and put to death in a manner that makes hanging, drawing and quartering seem a pleasant morning's outing. His torment lasted four days. He was hung from a pole, the strappado, suspended by his hands, which were tied behind his back. He was whipped until his body was an open wound. Salt was rubbed into those wounds. He was rolled into a ball, his limbs lashed together so he could not move, and he was left like that for a night. After this, he was again hung at the strappado and weights of two hundredweight or more were attached to his feet, almost ripping the joints of his arms from their sockets. The pits of his arms were branded with hot irons and a cloth soaked in alcohol was slapped on his wounds. Pieces of his flesh were torn, to the bone, from six parts of his body with pincers; boiling fat was poured over his back; carpenters' nails were driven under the nails of his fingers. His right hand – the hand that fired the shots – was burnt off with a red-hot iron. He was bowelled alive, his heart was cut from his body and thrown in his face. For good measure, he was quartered and beheaded, which must have been blessed release to him. Four days this torment took, gentlemen. Four days.'

Mills paused for his unrelenting description of Balthasar

Gerard's punishment to sink in, then continued: 'You may think this is no less than he deserved for so heinous a crime, and I would agree with you. But I wish you to imagine the state of mind of this wretched man. Curiously, Balthasar Gerard was brave in his own way and did not cry out or beg mercy. We know from the authorities in Delft that, even in the worst of his agonies, he seemed quite calm and was not given to screaming. But we also know that at times he became delirious and spoke as if in his sleep. He would not have been conscious. But what he did say may be of crucial importance to our own investigations. He said repeatedly, "We have slain Goliath, praise God. Oh, my friend, we have slain Goliath of Gath."' Mills paused for a sip of ale.

'The common belief is that Gerard acted alone, but I can tell you now that he most certainly had an accomplice. The Delft civil militia do not rule out a second assassin, out of sight, perhaps, or missed in the confusion. Did all three balls really come from one wheel-lock pistol? Why did Gerard say, "*We* have slain Goliath"? Why not "*I* have slain Goliath"?'

Walsingham broke in, his voice at once powerful and frail. 'This is where it becomes tenuous. If there *was* a second assassin, and I concur there probably was, how does that help us? What clues are there to his identity? And why have I come to the conclusion that he may be the same man sent by Mendoza to kill Drake? Mr Mills . . .'

Mills took another sip of small ale to wet his throat. 'There was in Delft at that time another murder committed, of a whore whose name is of no concern. You may think that there could be no possible connection between the killing of a loose woman and the murder of a prince – one of the finest princes in all Christendom at that. But there are compelling reasons to believe there was some link between the two cases.'

He paused again, looking in turn at the seated men, all of

whose eyes were trained on him. 'Gerard was a foolish, hot-headed young man and there were those who thought such a one could not have succeeded at his vile task alone. Enquiries eventually proved that, while planning his crime, he had lodged at an English-owned tavern in Rotterdam called The Mermaid, which, as the name suggests, was a bawdy-house. He was not alone in lodging there at that time. He was seen with another man, a man whom the women there remember well. This other man, a Fleming, had a taste for the whores, and paid gener-ously for their services. But his ways were strange. He asked the women to beat him. They are accustomed to unusual requests, including such acts of violence, but this man went too far. After being beaten by one of the women, he turned on her, tied her up and hurt her badly. She feared she might die. Her bawd, the landlord of The Mermaid, flung the man out of the tavern. Balthasar Gerard left the same day.

'A week later, a whore was discovered murdered in Delft, a few miles away. She had been beaten to death in a tenement lodging that had been rented by two men, one of them answer-ing to the description of Gerard, the other very much like his Flemish companion from The Mermaid in Rotterdam. The woman's injuries were similar to those suffered by the injured whore at The Mermaid – a severe beating that went too far and her wrists bound to the bed with ropes. One report says he had cut her, that religious symbols were carved into her body. No more was seen of either man until Gerard turned up less than a week later with his pistols at the Prinsenhof, the residence of William the Silent, where the prince was murdered ascend-ing the stairs. My assumption – and I believe the evidence is compelling – is that this other man was there, too. Or, if not actually there, was certainly involved in the detailed planning of the killing. One way or the other, Balthasar Gerard did not act alone.'

Shakespeare leant forward. In his mind he had a chilling vision: the corpse of Lady Blanche Howard lying cold on a slab in the crypt of St Paul's, the Searcher of the Dead, Joshua Peace, turning her over and revealing her back with a crucifix cut into it. Was it remotely possible that the man who had inflicted those wounds on her was the same man who in Delft had killed a whore and was accomplice to the shooting of William the Silent? But first, though, there was the connection with the killing of William and the plot against Drake. 'So you think this Fleming may be the so-called "dragon slayer" sent to kill the Vice-Admiral?'

Walsingham signalled to Phelippes. 'Thomas, if you will . . .'

Phelippes pushed his metal-rimmed glasses up his nose and consulted a paper on the table in front of him. 'Here,' he said, in his thin, birdlike voice, 'I have a message decoded last autumn, shortly after the Babington plotters came to trial. At the time we were not sure whether it was important or even what it meant, although it was clearly about the Spanish plans to send a fleet against us. Again, it was on its way to Philip, but this time the message was from the Duke of Parma rather than Ambassador Mendoza. I will read it to you: "What of Delft in the clearing of the seaways? One man with the eye of a falcon might be worth a hundred ships in the enterprise of God." The word "Delft", I suggest, refers in this instance to the assassination of Prince William. And the words "clearing of the seaways" are self-evident. They wish their fleet to be able to proceed along the Channel with no hindrance from the likes of Sir Francis Drake. If you accept this, then the meaning of Parma's message is clear: "Let us send the Delft assassin after Drake."'

'Thank you, Thomas,' Walsingham said. 'Now, John,' he turned to Shakespeare, 'you will need a description of this man and everything that is known of him. As Mr Mills said, he is a Fleming. We have descriptions of his person from the authorities in Delft and Rotterdam. He was a man of uncommon height, above six foot, slender but strong, habitually clean-shaven – though that could mean nothing for he may have affected a beard since then. He has a cold eye, almost black, is pale of skin and frequents whores. In Rotterdam he went by the name Hals Hasselbaink and claimed to be a Lutheran. It may be little, but it is more than we had. Send Slide into the stews, and go to them yourself, if need be. This Fleming has tastes that must be satisfied. Ask about. Have any women been attacked in such a way?'

He looked round the table. 'In particular, keep your thoughts on the weapon used in the assassination at Delft. I cannot emphasise enough my fears over the use of the wheel-lock pistol. The Queen is very concerned. Such weapons are too easy to conceal and especially lethal when employed at close quarters. If King Philip's hired killer is to use a pistol, there is every chance he has acquired it here. Go to the gunsmiths. In the meantime, I must insist that everyone in this room redoubles their vigilance. The death of the Scots devil changes everything and nothing. It will undoubtedly provoke a reaction from our enemies at home and abroad. Gentlemen, be prepared for the worst and pray for the best.'

Shakespeare was about to tell Walsingham of his suspicions that there might be a connection between the murder of William the Silent and the killing of Lady Blanche Howard, but before he could utter a word, Walsingham was out of the room. Shakespeare sighed and snapped his quill.

'He is expected at Greenwich,' Mills said, with a smile. 'He has a state funeral to arrange. Our sovereign lady is communicating once again. As the Mussulmans are wont to say, the dogs bark, the caravan moves on.'

Chapter 17

SHAKESPEARE KNOCKED AT the door of the house in Dowgate. He thought he heard noises inside, but no one answered. He began hammering impatiently and finally a woman came to open it. She looked at him with one eyebrow raised, as if in wonder that anyone could beat at the door quite so angrily. 'Forgive me for my tardiness, sir. I was putting the children to bed.'

Shakespeare grunted but did not apologise. 'I am come to see Mr Thomas Woode. Are you Mistress Woode?'

'No, sir,' she said, in a clear, low voice. 'There is no Mistress Woode, unless you mean my master's three-year-old daughter, Grace. I am Catherine Marvell, governess to the children. I believe Mr Woode is in his library.'

Suddenly Shakespeare took note of her look. Was she making jest at his expense? She was dark-haired with an oval face. At a time of year when skins were pallid and grey, hers was clear and had some colour. Her blue eyes met his and then she laughed at his sombre formality. He bristled. 'Tell him John Shakespeare wishes to speak with him on Queen's business.' His voice was stiff. He began to feel foolish. Too late he tried to smile, but was aware that it might have appeared as a grimace.

She curtsied and again he had the uncomfortable feeling that there was some mockery. 'Please come in to the ante-room while I ask if Mr Woode is available to see you.'

Shakespeare stepped into the welcoming warmth of the hall-way. It smelt of fresh-hewn oak and fine beeswax candles. On the walls were four or five portraits, probably of family. One in particular was more prominent than the others: a young woman with fair hair, wearing a dark gown and looking solemn. She had a white coif on her locks and a cross at her throat. She looked, he thought, devout, like a nun.

After a few moments, Catherine returned. For some reason, he found himself wishing to repair the damage wrought by his aggressive knocking and tone, but was tongue-tied. She led him to the library. Thomas Woode rose immediately from his table. 'Mr Shakespeare?'

Shakespeare shook the man's hand, which, he noted, was tremulous. 'Indeed, sir. I am come from Mr Secretary Walsingham. And you are Thomas Woode of the Stationers' Company, I believe.'

'Your servant. Catherine tells me you are here on Queen's busi-ness of some nature. May I offer you refreshment? Catherine, perhaps you would bring us some of the best claret.'

'Of course, master. May I remind you that the children are abed and would bid you good night?'

'In a few minutes.' As Catherine left he turned to Shakespeare. 'Now, how can I assist you, sir?'

Shakespeare did not wait to be asked before he seated himself at Thomas Woode's table. He observed his surroundings: fine wainscot panelling on the lower part of the wall, bookshelves full of weighty tomes, a white ceiling pargeted with Tudor roses. A rich tapestry on one wall, a Turkish carpet on another. An Italianate painting of the Virgin and babe. Thomas Woode was a wealthy man, of that there was no doubt. He sat now at the end of the table. Shakespeare turned to him. 'A fine house you are constructing here, Mr Woode.'

Woode put his hands flat on the table. 'It is for the children.

I had planned it these ten years past but lost the will to proceed with it when the Lord took my good wife, Margaret, three years ago. At last, though, I remembered the children needed a good home. I had more to think of than just myself.'

'I am sorry about your wife. Is that her portrait in the hallway?'

Woode smiled a grey, sad smile. 'I loved her very deeply. We had known each other since childhood. Our parents were friends. When I lost her I very nearly lost the will to live. But who are we to question the ways of the Lord?' He paused, apparently aware that he was straying into private grief in the presence of a stranger. 'God rest her soul,' he said quickly.

'From her portrait, I would say she was beautiful. Please forgive my intrusion.' Shakespeare laid out the paper and the type sorts retrieved from the burnt-out house in Shoreditch. 'I am told by Job Mallinson at Stationers' Hall that you are the man who knows more than any other in England about the provenance of letters and papers. I want you to tell me what you can about this paper and these type sorts.'

Thomas Woode did not need to look closely at the paper or the sorts: he knew them all too well. He felt the prickles of hair rising on his neck as he gazed upon them. He picked up the paper and looked at it this way and that in the light of a candle. He brought out a goldsmith's loupe from a drawer and held the paper and the type sorts close to his eye, one by one.

Shakespeare waited and watched, saying nothing. Catherine came back with two stoups of wine. Shakespeare gazed at her as she left again. She moved with quiet grace to the door, closing it soundlessly behind her. At last Thomas Woode put down his loupe.

Shakespeare took out the broadsheet. 'And this,' he said. 'Could it have been printed on the same paper and by the same press?'

Woode glanced at it.

'Well, Mr Woode?'

Woode nodded slowly. 'I can tell you a great deal about these papers and type sorts, Mr Shakespeare. May I ask you where you found them?'

'It is part of an investigation into a most grievous felony. I can offer you no more than that. But I can say that the broadsheet was bought from a street-seller.'

Woode moved the broadsheet to one side. 'Well, there is no connection. The broadsheet is poor stuff, but it most certainly has not been made with the same paper or press as the other scrap and sorts.'

'Then concentrate on the scrap, sir.'

Woode held the scrap of paper between them so that they could both see it clearly. 'What I can say first is that this is inferior quality paper and very bad printing. See how brown and stained it is. The paper has been made using turbid water, almost certainly at a mill downstream of a town. The manufacture of paper needs a lot of very clear, pure water, which is why paper mills should always be built on the higher reaches of rivers, upstream of towns where so much accumulated filth is dumped and so much river traffic stirs up the sediment. Muddy streams will stain the paper brown, as this is. The other requirement of good paper is good quality rag, which, as you may know, is the raw material of our industry. Good rag is hard to come by, which is why so many of us scratch our heads wondering what alternative material might be used. But as it is, we have nothing but rag and I can tell you plainly that whoever manufactured this paper did not have access to a good supply. That might, of course, lead one to think that the paper-maker was either very bad at his craft or, more probably, that he was working outside the law with whatever materials he had available.'

Shakespeare tapped his fingers on the table. He looked at Woode with a stern, impatient eye. Did the man take him for a fool? His hackles were rising. First the girl laughed at him, and now this. 'That might well be the case.'

If Woode saw the way Shakespeare was looking at him, he did not betray it, but continued with his theme: 'Now let us consider the type faces used on this piece of paper. These correspond with the selection of type sorts you have brought me. They are old and worn, which is why the print is so poor. Some letters are so degraded that you cannot, for instance, tell a D from a B. Type sorts are made of soft metal and wear down fast, which is why the great printers, such as Plantin of Antwerp – for whom I am an agent – replace them continually. Often it is difficult to get enough and they are very expensive. The use of such old thinned sorts would reinforce the suspicion that this was printed outside the law.

'Furthermore, we have here a curious selection of fonts from letter foundries all over Europe. You see these roman types? They are from Rouen and commonplace in England. But they are mixed up with others, such as this Black-letter, which I am certain is from Basle. No printer would use these together in the same line unless he had no option. For one thing they look odd – gothic with roman? – but mainly they will have been made to a different gauge and will have to be filed to size by the printer, an extremely time-consuming task. There are other fonts, too, some of them from Italy. It is a curious collection, like the sweepings of a printer's floor, Mr Shakespeare.'

Shakespeare drank some wine. It was remarkably good. Clearly, Thomas Woode had discerning taste as well as wealth. Unfortunately, he was also a dissembler. 'Can you, then, venture to suggest who did this printing?'

Thomas Woode put a hand to his furrowed brow, his soft gentleman's fingers flicking the grey at his temples. He seemed to be deep in thought, as if trying to work out who had made this paper or who had done the printing. But the truth was, he knew the answers to these questions: he had supplied the type and press, and the paper had been made by the old monk Ptolomeus on the Thames by Windsor. Who else could have made such a poor fist of it?

At last Woode sighed and shook his head. 'All I can say with certainty, Mr Shakespeare, is what I have already told you. This was not printed by a licensed printer. I would venture to suggest a wagon-back press, the sort that can be lifted and moved from hiding-place to hiding-place at a moment's notice, possibly concealed beneath haybales or canvas as it is transported. As for the paper, it would probably have been made near a town on the Thames or the Medway. A river setting not far from London. No one would bother to carry such a poor product any great distance, however malign their intent. Further than that, I can't say. It certainly hasn't been produced by any of the recognised paper-makers or printers licensed by the Council through Stationers' Hall.' He sighed and looked Shakespeare in the eye. 'I apologise for my inability to be more specific, but I hope I have been of some use to you.'

Shakespeare said nothing. He gave Woode a hard look. He didn't believe a word the older man had said. Woode was lying to him and he wasn't very good at it. When Shakespeare spoke, his tone was curt. 'You must come across many different printers, Mr Woode.'

The heat was rising in Woode's breast. It occurred to him suddenly that he was performing his part badly; very badly. He was under suspicion of something, but what? This agent of the state did not trust him and that was dangerous. He rose and went to the hearth to damp down the fire. 'Sir, I pride myself that I know all the legitimate printers in London and the counties close by. I can tell you for certain that none of them is responsible for this shoddy work. Are you sure that it was printed here in England, that it was not smuggled in by a colporteur?' Woode felt a bead of sweat on his brow. He was not made of the stuff of martyrs; he did not wish to die for his religion as others were prepared to do. He was merely the son of a successful printer who had learnt his trade well and become even more successful than his father. Apart from his Roman Catholicism, he was of no more interest to the state than any other wealthy merchant in this affluent city. Yet here, in this house, not far from this man sent by Walsingham – who could order torture and organise execution of anyone he wished – were hidden two renegade priests who could, with their discovery, bring him and his family to their doom.

At first, he had shrunk from telling Herrick he had to go; he had feared his reaction. But in the end he had approached him that morning after they had breakfasted. Woode explained his fears for the safety of his children. Herrick merely shrugged his shoulders, smiled and agreed it was time to move on. It had been good of Woode to have him here at all, he said, and he would be gone on the morrow. This, too, was to be Cotton's last night under their roof. He had another lodging to go to, in the house of a great lady who wished for a resident chaplain. In some ways Cotton had unnerved Woode the more; he so blatantly yearned for a martyr's death, as if life was nothing, the hereafter all. It was a way of thinking Woode could not comprehend. He would have given anything to have Margaret back with him, alive, in this world.

And now . . . what if Shakespeare should order in the pursuivants? It would be all too easy to find the priests. They would be here only a few more hours, but much could go wrong in such a short time. He needed to get Shakespeare out of his house.

'I am sure of nothing, Mr Woode. That is why I have come

to you,' Shakespeare said. 'Yet I feel you are not telling me all you know. Why is that? I came to you with one thought in mind: to use your extensive knowledge of print, but now I find myself wondering whether there is not something more to you than meets the eye. I have to tell you, sir, that I am not in the habit of delving into the recesses of men's souls, but neither am I willing to walk away and ignore my impression that you, for whatever reason, are holding something back from me.'

'Mr Shakespeare—'

'Spare me your protestations. I would have you tell me more about yourself and your circumstances. Some might imagine your business to be suffering since the fall of Antwerp to Parma's army, but you and I know that Mr Plantin is favoured by the Spanish King and that his business not only survives but thrives under the Spanish occupation. Why do you think he is so well looked on when many other Antwerp merchants have been forced to flee in the face of a pitiless enemy?'

Thomas Woode mopped the sweat from his brow with a gold-trimmed kerchief. 'This fire is over-zealous, Mr Shakespeare. Of course I will tell you everything I can. It is not my intention to hold anything back from you or Mr Secretary. But please forgive me while I attend to this fire.' He went to the door and called, 'Catherine.'

She reappeared in the room, her eyes keen.

'Catherine, please see to the fire. It is roasting us.'

Shakespeare threw her an enquiring look, as if to ask her whether she, too, found the fire hot, then said, 'I find the heat quite pleasant, Mistress Marvell. Perhaps Mr Woode has the sweating sickness.'

'Mr Shakespeare, you will find enough heat in the next life, I am sure. Let me turn it down a little in this.' Catherine went to the hearth and tried to reduce the heat.

Shakespeare watched her, then turned to Woode. He noticed

that he, too, was watching the governess intently and not, perhaps, in the way a master looks at a servant. 'You were saying?'

'I wish I could be of more assistance.'

'And about yourself. You have standing in the Stationers' Company?'

Thomas Woode could not help preening. 'I am indeed a member of the board of assistants. It is true I have standing in the company. I have worked hard over many years to earn the right to don its livery.'

'And has your Roman faith never hindered you?' It was an arrow shot in the dark, based on nothing more than a painting of the Virgin, and Shakespeare felt a pang of guilt for asking it, yet he needed a response. Woode froze like an ice statue.

Catherine hardly missed a beat. She turned from the fire, poker in hand. 'Mr Shakespeare? I wonder what your motive is in asking such a curious question.'

Shakespeare was taken aback. He stared at her, his brow crossed. 'Mistress Marvell?'

'Well, sir, you are invited into this house seeking assistance and then you pry into matters seeming unrelated. Are these Walsingham manners?'

'My motive, mistress, is to seek out some truth in this house. I think there is dissembling here.'

'And this from a guest who accepts our wine and hospitality?'

Shakespeare turned back to Woode. 'Your governess has a sharp tongue, sir. I am surprised you entrust your children to her care.'

'I think much of her care, Mr Shakespeare.'

'And do you think enough of your neck to answer my question? Would you deny your faith?'

Woode's mind was a pit of confusion. Did this Walsingham agent have some prior knowledge of his religious persuasion or was it simply a guess? Was it safer to admit it or try to equivocate as the Jesuits were taught? Once again, Catherine stepped forward boldly.

'I would not deny *my* faith, Mr Shakespeare. I am a Catholic and proud to be called so. But you will find me, also, a loyal subject of Her Majesty the Queen. I fear that being a loyal subject is not always a great help, though, is it? Did not Father Edmund Campion honour and pray for our Queen even as her men were tearing him apart like wild dogs?'

The words stung. It was the contradiction at the heart of John Shakespeare's work. He understood this well and could not escape it. Yet he knew that fire had to be used to fight fire, that this fragile reformation was susceptible to those who would bring wholesale torment and bloodshed to England's shores.

'You seem lost for words, Mr Shakespeare.'

'I am glad to hear that you are a loyal subject of the Crown, Mistress Marvell. To that end, I assume you accept Her Majesty as Supreme Head of the Church in England and would die to protect her from foreign potentates or the Pope himself. Nor will I ask whether you go to church, as required under the law, because I consider that a matter between you and your parish. I do not wish to delve into souls, though others might. But,' and here he addressed Woode, 'I will not be lied to. If you have information about the printing of that paper – or even, perhaps, the writing thereof – you will reveal it to me. And I promise you it were better to do so now, to me, than to others who might come after me. Do you understand my meaning, Mr Woode?' Shakespeare's voice was as cold as a Norse winter, but it was a curious rage, tainted with fury at himself for being led down this path and at finding himself in barbarous argument with

Catherine Marvell. He realised suddenly that he liked these people. He could tell that Thomas Woode was a good man. And as for Catherine Marvell, something about her moved and disturbed him. He was angry, too, because he feared for them should they find themselves in the hands of those with fewer scruples.

Woode was visibly trembling. 'I understand you very well, sir,' he said, 'but I swear to you that I have told you all I know. And, no, my faith has not been a hindrance to my career for I have not advertised it. As for Christophe Plantin of Antwerp, yes, he is a Catholic, but more than that he is a great craftsman, an artist, and he is a threat to no one, least of all England. Why, he is renowned for printing the Bible in Dutch. So far as I know, he was not considered an enemy by William of Orange and I do not see why he should be considered one now by you or Mr Secretary Walsingham or anyone else.' Woode paused to draw breath and, perhaps, for effect. 'And I, like Catherine, am a true subject of the Queen.'

Shakespeare rose from his chair, frustrated and with a gnawing sense of impotence in the face of this man's contradictions. 'Then I will leave you, Mr Woode. But I will return and I pray you may not live to regret it.'

As Catherine walked Shakespeare to the front door, Woode watched him in a kind of terror.

'You had better look to your master, mistress,' Shakespeare said, so that Woode could not hear. 'I fear he will choke on his own self-righteousness.'

'Better that than die of hypocrisy.'

Shakespeare turned to look at her. 'You have a viper's tongue in your head, mistress.'

'Aye. And an adder's teeth.'

Thomas Woode looked at her with fearful eyes. What was she saying to Shakespeare? Did she have any idea how dangerous this man could be to them? There could be no more delay: Cotton and Herrick would have to go this very evening, because if Shakespeare returned with the pursuivants to tear down their walls, there could be no protection for any of them.

Chapter 18

Parsimony field weighed the gold in her hands. Its brilliance and weight sent a chill of amazement and fear through her. The question was, how to turn it into coinage – and quickly? She was well aware that possession of such treasure could be a death sentence.

It had not been easy to secure it. Despite her threats, Starling Day wouldn't talk, and Alice was dead, choked on her own vomit. Time had been running out because Parsimony knew that Cogg's body would be found by someone else soon enough and then all hell would break loose. Put like that, there was no decision to make: she'd have to free Starling and bargain with her.

When she returned to the chamber where Starling was stretched out, the girl's breath was coming short and fast. She had been struggling against her bonds since Parsimony had left and was frantic now. Parsimony watched her from the door, knife in hand, and saw the rush of horror in the girl's eyes.

'No, dove, I'm not going to kill you. I'm going to set you loose. But I warn you, make one wrong move . . .'

As Parsimony cut the ropes, Starling closed her eyes, convinced that the knife would slide into her flesh at any moment.

'There, that wasn't so bad, was it?' Parsimony said at last.

Starling rubbed her wrists, scarcely able to believe she was free. She sat up on the bed, astonished to be alive.

'Well?'

'Thank you, Parsey. I thought you were going to do for me.'

'Would I harm my best girl? Come, let's do it. Half and half, you and me.'

'And Alice?'

Parsimony winced. 'Dove, your cousin's done for, drowned in her own puke while she was asleep.' She touched Starling's hand. 'That's the truth, dove.'

Starling looked at her. Had she killed Alice? Not that it mattered now. For better or worse they were in this thing together with one less person to share the loot. But she must never, ever, turn her back on Parsimony Field. Once Parsey had her grasp on the treasure, Starling was sure she herself would be as good as dead if she didn't move fast.

They spent the day looking for a tenement lodging. They had to get away from the Bel Savage whorehouse: it would be the first place anyone who knew Cogg would look for them and the treasure. Eventually they found a place across the river in Southwark. It wasn't much, just a room with a window on to the street, but it was in one of the better roads where they were less likely to be robbed. Once they had the stuff safely hidden, they had to sell it. Then they could go their separate ways. But first they had to retrieve the gold and jewels from Starling's hiding-place.

The churchyard behind the ruins of St Bartholomew the Great was a ghostly place at night. Starling led the way. There were still revellers about in Smith Field, drinking to the death of the Scots Queen, but the celebrations had been going on a long time so the watchmen had been ordered to clear the streets and impose a curfew. Any drunks found were to be beaten home with clubs; the government wanted no disturbances at this sensitive time when invasion or insurrection were real fears.

Starling and Parsimony dodged behind a wall at the northern end of Cock Lane. They stayed there, crouched down with the spades they had bought a couple of hours earlier.

When the way was clear, they darted across the great six-acre square as fast as they could. They heard a watchman calling after them but sprinted on regardless until they were safely at the far side by the rubble where the old church's nave had been pulled down fifty years ago.

'Where now, dove?' Parsimony said, panting.

'Round the back.'

The problem now was to dig up the treasure without being seen. Starling and Alice had buried it in a new grave where the earth was fresh-turned. They had planted it two feet down, probably a couple of feet above the corpse. Starling and Parsimony worked by moonlight; they didn't use pitch torches for fear of being spotted by the watch.

They took it in turns to dig. The earth was heavy and cloying. Starling hit an old stone from the demolished church nave and the spade clanged. 'Quiet!' Parsimony whispered. 'Do you want to get us strung up?'

'We must be there near enough,' Starling said. 'We didn't bury it too deep.' Suddenly she was on her knees, scrabbling in the earth with her hands. 'Here it is,' she said, grasping the handles of the carpet bag. She yanked hard and it came out. She held it up and brushed off the mud. 'Here, Parsey, we got it.'

Something in the glint of Parsimony's eye, silvery black in the moonlight, told Starling she had let her guard down again. Just as Parsimony lunged forward, Starling sidestepped, and tripped her, flailing, into the cold, damp earth.

She dropped the bag and leapt on to the other woman's back, pushing her head into the mud as though to suffocate her – as, she was sure, Parsimony had choked Alice. It would be a fitting end for her.

But Parsimony was stronger and wrenched her off. Thrashing about in the thick, wet clay, they hit each other, tore hair, twisted limbs and scratched. They fought to the point of exhaustion. Eventually neither could raise another punch and they lay back, panting for breath on the soft ground, side by side, their clothes filthy and torn.

'By God's little finger, dove, I never thought you had it in you to put up such a fight.'

Neither had Starling; she rather wished she had had half as much fight a while back in Strelley when she was being beaten as black as coal by Edward. 'It's my one chance, Parsey, and you're not taking it from me.'

As they lay there, gasping, respect arose between them. More than that, they both realised they needed each other. It would be impossible for one to conceal and sell all this treasure. Perhaps they could work together.

'Well, Parsey? Shall we do it together? We could even buy a place with this plunder.'

Parsimony thought for a moment. 'I've always wanted my own stew. You seem a likely partner, dove.'

'We could have a palace of a place.'

'Get the gentry in. Gaming too. The best place in town. All we need do is find ourselves a good broker and turn this into coin. What a place we will have!'

Starling laughed. 'We could call it Queens – because we'd be a couple of queen bees, mistresses of the game.'

Parsimony struggled to her feet and brushed herself down as best she could. 'Or we could call it The Queen's Legs – we never close! You know, dove, it's a shame you didn't get to know Cogg better. He'd have loved you. You're just his sort, you are. Who was it killed him? It looked like his eyes had been poked out.'

'He was a horrible man in dark clothes. Cold as a Christ-tide frost. He had this thin, black-handled skene. Stabbed Cogg twice as I saw – once in each eye, up to the hilt. Kill you as soon as swive you, that one.' Starling was standing now, the carpet bag gripped in her left hand. She looked at it and then, in a moment of trust, held it out for Parsimony to take.

Parsimony took the bag, fished out two gold bars and felt their weight, then put them back in the bag. 'No, you carry it, dove.'

'One more thing, Parsey. That killer, after he put his skene through Cogg's eyes . . .' she paused, wide-eyed, rememberin' '. . . he crossed himself like a fucking priest.'

Chapter 19

WALKING ALONG DEPTFORD Strand among the bustle of sailors, sailmakers, carpenters, shipwrights and whores, no one would have noticed Miles Herrick in his workman's jerkin with the tools of his trade slung in a bag over his shoulder.

It was a crisp, bright February day, almost spring-like. The last of the snow had melted or been washed away by the rain and there was new fire in men's bellies. The world seemed brave and worth getting out of bed for. Herrick looked around him and examined the houses and shops that fronted the riverbank. His eye fixed on a chandlery, an ancient, leaning building on three storeys with small windows. A sign outside said, 'Room to let'. That would do. He ducked into the shop.

It was thick with lung-clogging sotweed smoke. Through the fug, among the cordage, the sail gear, the galley pots, the barrels of hard biscuit, dried peas and salt beef, and all the other essentials of a voyage, he saw two men in conversation, strong working men, who seemed to be arguing over some detail of a shipwright's plans for a caravel spread over a trestle. As he approached, they stopped talking and turned his way, pipes of sotweed in their mouths, belching smoke like autumn bonfires.

'Are you the master of this chandlery?' Herrick asked the

taller of the two, who seemed the more assured. 'I am looking for lodging and saw your sign. Is the room still free?'

'It might be free of tenants,' the taller man replied, 'but it would certainly never be free of charge.'

Herrick smiled thinly at the attempt at humour. He took his purse and loosened the drawstring. 'I can pay well. I am here from the Low Countries, looking for work with armaments.' He enjoyed the irony; 'armaments' made him sound plausible. He knew, too, that such a claim would never be checked.

'Well, there is plenty of work to be had. The admirals will be glad of another armaments journeyman. Come with me and see the room.'

It was on the second floor under the pitch of the roof. Exactly what he required. He heard rats or birds scuttling behind the plasterwork, in the eaves. There was a bare palliasse, a small table and three-legged stool. Nothing else. But there was a small casement window that gave out over the river. Herrick stood at it a long moment, then turned back into the room. God's work. *Thy will be done.* 'I will take it.'

The landlord reached up to brush some cobwebs down from above the low door. 'My name is Bob Roberts. I'll supply you with blankets and a pot to piss in. Two shillings and sixpence a week, but you can have it for half a crown.'

Herrick put his bag of tools on the floor as casually as a good-wife depositing a basket of laundry, and shook hands with the landlord to seal the agreement. 'Henrik van Leiden.'

'Well, Henrik, share a stoup of ale with us and you can pay me the first week's rent,' the landlord said, and turned to leave. 'If you need any names of captains for work I will happily help you.'

'What of Drake, the greatest of all?'

The landlord laughed. 'Aye, what of him? Work for him? He will give you no rest and no pay.'

'So he is in these parts?'

'Every day. Never have I seen a captain put so much into preparation. If our fleet is not ready for the armada, it will not be for want of Drake's efforts. But beware, after a few days in his employ you might wish yourself an oarsman slave, manacled and thrashed daily on a Spanish galley.'

Herrick smiled. 'I understand. But it would be a great honour to make his acquaintance.'

'Then I wish you well, Henrik, but beware. He will press you into service as soon as shake your hand.'

As the door closed behind the landlord, Herrick stepped once more to the window. The sill was three feet off the floor. The window was two feet wide and three and a half from top to bottom. It was perfect for his purpose. He crossed himself, then knelt and prayed.

Chapter 20

THE FACE OF Catherine Marvell haunted John Shakespeare. What was she? A Catholic governess, probably a recusant, in a household of secrets. Was she more than a governess to Thomas Woode? She was certainly familiar in his presence. Shakespeare kicked his horse with a violence that, on another day, would have shamed him. He would dismiss her from his thoughts.

He rode on to the bridge to Southwark. He was still full of unreasoning anger. He was angry with Thomas Woode for his foolish lies; he was angry with the intruder who had broken down the door to his home and ransacked the papers in his solar, he was angry with himself, though he was not sure why.

When he got home, Slide had been waiting. He had brought with him another copy of *The London Informer*, which carried a lurid story describing the last minutes of Mary, Queen of Scots. Shakespeare read the story slowly. It told him nothing that he didn't already know, grisly details of the head rolling out of the hand of Executioner Bull. That did not surprise Shakespeare: Bull was incompetent at the best of times. He read on: the blood-red martyr's garb she wore; tittle-tattle about the dog cowering among her petticoats; a few lines on the great rejoicing of London and the fears of a Spanish invasion fleet being despatched imminently.

'How did he get this paper printed?' Shakespeare exploded, tearing it into pieces and throwing them to the floor. 'I thought his press had been broken up by the Stationers' Company.'

'Perhaps he had access to another.'

'Well, find him, Harry,' Shakespeare growled. 'I want Walstan Glebe locked up and fettered until I have questioned him.'

Slide bowed. He would, of course, do his best, he said, and he was sure it was only a matter of time before Glebe was apprehended.

'And I want the Jesuit Southwell incarcerated. You said you could deliver him, so where is he? You have money on account, Harry. Bring him in! Mr Secretary will want my own head on a platter if we don't have him soon.'

Slide took Shakespeare's rage without flinching. He still looked battered from the attack he had suffered. The cuts were clotting to scabs and the bruises turning yellow, but he was a mess. He assured Shakespeare, however, that he was well enough in himself. He didn't mention that his leads to Southwell had gone cold, which would have done nothing to calm the storm.

'I want you to get out into the stews, Harry. Find out if the bawdy baskets have been lashing any strange clients, or have been berayed unkindly in their turn. Have they entertained any Flemings, or men with Dutch or German accents? If there are any strange customers about, I want to know – and quickly. Keep asking about Blanche Howard, too. Did she move in dissident circles? Was she close to any foreign men, particularly Flemings? I think there is some connection here. Return to me with information as soon as possible.'

'Consider it done, Mr Shakespeare.'

'And, Harry, what do you know of a Thomas Woode, merchant? Is there any talk about him?'

'Well, of course I have heard of him. He is wealthy, though not ostentatious. A little puritanical, on the Presbyterian side, I would think, from the way he lives. Perhaps he is of the same persuasion as Mr Secretary.'

Shakespeare laughed without humour. 'I think not, Harry. Woode is of the Romish persuasion. Mr Secretary would not be amused at the suggestion that he shared anything in common with Mr Woode.'

'Ah . . .'

'But find out what more you can. Anything in Thomas Woode's past, any contact he has with merchant strangers. Who are his friends? And he has a governess for his children, one Catherine Marvell. Find out what you may about her.'

Slide tried to offer his winning smile, but his face was still crooked from his beating. 'Of course.' He hesitated a moment, then added, 'Forgive me, sir, for bringing up such a delicate subject . . . this is not the time to make such a request, but I am sore in need of funds.'

Shakespeare bared his teeth. He was about to say something, which he suddenly realised he might well regret; he needed Slide now. Badly. He could not afford to lose him. And, clearly, the man had to have gold. 'How much?'

'Fifteen marks. If I am to go to the stews, the apple-squires and whores will not talk without sweetening. You must know that, Mr Shakespeare.'

'Indeed. Forgive me, Harry, but I fear my knowledge of the ways of bawdy-houses is scant. I am sure, though, that you are well versed in such matters and could educate me over a quart of ale some day. But not now.' He opened his purse and counted out coins, then handed them to Slide without ceremony. 'I expect results, Harry. Go.'

Now, an hour after that conversation, Shakespeare reined in his horse by the Marshalsea. He told himself he would have to go back to Dowgate later that day, to talk once more to Thomas Woode and bring him in for interrogation, if need be. He also had a curious compulsion to see Catherine Marvell again. Had he been thinking more clearly, he might have recognised the symptoms: at the age of twenty-eight, a time when most men were settled into comfortable marriage and fatherhood, he was still in need of a wife. All he could think was that he was a poltroon, a fool for a girl he had scarcely even talked with. And there was nothing he could do about it.

The Marshalsea gaoler was a giant of a man, yet when Shakespeare announced he was there on Queen's business, he thought the man seemed uneasy. 'I would see John Doughty, turnkey.'

The gaoler seemed puzzled. 'I know no one of that name, sir.'

'Come, come. He had plans to kill Sir Francis Drake. He has been here these five years past.'

The gaoler shook his head. 'No, sir. I have been here myself for three, and I do not recall a prisoner of that name or similar.'

'Let me see your records.'

The gaoler gave Shakespeare a bewildered look.

'You do have a black book, man?'

'Of course, sir. But how could that help if the prisoner you seek isn't here?'

'Let me look at it.'

The gaoler's room offered little respite from the gloomy atmosphere of the building. He had a table, two stools, a fire and the tools of his trade: bunches of great keys, lashes and canes, brutish manacles and deadweight chains. He reached up to a dusty shelf and brought down a tome, which he dropped with a thud on the table next to his half-eaten trencher of food.

Shakespeare turned the thick pages of the black book back

to 1582, when Doughty should have been brought here. There it was: Doughty, John, for conspiracy to do murder; close confinement.

'Here is our man, turnkey.'

The gaoler clanked his keys nervously. 'Never did hear of him, sir. You'd be welcome to look in all the cells and talk to whomsoever you please, but I defy you to find someone of that name here.'

Shakespeare looked the gaoler in the eye. Despite his unease, he was telling the truth. So what had happened to Doughty? 'Do you have any prisoners who have been here five years or more, someone who might recall this man?'

'Aye. Davy Bellard, sir. He's been here fifteen years or more for counterfeiting. As fine and clever a man as you could meet, Mr Shakespeare.'

Bellard was a short fellow with long, unkempt hair and beard that had evidently not been trimmed during all his years of incarceration. But his eyes were still bright and alert. 'Yes, I recall John Doughty,' he said. 'Angriest man I ever did know, Mr Shakespeare. Wanted to kill the whole world for the injustices suffered by him and his brother. I made the mistake of laughing at him, I'm afraid, and he tried to kill me.' Bellard lifted the tattered remnants of his shirt. 'See that scar? He had a buttriss for paring horses' hooves and stuck me with it. Lucky for Davy Bellard, his aim was poor and the blade glanced off my ribs. I avoided John Doughty after that. He was a man beyond reasoning.'

Shakespeare examined the scar. It had been a jagged gash and very unpleasant. 'What happened to him?'

'That's the curious thing, sir. We thought he'd be hanged for certain. Conspiring to commit a murder must be a gallows offence, or so we did believe. But if he was hanged, we heard nothing of it. One fine summer's day, a few weeks after he arrived, he just weren't here any more. He might have been moved to another prison, but I couldn't say. Nor would I know whether he was strung up or set free. It was a mystery to us all and still is, sir. Not that we gave it much thought. I, for one, was glad to see the back of him.'

'Thank you, Mr Bellard.' Shakespeare handed him a shilling. 'What is your sentence?'

Bellard glanced around to make sure the gaoler was out of earshot. 'Ten years, sir, but don't tell the gaoler, sir, or he might throw me out. I do well here, sir. I don't want to leave.'

Shakespeare managed a smile, the first of the day. 'Fear not, Mr Bellard, your secret is safe with me. And if you hear anything of any interest to me within these four walls, I would be pleased if you would somehow get the information to me at Mr Secretary Walsingham's department.'

Bellard tapped the side of his nose conspiratorially. 'Intelligencing, is it, sir?'

'Something like that. In particular, I would like to know of any Flemings you might have word of. And any Jesuits . . .' Shakespeare left the prisoner and asked the gaoler to take him, separately, to see Piggott and Plummer, the two priests of whom Harry Slide had told him. It was a long shot, but Shakespeare was more than a little interested in the guests at the mass and dinner of which Slide had told him. There might, just, be more information to be had from these men. If they could lead him to the Jesuit Southwell it would be one rod off his back.

Plummer was first. 'Ah, Mr Shakespeare. Harry Slide has told me of you.'

'And he has told me of you, too, Mr Plummer. You give him information from time to time, I believe.'

'Indeed I do, sir.'

'I would know more of the mass that was held here. Yourself,

Piggott, three ladies – Anne Bellamy, Lady Frances Browne and the Lady Tanahill, I believe.'

'And a Jesuit called Cotton.'

'Are you sure that was his real name?'

Plummer scratched his privies as if he had the French pox – which, for all Shakespeare knew, he might – and made a face as if he were in extreme discomfort. 'Now how could I know that? I would say it was highly unlikely that he was using his real name. Few of us sent over from the English colleges do.'

'I understand. Could he, then, have been Father Robert Southwell?'

'Again, how could I know? I have heard of Southwell. He is a poet and was renowned among the Popish fraternity for his saintliness even before he came to England last summer. But I was not at Douai or Rome with him so I have not made his acquaintance.'

'We have a description of him from his younger days. It is said he was not tall, nor of a very great weight, his hair a flame-golden colour and his eyes green or blue. Could that have been the man Cotton?'

Plummer did not have to think hard. 'It most certainly could, though I would have said his eyes were grey.'

'And did he give you any inkling of his movements, where he lodges, who he sees?'

Plummer shook his head. 'Nothing. Jesuits are cleverer than that.'

'And the ladies at the mass, did they know him?'

'I think the Bellamy girl did, but not the other ladies, though I would say they seemed much taken with him. As was I. He was an uncommon man and likeable. I could see how he might attract people to him and bring them into the Roman faith. Mr Shakespeare, he would draw them all in.'

'What of your colleague, Piggott?'

'I don't like him. I don't trust him and he doesn't trust me. He was very familiar with Cotton, clutched him to his foul, pox-ridden breast and whispered secrets in his ear. If you want to know more of Cotton, you had best speak with him. He is your man for that. I think he could be dangerous.'

'And the three ladies at the dinner?'

'Simpering, stupid women who would rather be occupied by God in heaven than enjoy a decent fucking here on earth. I fear they are all on a mission to die, for which I am sorry. They are harmless fools posing no threat to the estate.'

Shakespeare made to leave. 'I will see you are recompensed for this, Plummer. Keep your ears and eyes wide. I want word of a Fleming, one with a taste for being beaten by women, and beating them in turn. And tell me one more thing: the gaoler seemed nervous when I arrived. Why do you think that might be?'

Plummer scratched his stones once more, then put his hand down the back of his woollen smock to rub his neck. 'Fleas, sir. The place is alive with them. I fear they live on the rats, which are as fat as well-fed cats. Yes, the gaoler. A good man, runs a decent prison except for the fleas. But he has a little secret. Can't quite let go of the old faith. And, sir, there is another thing that might have set his nerves on edge. You are not our only visitor today.'

'Really? Who else has been here?'

'Richard Topcliffe. Like you, he was asking questions about our little supper party and mass. I am happy to admit to you, sir, that he scared me half witless.'

Every muscle in Shakespeare's tall, lean body clenched. 'Topcliffe?'

'Like you, he seemed most interested in the ladies and Cotton. threatened me with the rack if I did not speak plain, so I told him everything I could without demur.'

'Did you mention the work you do for Slide?'

'No. I am not such a cony as that. But I did mention he might get far more information from Piggott. I fear Father Piggott may now be even less kindly disposed towards me . . .'

'Thank you, Mr Plummer. Please use my name if you are in danger and need assistance. You may find it does not work miracles with Richard Topcliffe, though.'

Plummer took Shakespeare's hand and held it. 'Thank you. And I hope I have not given you my fleas to take home.'

Outside the cell, the gaoler was waiting, and walked with Shakespeare the few steps to Piggott's dungeon. Piggott was in a corner of his cell, hunched into himself like a wren in a hard frost. He did not move or utter a sound when Shakespeare entered and clanged shut the door.

'Father Piggott?'

Piggott did not move.

'Father Piggott, I will talk with you whether you wish it or not.'

Still no movement. Shakespeare grasped the collar of his coarse woollen smock and pulled him up sharply. As he did so, Piggott's head flopped into view and Shakespeare recoiled in shock: it was a bloody pulp. His nose looked broken, his eyes swollen red dumplings with pinpricks of light. The man tried to sit up, but groaned as if his ribs were cracked.

Shakespeare moved his hand forward to help him, but Piggott shied away as if he would be hit. He tried to speak, but no human sound came from his mouth. Shakespeare went back to the door and ordered the gaoler to bring water and rags to wash the wounds.

The gaoler was reluctant to comply. He stood there, dumb and inert.

'If you have any sense, gaoler, you will do as I say. Or perhaps you would like me to put out your little secret? I am sure Mr Topcliffe would like to hear of your Romish leanings.' It was a low trick, but it worked. The gaoler looked shocked for a moment, then lumbered off. He returned quickly with all that Shakespeare required. 'Now clean the blood from the prisoner.'

The gaoler looked at Shakespeare as though he were mad. Why would anyone wish to clean the blood from a prisoner's face? But when he saw the scowl in Shakespeare's eyes he sighed in submission and advanced on Piggott, grumbling as he roughly wiped away the clotted blood. When he was at least partially clean, Shakespeare handed the gaoler twopence and told him to go to the nearest apothecary for muslin bandages to wrap Piggott's injured chest.

'I cannot leave my post.'

'Then send one of your turnkeys. Do I have to remind you this is Queen's business? Would you have me draw your neglect to the attention of Mr Secretary Walsingham?'

'It seems everyone is on Queen's business today,' the gaoler mumbled as he trundled off once more.

'Now, Piggott, we are alone,' Shakespeare said, in a low, urgent voice, as he stood over the prisoner who, he had to admit, did not look much better cleaned up. He was an ill-favoured individual with heavily pitted skin and thinning, lank hair. 'Be straight with me or I will have you in the Tower this day, where you will be confined to Little Ease before questioning under duress. This is a matter of state and I will be answered.' Little Ease: a cell so small that a prisoner could neither stand, lie down nor even sit properly. 'Little Ease, Piggott. Discomfort so severe that you would beg for the back-breaking pain of the pillory in exchange.'

Piggott picked a stray clot of blood from his nostril. He looked like a dog that had been whipped to the point of death. His voice was a hoarse whisper. 'I'll tell you everything I told Topcliffe.' He winced and put a hand to his injured jaw.

'Well?'

'I told him I had a message to pass on. It was a message for a priest whose name I do not know. All I know is that he is lodged with Father Cotton.'

'And what was the message?'

'Cogg of Cow Lane. Just that and no more.'

'And who gave you this message to pass on?'

'I – I do not know.'

'I could have you on the rack this day, Piggott. Do you know what it does to men's bodies?'

Piggott nodded sullenly. He knew that the rack could pull bones from joints, that it could tear muscles and tendons irrevocably so that the victim would never walk or use his arms again.

'So answer me. Who gave you this message to pass on?'

'It was a Frenchie. I do not know his name. He came to me here and said he was sent by Dr Allen. He may have been from the embassy of France. In truth, Mr Shakespeare, I do not know. That was enough for me. He gave me money, two marks, the difference between life and death in a place like this.'

'And what did you consider the message to mean?'

Piggott was in so deep now that all he could think of was staying alive. He would sacrifice the Pope, Cardinal Allen and the English College at Rheims for the slim chance of life. His voice grew even lower and seemed to scour his mouth. 'I took it to be the whereabouts of a weapon. A dag, perhaps. That is the way to kill princes these days, I believe.'

Oh, yes, thought Shakespeare, a wheel-lock pistol is certainly the way to murder princes. It had worked with William the Silent and now Elizabeth feared it would work its evil on her. A wheel-lock pistol could be ready primed and was small enough to be hidden in a gown or sleeve. That was why wheel-lock pistols – dags – were barred from the precincts of royal palaces. 'Is that merely your surmise? Or do you have some reason for believing this?'

Piggott shook his head wearily. 'Surmise, sir, merely surmise.' He turned his head once more to the wall and slumped back into the foetal position, the only sign left of life being the fast and harsh sound of his painful breathing.

Chapter 21

Two heavily armed men stood at the doorway to Cogg's property in Cow Lane. Shakespeare dismounted and approached them. 'Is Topcliffe here?' he demanded.

They winked at each other, then turned to him and smirked. 'No entry,' one said, with studied nonchalance.

'Do you know who I am?'

'You could be the King of Sweden's monkey for all I care. No entry.'

'I am John Shakespeare, secretary to Sir Francis Walsingham. I am here on official business and I will be admitted.'

'Try it, if you like.'

Shakespeare stepped forward. Immediately the two men moved closer to each other to form an impenetrable wall. They wore thick doublets of ox-hide, which would deflect most knife blows. They carried skenes and wheel-locks in their belts and swords in scabbards, which they did not bother to draw. They were both strong of arm and broad of chest. 'If you do not let me pass, you will answer to Her Majesty's Principal Secretary. Do you understand what that means?'

'Look, whoever you are, do you think we're worried about you or bloody Walsingham? We answer to Mr Topcliffe and he answers directly to the Queen. Do you understand what *that* means? Now, then, which of them two would scare *you* more?'

At that moment the front door opened. Topcliffe stood there. He glowered at Shakespeare, then diverted his attention to the two guards. 'Get a handcart,' he ordered. 'We've a body to move.'

The more vocal of the two guards bowed obediently, then shuffled away.

'Topcliffe,' Shakespeare said, 'what is going on here?'

Topcliffe was about to turn back into the building but he thought better of it and stopped. 'What's it to you?'

'You know very well. I am in the middle of an official investigation.'

'And, by God, you're slow. Would you have found Cogg without me? Would the foul priest Piggott have talked to you if I had not softened him first? I doubt you could find a cunny in a whorehouse.'

'Topcliffe, we must work together. We may not employ the same methods but I know we share the same ends – the security of our Queen and country.'

'And what sort of milk-livered country will that be with the likes of you fighting for it? A country of men who would rather kneel and kiss the feet of the Antichrist than wash their hands in the blood of the Queen's foe. I would rather spill every last drop of Popish blood than see a single hair on her body harmed. Would you? Which church does your father go to on Sunday, Shakespeare? Tell me that.' Topcliffe spat on the ground between them. 'Come in, then, boy. Come and see what we have found and explain to your Walsingham why you always follow where Topcliffe leads.'

Shakespeare's heart was pounding with rage, but he swallowed his pride and stepped into the building. A large body lay beside a barrel, its head a mask of caked blood. Flies feasted and buzzed.

'Stabbed through the glaziers,' Topcliffe said. 'Looks like a pig, don't you think? Get him down the shambles and turn him into pies, no one would know the difference.'

'Who is it? Cogg?'

'Oh, yes, that's Cogg. Whoremonger, broker of stolen goods, wild rogue with a taste for meat and venery.'

'I take it you knew him.'

Topcliffe put his heavy boot square on Cogg's chest and leant forward so that Shakespeare could smell him. 'He could get you anything you desired. He was dangerous but he had his uses. Sometimes. He didn't always choose his friends wisely, as you can see. But we know who did this to him, don't we?'

'You think it was Southwell?'

'I know it's the boy-girl. And I know *why*. A dag. He bought a dag from Cogg to kill our Queen, and then tried to cover his tracks by killing him. We both know that the Popish beast Southwell did this, but you will flounder like a fish in a bowl while I will catch him and make sure he departs this life in great pain and torment, wriggling like an eel as I remove his pizzle and sweetbreads and hold them, dripping, before his bulging eyes. And I will do so before he harms the Queen.'

Shakespeare had more to say, but held his counsel. He knew that it would all be so much wasted breath. It was impossible to talk to Topcliffe: he was set in his brutish ways. Like a terrier with game in its jaws, nothing would prise him from his belief that Southwell was on a killing spree, with Elizabeth his ultimate target. For one brief moment, Shakespeare felt a flicker of doubt. Perhaps Topcliffe was right in this. The moment passed. Yet he had to ask one more question. 'Topcliffe, you took my witnesses. Where are they? I must talk to them.'

'What witnesses would they be?'

'You know very well. The vagabonds from Hog Lane. You removed them from Bridewell where I had sent them in custody.'

'Vagabonds? I know nothing of any vagabonds, Shakespeare. And if I did, I'd rack them, every one, then hang them. I'd clear our country of such foul slurry.'

'Are you denying that you had them removed?'

Topcliffe said nothing, merely stared at Shakespeare with scorn, then went back to his work.

There was nothing Shakespeare could do. He could not prove anything against Topcliffe. And even if he did, who would care? Most people in this town would consider the disappearance of four vagabonds a good thing and shake Topcliffe's hand.

Shakespeare searched the house, impeded at times by Topcliffe's men, who delighted in trying to trip him and bar his way. He wasn't certain what he was looking for. After an hour, he left and set off for Seething Lane. He wanted to see Harry Slide. Something had been nagging at him since his visit to the Marshalsea. How had Topcliffe heard of Piggott, Plummer and the mass said by the Jesuit priest Cotton? Painful though it was to come to such a conclusion, it seemed to Shakespeare that probably Slide had told him.

Slide was waiting for him, but he wasn't alone. He had with him a constable and Walstan Glebe, publisher of *The London Informer*. Glebe's hands were bound and he was restrained by the constable. He tried to protest at his detention, but Shakespeare would not listen. He ordered the constable to wait with Glebe in the ante-room, then took Slide to the solar, now nearly restored to the condition it had been in before it was ransacked. 'Harry, before we speak of Glebe, I must ask you this. How did Topcliffe know about the Marshalsea mass?'

Slide looked genuinely shocked. 'Topcliffe knew?'

'Oh, yes. He got there before me. He beat Piggott half to death. Have you been dealing with him?'

'Mr Shakespeare, no. I have never dealt with him.'

'I couldn't help but wonder about your injuries . . .'

'In God's name, no. No! That was as I told you. I was robbed and beaten in the street by an unknown attacker.'

'So I would be wrong in wondering whether Topcliffe beat the information out of you as he beats everyone else to get what he wants?'

Slide shook his head vehemently.

'How do you think he knew?'

Harry Slide sat down. He looked distraught, but Shakespeare knew all too well how he could dissemble. Walsingham had once said that if Slide ever gave up intelligencing he could get work as a player with Mr Burbage at the Theatre, so clever was he at playing a part. 'Anyone could have told Topcliffe,' Slide said. 'The gaoler, one of his turnkeys, a visitor, prisoners. They come and go, Mr Shakespeare. The Marshalsea is not the Tower. It is as tight as a goodwife's sieve.'

Shakespeare sat down beside him. He wasn't by any means certain that he believed him, but he was sure he needed him. 'All right. Leave it at that. I will accept your denial. But let me tell you, Slide, that if ever you do consort with Topcliffe you will make an enemy of me, and an enemy of Mr Secretary, who prizes loyalty above all else. Now, tell me what you know about Cogg of Cow Lane.'

A painful smile forced its way on to Slide's yellow-bruised face. 'Gilbert Cogg! The fattest, greediest felon in all London, but a jovial fellow.'

'A dead fellow now. Murdered. Stabbed in the eyes with some thin blade.'

Slide did not seem surprised. 'Ah, a sadness. Not a great shock, though. He dealt with dangerous people. He loved gold more than anything. More than meat, drink or lechery. Gold and rare stones were his passion and he would do anything to acquire them.'

'Such as supply a pistol to a hired Spanish killer?'

Slide's eyes met Shakespeare's. 'So that is what this is about. Is there some connection with Piggott?'

'He was the intermediary. Whoever organised Cogg to supply the weapon sent the message to his assassin that it was ready through Piggott. So now we have a killer loose with a weapon, the like of which we can only imagine. To stop a determined man with a wheel-lock, we would have to keep Drake hidden in his cabin, seeing no one until he is safe at sea. I fear that is most unlikely. And with Cogg dead there is no witness to identify him.'

'What of the Jesuit Southwell?'

Shakespeare laughed humourlessly. 'Is he the killer? Everything we know about him suggests not. Tell me this, though, Harry. If Cogg was so wealthy, where was his gold? I searched his house thoroughly. Topcliffe did, too. There was no sign of it.'

'Cogg *was* wealthy. Maybe Topcliffe found it and kept it for himself. Or perhaps he banked his treasure elsewhere. He had a whorehouse beside the Bel Savage, much to the irritation of the city aldermen. They found it far too close for comfort, though many were not above making use of its services.'

'Take me there one day, Harry. It might be an education. Sometimes I think I have lived far too innocent. But in the meantime go there and make enquiries. The geese might know something. First, though, let us speak with Mr Glebe and see if we can't find some reason to give him a spell in the pillory. A spattering of eggs and a back that aches beyond enduring might make a better man of him. Where did you find him?'

'At Fleet Lane. He was trying to take apart his press to get it out of there. Evidently your friends at Stationers' Hall were slow off the mark.'

In the ante-room, Glebe hung his head sullenly. His hands were bound but he could use his fingers as a comb, teasing his thick, wiry hair into a fringe to conceal the branded L. He looked up as Shakespeare and Slide entered the room, then held up his bound hands in front of him. 'Please untie me, Mr Shakespeare. I am not going anywhere.'

Shakespeare nodded and the constable proceeded to cut him loose. He picked up a small bell from a coffer and rang it. Jane quickly appeared. 'Some ale, please.' Slowly he began to pace the room. Glebe's eyes followed him expectantly. Finally Shakespeare turned to him. 'Well, Glebe, it seems your days of beslubbering reputations are over. At the very least I have you on charges of illicit printing and resisting arrest. With your previous record, the least you can expect is the loss of a hand, both ears and ten years with hard labour.'

'Mr Shakespeare . . .'

'Have you anything to say to me before I consign you to Newgate and let the law take its course?'

'What can I tell you, sir? All I have done is repeat gossip I heard in the taverns and alehouses.'

Jane returned with ale. She poured some for Shakespeare, Slide and the constable but hesitated before giving any to Glebe until Shakespeare nodded.

'No, Glebe, that is not all you have done. Someone who knows about the murder of Lady Blanche Howard has spoken to you. I think a spell in Newgate and the thought of what is likely to befall you might concentrate your mind. I do not have time to listen to your denials.'

Glebe looked sour, as though he had swallowed unripe medlar fruit. 'Sir,' he protested, 'what have I done wrong? I merely wish to exercise my rights as a freeborn Englishman. Are we slaves? Have you forgotten the Great Charter?'

'This has nothing to do with slavery. You know as well as I do that all printed works must be licensed. Yours are not so you will pay the penalty. Had you co-operated with us, we could have let you go about your business, but this matter involves the murder of a cousin of the Queen – and we need to find out who is responsible. Once you are in the cage, there will be no way out, Glebe. No appeal. I am sure you understand.'

Glebe shrugged his sloping shoulders. 'I have nothing more to say. Do your worst.'

For a moment, Shakespeare was caught off guard. He had expected Glebe to crumple and talk. Surely a man who has known the stench of his own burnt flesh and the pain associated with it might wish to avoid further internment and possible mutilation? 'Take him to Newgate, constable. Make sure he is shackled to the floor and given nothing but porridge and water. And tell no one he is there.'

Chapter 22

THE *ELIZABETH BONAVENTURE*, a royal ship of six hundred tons with thirty-four guns and a crew of two hundred and fifty, slipped away from the quay at Gravesend on the tide and made sail with the wind. It was a chilly morning, just past break of day, and a brisk breeze stretched the ship's pennants bravely and churned the grey surface of the Thames.

The sailors set to work, coiling ropes, scrubbing the decks of all the land detritus that had collected in port. Behind them, growing more and more distant, the smoke of London spiralled hazily into the sky. Gradually the river became broader and the great ship moved elegantly onwards through the turbulent flood on her way down to the sea. As the wind freshened, it whistled through the shrouds and sails, casting a curious spell that, for a while, rendered all aboard silent in their toil.

Boltfoot Cooper rested his left arm on the polished oak bulwark and watched Vice-Admiral Drake from a distance of not more than forty feet. He had his right hand on the hilt of his cutlass, which was thrust loosely through his belt. At last, in the early afternoon, they reached the gaping mouth of the river and flew before the wind into the narrow sea.

'Cooper!' Drake's gruff voice rang out above the wind. 'Drag yourself here, man!'

Boltfoot moved resignedly towards his former captain. He

had vowed never to take orders from him again and never to set foot aboard another of his vessels.

'Report to the carpenter, Mr Cooper. There will be plenty of work to do on the spars and casks. Make yourself useful. I don't need watching like a babe out here.'

Boltfoot stood his ground. 'I am ordered to remain with you at all times. Who is to say that one of this crew is not a hireling of Spain?'

'By the bones of the deep, Mr Cooper, would you disobey an order of your captain? I'll have you hanged at the yardarm.'

'My captain is Mr Shakespeare and my admiral is Mr Secretary Walsingham, as you know, sir. I am answerable to them, and to them only, save the Queen and God.'

'Huh! You have a fine spirit this cold morning, Cooper. Take a tot of brandy.' Drake turned to his lieutenant. 'Captain Stanley, be good enough to ask the galley steward to bring us a bottle of Aquitaine liquor.'

Stanley, thought Boltfoot, seemed a little bit put out, as if it were not his place to call upon a steward to serve them, especially with Boltfoot and Diego in close attendance. But though Stanley might have felt slighted, he did not complain. When the brandy arrived Boltfoot insisted on tasting Drake's first, for poison. Drake scowled at him. 'You think me as womanly as a Spaniard, Mr Cooper?'

Boltfoot glared back and grumbled, 'Marry, if it were mine to choose I would poison it myself.'

'And I would gladly make you drink it, Cooper!'

Diego clapped Boltfoot on the back. 'Do not listen to him, Boltfoot. I think he loves you. Let us drink a toast to the *Elizabeth Bonaventure*.'

'Is she not yare, gentlemen?' said Drake. 'Mr Hawkins has done a splendid job here. Low to the sea, fast and responsive. She has the narrow waist of a wanton. It will be a rare Spanish galleon can match the *Lizzie* when we have the weather gauge. Now, Captain, bring forth the master gunner and let us prepare for some sport with the ordnance. We will soon be upon the target hulk.'

They were moving on a broad curve northwards, close to the tidal sands of Pig's Bay near Shoebury Ness. A coaster with coals from the north tacked southwards past them and disappeared slowly into the Thames. The *Lizzie* had been Drake's flagship sixteen months earlier on his Caribbean raid. She was already a quarter of a century old on that voyage, but John Hawkins had streamlined her and made a new ship of her. Since then, with advice from Drake, he had made more adjustments to improve her speed and manoeuvrability. Sleek, fast, like a wisp in the wind but with the firepower of a dragon, she was a Spanish galleon commander's nightmare.

At last a boy at the top of the mainmast called, 'Hulk ahoy.' And soon they saw it, a weathered old vessel stuck fast in the sand with nothing left but its hull and a broken skeleton of spars and masts, dating back to the turn of the century or before.

'We will take six turns, master gunner. First turn long range, five hundred yards,' Drake announced. The master gunner, a short, broad-shouldered man of thirty, bowed to his vice-admiral and went straightway to the gun-deck where he issued orders.

As they came round for the first turn and as the great cannons boomed and recoiled on their four-wheeled carriages, the smoke of gunpowder choked out the sun, like a crackling bonfire of greenwood in autumn. Boltfoot watched Drake and remembered the long days of the circumnavigation in the great oceans with a curious nostalgia he had thought never to feel again.

In his mind's eye, he could see the vastness of the open sea, when you knew there was a God in Heaven and that He was very close. On a clear day, the ocean was a glory to behold. The rolling waves, higher than the bowsprit of the *Golden Hind*, reaching as far as a man could see, north, south, east and west; immense in their splendour. As the *Hind* had descended from one wave into a long, dipping trough, the next wave came up like a tall, grey cathedral before them and the ship rose to meet it, before falling once more down a wall of water into an enormous, foam-racked trough. Such days had terrified many mariners, but Boltfoot had loved them; he had forgotten how much.

'Regrets, Cooper?' Drake bellowed, just after the second boom of the *Elizabeth Bonaventure*'s guns, as if he had read Boltfoot's mind.

Yes, that you cheated me out of my plunder, Boltfoot thought, but said nothing.

The ship continued its long sweeps across the hulk, turning with grace and speed, its bows low and eager to please, then firing with increasing accuracy from different ranges, crashing the hulk to splinters. Finally, when the supply of balls was exhausted and the hulk had all but disappeared, Drake ordered the master to take them home. 'We will make for Deptford, where you will land me, and you will take her back to Gravesend with Captain Stanley.'

They arrived back soon after a limpid sun rose the next day, the *Elizabeth Bonaventure*'s sails gleaming in the low eastern light. Boltfoot had spent the night outside the great cabin in the sterncastle, taking turns with Diego to sleep in a hastily raised hammock. This was also how he kept watch in Drake's home in Elbow Lane and at court when they stayed there. Despite his reservations about being protected, Drake allowed Boltfoot and Diego to sleep outside the chamber he shared with his wife.

They dropped anchor in midstream, some way from the landing steps at Deptford. The coxswain, Matthew, lowered the captain's boat and brought it into position. When the oarsmen were at their stations, Drake descended the rope ladder, a small, indistinct figure against the vastness of the sleek, oiled oak of the bulwarks and the pitch-blackened hull below. Boltfoot followed, then Diego.

Herrick, in his room above the chandlery on the Strand at Deptford, had been awake and watchful since first light. He had seen the *Elizabeth Bonaventure* from some way off. She was every inch a royal ship, proudly bearing flags with the white cross of St George and silken pennants of gold and silver flying thirty yards or more from the masts. And then, as she came closer, he could see the rose shield of the Tudors adorning the low, race-built forecastle – the diminutive structure that made her so vulnerable to boarding yet as nimble and quick as a wild cat.

For a moment Herrick found himself admiring her lines. She was majestic, and it occurred to him that if the English had many more such ships they could trouble, if not match, any armada Philip could muster and put to sea. He resolved that when this holy mission was done, he would go to Mendoza in Paris with information on what he had seen here. His Spanish masters should know the truth about this English fleet.

From the bag he took the two pieces of the gun, the mechanism and the barrel in one piece, the stock separate. They clipped together easily. He primed the weapon with the fine willow powder and rammed one of the balls into the muzzle. It fitted perfectly, as required. Herrick removed his sighting stand from below the bed. It was short, no more than two feet. He had crafted it himself from wood he had found discarded outside the dockyard timber merchant nearby. At its top was a notch he had cut, on which he could rest the muzzle.

He opened the little window and looked out. Beneath him

the early-morning throng was going about its business. No one looked up. Herrick took his pillow from the bed and and put it on the floor close by the window, where he placed it beneath one knee, crouching low so that his head would not be visible from the street. He had a clear, unimpeded view of the steps where Drake would land.

He could see the cockboat now, rowed hard and in time by four oarsmen. The coxswain stood, directing their strokes. In the back, the captain sat in splendour, talking to a dark-skinned man to his left. On the other side of him sat a thick-set fellow who looked for all the world like a broadsheet version of a pirate. Herrick studied the captain. Was it Drake? If his information was correct that Drake would come ashore from the *Elizabeth Bonaventure* this day – and Herrick had no reason to doubt it – it had to be him. He took the portrait from his doublet and studied it briefly. The man before him fitted every description of Drake: the proud, puffed-out chest; the stocky stature; the jutting, sharp-cut golden beard; the curling flame-red hair; the arrogance. This was Drake. Herrick discarded any doubts.

They were about two hundred yards away. Herrick rested the barrel of his snaphaunce musket on the makeshift stand, its muzzle protruding no more than an inch over the sill of the window.

He knew it to be a remarkable weapon. Before he had come to this eyrie in Deptford he had taken the gun, concealed in his bag, out to the woods past Islington ponds, where he had expended three-quarters of the twenty-four specially manu-factured balls in target practice. It was as accurate as claimed by its maker, Opel. He knew he could easily hit a man's head from a hundred yards, probably one-fifty, and possibly even two hundred. With such a weapon ranged against them, no prince or captain-general would ever be safe again.

Herrick lined up the sights of the gun on his target and

squinted down the barrel at Drake. He could take him now, literally a sitting target. But he held back: the boat was swaying in the choppy swell. Herrick could wait. He had been at this window for sixty hours now, watching Deptford Strand, the river and the moored ships almost every moment of daylight, barely breaking for food or drink. Wait until Drake was closer to shore but not yet landed, that was the thing. This was the place, his man had assured him.

Drake's head was in his sights now; as big as the water-melons in the market at the bottom of the Capitoline Hill, near the English College. He let the muzzle drop and lined up on Drake's chest. Aim for the biggest target, the body, not the head.

They were close enough. The boat was in calmer water and there was no obstacle between the muzzle of Herrick's gun and the body of England's greatest mariner. Herrick held the stock hard into his shoulder to minimise recoil, then pulled the trigger.

The explosion in the small room was deafening. The recoil threw him back. Smoke billowed from the muzzle. Herrick put the weapon aside on the bare boards of the floor, then looked out of the window, trying to see the boat. There was a mass of confusion and the vessel was rocking madly. The oarsmen were all now standing; they seemed to be crowded around Drake. Was he dead? He had to be. There was no time to lose. Herrick had to move fast. He couldn't get back to London by boat. The river would be closed immediately. He had a horse liveried at a tavern stable inland, half a mile to the south, towards the gabled manor house, Sayers Court. His plan was to ride to Southwark where there was a safe-house until the hue and cry died down. Perhaps a week, maybe more. The ports had been closed anyway since the death of Mary, Queen of Scots, and the searches of any foreigners trying to get across the Channel would now be redoubled. Herrick must keep his head, stay low and wait.

He dismantled his weapon, put it back into the bag and stowed it beneath the bed. No need of it now. He had no other belongings, merely the clothes he stood in, the wheel-lock pistol at his belt, his thin-bladed skene and a rapier. He shut the door of the room behind him and walked down the creaking staircase to the shop below.

Bob Roberts, his landlord, was there, standing at the doorway. He turned and smiled broadly at Herrick, clutching the base of his fume-belching pipe. 'There's quite a to-do out there, Mr van Leiden,' he said, carelessly blowing smoke in Herrick's face.

'What is it, Bob?'

'Hard to say. Looks like someone's been hurt.' Roberts looked curiously at Herrick. 'Are you all right, Mr van Leiden? I heard a noise from upstairs. Thought you must have fallen out of bed.'

Herrick laughed. 'That I did, Bob. And now I must take my leave of you and try again for some work. I will see you at dusk.' He stepped out from the doorway, intending to hurry to the stables, but first he would join the throng at the waterfront to make sure that Drake was dead.

Boltfoot was drenched. He stood on the quayside, eyes focused on a small window. Just before the shot had rung out, he had caught a dull glint from that window, in the middle of the row of shops and suppliers at the back of Deptford Strand. The glint had become a puff of smoke, quickly followed by the familiar sound of a charge of gunpowder exploding. At that moment, Matt, the coxswain, had moved to the side with the landing hook to pull the boat into the steps when she came along-side. He took the bullet in the lower abdomen and crumpled backwards into Drake's lap.

Boltfoot's eyes turned briefly from the window to Matt, then back to the window. As the puff of smoke cleared, a face appeared. It was clean-shaven, as pale as a carved marble bust, and it was peering towards them. After the initial shock, the oarsmen and Diego clustered round Matt, moving him off the vice-admiral's lap and laying him in the bottom of the boat where they could tend to him. Drake took control of the situation. Boltfoot scrambled out of the boat, dragging himself through the water to the steps, which, at this high tide, were below the surface of the river.

He pulled himself up to the quay, his clothes dripping. Crowds were now milling around, trying to see what had happened in the cockboat. After a moment on the quay to get his bearings, Boltfoot pushed his way through the throng and looked to the window he had seen. The face was no longer there. He started to stride towards the building. He was surprisingly quick, even with his club foot. His cutlass was now drawn and hanging loose in his hand at his side. The chandlery where he had seen the face at the window was sixty or seventy yards away. There was a man at the doorway now. He was bearded and looked for all the world like a casual onlooker. Another man appeared beside him, clean-shaven, like the face at the window. It *was* the face at the window. Boltfoot's pace quickened.

Herrick's eye caught Boltfoot's as soon as he stepped out from the doorway. He recognised him instantly as the piratical figure beside Drake in the cockboat. His cutlass was drawn and he was coming straight towards him in a difficult, loping stride, one leg dragging as if it were injured. Had he been hurt in the mêlée when Drake was hit? Herrick switched plan: he would not go to the waterfront. This man was coming for him. Swiftly, he turned right and ducked down an alley, barging past a water-seller, knocking the great conical butt from his shoulders to the ground. The butt was well hooped for strength and did not shatter but the water flowed forth. The man cursed, but Herrick was already gone.

Boltfoot appeared in the alley as the water-bearer was lifting his ungainly butt back on to his shoulders.

'Where did he go?'

The man, grey-haired with a stoop, pointed down the alley and indicated that the fugitive had turned right at the end. 'And give the whoreson a bloody nose from me!'

Boltfoot had unslung his caliver and was priming it. He loped on. At the end of the alley he turned right and saw the back of the intruder, perhaps thirty yards ahead of him. It was an impossible shot, but Boltfoot knew he would never catch the man on foot. He stopped, knelt, held the wheel-lock gun in his right hand, resting on his left forearm, took aim as well as his heaving lungs would allow, and fired.

Herrick felt a searing pain in his side, just below his left armpit, and arced forward. But he did not falter in his run. His right hand clutched the wound. His fingers were wet with blood but that would not stop him. At most, he reckoned, the ball had torn a bit of flesh but ricocheted off his ribs. He had been lucky. He ran on.

The alleys were dense and maze-like with jettied overhangs from the crowded buildings, many of which were in some way connected to the trade that was the essence of this town: sailors' lodgings, ale-houses, stews, chandlers. Herrick pushed on, like a wolf evading a shepherd whose lambs it had just slaughtered. He was fit but his chest and lungs hurt. At last he came out of the main part of Deptford. He ran across a road, then another, narrowly avoiding a horseman who had to rein in sharply. Ahead he saw the stable and slowed to a walk.

One of the ostlers was leading his mount out into the cobbled yard. He saw Herrick. 'Good morrow, master. Fine timing, sir. Your mount is ready for your morning ride.'

Herrick caught his breath. He took the reins from the man and accepted his cupped hands as a step-up, then swung himself on to the horse. Slow down now, he told himself. Don't arouse suspicion. He managed to smile at the ostler and found a coin for him in his purse.

'Thank you, sir.' Then, 'It seems you have hurt yourself, sir.'

'I fell and caught my side on a piece of iron. I think it was an old spoke from a carter's wheel.'

'Too much of the falling-down juice, is it, sir?'

Herrick laughed. 'Perhaps.' Over the ostler's shoulder he saw, in the distance, the advancing figure of the limping gunman who had just shot him; his awkward running style was unmistakable. Herrick dug his heels into the horse's flank, shook the reins, wheeled and was gone.

Chapter 23

THE MUFFLED BEAT of drums hung in the air, like the distant thunder of war. All roads through London were blocked to traffic. Every street was thronged with sombre crowds, come to honour their valiant knight and poet, Sir Philip Sidney.

He had died of the black rot following a shot in the thigh when he and his troops were ambushed by the Duke of Parma's Spanish forces at Zutphen in the Lowlands the previous October. His body had been embalmed and brought back to England in a ship with black sails, and for months he had lain in state at the Minories close to the Tower, awaiting England's first state funeral for someone not of the blood royal.

Now the day had arrived. Sir Philip had been Walsingham's son-in-law and Mr Secretary was paying for the extravagant procession with funds he could scarce afford. It was an occasion of symbolism: the laying to rest of a champion of the Protestant reformation. Seven hundred official mourners followed the cortège as it wove slowly through the streets from Aldgate to St Paul's. At the head of the procession, dominating all, was the catafalque, covered with velvet and flags and surrounded by close members of the Sidney and Walsingham families. The great of the land were there, including Sir Philip's uncle, the Earl of Leicester, tired and wan as though the fight had left him, and Leicester's stepson, the Earl of Essex, new-blooded hero of the Lowlands war. Of the ruling élite, only the Queen herself was missing, still raging over the execution of Mary Stuart, it was said, in her privy chamber at Greenwich Palace.

The crowd applauded the funeral cortège with tears rolling down their cheeks, their emotions heightened by news of the attempt on the life of their other great hero, Drake. Many called out tributes to Sidney, this most loved son of England; others called for vengeance on Parma, King Philip and Spain.

John Shakespeare watched for a while. The sight of Topcliffe, up with the vanguard of mourners, was too much for him. Their eyes met and Topcliffe seemed to smirk, his brown teeth bared like fangs. Shakespeare turned away; there was work to be done. He needed to see Catherine Marvell and Thomas Woode again, and he had to travel to Deptford to talk with those who had encountered Drake's assailant. He had another task at Deptford, too: to try to talk with the Lord Admiral when he returned from the funeral. There must be more he could learn from him about Lady Blanche. As Shakespeare walked towards Dowgate, the scent of hot chestnuts roasting in a brazier enticed him and he bought a few, then strode on, peeling and eating them as he went. The muffled drums, draped in black, beat out their death march, fading slowly into the haze behind him.

Catherine was at home but Woode was not. She did not seem pleased to see Shakespeare. 'I am surprised you are not at St Paul's mourning the heroic Sir Philip,' she said. 'Everyone else in London seems to be.'

'Do you not think him heroic, Mistress Marvell?'

'Oh, indeed I do, sir. He was a very perfect, gentle knight. It is the timing of his funeral that interests me. The day was chosen by your own Mr Secretary Walsingham, I do believe. How curious that it should come so close after the despatch of the Queen of Scots.'

Shakespeare had heard the scurrilous mutterings about the choice of date. In fact, he had wondered about it himself, for this great funeral of Sir Philip Sidney was indeed a most convenient way of deflecting public interest from Mary's execution. It was one thing to have such thoughts, but quite another to voice them openly as Catherine Marvell had. 'You should beware your tongue, mistress, lest it attract unwanted attention to this household.'

'Have they passed a law now making it a capital offence to call myself Catholic?'

Shakespeare bridled. 'You may call yourself what you wish, so long as you attend your parish church and do not harbour priests come here from abroad. You must know that it is a treasonable crime for a Popish priest to enter England.'

'Well, then, Mr Shakespeare, I must take care not to harbour any.'

'As for the Scots Queen, I am surprised you have tears to spare for her. Was she not an adulteress? Did she not kill a husband in cold blood? Do you doubt she meant to murder the Queen of England?'

'I will let God be the judge of that, yet I do believe she died a Christian.'

This was a bad start. Shakespeare had no desire to cross swords with her. He stood there awkwardly, like a grammar-school boy, not sure what to do or say next. He did not want to play the heavy government agent with her.

'I am sorry, Mr Shakespeare,' she said at last, a smile lighting her blue eyes. She wore a long dress of fine burgundy-red wool with a matching bodice. Her ruff was simple and her long dark hair uncovered. The effect was to accentuate the unwavering character in her eyes and mouth and the slenderness of her figure. 'I am sure you did not come here to be berated so. It is unforgivable to leave you on the doorstep in the cold. Please, do come in.'

He thanked her and stepped into the warmth of the house. From within, he heard the sound of children laughing and playing.

'They are master Mr Woode's. Would you like to meet them? Perchance they have been harbouring priests.'

Shakespeare found himself smiling. 'Your sense of comedy may well prove your undoing, mistress.'

'Well, that is who I am, sir. If speaking my mind leads me to Tyburn, it will say a powerful lot more about you and Walsingham than it will about me. I am sure of that.'

Shakespeare sighed deliberately and dismissively, the way his old school teacher had when a pupil gave a poor excuse for being late on a winter's morning. 'That, as you know well, is not the point. And it is not I who would bring you to the headsman's axe. There are . . . others . . . others less understanding, less mindful of your welfare.'

'Perhaps. But you are in bed with them, Mr Shakespeare, and you cannot so easily distance yourself from your bedfellows.'

'Nor you, mistress. For you must know that the Romish priest Ballard conspired to kill our sovereign lady. You must know that the Pope himself has condoned the Queen's murder and sends seditious young men from the serpents' nest of the English College in Rome to undermine her realm. Are these *your* bedfellows?'

Catherine's eyes burnt bright. 'I have *no* bedfellows, sir. I am a maiden. Come, let us go to the children. They offer better conversation.' She led the way to the nursery. The boy, Andrew, ran to her and threw himself into her arms. He was a hefty six-year-old with fair hair like his father's and the same broad brow. The girl, Grace, looked to Shakespeare like a younger version of the portrait in the hall of Woode's late wife. She also ran to Catherine, dragging a wooden doll along the timbered floor by its remaining arm. Catherine put her arms round them and crouched to their level to kiss them. Suddenly the children noticed Shakespeare and drew closer to her.

'Andrew, Grace, this is Mr Shakespeare. Will you please greet him as you should.'

'Good morrow, sir,' the boy said firmly, as he had been taught.

Shakespeare bent and shook his hand. 'And good morrow to you, Mr Andrew.'

Grace turned away her head coyly and would say nothing.

'I'm sure she has far more important things to do in caring for her doll than talking with tedious adults,' Shakespeare said.

Catherine removed the two children gently from her arms and patted them. 'Go and play while I talk with Mr Shakespeare, please.'

The children ran across the room, as far from him as they could go.

'Now, may I offer you some refreshment, Mr Shakespeare? Perhaps some hot spiced malmsey?'

'No, thank you. Do not put yourself to any trouble. I have one or two questions, that is all.'

'And how should I answer you? Truthfully and risk my head? With comedy and set myself on the road to Tyburn? Or should I dissemble and stay alive?'

Shakespeare ignored her barbed remark. He knew he could match her, atrocity for atrocity and more. He could mention the French Catholics' slaughter of thousands of Protestant Huguenots on St Bartholomew's Day; he could regale her with the horrors of Torquemada's Inquisition burnings. Instead he went straight to the point. 'Did you know Lady Blanche Howard?'

Catherine barely hesitated, but it was enough for Shakespeare to notice. 'I did, Mr Shakespeare. I loved her like a sister.'

The honesty of the answer caught him off-guard. 'Why did you not mention this before?'

'Why, sir, I did not know it was pertinent to your enquiries and, anyway, you did not ask me.'

'Please, tell me how you knew her.'

Catherine stepped towards the door. 'Come, let us sit in the library while we talk. We will not be disturbed there by the children's prattle. Are you sure you will not take refreshment?'

Shakespeare thanked her and said that he would, after all, take some hot malmsey. While he waited for Catherine to return with his drink, he paced the library, examining Woode's extensive collection of books, many of them Italian. From somewhere, in another part of the house, he could hear hammering. When Catherine reappeared a few minutes later he thanked her for the wine and asked about the noise.

'This house is not yet finished, Mr Shakespeare. The carpenters and stonemasons are still working on the area to the west of the court.'

'It seems curious to me that such a large house should have so few servants.'

'That has been the way while the construction work has been continuing. Mr Woode did not want to move away and disturb the children, so we stayed here and he reduced the household; I confess we have lived in a rather confined space. It is only recently that we have had so much room. Maids and cooks come in by day, and I direct them. Happily, I believe we will have more when the work is complete.'

Shakespeare gathered his thoughts. 'Mistress, you were telling me about Lady Blanche. I confess I am surprised that you knew her. She was a lady of the court. You are governess to a merchant's children.'

'You are trying to say that I was not of her standing . . .'

Shakespeare reddened. 'Forgive me, I did not mean to imply such a thing.'

'Really? I am sure that is exactly what you meant to imply.

And you are quite right. I am a humble school teacher's daughter from York, Mr Shakespeare. I have no fortune and few prospects. Blanche was the daughter of one of England's great families and might have expected to marry an earl or a duke. How could there be any common ground between us?'

'Well?'

Catherine tilted her head. 'I feel sure you have already divined that. It was, of course, our religion. Blanche had lately returned to the Roman church and we met at mass.'

'Where, pray, was this mass held?'

'Mr Shakespeare, you must know I cannot tell you that. I am only giving you this much because I wish the perpetrator of the terrible crime to be caught. And . . .'

She looked away from him to the window. The sky outside was winter white. Shakespeare waited. She turned back.

'And because I trust you, Mr Shakespeare.'

Her words sent a shiver down his spine. The intelligencer in him, the state agent, feared her trust. The last thing he wanted was to be drawn into secrets he could not keep. He sipped the wine and savoured its warm sweetness. 'Mistress,' he said at last, 'you must realise that I cannot promise to keep secret anything you tell me. My first duty is to Mr Secretary and Her Majesty the Queen.'

Catherine laughed drily. 'I do not intend to compromise you. All I mean is that I trust you to use judiciously whatever I say to you.'

'Then tell me more about Lady Blanche.'

'Well, she seemed very young at times, full of life and laughter. At others she was serious and devout. She had ideas of going to Italy or France to join a convent, then changed her mind. At the time I did not understand what had altered. Now, of course, I know. She fell in love.'

'The father of her unborn child?'

Catherine closed her eyes and held her hands to her face, like a girl at the bear-baiting who averts her eyes from the sight of blood. 'I think so,' she said quietly. 'I did not know she was expecting a baby until I heard the news of her death. Please do not ask me more. I cannot name him.'

'What sort of man was he? Was he a stranger to these shores? A friend of yours? Another Papist?'

'Please . . .'

'But you want me to find her killer. I cannot work with shadows. Shed some light on this dark affair for me. I must tell you that there might be a great deal more to this tragedy than meets the eye. I have reason to believe that her killer was sent by Spain and is conspiring against the realm. Perhaps she found out more than she should have and became a threat to him. You say you are a loyal subject of the Crown. Now is the time to prove it. If the man who killed Lady Blanche is the same who brought her with child, then it is your duty as an Englishwoman to tell me his name. Also – and I have no desire for this to sound like a threat – you must know the danger to yourself and this household if you hold back important evidence.'

She shook her head vehemently. 'The man she loved would not hurt a mouse. He is a gentle soul. It was a sadness that they could never have married.'

'Then you know him?'

She nodded slowly. 'Indeed I do. But I will not reveal his name to you.'

'How do you know he did not kill her? Only God can see into the heart.'

'Mr Shakespeare, I am no gull. I am trusting you as far as I may, so please trust me now. The man she loved did not kill her.'

'Do you know who did?'

Outside, a bird drifted lazily across the sky; a crow, perhaps, or a kite, looking for carrion. There were jarring sounds: the hammering of carpenters driving nails into rafters and joists; the slow beat of funeral drums somewhere to the west. She thought for a while. She had her suspicions, but no proof. And she could not speak her fears for that would be a betrayal of those she loved. 'No,' she said softly. 'I do not know who killed her.'

'But you have an idea, don't you?'

'If I have suspicions, they are without evidence so must be considered unfounded. It would be pointless to tell you.'

'Will you let me be the judge of that?'

'I cannot.'

Shakespeare gritted his teeth. He was beside himself with frustration. By now, with any other witness, he would have brought her into custody for hard questioning. Why was this woman so different from Walstan Glebe, presently languishing in Newgate's dungeon, threatened with mutilation and years of hard labour? Perhaps Topcliffe was right: he was too soft for this work. He scowled at her. 'Very well, mistress, we will come back to that. But, for the present, let us move on to other matters. What connection did Lady Blanche Howard have with the printing of seditious tracts? Are you and Mr Woode involved in this?'

'I know nothing of printing. And I have no knowledge of whether or not Lady Blanche was involved in anything like that either.'

'But Mr Woode knows something. Of that I am sure. I saw his reaction when I questioned him. He recognised the paper, the printing or both.'

'That is something you will have to ask Mr Woode himself. I cannot answer for him.'

'What, then, of the house in Hog Lane, where Lady Blanche's body was found?'

'Again, nothing. I have never been to a house in Hog Lane. I had not even heard of the place and certainly could not tell you where it is.'

'Is there anything you do wish to tell me? Any information that may help us find this foul murderer?'

'Mr Shakespeare, please believe me. If I knew the name of the killer I would tell you his – or her – name without a moment's hesitation. I want the perpetrator of this wicked crime brought to justice so that they will never do such a thing again.'

Catherine had spoken firmly, yet even as she said the words she felt a chill inside. For though she had been careful not to lie, she was horribly aware that she had not been quite truthful either.

Chapter 24

Rose Downie reached up to the cheese cratch in the buttery and brought down the Parmesan, the Cheshire, a small sheep's cheese and a soft pungent one from Rouen. She also found a piece of spermyse, a creamy, herb cheese, but it had gone mouldy so she set it aside for the pig. Tonight, she had been told, there was an important dinner and the Countess was expecting a fine spread.

She laid out the cheeses on a big wooden trencher, then set to cutting some cold meats to go alongside them. Like the other two maidservants in this huge and rambling old house in the ward of Farringdon, Rose was curious as to who her mistress, Anne, the Lady Tanahill, might be entertaining this evening. Such an event was rare these days: since the Countess's lord, Philip, had been consigned to the Tower two years ago, she and her small child had lived an isolated, sad life. Though tall with fair hair and skin that glowed like that of a girl half her thirty years, she was shy and thin. And yet she had a grace that Rose loved and admired.

The house was pleasant, if old and in need of attention. It had been the town house of bishops and other men of distinction before passing into the hands of the earls of Tanahill some forty years earlier. It had a long, broad garden leading down to the Thames, where it had its own landing-stage. It stood brazenly close to the grand mansion of the Earl of Leicester and the Queen's palace, Somerset House, which was not a comfortable position for a family that clung to the old faith, when so many of those around were steeped in the new.

Usually the maids, the manservant and their mistress took to their beds as soon as dusk fell, but tonight there was candlelight throughout Tanahill House. Amy Spynke, the housekeeper, had organised the cooking of two fowls and a rump of beef. There was a broth, too, winter vegetables and sweetmeats.

At seven, the guests came. First the Vaux family, then the Brownes, followed by the Treshams and Mr Swithin Wells, grey and stooped. Mr Wells was the Countess's most regular visitor now. Rose knew them all well and that they were Papists, every one, but that had never concerned her. They were kind to her and treated her with respect. She had no interest in religious mutterings; she went to the Anglican parish church each Sunday because failure so to do would cost her a fine under the recusancy laws, but that was all.

The last two guests were not known to Rose, but they were introduced as Mr Cotton and Mr Woode. She curtsied to them, for they were dressed in the fine clothes of the gentry. As the three maids – Rose, Mistress Spynke and the girl Beatrice Fallow, who was only eleven – retired from the dining hall to the buttery, the baby wailed upstairs in Rose's room. She froze in mid-step. 'Oh, please, not again,' she said, beneath her breath. Every muscle in her body tensed. She would have to go to him, though she knew that no amount of cradling would bring an end to his unearthly cries. The only thing that might bring relief from the cat-like wailing was her milk and, eventually, sleep. But he had slept these past two hours and would be unlikely to sleep again until after midnight.

'I'll have to go to him, Amy,' she said. 'Tonight of all nights.'

Amy nodded. 'All right, Rose, love. Get back when you can. Beatrice and I will manage.'

In her small room at the top of the house, Rose stood over the baby's basket. For a minute she just gazed at the round face with its low ears. Its curious froglike black eyes, so widely spaced, stared back at her uncomprehendingly. Its mouth was fixed wide open in a scream. She thought it monstrous, like some animal she had never encountered. With the cushion from her bed, she could snuff out its life like a candle this moment. There were times when she wondered whether she had been visited at night by an incubus that had put this thing in her womb, but then she remembered it was not hers and that it had never been in her belly, that her baby was called William Edmund and he was beautiful. Who had taken him and replaced him with this – *thing*?

She loosened her blouse and brought the baby from the basket to her breast. Its mouth, open and demanding like a new-born sparrow in the nest, took her teat and sucked ferociously. It occurred to her that she should give it a name. She couldn't call it Edmund or William because they were her own baby's names. Perhaps she might call him Robert after her late father. Had it even been christened?

Rose lay back on the cushion with the child at her breast, letting these thoughts and questions wash over her until she became drowsy. She had almost drifted off when there was a soft knock at her door. 'It's Amy. M'lady has asked that you bring the baby downstairs.'

Straightway the child set to wailing once more. 'Why would she want me to bring him down when she has guests?' Rose sighed. She owed a huge debt of gratitude to the Countess. Many employers would not have taken back a young widow with a child as she had.

She arrived downstairs to find the table cleared and the

guests talking quietly, sipping wine. Rose stood in the doorway, cradling the swaddled baby in her arms. He was screaming at the top of his high-pitched voice now, an urgent monotone that pierced her ears. The guests turned to look at her. Lady Tanahill stood up from her chair and walked over to her. She touched her and guided her to the table. Smiling, she took the baby from Rose's arms and held him out for all to see. 'This is Rose's foundling child,' she said, ignoring the incessant wailing. 'Her own baby was taken from her while she was at the market and this one was left in his place. I am afraid that the courts and the constable have done nothing to help her find her child, William Edmund, but Rose has cared for this infant with fortitude. In this she has shown true godliness, for this also is one of His creatures, and she is to be commended.' She smiled at Rose. 'I hope I do not make light of your tribulations. It can be no easy thing to lose a child in this way. Many a woman would not have accepted the burden of feeding and taking care of someone else's, as you have done.' She held the baby's head up for closer inspection by the guests. 'As you can see, this child is not as others.'

The guests peered at him with interest and sympathy. The women rose from their seats and crowded around to look closely and to touch his face. Rose Downie watched them, astonished. She had not thought this grotesque infant could elicit such interest and compassion from others.

'Father Cotton,' the Countess said at last, 'will you bless this child?'

Cotton took him from her arms. He stroked the small face softly with one hand, while cradling the baby in the other arm. Then he murmured some words in Latin and made the sign of the cross over his forehead. The baby ceased crying. Then he handed it back to Rose Downie. '*Pax vobiscum*, my child,' he said to her. 'Truly you are blessed among women, for He has chosen you to care for this child, as once the Holy Mother was chosen.'

Rose said nothing. She didn't know what to say. They were smiling at her yet she felt small and insignificant in their presence, especially this holy man with his gift. If she hadn't realised he was a Papist priest, she would have thought him a sorcerer for silencing the baby so. Uneasily, she curtsied to the Countess, then backed out of the room. She was met by Amy and Beatrice, who had been watching at the door.

'How did he do that?' asked Beatrice. 'It's some trick, that is.'

'I confess it seemed like conjuring to me,' said Amy, 'but if it gives you a night's sleep . . .' She moved closer to Rose and whispered in her ear, 'And he'll be staying here, hidden away, but not a word to anyone or we'll all be in trouble. I know you do not share our faith, but you are a good person. With luck, Father Cotton might keep the baby quiet for you when you need a rest.'

Rose felt sick and ashamed for the terrible thoughts churning in her mind. She knew that Father Cotton, the saintly priest of the Roman church, was the man Richard Topcliffe was so desperate to find. And she believed that Topcliffe in his turn had the power to find William Edmund for her and return him safe to her arms. If it meant allowing him to occupy her body whenever he pleased and if it meant betraying not only Cotton but her benefactress and the whole household, so be it. What mother in the world would not do *anything* – at whatever cost to themselves or those around them – for their child?

The baby was still sleeping soundly and she went back upstairs to put him in his cot. Then she gathered her warm woollen cloak and hood about her and slipped silently down the back stairs. Outside, the high, crenellated towers of Tanahill House blotted out the light of the moon, but there was enough candlelight through the leaded windows of the great houses along the Strand for her to see as she hurried westwards the few hundred yards to Charing Cross, then down through Whitehall Palace towards Westminster.

Chapter 25

THE IRON FIST of Topcliffe and his pursuivants came just before first light, as Cotton was saying mass for the Countess, her small child and her staff in a first-floor chamber. The manservant, Joe Fletcher, raced down the small flight of stone steps at the back of the hall, but by the time he reached the front door it had already been flattened by a battering log. He stopped dead in his tracks, confronted by a wall of dazzling blades, blazing pitch torches, solid leather chest armour bearing the Queen's escutcheon and heads encased in steel morions.

Topcliffe stood at the forefront of ten dark-clad men, casting a menacing, moving shadow from the light of the torches fanned out behind him. Those with him included London's chief pursuivant, Newall. All but Topcliffe had their swords drawn and there was much shouting and stamping of boots. Acrid smoke streamed from the torches, and from the sotweed pipe stuck hard between Topcliffe's teeth.

Topcliffe took a step towards Fletcher so that their faces were no more than a foot apart. He was half a head shorter than the servant, but exuded twice the power. 'Where are they?' he growled, smoke billowing. 'Bring me straight to them or I will kill you where you stand.'

*

Upstairs, Lady Tanahill's hands shook as she cleared away the sacred vessels. Cotton gathered up his vestments, ducked through into the stairwell and climbed two steps at a time to the second floor. His heart pounding, he went through a great chamber into a garde-robe tower, and up a few more steps into the cramped privy closet that housed the jakes. There was something wrong with the pipework for the stench of human waste was atrocious.

He flicked open a concealed hinge and lifted the jakes, revealing a hole in the floor. The Countess had shown him this place after the other dinner guests had gone. The hole was big enough for a man to slip through but no more. Cotton half turned and sank to his haunches, then dropped into the hole, pulling the jakes back into place above him. Immediately he was enveloped in darkness. He had no candle with him and even if he'd had one he could not have used it for the smell of burning wax would give him away. He prayed that the Countess – the only other person in the house to know of this place – would remember to replace the concealed hinge.

Joe Fletcher backed away from Topcliffe and the pursuivants, fearful for his life but saying nothing. Suddenly Beatrice appeared at the bottom of the stairs. She was not tall and it must have been obvious to the men that she was merely a child. 'Put down your swords,' she said, in a firm voice that showed remarkable self-possession and courage. 'Put them down, I say!'

The Countess was now standing at the bottom of the stairs, behind her young maidservant.

'Who are you?' Topcliffe bellowed at Beatrice.

'I am Beatrice, maid to the Lady Tanahill,' she said boldly. 'Who are *you*, sir?'

'Never mind who I am, girl. Where is your mistress?'

Topcliffe saw the Countess framed in the doorway by the stairs. She was slight and frail. 'Ah, Lady Tanahill, what a pleasure. Where is Southwell?'

'Southwell?' she said. Her voice was faint, barely audible.

'Tell me now where he is or I will tear this house apart, board by board, panel by panel, brick by brick, for I know he is here. And I will have him, however long it takes.'

The Countess could scarcely breathe. Topcliffe had been there before, to taunt her over her husband's imprisonment and to seek evidence against him in his papers. He had found nothing, though he had searched for a day and a half. It was after that visit that she had had the hole built beneath the jakes by a carpenter introduced to her by her friends in the Church of Rome. It was a construction of breathtaking complexity and ingenuity, so hidden within the fabric of the house as to be undetectable. To find it, a pursuivant would, indeed, have to tear the place apart brick by brick and stone by stone until nothing was left.

Topcliffe confined the servants to the kitchen and Lady Tanahill to her chamber. Outside the house he had fifteen more men, who surrounded it on all sides, watching over every doorway and window as the sun came up. Systematically, he and his cohort began to search, stamping heavy-booted through the multitude of rooms. He looked in and under every coffer, bed and cupboard. His men hammered or tapped on every panel of the wainscot listening for one that sounded different. In the library he cast down all the books in his quest for a false bookcase that hid a doorway. He took each servant aside one by one and threatened them with torture and execution. 'If you tell me now where he is, you will be spared. If we find him and you have not divulged his whereabouts, you will be racked and executed for treason with all that that entails.' These words he even used on Beatrice.

When it was Rose Downie's turn to be taken into another room for questioning he handled her even more roughly than the others until they were alone. He told her to sit down and poured her some wine.

'You're a pretty girl, Rose,' he said.

'Thank you, Mr Topcliffe.' Rose sat down, the baby in her arms.

'Is it difficult for you working among these base and filthy Papists?'

'It is easy enough, sir. They are good people. They do me no harm.'

'But they harbour traitors, Rose. Jesuits. These are men who would kill our beloved Queen Elizabeth.'

Rose hung her head.

'And they won't help you find your baby . . .'

She looked up at him expectantly, eyes brimming with hope.

'Now, Rose, where is this man?'

'My baby, sir?'

'All in good time. First, Southwell.'

Rose clutched the foundling baby to her breast. She had noticed strange looks from the other servants. She could not meet their eyes. 'I promise you, sir, I do not know where he is hid. I only know he is here. They told me he was staying. I beg of you, believe me . . .'

'God's teeth, Rose, that is not good enough. Talk to the others. Find out what they know.' Without warning, he raised his fist and hit her full in the mouth. The blow knocked her down and the baby slid across the floor. It began to scream. Rose scrabbled around, dazed, until her hands located him and picked him up. Her hands were bloody, and the blood stained the baby's swaddling wraps. Blood was dripping from her mouth and a front tooth was loose. 'That was to prove to the others that you have not betrayed them, Rose. Now get back out there and discover where this priest is.'

In the black hole, the stink was overpowering and, at first, Cotton gagged, bile rising in his throat. The hole was five foot square and seven feet high. There was a cold brick seat and nothing else, nothing of comfort. All there was by way of sustenance was a pail of water and a beaker with which to drink it. It seemed to Cotton that the air was stale and there wasn't enough of it circulating in here. How would he breathe if he was forced to stay here any length of time? He had never known such darkness. It was darker than the blackest night; it made no difference whether his eyes were open or closed. This is what the tomb is like, he thought. This is what it was like for Christ when first he rose in the grave. He felt ashamed of the thought and put it aside. How dare he compare his own plight to the suffering of the Messiah?

He tried to still himself, to quieten his breathing and his heart so that the air might last longer. He drank some water and counted the seconds, then the minutes. The minutes stretched to an hour and then many hours. From all around he heard hammering and cracking, the splintering of wood as panelling and floorboards were jemmied and smashed. He knew he must not make a sound. At one point they were close to him, laughing and joking, swearing and threatening. How could they not hear his racing heart? 'Come out, you Popish dog,' one called. 'You smell like a dungheap!' Then they laughed, and one of the pursuivants, barely two feet from him, used the jakes to defecate, jeered on by the others as he strained. It seemed to Cotton that the foul smell redoubled. The same words kept churning in his mouth, though he never uttered them aloud: *'Fiat voluntas dei, fiat voluntas dei, fiat voluntas dei . . .'* God's will be done.

After sixteen hours, Topcliffe brought in a new squadron of

men and sent his first troop home to their beds. Yet he stayed. He would remain throughout the night. The hammering and breaking, the shredding of great tapestries and the smashing of glass continued all through the dark hours. In the morning, Topcliffe sent for two builders. When they arrived at the devastated house he ordered them to take measurements of every wall and every floor in the building to find a hidden cavity. For many hours they took measurements, arguing and scratching their heads. At one point they were certain they had discovered a space that was not accounted for. When Topcliffe's men were breaking through the wall, it began to move perilously and they had to run for props to shore it up. Finally they got through, only to find themselves in the larder. Angrily, Topcliffe sent them away without pay. When they protested, he told them to send their reckoning to the Lady Tanahill.

On the second night, Topcliffe called his men off but left several guards outside and one in the great hall. 'I will return at dawn,' he told the Countess. 'Do not even think of trying to get him out of the house.'

In his hole, Cotton slept fitfully. The hours passed and he lost track of whether it was day or night. He leant on the bench against the wall, fearful he would snore or talk in his sleep. He shivered with cold, but that did not concern him much for he had learnt about harsh living and deprivation at the Jesuit colleges. The hunger gnawed at his belly, but neither was that new, for he had fasted often. He spent much of his time in prayer and he thought at length of what would happen to him if – when – he was caught. Would he be able to endure a martyr's death? Many failed, even to the extent of yielding up the names of their fellows. Some men could take the rack without begging for mercy and telling their tormentors all they wanted to know, but most could not. Which category of man would he fall into? It was well and good to long for a martyr's death when one was not suffering, quite another to hold firm when it was close.

In the absence of light, his sense of hearing and of touch became more acute. He seemed to hear every sound in the house and he could soon move with absolute silence in his cramped hole, feeling his way brick by brick. Mercifully his sense of smell dulled, so that he longer noticed the stench of the ordure that permeated from the jakes, or of his own, dumped as carefully as possible in one small corner of the hole.

Most of all, in the endless hours, he longed for light and reading material. He comforted himself by reciting poems and tracts from the Bible in his head.

And then, in his mind, he began to compose a letter. It was an uncompromising letter to an imaginary prisoner: perhaps to Philip, Earl of Tanahill, whom he had never met, now languishing in the Tower, sentenced to a traitor's death; perhaps to those other sacred brothers from the Society of Jesus, such as Campion, who had been here before him and had suffered grievously for it, or to those who were yet to come; perhaps to his friend and companion on this journey, Henry Garnet, now at large somewhere outside London; perhaps to himself, to convince himself yet again that this was God's will and that He would enable him to endure.

Let neither fury nor fiction nor the sword, nor glory of splendid attire, nor bribes, nor entreaties, nor any other violence seduce you from the charity of Christ. You were born to be God's; by Him you live, and for Him you are to die. It is a death that will confirm the wavering and make the strong yet stronger. The cause is God's, the conflict short, the reward eternal. The contrition of a humble heart, expressed by your bloodshed in this cause, will remit all sins as fully as in baptism, so great is the prerogative of martyrdom.

Martyrdom. The very word made him shudder. The extreme mortification of the flesh that would bring him as close to the love of God as it was possible to be. How often had he dreamt of martyrdom in the long nights of his college years?

After nearly two days in the hole, he heard a whisper and wondered whether it was the voice of God or an angel come for him. It was a woman's voice, as sweet as the sound of church bells on a summer's day. And then, above him, he saw a chink of light – more blinding than he had ever seen – and he closed his eyes tightly, covering his face with his hands.

'Father Cotton, it is Anne.' Her voice was very quiet.

'Is it safe?'

'No, they are still here. But it is late and they are playing cards in the great hall while Topcliffe is away. I have brought you food.'

'I cannot look at the light. It is too bright.'

The Countess recoiled from the smell. 'Father, I am so sorry you have been brought to this.'

'*Fiat voluntas dei*, my dear Anne.'

She had a cloth with some food – bread, cheese, pieces of cold meat, some wine – very little because Topcliffe's men were keeping a close watch on the larder. She and Amy had gathered it together hastily in the remains of the kitchen while Rose Downie was in her room with the baby. They would not have believed that Rose could do such a thing, yet she would not meet their eyes.

'Thank you for this food. It is most welcome. And, please, do not fret for me. If it is God's will, I shall be safe. If you feel that any here in this house are in danger because of my presence, you must tell the pursuivants. You must save them before me.'

'I cannot do that, Father. Nothing we could do would save us from the wrath of Topcliffe now.'

'Topcliffe? I have heard of him.'

'He is a cruel man, Father. He will not desist in his search for you until this house is rubble, for he knows you are here. We are fortunate that this hole is so secure, but it was difficult for me to get here to fasten and conceal the hinges before it was found. I think you would have been discovered if I had not done so.'

Her voice was choked and feeble. He feared she was in a worse state than he was. 'I beseech you, Anne, endure, for this *will* end.' He tried to open an eye, yet it merely watered and he closed it once more. He made the sign of the cross and blessed her before she closed the trapdoor and secured the hinges.

In the blackness of the hole, the fresh air and food brought Cotton new hope. With the wine and bread, he spoke mass, then said grace over the food and began, slowly, to eat and drink.

Topcliffe summoned Rose Downie again.

'Tell me more about this gathering. Did the Jesuit priest come alone?'

Rose's mouth was bruised and swollen. Her face was streaked with dirt and tears. 'He arrived with another man, Mr Topcliffe, called Thomas Woode. I had never met him before but we were introduced to him.'

Thomas Woode? The name was familiar. 'What more can you tell me? What did he look like? What did he say?' Topcliffe pressed her.

Rose described him as best she could but said that he had spoken little. Then, tentatively, she said, 'What of my baby, Mr Topcliffe, sir?'

'Your baby is safe and well, Rose. That is all I will to tell you for now. When Southwell is delivered into my hands, alive or dead, I will reunite you with William Edmund. Do you understand me, Rose?'

'But I have done all you asked! I know he is here. I know they were having their mass when you and your men arrived. He must be in this house unless . . .' She stopped, seeing the blood rise in Topcliffe's face.

'Unless?'

She had been about to say 'unless you let him slip away' but thought better of it. 'Unless he has somehow managed to get away, Mr Topcliffe. Perhaps there are tunnels from the cellars. I have completed my side of the bargain, sir. Please let me have my baby back.'

'All in good time, Rose. All in good time.'

Chapter 26

LORD HOWARD OF Effingham, the Lord Admiral of the Navy and adoptive father to Lady Blanche Howard, was not at home.

His steward, Robin Johnson, welcomed John Shakespeare into the grand entrance hall of the imposing house that Howard often used in these days. Standing tall on the edge of Deptford Green, close to the scene of the attempt on Drake's life, it was perfectly located for Howard's work in preparing the navy in case the Spanish launched their infernal war fleet, and also for his frequent visits to court at Greenwich Palace, less than a mile to the east, across Deptford Creek. Johnson was a man of charm and ease. He offered to take Shakespeare to meet his lordship at the Royal Dock, where he was overseeing provisioning. Together the two men set out across the green.

'These are difficult days for your master, Johnson.'

'Indeed, sir. The household is in mourning for Lady Blanche.'

A fresh breeze blew up the Thames from the east. Gulls played in the wind, holding themselves against its force by slight movements of their wings so that it seemed they were stationary in the air.

'Do you have any theories about who might have done this terrible thing to her?'

'I fear not, sir. I only wish that whoever did it might be

brought to justice as soon as possible.' Johnson stopped. 'Ah, here we are. I see his lordship now.' He pointed to a bark where some men were gathered on the quarterdeck. In their centre was the tall figure of Howard of Effingham, his shock of snow-white hair unmistakable.

Shakespeare strode to the ship. Howard was standing with Diego, Captain Stanley and three other men, while Drake knelt on the deck, scratching plans of attack on parchment. Shakespeare wished he would think to do such work below decks where he was out of musket range. A little way off, Boltfoot Cooper was watching them and surveying the crowded quay-side. He spotted Shakespeare immediately and raised his head in recognition. At least he was suitably alert. But it was obvious that Drake was as exposed, nonchalant and vulnerable as ever. The attempt on his life had bothered him not a whit.

Drake looked up from his sketchings. 'Well, Mr Shakespeare, how do you do?' he boomed. 'Come to see that I'm still alive? Well, damn it, I am. And so, unfortunately, is the accursed Cooper.'

'Sir Francis, it is indeed good to see you alive and well. How is your coxswain?'

'Not well, but the surgeon says he may live. As with all things, God will decide. What do you want with me?'

'To ask you a question, Sir Francis. How did your would-be murderer know when and where you were to disembark and land?'

Drake tossed the question aside. 'I imagine he watched and waited. I am always here. I am a sea-captain. This is where my ships are.'

Shakespeare was not impressed by this explanation but let it pass. He knew there was no point in gainsaying Sir Francis Drake. He thanked him and turned to Lord Howard of Effingham. Their previous meeting had been unsatisfactory;

this time he would not be brushed off. Howard must have more information to give about his adopted daughter. 'Might I have a word with you alone, my lord?'

Howard led Shakespeare below decks to the great cabin and closed the door. A flask of brandy stood on the captain's table and Howard poured two goblets. 'How do your investigations proceed?'

'We have progressed, my lord.'

'But you have not yet apprehended the murderer?'

'No, my lord.' Shakespeare hesitated. How much could Howard bear to hear?

As if reading his thoughts, Howard smiled faintly. 'Please, Mr Shakespeare, do not try to spare me. It is enough that she is dead.'

Shakespeare bowed. 'I fear I must tell you there is possibly more to the killing of Lady Blanche than we had first thought. I have discovered that she had recently taken up with a group of Roman Catholics. She was following the old faith, my lord.'

Howard laughed humourlessly, a short yap like that of a small dog. 'Mr Shakespeare, that is no surprise to me. It is a family failing of the Howards. I told you before that she had been associating with people of whom I disapproved.'

'But there is more. She had certain injuries . . .'

'Yes?'

'A crucifix cut into her back . . . after death. I had not noticed it at first. And she had been bound, too, for there were rope marks round her wrists.'

Howard looked aghast.

'I mention it only because I suspect there to be a religious significance and wanted to know whether you have any ideas on the matter. My lord, I fear that the assailant may be the same assassin who has been sent by Spain to kill Sir Francis.'

Howard was incredulous. 'What possible connection could there be between Blanche and a plot against Drake? Have you taken leave of your senses, Mr Shakespeare?'

'There are certain curious connections that lead me to this belief.' Shakespeare outlined his theory, including the conspirator's viciousness towards whores in Delft and Rotterdam.

For a moment, Howard glared at him, as if trying to decide whether he had heard him correctly. 'Did you say whores, Mr Shakespeare?' he said at last. And then he exploded. 'Are you suggesting that my daughter was a *whore*?'

Shakespeare held up his hands defensively. 'My lord, certainly not.'

'How dare you come to me with such scandalous imaginings?'

'My lord, you misconstrue me. Lady Blanche was a devout young woman, of that I have no doubt. There is not the slightest suggestion that she was a whore. But I do believe she may have known this man. And if this man is in London, as I believe, there is no reason to suspect he has changed his brutal treatment of women. *All* women, not only whores. The nature of Lady Blanche's injuries, the fact that she was moving in Catholic circles where the assassin might have sought sanctuary, these lead me to the possibility of a link. It is tenuous but I cannot ignore it. Perhaps she had discovered something and he killed her to silence her.'

Howard's face was still set in fury, but his rage had subsided. 'So you believe the man who killed Blanche may be the same man who shot at Drake and wounded his coxswain?'

'It is possible. I can put it no stronger than that.' Shakespeare downed the remainder of his brandy. 'Now I must ask you, my lord, whether you know the name of the man with whom Lady Blanche was consorting and by whom she came to be with child.'

Howard continued to glare at him. 'I do not like this line of questioning. It is . . . indecent. Poor Blanche is not yet interred and yet you spread tittle-tattle about her.'

'No, my lord. That is not so. I have spread no word about her.'

'But someone has. The broadsheets have been brought to my attention with their scurrilous stories.'

'I am investigating that, sir. I already have the most notorious of these people, one Walstan Glebe, in Newgate, awaiting trial on a number of charges. He is likely to lose his ears, his liberty and his right hand.'

'Then let us leave it at that. Find Blanche's murderer, Mr Shakespeare, and when he hangs at Tyburn, you shall have my gratitude. Good day to you.'

Shakespeare wanted to press for more information, for any clues in the background of Lady Blanche, any word of her friends and acquaintances, but it was clear that Howard considered the interview over. Shakespeare knew only too well that there was no profit in pushing matters with such men of power. He bowed, thanked Howard and together they left the cabin.

On deck, Drake was standing up, jabbing his finger at the parchment and muttering something about the weather gauge. Shakespeare left Lord Howard with his naval consorts and went to Boltfoot Cooper. 'I trust you are well.'

Boltfoot made an indeterminate noise from the back of his throat.

'It sounds as if we nearly lost our vice-admiral. The Royal Armoury has looked at the weapon you found. They tell me they had never seen anything like it. Accurate to an extreme degree. Made to order by a Bavarian named Opel for Gilbert Cogg. It was clearly constructed with only one purpose in mind and should have been brought to our attention. Mr Opel has one of two choices: expulsion from these shores or he can work for the Armoury.'

Boltfoot lifted his head in the direction of Deptford Strand. 'You should talk to them in Roberts Chandlery over there, sir. Bob Roberts. And the ostler, Perkins, of the livery stables at the Eagle Tavern by Sayers Court. They'll tell you more about the man who fired the shot. They saw and spoke with him.'

'I met them both on the way here. They gave me good descriptions of our man, but no clue as to where he has gone. The horse he rode has not been seen again. I believe you hit him, Boltfoot?'

Boltfoot shook his head. 'No more than a small hole in his side. He was too far away. I should have got him straight through the back but I was losing ground against him.'

'I am sure you did well to hit him at all. Did you get a good look at him?'

'No. But I might recognise him running. All I know is that he didn't have a beard and he was tall, slender and could move quick.'

'Stay vigilant. I have put out word to the surgeons, physicians and apothecaries in case he should seek treatment.'

Shakespeare left the teeming Royal Dock and walked through the crowds towards Deptford Strand for the tiltboat to London. He stopped and changed his mind, turning instead towards Howard of Effingham's house by the green.

Robin Johnson, the steward, answered the door. He did not seem surprised to see Shakespeare again. 'I trust the Lord Admiral was not too harsh with you, Mr Shakespeare.'

'No, no.'

'I am sure he wishes the matter to be resolved as much as any man, but he worries about the effect on his family's reputation. These have not been easy times for the Howards, as I am sure you understand.'

Shakespeare did. Too many Howard heads on pikes had decorated the gatehouse to London Bridge in the past half-century.

'Quite. But it is you I wish to speak to now, Johnson. Is there somewhere quiet where we can talk awhile?'

Johnson led the way through the hall into a side corridor, then down to his own room in the servants' quarters. It was bare by comparison to his master's sumptuous hall, but it was warmed by a fire and had chairs and a small oak table. 'This is my sanctuary,' Johnson said, 'where I escape from the trials of the day and plan the work of the other servents.'

He wore the livery of his station as steward to one of the most important men in England: a white satin doublet with gold trimming and black hose. He was a handsome man in his late twenties or early thirties, of medium height with dark hair and a trimmed beard. His good looks and easy charm had made Shakespeare think twice. And he had recalled, also, something that Catherine Marvell had said almost in passing – that Lady Blanche and her lover could never have married. A woman of noble blood could not wed a servant.

'So, Mr Shakespeare, how can I help you?'

'I would like to know more about Lady Blanche.'

'As I said, sir, her loss was felt by us all.'

'How long have you been in the service of Lord Howard?'

Johnson was as stiff as an oak stave. 'Since I was a boy, sir. My mother worked in his lordship's kitchens and I was brought up in the household. I have worked my way up to steward.'

'I am sure you have been diligent. You are a good-humoured man, Johnson. I am sure the household likes you well.'

'I hope so, sir.'

'Perhaps the Lady Blanche was fond of you, too.'

'What do you mean, Mr Shakespeare?'

'You were her lover, were you not?'

Johnson was shocked into silence. Then he said, 'I wonder, sir, if I were to speak openly, whether I might prevail upon you not to reveal to his lordship what I say.'

Shakespeare studied his eyes and saw some kind of honesty, but that was not enough. 'I can promise no such thing, Johnson, as you know. But I would have you speak your heart to me. It will be better for you to proceed thus. I respect openness. The alternative would be questioning under duress, which I am loath to do.'

Johnson nodded slowly. The ghost of a smile crossed his lips. 'I understand, I hope. And yes, Mr Shakespeare, I was her lover. But, more than that, we were in love. Her death has torn out my heart, sir.'

'You would have become the father of her child had she lived?'

Johnson seemed close to tears, but he held them back. 'Yes. But things would have been difficult for us. His lordship would never have countenanced her union with a commoner. We had talked of running away, perhaps across the sea to France, but I fear that would have been impossible. How would we have lived?'

'Did you bring her to the Church of Rome?'

Johnson looked away so that Shakespeare might not witness his distress. 'It was not quite like that. We were always talking. She was lonely for a long time, not accepted by many in the family apart from his lordship. She used to seek me out in this my sanctuary, where we would spend hours together, talking about everything – religion, music, exploration. Serious subjects, I suppose, for young people, but we were intensely interested in the world around us. We had much in common, since we were both outsiders in the household. One day she asked whether I was a Papist because, I suppose, it must have been obvious from the way I spoke on certain matters. I admitted that I was. She expressed an interest and I agreed to take her to mass. That was how she met Catherine Marvell, whom I understand is known to you, and various others.'

'But you were not lovers at this time?'

'No. That happened at the end of last summer. For a while Blanche had been talking of entering the novitiate in an Italian convent. But she changed her mind. I could tell then that her feelings for me were the same as mine for her. We became lovers soon after that.' He paused, then said more quietly, 'I beg you not to judge us too harshly.'

'That depends upon how much help you give me. Tell me about these secret masses. Who was there? Was a Fleming among their number? Which priests said the mass?'

'I cannot tell you any of that, Mr Shakespeare.'

'I need this information. It is imperative that you tell me.'

'Mr Shakespeare, I cannot. Would you have me betray those who have laid their trust in me?'

'Yes, Johnson, I would. This is a matter of state. I believe a Fleming is at large who is a danger to the realm. I would know his name and whereabouts. I believe you can help me.'

'I am sorry, I can say no more.'

'Then, Mr Johnson, I must consider you my main suspect in the murder of Lady Blanche Howard. You had the motive. The next you see of me will be in Newgate where I will inter-rogate you with all the powers invested in me by Her Majesty the Queen. I have no time for niceties.'

'Mr Shakespeare, please—'

'A warrant will be issued by day's end and the sheriff or his constables will come for you. In the meantime, do not leave this house or, I promise you, you will suffer the worse for it when you are taken.' Shakespeare walked towards the door.

'Mr Shakespeare, wait—'

He stopped and turned. 'Yes?'

Johnson opened his mouth as if to say something, but closed it again and shook his head in despair.

Shakespeare turned like an enraged bull and and barged his way out. He was angry: angry with Johnson for putting him in this position, angry with himself for using the threat of violence against a man who deserved better. But this killer had already made one serious attempt on Drake's life. How long before he made his next?

Chapter 27

Thomas woode awoke in such terror that he thought he would never draw breath again. A hand was at his throat and two other powerful hands pinned his arms to the bed. He twisted his body with all his strength to free himself, but could not move.

It was dead of night. Midnight. Somewhere in the distance he could hear the watchman calling the hour. One minute a comforting dream of lust, as every man has, the next a waking nightmare. He fought for breath. The hand at his throat was crushing his Adam's apple and windpipe.

'Woode? Thomas Woode?' The voice was coarse and blunt, and smelt of pain. The hand clasped Woode's throat and pulled him from the pillow. His arms were wrenched behind his back and fastened with rough ropes by a second intruder. At last the hand moved away from his throat and he gasped, his mouth opening and closing like that of a tench pulled by hook from the water.

Woode was sitting up in the middle of his sumptuous four-poster bed, with rich damask drapes on all sides and bedding of gold and crimson. His chamber was large and entirely panelled in fine wood. He was dressed in a white lawn nightgown and cap. But now this fine room was lit by the flickering tar torches of six brutal men. The one closest to him, the one who had spoken, eyed him up and down with disdain. Woode tried to say something, to protest, but nothing except a low hiss emanated from his throat.

'Thomas Woode?'

Woode nodded and tried to say, 'Yes.'

'Thomas Woode, you have committed a felony and you are under arrest. You will be taken from here to be questioned, then brought to trial by jury of your peers, where you will be found guilty and hanged.'

'What? What felony?' Woode rasped.

'Larceny, Woode, larceny of timbers destined for Her Majesty's ships. We know how you've built this pretty pile.'

'What are you saying?'

The man stood back. He was wearing a dark cape of black fur. 'You know well what I am saying, Woode. You have used navy timbers in the building of this house. They have been identified as such and there is no doubt. You build a fine house and the Spaniard sends his ships of invasion in safety.'

'It is a lie!'

'So, you have found your voice.'

'I tell you these timbers are brought here by my carpenters, who are reputable masters of their craft. I have stolen nothing, Mr . . . Who are you?'

'Topcliffe. And the jury will decide who tells the truth, Woode. You will come with us.' He turned to his men. 'Take him away.'

After three days in the fetid hole, Father Cotton began to see in the dark. He saw strange things: angels with blue spider-thread wings, demons with seven-clawed feet and red raw cocks that caught the light like blades. He saw women, naked and pink, sprawled on sheets of white linen. He saw feasts of forbidden fruit and meat that stank of morbidity, like autumn apples hung too long.

When he saw them he closed his eyes and prayed. But closing his eyes did not remove his sight. He still saw these things. After a while he could not tell whether his eyes were open or shut.

At times he put his hands beneath his vestments to see if his body was still there. It occurred to him that he was dead. More than that, at times he was certain he was dead. When the senses are denied, how can a man tell which side of the line he stands between life and death?

The food had not lasted long, though he still kept a mouldy piece of cheese, which he cut in half every time he had to eat. It gave him comfort to feel his body working, digesting. He wondered how many times you could cut a piece of cheese in half before it disappeared. Hunger was not the most insistent of his needs. He knew he had to drink to survive, so he drank constantly and pissed frequently in the corner.

The noises from outside this stinking hole were becoming fainter and less frequent. He knew now that he would not die from lack of air. He longed for the freshness of the outdoors, but it was clear that whoever had designed and built this hiding place was no fool and had factored ventilation into his plans.

At times he wondered whether anyone was still in the house. Were Topcliffe's guards still there? If not, why had the Countess not come to release him? Perhaps she herself had been taken. When this thought entered his head he breathed in short, sharp gasps of fear. Perchance this would be his tomb. Without the Countess to free him, he could die here and no one would be the wiser. He prayed often, most commonly, 'O Lord, my work here is not yet done. Release your humble servant that I might go out into the world like a shepherd among wolves and bring your flock home.'

He tried composing poetry, as he had done during his eight years in Rome. As in a dream, he thought at times of his days there and of his idyllic Norfolk childhood, paddling in the crystal clear Hor, a stream that meandered through the villages north of Norwich. He had always been a quiet, thoughtful child, not given to some of the rougher games of his fellows. So sombre a child was he that he recalled his own father calling him 'Father Robert' from a young age. And, yes, he had been solemn, perhaps thinking too much on the cares of God and the world when he should have been kicking a pig's bladder through the fields or hawking for rabbits like his elder brothers.

The gaunt ruins of St Faith's Priory entered his mind's eye. He had lived in their shadow half his life. The old Benedictine monastery had been torn down by his own grandfather, Sir Richard, on the orders of Great Henry, and the family had prospered as a result with the reward of church lands and property. Sir Richard had built a fine manor, yet the stones of the old priory remained as a constant reminder of where the riches had come from. Wealth garnered in such a way, at cost to the true faith, could never go unpunished. For as long as he could remember, he had known that one day he would have to accept the burden, to seek redemption in order to remit the sins of his family.

His back and shoulders were racked with pain and his legs felt shaky and unsteady. He was perpetually cold and could never find comfort. How long had he been here? Night and day melded into one long night. He would go mad before he died.

He fell once more to his knees, clasped his hands together in supplication and prayed.

By early afternoon, word reached Shakespeare from the Deptford constable that Robin Johnson was no longer at Howard of Effingham's house. Shakespeare was dismayed and cursed Johnson for a cogging fool. He sent the messenger back to Deptford with orders to raise a hue and cry and bring the steward to Newgate in chains.

After the man had left, he sat on the settle in his solar, enjoying the last wispy hour of daylight. He had much to consider.

The main question was whether a link existed between the killing of Blanche Howard and the attempt on the life of Sir Francis Drake, or whether fancy had taken flight in Shakespeare's overwrought imaginings. Beyond that, he needed to know the meaning of the papers he had found at the burnt-out house in Hog Lane. Was it something to do with an illegal printworks – and, if so, how was Thomas Woode involved? He knew that Woode's governess, Catherine Marvell, was acquainted with Lady Blanche and with Howard of Effingham's steward, Robin Johnson, who was now revealed as Lady Blanche's lover. What was unclear was whether any of them were in any way involved in Blanche's death. Could Johnson have been her killer? Shakespeare's instinct told him no. So who, then? There was a similarity between Blanche's injuries and those inflicted on the whores in Holland. So, was the Spanish King's mercenary, who, he now knew, had stayed in Deptford under the name of van Leiden, responsible? If so, why kill the girl? Why draw attention to himself?

As he was pondering all this, there was a knock at the solar door and Jane entered. 'A Mistress Catherine Marvell is here, sir. I told her you were busy, but she insisted it was urgent and that you would see her.' She gave him a long look and Shakespeare found himself reddening.

'Yes, Jane,' he said. 'Please show her in.'

He saw instantly that Catherine was out of sorts. She was breathless as if she had run from Dowgate. Her hair was tousled and her eyes were wild.

'Mistress Marvell—'

'Why have you done this to us?'

Shakespeare was taken aback. 'Done what?'

'I trusted you!'

'Mistress, what is this? I do not know what you are saying. What do you think I have done to you?'

She stepped close to him, her bright eyes staring angrily into his, and raised her hands, beating him on the chest with surprising strength. He reeled back but did not respond. In the background, framed in the doorway, he caught sight of Jane, smiling the knowing smile of a woman who sees things that men don't. At last, Shakespeare took Catherine by the wrists, and led her to the settle, where he sat her down. She slumped, head in her hands.

'Mistress, try to start from the beginning. I am sure I have done nothing to offend you.' He nodded to his maid. 'Jane, please fetch some strong wine or brandy for us.'

Catherine looked up. 'Are you saying you know nothing about the pursuivants who came for Mr Woode? They have taken him away in brutal fashion, accused of God knows what.'

Shakespeare's mouth set hard. 'Was it Topcliffe?'

'Of course it was the foul Topcliffe. And his henchmen, Young and Newall. You must know all this for you must have sent them.'

'No. Topcliffe is no friend of mine.'

'Then you told Walsingham about us and he sent them.'

'No.'

'They came at midnight like thieves and housebreakers and took him from his bedchamber. They woke the children so that they could see their father marched away in ropes by men with swords and daggers. This is the state you work for, Mr Shakespeare. These are your bedfellows.'

'Did they say where they were taking him?'

'No.'

'Did they say anything to you?'

'They cursed me and jeered at me. Topcliffe tried to touch

me, but I pushed him away. He called me a Popish whore and damned me to hell. He said he would have the children taken to Bridewell where they might be put to useful employment.'

'But he didn't do that?'

'No.'

'Have you spoken to anyone about this?'

'I have been at Lincoln's Inn with a lawyer all day. Cornelius Bligh. He is an old friend of Mr Woode. He has tried to discover where Thomas – Mr Woode – is being held, but so far without success.'

'And where are the children?'

'They are here. I have left them in your ante-room. I wanted to keep them with me.'

'I will ask Jane to bring them in – they must be distraught and should stay close to you. I will ask her to fetch them some cake, too, and something to drink.'

'I think she is already doing that.'

Shakespeare walked back to his table to create some distance between himself and Catherine. He had to tread carefully. Any intervention might make matters worse for everyone, especially where Topcliffe was concerned. Topcliffe had become a law unto himself, answerable only to the Queen, and neither Walsingham nor the Lord Treasurer, Burghley, seemed able to exert much control over him. Nor did the courts.

'Let us try to think about this clearly. Had Mr Woode crossed Topcliffe before?'

'Not that I know of. I thought straightway it must have been your doing. But if not, then all I can think is that it must have something to do with my master's association with Lady Tanahill. They are friends of old. He went to sup there the night of the raid.'

'Ah, yes, I know of that. All London is talking of it. So Woode was there?'

Catherine shook her head. 'Not at the time of the raid, but earlier. I think Topcliffe is looking for a priest, and is tearing the house down from what I have heard.'

'Yes. He is looking for the Jesuit Robert Southwell, as am I. But I think the Queen is like to intervene. Even she cannot stomach the destruction of one of the great houses to no end.'

'I suppose someone must have told Topcliffe that Mr Woode was there.'

'That seems likely. And I fear he will be questioned under great duress as to the whereabouts of Southwell. It is Topcliffe's way . . .'

'It is too awful to imagine.'

'Mistress, if you have any information on the whereabouts of Jesuit priests in England you would do well to tell me now. The sooner we find them, the sooner may end the torment of Mr Woode and the tribulations of Lady Tanahill. Yes, I am looking for this Southwell but also looking for another Jesuit or one associated with the Society of Jesus. I do not know his name for certain, though he has called himself van Leiden. He is a Fleming and is not what he seems. The chances are, however, that he is known by Southwell, for these people arrive in pairs and support each other.' As he spoke he studied her closely for a reaction, but just then Jane arrived with fortified wine and Shakespeare asked her to bring the children through with cakes.

'Well, mistress,' Shakespeare said, after Jane had gone, 'do you know any Jesuit?'

'I do not.' They were the most difficult three words Catherine had ever spoken. They were a lie, and no amount of equivocation could disguise that in her mind. Her parents would be horrified that she had had to stoop to this. And yet the alternative was betrayal of all those she knew in the Church of Rome. Her friends.

Shakespeare did not believe her, but all he did was nod. 'Good. Well, the first thing to be done is to find out where Woode is being held. I will make enquiries. In the meantime, what will you do, mistress?'

'I will return to the house in Dowgate with the children.'

'Will you be safe there?'

'I can only pray – if I am still allowed to – that I will be.'

Chapter 28

Topcliffe cracked the silver-weighted end of his black-thorn stick into one of the few remaining window panes at Tanahill House. The glass shattered, sending shards crash-ing into the entrance hall. On the orders of the Queen, he was leaving. Reluctantly. After four days he was still convinced that Robert Southwell was hidden in the house, but Elizabeth had told him to call off his hounds.

He stood directly in front of Lady Tanahill and scowled at her. 'I will be back,' he said, 'and I will have this house as my own. Listen carefully to my words, you Popish whore-bitch. This will be mine and you and yours will be broken.'

'And I will pray to God for you, Mr Topcliffe, that He may teach you the error of your ways.'

He spat at her and stormed off. Anne Tanahill wiped his spit from her soft ruff, then turned back into the house. She felt that nothing could hurt her any more. As she surveyed the wreck-age, she could hardly believe that this had once been a beautiful family home. In the quieter days, before Philip was taken to the Tower, they had spent long hours of joy within these walls; now, as she walked from room to room and from floor to floor, she saw only rubble and broken woodwork. Every panel had been torn out and thrown aside, every floorboard jemmied up but not replaced. The backs of every fireplace had been hammered into with heavy mallets, shattering the brickwork, as had the backs of cupboards and spaces under the eaves. Even plastered ceilings, exquisitely crafted, had been destroyed.

'How can they be allowed to do this, m'lady?' her house-keeper, Amy Spynke, said, when they had finished their tour and returned to the kitchens, where they all spent most of their time now. 'Surely they must make reparations to you.'

The Countess laughed without humour. 'That is about as likely as peace on earth, Amy. Topcliffe has made plain he will not rest until this house is his. That is what this has been about. The people who make the accusations take the property of the accused. It is all vanity.'

Rose Downie sat huddled in a far corner, by the fire, cra-dling the baby that was not hers. She still could not meet their eyes.

Amy and Joe Fletcher, the manservant, had interrogated Rose, but she had refused to say a word, either of denial or confession. Every day, they had demanded whether she had brought Topcliffe and every day when she refused to answer they knew she had. And yet they also knew Topcliffe had hit her in the face with great savagery, so there was still sympathy for her and a sliver of doubt in their hearts.

'She must answer to God, not us,' said Lady Tanahill, to Amy, in a low voice, looking at Rose. 'But we must never trust her again. She must be kept away from all aspects of our faith – and, in particular, she must never catch sight of any priests who might come here. Topcliffe will keep a constant watch on this house.'

A little later, when the household sat down to eat, exhausted by the start of the clearing-up, the Countess left them in the kitchen and went up to take Father Cotton fresh food and water. She feared he was in desperate straits, but felt that he should stay in the hole a few days more, then escape at night to a safer house. The Bellamys and the Vaux family would take him in. But he had other sanctuaries of his own.

She raised the jakes, prised up the trapdoor and peered in. By the light of her candle she could see Father Cotton sitting on the brick bench, legs hunched up with his arms round them, head into his chest. He was shivering and she could hear his teeth rattling.

'Father, we believe it is safe now. They have gone.'

He made no move, nor signalled in any way that he had heard her. 'Father?'

She knew he was alive by the violent shaking of his body, but apart from that there was no movement. The smell in the place was repulsive, but she slid down into the hole with him, leaving the candle standing above her on the lip of the trapway. She sat beside him on the brick bench and put her arm round his shoulders. His body was as cold as stone yet he shook as if he had a fever. She stroked his forehead like a mother with a child, combing his lank hair with her fingers.

She thought she heard him say something but it was so quiet she could not make it out. She talked to him with soft, reassuring words. Once more he seemed to say something, so faint she could scarcely hear him, but she thought it was 'I have seen God.' She felt her skin prickle and held him closer. She could not leave him in this hole a moment longer.

Harry Slide swept into John Shakespeare's house in Seething Lane with his usual flourish. All he needed to complete the regal touch was a herald to announce his coming. 'I have juicy titbits for you today, Mr Shakespeare,' he announced, with no preamble. 'First, it seems our friend Walstan Glebe, publisher of *The London Informer*, is willing to talk in return for his freedom.'

'Well, that was what we wanted.' Shakespeare rose from the

table where he had been writing a report on his investigation for Walsingham and shook Slide's hand. 'But I shall not let him out of prison until I hear the quality of what he has to say. We'll see him at Newgate. What other news?'

'Two of the Winchester geese from Cogg's bawdy-house have flown the nest – and a third is dead.'

'Now, that is interesting. Tell me more.'

'The dead one is Alice Hammond. There is nothing sinister about her death. She drank herself into oblivion and choked on her puke. However, it is curious to note that her cousin, Starling Day, and the procuror of the bawdy-house, Parsimony Field, are missing. Girls like them go missing all the time, of course, but I am told that Parsimony and Cogg were as close as two stoats in a hole. If anyone might have known his secrets it is she.'

'Do we know where they have gone?'

'I fear not. The trail is cold. But I have word out that we are looking and that any information will be well rewarded. Unfortunately we are not alone in our search. Topcliffe is hunting for them, too.'

Shakespeare closed his eyes and groaned inwardly. He wasn't surprised, of course; he knew of Topcliffe's interest in the murder of Cogg. But why would Topcliffe be concerned with preserving the health of Sir Francis Drake? His only interests usually were the evisceration and butchery of Papist priests and the accumulation of riches. 'Well, let us find out what has happened to these two young women. Perhaps they murdered Cogg. We must not lose sight of our targets, Harry. We are to find the murderer of Lady Blanche and to discover and dispose of the would-be killer of Sir Francis Drake. Nothing more, nothing less. There is, however, one other matter of interest to me: have you heard anything of the whereabouts of Thomas Woode?'

Slide was in ebullient mood. 'I may. What might it be worth to you, Mr Shakespeare?'

Shakespeare winced. 'How much do you think it's worth, Harry?'

'Four marks. Plus two for the news about Walstan Glebe and Cogg. And I have expenses. The whores had to be paid to talk.'

'And for what else? Three marks, for all your pieces of intelligence. I would have found out about Glebe's change of heart anyway. And half a crown for garnishing the whores.'

'You are a hard man, but I will accept your offer with grace. Talking of grace, did I tell you what I heard about his grace the Archbishop of Canterbury?'

'Yes, Harry, you said he was caught swiving a member of his flock, then had her for lunch with mint the next day. A good tale, but an old one.'

'No, Mr Shakespeare, this is better. It seems he didn't eat her after all. Instead he has set her up as his mistress in the gardens at Lambeth Palace. All the swiving he wants is there when he likes, she doesn't answer back and the grass is kept nice and short. Oh, and he'll have some warm woollen nether-stocks when shearing time comes round – so long as he can teach her to weave. Seems he's promised to marry her to make her honest, but I expect he says that to all the girls.'

'Harry Slide, you will find yourself carried westward to Paddington Fair if you continue with these slanderous jibes. Just be sure you don't tell your stories to the wrong person. Now, where has Topcliffe taken Thomas Woode?'

'Home, Mr Shakespeare. He's taken him home.'

'Back to Dowgate? I had not heard—'

'No, no, to *his* home. In Westminster.'

'I have no time for this, Harry.'

'I speak the truth. He has taken him to his home. The Council has licensed it as a holding prison for questioning. He has a strong chamber there, with his own rack and wall.'

Shakespeare was aghast. 'Do you believe the Queen knows of it?'

Slide smiled strangely. 'It is said Topcliffe is the Queen's dog, Mr Shakespeare. Beyond that I cannot say.'

'But that should not mean he is beyond the law. The question I would ask is, how can habeas corpus be effected if a prisoner is held there? Who has jurisdiction over such a place?'

'I am not a lawyer, Mr Shakespeare. I know little of such things.'

Shakespeare was horrified. He had not realised this. If the Council had agreed to it, Walsingham must know – but why would they do such a thing? 'Needs must,' Walsingham had said to him. 'Needs must in these days of threatened war and invasion.' Did that mean anything was permissible in the struggle against Rome and the Escorial?

'God's Body, Harry, these are difficult days. Come, let us ride to Newgate together.'

Besides the Tower, Newgate was London's most feared prison. This was where condemned men found themselves in a foul hole called Limbo, awaiting their last journey to the scaffold, usually at Tyburn by the village of Paddington, but also in London itself at Smith Field, Holborn and Fleet Street.

Walstan Glebe was not with the condemned, but in a hole with those awaiting trial, about forty or fifty in all, mostly men but a few women too. All were fettered to the floor or walls, languishing in stinking, dung-clogged straw. Glebe was in a bad way. His head was bandaged with a dirty rag and one eye was closed. His clothes were alive with fleas and other insects. Rats scurried among the prisoners at will, though occasionally one would be caught and dashed to death for a tasty addition to lunch.

'You seem to have done yourself an injury, Glebe,' Shakespeare said, by way of greeting.

'The tipstaff decided to play tennis with my head, using his cudgel as a racquet, Mr Shakespeare.'

'And I trust they are feeding you well.'

'Most certainly. I have developed quite a taste for raw cat, sir. As for the gruel, it passes in one hole and out the other without noticeable change of smell or texture.'

Shakespeare turned to Slide. 'Mr Glebe has things too easy here, Harry. He retains his humour. Perchance we should move him to Little Ease in the Tower . . .'

Slide chuckled. 'I hear the hole in Wood Street Counter is particularly unpleasant at this time of year.'

Shakespeare turned back to the prisoner. 'So, then, Glebe, I am told you have information you now wish to pass on to me. I trust you have not wasted my time in bringing me here, for if you have, it will be the worse for you.'

Glebe scratched his lice-ridden hair and a couple of plump grubs fell out. He picked one up and ate it. When Shakespeare raised an eyebrow he smiled sheepishly. 'It is all nourishment, sir. What they give us would not keep a mouse alive.'

'Well? What have you to tell me?'

'Do I have your word that I will be freed when you have what you want?'

'Only after I have checked it thoroughly.'

'And will I have my press back?'

'No, Glebe. By now it should be firewood. But if I like what you say I will leave a little silver so you will be fed.'

Glebe shrugged helplessly. 'Then I have no alternative but to accept your terms. You wanted to know how I heard about Lady Blanche Howard's death. I'll tell you. It was the famous Mother Davis herself who did give me that information about the piece of bone and the silver crucifix said to have been found within the lady's person. I take it this is what you wished to know.'

'Mother Davis? Which Mother Davis would this be, Glebe?'

'*The* Mother Davis. Is there more than one? The same sorceress said to have made lusty potions for the Earl of Leicester.'

'Are you saying the woman exists?' Shakespeare was exasperated. He wanted information, not superstitious rumour.

'Of course, Mr Shakespeare. I depend on her for much of my gossip.'

'I had thought she was plucked from some Papist's fevered imagination.'

'No, indeed, sir. She is real enough. A notorious witch who can conjure you wealth or depravity, love or murder, whichever you require. But you will always pay her a heavy price, as I am doing now.'

'Are you suggesting, Glebe, that your present predicament is something to do with this Mother Davis?'

'Of course. I failed to pay her the full sum she asked. Not an error I will make again, Mr Shakespeare . . .'

'And where might I find this witch?'

Glebe laughed bleakly. 'You will not find her, sir. She will find you.'

'And how, pray, will she know I am looking for her?'

'Because she is a witch, sir. She knows things that others do not.'

Shakespeare turned to Slide. 'Have you heard of this woman?'

He nodded slowly. 'I would not like to be on the wrong side of her.'

Shakespeare's instinct was to disbelieve such tales. Yet even if she was no witch, she knew something of the murder of Lady Blanche. 'Will she contact me soon, Glebe?'

'Very soon.'

'And where does she live?'

'In the air, sir.'

'What scurrilous nonsense you talk! What does this woman look like?'

'One day she might be a foul hag who would not be out of place here in Newgate, another she might be a beautiful, nubile wench.'

'And which of these forms did she take when you met her?'

'Well, to tell truth, sir, she was rather like my mother. But I know that sometimes she does take the shape of a cat, which is her familiar.'

At that, Shakespeare laughed so loudly that the other prisoners turned to see who could find anything of amusement in this dungeon. 'A cat! Then perchance you have eaten her, Glebe. You will stay here. Your only hope of release is if this Mother Davis – of whom I have grave doubts – contacts me and if she then makes any sense. Good day to you. I will leave a shilling with the turnkey for some food, which is more than you deserve.'

Chapter 29

JANE WAS AT the door when Shakespeare arrived home in Seething Lane.

'Mistress Marvell called on you again, sir. She wished to speak with you on a matter of urgency.'

'Anything else?'

'Yes, sir, this.' Jane handed him a sealed letter. 'A messenger brought it to you an hour since.'

Shakespeare broke the seal. Inside was a short missive. 'If you desire to know the truth of certain matters, come at three of the clock. You will be met in the Bear Garden, at the main entrance to the Baiting Pit. MD.'

MD. Mother Davis. The hair rose on the nape of his neck. He would have to go, of course, though his instinct was to rush straight for Dowgate to see Catherine Marvell. But that would have to wait. If the witch really knew something, she was the key to the murder of Lady Blanche and perhaps – if his surmise was correct – the attempt on Drake's life. Only the killer or someone close to him could have known about the objects found inside Lady Blanche's body.

'There was one more thing, master. Your brother William was here.'

Shakespeare frowned. 'William?'

'He is with a players' company, the Queen's Men. They have come to London.'

'Ah. Well, I shall seek him out. In due course.' The arrival of his younger brother was a distraction Shakespeare did not need.

He took horse and rode across the bridge, turning right after the Great Stone Gate, along through the mass of narrow streets and poor housing that crowded the Stews Bank area of Southwark. A modest wedding party was stepping out joyously from the porch of St Saviour's as he trotted past and he raised his hat to the plump bride. It was good to see some normality in these straitened times; it reminded him of all that he was fighting for in Walsingham's war of secrets. For a moment a picture came into his mind, an image of Catherine Marvell in a silken gown of ivory and damson, trimmed with gold and sable, her dark hair cascading across her shoulders. But he shook the vision from his head and trotted on. Such thoughts had no place in this day's work.

The Bear Baiting Pit was closed and the gardens looked skeletal and out of sorts, but in a few weeks' time, when spring arrived, the dreariness would disappear and jollity would begin afresh as the much-loved bears – Harry Hunks, Bold Tarquin and the others – came out every Wednesday and Sunday to perform. Then the people would throng this park and, on a baiting day, hawkers selling nuts, fruit and saffron cakes would shout their wares while minstrels sang and played for tossed farthings.

A woman was waiting at the gate as promised in the letter. Though wrapped in a cloak from head to foot, she was striking to look at. Shakespeare took her to be of African blood for she was dark-skinned. He leant from his saddle. 'I take it, mistress, that you are not Mother Davis?'

She smiled a beautiful smile. '*Mais non*. My name is Isabella

Clermont, but I am here on behalf of Mother Davis. Won't you please accompany me to meet her?' The accent was husky and richly French. Shakespeare bowed in acknowledgement, then dismounted and took his horse by the rein as he followed her back to Long Southwark, then along Bermondsey Street, turning northwards into the maze of back-streets that crowded near the water downstream of the bridge.

As they walked, he wondered about Mother Davis. He tried to recall all he had read in the seditious tract known as *Leicester's Commonwealth*, published illegally two years earlier. It was a vicious attack on Leicester – Robert Dudley – renowned as the Queen's favourite courtier and, it was alleged by some, her secret lover.

The tract had been banned, but everyone in London seemed to know its content. It alleged that he had used the services of Mother Davis to fashion a love potion for him so that he might seduce a young married woman, commonly believed to be the beautiful Lady Douglass Sheffield. The ingredients of the potion were young martins – which Leicester had been required to take from their nest – and his own seed, which he had spilled at Mother Davis's behest.

Mother Davis then distilled the birds with his essence and some herbs into a powerful potion, which Leicester gave to Lady Douglass in a glass of wine. When the potion had taken effect, she succumbed to him willingly. One rumour even said that her then husband, John Sheffield, had caught the lovers in a frenzy of lust in the marital bed. It was also put about that later Leicester had poisoned Lord Sheffield. But then who hadn't Leicester been accused of poisoning? Some said, too, that Leicester and Douglass went on to wed in secret to avoid fomenting a jealous rage in the Queen. Naturally she discovered the truth eventually and exploded into a towering fury. Then, as the fall of the leaf follows summer, Leicester tired of Douglass and cast her aside with cruel indifference. She was said to hate him now, seething in her Paris exile with her new husband, England's ambassador Sir Edward Stafford, who loathed Leicester with a fervour equal to his wife's. For the common people, though, the story was the stuff of great mirth. Whenever Leicester passed in a procession through the city, the apprentices would call out, 'Fresh martins for sale! Get your fresh martins here, your lordship!' and would fall about laughing. Leicester could ignore such jibes, yet when he saw his peers sniggering into their ermine collars he noted their names and vowed vengeance one day. Exacting retribution on all who had mocked him was likely to take several lifetimes.

As for Mother Davis, the tract gave no more information except to say that she was a famous sorceress and lived across the river from St Paul's. Shakespeare had taken little note of the pamphlet; he had never believed Mother Davis existed or that the event with the martins had taken place. He found it laughable that the seed of a man's loins mixed with the distillation of young birds could make a woman fall for a man; if there was any truth in such dark things, it made a mockery of all that was Christian and good.

Within fifteen minutes, Shakespeare and the Frenchwoman were outside a large old galleried building, which gave the impression that it had, at one time, served as a warehouse. Still following Isabella, who had said not a word on the journey, he walked his horse through into the cobbled courtyard where an ostler took the rein and tethered it by a trough.

Isabella signalled with her elegant hand. 'Come with me, please, monsieur.'

She led the way through a postern door. From further inside the building he heard music and laughter. They went up a narrow staircase to the second floor. Isabella pushed open a door and they entered a small room with a blazing open fire and a dozen or more flickering candles. 'Please, monsieur, would you wait here a short while. Madame is a little delayed. Would you like something to drink?'

Shakespeare was irritated. He wished himself elsewhere – in Dowgate with Catherine Marvell, to be precise. He certainly did not want to be kept waiting by the ludicrous Mother Davis and her heathen trickery. 'I'll wait,' he said shortly. 'And you may bring me some brandy, mistress.'

She nodded and went out, and he sat close to the crackling flames and looked at his surroundings. The walls were hung with opulent, inviting tapestries. Over the fireplace, he noticed a series of small, framed pictures, ranged in two rows of eight. He rose for a closer look and was taken aback by their content. It was not the first time he had seen pictures of men and women fornicating, but these were of a different order from the laughable stuff that could be bought for a crown or so from the sellers around St Paul's. They were originals drawn in ink, rather than poor woodcut prints, and the execution was exquisite, which served only to heighten their erotic content. It would be difficult not to be aroused by such highly charged images. Feeling self-conscious, he sat down again.

The door opened and a woman entered, carrying a tray with a glass of warm spirit. Shakespeare stared, astonished. She was slender, fair and naked. He could not take his eyes from her breasts. She brought the drink over and handed it to him. He took it, as if in a trance, and drank.

'Would you like anything else, master?' she asked. Her hand touched his as she spoke.

'No,' he said. 'That will be all.'

'Are you certain, master?' She guided his hand to the softness of her inner thigh. The effect on Shakespeare was dramatic and he pulled away. Yet all the pent-up frustration of these past days welled within him and his hand moved back, guiltily, to touch her there again. She pushed herself towards him. He wanted to caress every inch of her smooth skin.

He closed his eyes, drinking in the sensation. And then he pulled away, though he could hardly bear to do so. 'No. Go now.'

She hesitated a moment and reached once more for his hand, but this time he did not react, so she bowed and left the room. He downed the remains of the brandy and gasped at its potency. What was this all about? He began to panic. He had made a wrong decision in coming here, especially alone. He should have brought Slide with him.

What to do now? He couldn't just sit here, waiting for Mother Davis to deign to appear. Would she be five minutes, five hours? He put the glass by the fire, which seemed to be burning more ferociously. The room was too hot and a bead of sweat dripped off his forehead, down his cheek and into his ruff.

He went to the door and lifted the latch, opening it a fraction, then fully. It gave on to a corridor, lit by sconces with broad candles. He stepped out and walked down it. At the other end he came to another, closed door. Behind the door was music and strange sounds, laughter and moans.

The door opened easily. He stood on the threshold looking on to a scene that might, he thought, have come from someone's sordid imagining of hell. Nine years ago, at the age of twenty when he was a young lawyer, he had travelled to Venice and Verona and he had encountered many engravings and paintings based on the infernal visions of the great poet Dante Alighieri. He had also seen paintings of orgies during his travels and, indeed, here in London, and he was no virgin, yet he had never seen such a scene of debauchery in the flesh. A dozen women of every hue of hair and skin, each one naked, were entwined with each other on a bed large enough for a monarch. It was hung with red draperies and bedding that glowed like blood in the firelight. Frankincense infused the air with its luscious scent. The girls were writhing like overheated snakes in May, employing tongues, fingers, limbs and implements made to represent the male pizzle, in all manner of positions. They moaned and mouthed obscenities, seemingly oblivious to his presence. In a corner, two naked women played a lyre and a harp. No man could watch this unaffected. As Shakespeare stood there, transfixed, he realised suddenly that this was all for his benefit.

With a mighty effort, he slammed the door. He was shaking. He closed his eyes but could not dismiss the vision of that bed of flesh. He turned quickly and came face to face with the seductive smile of Isabella Clermont.

'That was very pleasurable, no?'

'You presume too much upon my forbearance, mistress.'

She feigned surprise. 'I am sorry, monsieur.'

'I tell you what would be pleasurable: this place closed and everyone in it thrown into Bridewell, yourself and the famed Mother Davis included. And I will ensure you tread the wheel day after day until you are fully cleansed of this wanton depravity.'

'Forgive me, sir. Most men enjoy this. They like to see beautiful women taking pleasure from their bodies. Perhaps you prefer boys. We could arrange that.'

'I shall leave now and I will be back with the sheriff and constables.'

'But, monsieur, Mother Davis has arrived and would speak with you. Do you not wish it?'

'And how long will you keep me waiting this time?'

'No, please, come with me now.' She took his hand, but he pulled it away from her. He did, however, follow her away from the ante-room and the chamber of naked women. Shortly they came to another room, where a small, well-rounded woman with grey hair sat by the fire, alone. She was dressed modestly and her hands rested demurely in her lap. If this was Mother Davis she was, indeed, as Walstan Glebe had suggested, rather like any man's mother.

'Monsieur, may I introduce you to Mother Davis.' Isabella extended her palm by way of introduction.

'Mr Shakespeare, I have so wanted to meet you,' said Mother Davis. 'I have heard so much about you and your good work for the safety of our beloved Queen and this England, which we love so dearly. Please, won't you come and sit here beside me?' She patted the cushioned day-bed at her side.

Shakespeare moved closer to her, but did not sit. He spoke stiffly. 'Mistress, I have no idea what sort of house you run, but I will do my utmost to close it. In the meantime, I am led to believe you have information for me concerning a heinous crime. I demand that you pass it to me forthwith or face the full force of the law.'

Her voice was warm and cooing. 'I will do all I can to help you, but I am just a poor old woman so I am not sure how much assistance I can be. Please sit, Mr Shakespeare. You seem so uncomfortable standing there.'

'I will continue to stand.' He knew he sounded brittle, but he wished it to be so. This woman was a succubus and he would not be drawn in. 'Will you tell me about the information you gave to Walstan Glebe about the murder of Lady Blanche Howard? How did you come across this intelligence?'

'All in good time, sir. I am sure we have much to talk about.'

'We have nothing to talk about. You have information. I want it.'

The old woman shook her head. 'I fear I have upset you. Forgive me. Something is building within you, Mr Shakespeare, and I worry that if you do not release it you will explode like a cannon. I was sorry you did not want any of my girls. They are so lovely, so kind, and I do believe that one would have done you a great deal of good. But at least take some refreshment with me. Isabella, some malmsey, please.'

Shakespeare paced the room, conscious of the old woman's eyes following his every move. 'Will you tell me or no?' he demanded. 'Must I fetch the pursuivants?'

Isabella reappeared with the malmsey and a platter of sweet-meats. She offered them to Shakespeare but he waved them away.

Now he was losing what little patience he had and spoke sharply. 'Mother Davis, you brought me to this place. If you have aught to say, then say it now.'

'I will tell you this, Mr Shakespeare. There is plot and counter-plot. Who plots with one plots with another against the first. And the first plots with the third against the second. The man you want has ill-used my Isabella, who led you here. The devil and his demons are welcome to him and you shall know his name.'

'Then tell me. I do not need your riddles and potions and foul practices. Just the name.'

Mother Davis signalled to Isabella. She clapped her hands and two maids appeared and started immediately to remove her rich blue dress of silk and satin.

'I hope this does not disturb you, Mr Shakespeare,' Mother Davis said, her old eyes sharp, 'but I vouchsafe it is necessary.'

When Isabella was naked, her dark skin glowing a rich golden brown in the light of the fire and candles, she stretched out her arms in the shape of a cross.

Shakespeare watched, unwillingly beguiled. His gaze went to her wrists. Though her skin was dark, he could see a raised purple weal round each one, like those on Blanche Howard. His eyes turned to Mother Davis. She smiled comfortingly and nodded to Isabella, who turned. A cross was cut into her back. It did not seem a bad wound, difficult to say how deep it had been, but there was no doubting its form: it was very like the crucifix carved into Blanche's dead body.

'Enough!' Shakespeare said to Isabella. 'Cover yourself.'

Mother Davis signalled to the maids, who began to dress her. 'Well, Mr Shakespeare, does this give you pause for thought?'

Shakespeare no longer felt uncomfortable. He was angry. 'You have not told me what I need to know, mistress. You passed information to Walstan Glebe. Where did you hear it? And what was the name of the man who did these things to Isabella?'

'It was Isabella herself who gave me this information. Isabella, show Mr Shakespeare the items.'

Isabella went to the mantel. From it, she took a silver crucifix and a piece of bone. She handed them to Shakespeare, who turned them in his hands, but the objects alone meant nothing. 'Whence came these objects?'

Mother Davis did not smile. Neither did her eyes leave John Shakespeare's. 'They came from within her, sir. They were placed there, most savagely, by a man who gave his name as Southwell.'

'The Jesuit priest?'

'We believe so, Mr Shakespeare. At the time we did not know of him, but we have since heard tell that he is sought by Mr Secretary among others. That is why we are talking with you. We thought this intelligence might be important to the safety of the realm.'

'But where is the connection to the murder of Lady Blanche? You gave Glebe the information about the crucifix and bone in relation to the murder of Lady Blanche Howard.'

Now Mother Davis did smile. 'For a very good reason, Mr Shakespeare, and one that I cannot yet divulge. But before you delve too deep, let Isabella tell you her story. Isabella, please . . .'

Isabella was almost dressed now. The maids fussed over her stays and hooks. 'He came to me two days ago, Monsieur Shakespeare. At first he asked me to beat him. That is not unusual. There are many men in the world – particularly those of a religious nature – who ask this.' She shrugged. 'But if they pay, it is none of my business and I am more than willing to comply. This Southwell asked me to tie him down and then I whipped him. I do not do it hard because I do not wish to cause real harm. He seemed to enjoy it well enough – at least, I thought he was satisfied. But then, when I loosed him, he seized me and tied me down in his place, my wrists bound tight in the ropes. That was when he did his evil work, thrusting those things into me and cutting my back with his poniard. I feared he would kill me.'

'But he did not. Now, why would that be if he killed Lady Blanche? Why would he free you?'

'Because of me,' Mother Davis said. 'I look after my girls, Mr Shakespeare. I heard Isabella's screams and came in while the brute was about this Popish business. When I called for help, he ran and that was the last we saw of him.'

Shakespeare laughed, a strange, high-pitched giggle that came unbidden, and wondered why he was laughing. A woman is nearly killed and I am laughing, he thought. But the thought made him laugh all the more. He put a hand to his mouth, trying to focus. 'Can you describe this Southwell?'

Mother Davis looked at him. 'We both saw him. He was a pretty boy,' she said. 'Half man, half girl, with golden hair, scarce bearded. Not tall, not short. He spoke precisely, perhaps too precisely. I am sure we would both recognise him again. Catch him and we will identify him for you, then bear witness against him in a court of law.'

'And you, mistress, how would you describe the man?' His words came out oddly, twittering and light. He needed to sit down. His legs were wobbly, as if he had drunk too much strong ale. He was swaying.

'Much as Mother Davis has. I would also say that his eyes were green, though it is never easy to be certain of such things. It might have been a trick of the light. For a *religieux*, it seemed he was strong in the arm. I could not have fought him off.'

Shakespeare giggled as he sat beside Mother Davis. He leant forward, head in his hands, and closed his eyes. She stroked his hair. 'Mr Shakespeare, what is the matter?'

'I – I am out of sorts. I will lie down for a few minutes.'

'Of course. Isabella, fetch help. Have a bed prepared immediately.'

The room seemed to be expanding. He began to feel smaller, as if he was shrinking to the size of a cat. He was vaguely aware that his mind was no longer functioning as it should. Where was he? Who were these people? After that, darkness fell and he remembered nothing.

Chapter 30

HE AWOKE IN a crimson bed with blood-red sheets. His body was weak. He was too tired to move. Hazily, he realised it was the bed in which Mother Davis's women had performed their squalid tableau of an orgy for him. Now he was alone. It occurred to him that he should leave this place, but he could not move. He raised his head from the cushions, just long enough to see that he was not alone after all. Isabella Clermont was sitting quietly on a wooden chair in a corner of the room. His head fell back.

'Monsieur, you are awake.'

He tried to reply but could not. His mouth moved like a fish's but no sound came forth. He felt blissful; there was nothing to concern him in the world. He could hear his breathing and it was like listening to the calm lapping of the sea on the shore. All he had to do was close his eyes again and drift away.

'I shall fetch Mother Davis.'

Yes, he thought. Fetch Mother. A picture of his mother came into his mind. She was smiling at him beatifically and he was a little boy again, back in their lovely house on a summer's day, with flowers growing round the doors and windows.

When next he opened his eyes, Mother Davis was at the side of the bed with Isabella. 'How are you now, Mr Shakespeare?'

He looked at her eyes and noticed they didn't smile. It was

her mouth that smiled, not her eyes. They held secrets and dark things, things he didn't wish to know.

She held up a small glass vial between the thumb and forefinger of her left hand. 'I have your essence here, Mr Shakespeare. Isabella procured it from you. I think its release has been good for you. Something *was* building within you and it did, indeed, explode like a cannon. You will feel much the better for it, I am sure. These things are better expended than held in.'

Through the haze, it registered with Shakespeare that she held a vial containing his seed. Why? As if reading his mind, she said, 'It is by way of payment, Mr Shakespeare. There is always a price. Hear this and remember it.'

As he watched, unable to speak or communicate, Mother Davis closed her eyes and her voice became high and ethereal: 'The Fathers plot and the vain ones play, yet a man called Death is on his way. Heed what I say, John Shakespeare, or pay. For a price there is, though you say nay. And the price you will pay, in love, is named Decay.'

She patted his hand. 'There. Be clever. I have your seed. I still have Leicester's seed and he is for ever mine. Always remember the price. Walstan Glebe forgot it and now he shivers and thirsts in Newgate. In return you have the name of your killer. All you must do is find him. The key is with you. You can unlock the doors if you desire, but never betray the messenger, Mr Shakespeare. Never do anything to harm Mother Davis.'

He slept. When he woke again, the room was cold and lit by a single candle that had burnt down to less than an inch. This time he was alone. He found he could now rise from the bed, though his head hurt. The paralysing torpor had gone.

He was naked. His clothes were on the chair where Isabella had been sitting watching him. As he dressed himself, he remembered they had taken his seed. He listened for sounds, but none was forthcoming. He picked up the candle and walked to the door. A looking-glass hung from the wall and he caught his reflection in it. He gasped: his right eyebrow was missing, shaved clean off. What spells was the witch Davis weaving?

The corridor outside was dark, but for his rapidly diminishing candle. It was just enough to get him to the ante-chamber where he had first waited and had seen the pictures of fornication on the wall, before the flame guttered and died. In the ante-chamber, the fire was reduced to glowing embers, but that gave him some light, enough to find another half-burnt candle, which he lit from the embers. He walked back down the corridor to the room where he had met Mother Davis. All was emptiness and darkness. What time was it? From the embers, assuming no more wood had been thrown on to the fire, he guessed it must be early evening.

Suddenly he thought of Catherine. She had been desperate to see him. He had to go to her. A wave of guilt crashed over him as a flickering image came into his head of Isabella Clermont kneeling astride him, toying with his tumescent member, harvesting his seed.

And still he did not know how Walstan Glebe had come by the information he had written concerning Lady Blanche Howard's injuries.

As he arrived back at Seething Lane, he was groggy. He had ridden across the bridge slowly, fearing he might fall. Once home, he walked his mount round to the mews, where a groom took the reins. He then moved unsteadily towards his front door.

A cowled figure emerged from the shadows and his hand went to the hilt of his sword. He breathed a sigh of relief and slid the weapon back into its scabbard. It was Catherine. 'Mistress, I was about to come to you.'

'I couldn't wait. I have heard nothing from you about Mr Woode. I am desperate with worry.'

'Come in.'

Indoors, Jane took their cloaks and offered them food and drink. 'What happened to your eyebrow, master?'

Shakespeare scowled at her.

'I'm sorry, mistress,' he said, when Jane had left. 'I have not been able to come to Dowgate. But you are welcome here.' Seeing her, Shakespeare's thoughts returned to the events in Southwark. He felt shabby and unclean, wanted nothing more than a bowl of water and a cloth to wash his body from head to toe. He felt very tired, his head was throbbing and he longed for his bed.

He took Catherine to his small library. It was his place and his alone, a place to think and pray, when the humour took him. He was waking fast now and it was clear that Catherine was deeply distressed. Her hair had not been combed and her eyes were lined with dark shadows. Yet still she contrived to be beautiful.

'We must save Mr Woode from the clutches of that monster,' she said. 'Where has Topcliffe taken him? Is he alive or dead?'

Shakespeare had never imagined her like this. Her character was all fire and defiance but now she was almost begging, though not for herself.

'Mistress,' he said gently, 'I have discovered the whereabouts of Mr Woode and it is not news that will comfort you. He is being held in Topcliffe's own home in Westminster. I am told he has there a strong chamber with a rack. There is no way to remove your master from this place. We can only wait until he is brought to trial on whatever charges Topcliffe can muster, then ask Mr Woode's lawyer to do his best. This is bad, but I must speak plain with you.'

He half expected Catherine to erupt in tears or to collapse swooning in a heap, but she looked him square in the eye. 'I will not believe that all is lost. We must bring my master out of that place. I have a proposition for you. And a confession. I will tell you things, trusting in your Christian goodness and in my belief, which I pray will not prove misguided, that a human heart beats within your chest.'

He held her eye for a few seconds, then nodded. 'Sit down and speak. I will listen.'

She lowered herself on to the cushioned window-seat where he often sat to read. Her fists were balled, but she spoke firmly and directly. 'I have not been honest with you, Mr Shakespeare. I told you I did not know anything of Jesuit priests, but that was a lie. The truth is I know two such priests, one of whom concerns me greatly. It pains me to say such a thing, for I am betraying a trust placed in me, but I now believe it would be better for all if he were apprehended. I am afraid he may be capable of terrible crimes, which will sow discord rather than harmony. I fear, too, that it is possible he may have been responsible for the murder of Blanche.'

'Do you have evidence that this is so?'

'Only circumstance. And my instincts, which are powerful. I am proposing a trade. I will take you to meet the other priest, of whose character I have no doubt. He has agreed to talk to you and will, I believe, provide you with intelligence that might bring a conclusion to these unhappy events. For me to do this thing, you must vouchsafe not to arrest him. But first you must do everything within your power – which I know to be considerable – to effect the release of Mr Woode. If that involves prostrating yourself before Mr Secretary or petitioning the Queen, then you must do it. My master is a good and innocent man and does not deserve this. His life and the future of two small children are at stake.'

Shakespeare's head was clearing fast now. He was angry with Catherine for her lies, yet he had suspected all along that she knew the whereabouts of the hunted Jesuits, had helped to harbour them, even. For her now to offer one in return for the life of her master, she must indeed have severe doubts about the priest. She must also, he realised with dismay, have a deep affection for Thomas Woode. What did their relationship amount to? Were they lovers? If not, did she wish it so? For one brief, unworthy moment it occurred to Shakespeare that it would serve his purposes to let Woode die, leaving the way clear for him to woo Catherine. And then, discomfited, he recalled the Old Testament tale of David and Bathsheba. Was he, like David, willing to allow another to die for his own happiness? The words of Mother Davis came back to him: 'The price you will pay, in love, is named Decay.' He shuddered.

'Yes,' he said. 'I will do all within my power to save your master from Topcliffe. Yet if there are charges against him, I cannot protect him from the law. If he has harboured traitors he must pay the price.'

'I understand that.'

'But first tell me this: what is his connection with the tract we found close to the body of Lady Blanche? There was something in the printing of the lettering that he recognised.'

'When you get to him, Mr Shakespeare, you can ask him yourself. I am sure he will tell you what you wish to know, for he loves me and will be influenced by me. Just say to him, 'I bring you solace, Mr Woode.''

Chapter 31

WALSINGHAM WAS RELUCTANT to provide Shakespeare with the warrant he required. He looked at his chief intelligencer curiously, but did not see fit to comment on the missing eyebrow; he had weightier matters on his mind. 'I do not like to cross Mr Topcliffe, John. These are not days for such politicking between ourselves. Fight the enemy, not each other. If Woode has information, Topcliffe will discover it.'

Shakespeare had to argue his case forcefully. It was, he said, critical that *he* see him for, unwittingly, he might have the key to finding the killer of Lady Blanche and the mercenary sent after Drake. He did not elaborate on the source of his intelligence, or that it involved Southwell; he did not want to incriminate Catherine Marvell. But he did explain his theory concerning the link between the two crimes and his belief that Woode might reveal things to him that he would not to Topcliffe.

Walsingham was not convinced, yet he saw Shakespeare's determination and relented. 'But this warrant will only provide you with leave to talk to Woode, not to carry him away from Topcliffe. Go today and I will ensure Topcliffe expects you and obeys the warrant. And be civil, John.'

'And do you think Topcliffe will be civil to me?'

Walsingham did not reply.

*

Shakespeare rode through the chill streets clutching his warrant in his doublet. He was not expecting Topcliffe to grant him admission to his house but knew he must try.

Topcliffe was waiting for him and seemed uncharacteristically good-humoured. 'Welcome, Mr Shakespeare. Welcome to my humble abode.' He held back the great oaken door to give Shakespeare admittance. 'Can I provide you with aught to take away the cold of the day? A tot of brandy, perchance?'

Shakespeare thought he would rather sup with the devil than with Topcliffe and declined. 'I am here to see Mr Thomas Woode.' He was brisk and to the point.

'And I am more than pleased to show him to you. Perhaps you would like to see inside my strong chamber. It is a remarkable piece of work. The Tower has nothing to compare, I believe.'

'Is he there? Have you tormented him?'

'Come.'

Topcliffe led the way along a short passage to a door with heavy iron ties and straps that gave it a look of impregnability. He threw open the door to reveal a room of darkness relieved only by the guttering light of a few pitch sconces and a small, grubby skylight. The windows to the street were boarded.

'Step inside, Mr Shakespeare, do not be afraid. I will not eat you.'

'I promise you this, Topcliffe. Whatever I might feel about you, it is not fear.'

Topcliffe barked his mongrel laugh. Shakespeare stepped inside and peered around the gloom. The room was dominated by the rack, a grotesque bed-like structure constructed of bright new timber and measuring ten foot by four. At each end was a roller, with thick ropes for attaching to the wrists and ankles.

'Brand new, Mr Shakespeare. Do you like it? I paid for it

from my own purse,' Topcliffe said. 'Twenty-one pounds, fif-teen shillings. How much have you paid of your money in the defence of the realm?'

In a corner was a brazier with dead coals and ash from another day. On the wall a bar was attached to two iron rings, bolted firmly into place just below the ceiling. Topcliffe saw Shakespeare's eyes move there. 'Now, *that*, Mr Shakespeare, is my pride and joy. All you must do is put a pair of fetters to their wrists with a metal point pressing into the flesh, then hang them by the hands from that bar. In haste, I'll hang them loose, but usually I take my time, so I'll let them touch their back to the wall or have their toes touching the ground. Then they don't die so quickly. The pain that such a simple device can provide is a mighty thing to behold. They go mad with it, Shakespeare, mad as Bedlam fools. It does grip their torso most, their belly and chest, a crushing pain worse than any can endure. They believe blood is leaking like sweat from their hands and fingers, though it is not. But they can scarcely say a word while they're up there, so I cannot tell when they wish to provide the infor-mation I require. But I let them down every once in a while to see whether they wish to talk. Usually they do.'

'I am here to see Mr Woode, not to discuss the merits of your unchristian instruments.'

Topcliffe seemed satisfied with the impression his chamber had made. 'Ah, yes, Woode. Now there is a gentleman most fearful. He is a talker. He told me everything I wanted to know and more. I now know the name of his aunt Agnes's best milk-producing cow. And, of course, the truth of the priests he has had at his house. He has admitted everything, names, dates, descriptions, present whereabouts. He tells me Robert Southwell was among them and that he was at Tanahill House while I was searching, Proof enough that I was right not to stop looking and proof that her ladyship is in league with the Romish anti-Christ and all his devilish works. I hope Southwell starved to death in his dismal hole and that his rotting flesh stinks the place out.'

'I have a warrant allowing me to talk to Mr Woode.'

Topcliffe took a cold branding iron from the brazier and idly slapped it on his hand. 'There is no need, Shakespeare. He has told me all, as if I was his priest in the confession box and he was revealing all his secrets. Why, he even admitted stealing timbers from the Royal Docks. Now if that isn't a treasonable offence, I'm a Dutchman's donkey.'

'A man will testify that black is white under torture. Now, take me to Woode or answer to Mr Secretary.'

Topcliffe bared his teeth with contempt. He threw the iron back into the brazier. 'Very well. Come, boy, through here.'

There was a door in the side of the strong chamber, set into a brick wall. Topcliffe unlatched the bolt and kicked it open. There was no light except the flickering of the torture room's torches. Shakespeare could see nothing at first, but then, as his sight adjusted, he saw a mound, like a sack of beets, in the far corner. He strove not to recoil at the habitual prison stench of ordure and stepped forward into the straw-strewn room.

'Mr Woode?'

There was no reply. He could hear breathing, coming in short, painful gasps.

'Mr Woode, it is John Shakespeare. I am here to talk to you.' Shakespeare turned to Topcliffe. 'Do you have drink for this man?'

'He has water. If he doesn't like it, he can drink his piss.'

'I would speak with him.'

'Then do so.'

'Alone.'

'As you will.' Topcliffe stepped away and was about to slam the door when Shakespeare intervened with his foot.

'I want light in here. And provide this man with good food and some small ale or I will write to the Queen giving details of how you care for those you question in her name.'

'Your threats mean nothing to me. She knows what I do for her and revels in it.'

'What febrile nonsense you talk.'

'Oh, but she does, Shakespeare. I tell her all about it when I'm on top of her thrusting in and out. How that do work her up into a frenzy until she cries out in pleasure.' Topcliffe laughed, but Shakespeare wasn't deceived. He knew he had touched a raw nerve, that Topcliffe's relationship with the Queen was the one area in which he might be vulnerable. Elizabeth would never allow herself to be shamed by one of her hirelings.

'Would you wish me to tell her you said that?'

'Would you wish your head broken with an iron bar? Would you wish me to bruit abroad to Mr Secretary your bedtime cavortings? Tell me, Shakespeare, what did become of your right eyebrow? Hah! I know everything about you. You're as bad as one of those Popish girl-boys. God's blood, have your damned candle and food. Perhaps the prisoner would care for a baked pie of elvers and thrushes, with some dainty marchpane sweetmeats to follow . . .'

Shakespeare's colour rose. How did Topcliffe know about Mother Davis and Isabella Clermont? Had he followed him? Had she told him? And, if so, why?

As Topcliffe went to order some scraps from one of his servants, Shakespeare took a deep breath and went to the huddled figure in the corner. His clothes were still those of a gentleman, but covered with the dust and filth of this hellish cell. Shakespeare put an arm round him.

'Mr Woode, can you speak, sir?'

Woode's eyes shone in the gloom. 'Yes, but I will not.' The

voice rattled like a bag of beans, but it was strong enough and more than a whisper.

'I am here to help you.'

'Another Walsingham trick, I presume.'

'Catherine – Mistress Marvell – has told me you are an innocent man.'

'And what difference does that make? My body is already broken. That is what the law of England does: it breaks innocent men until they confess to things they did not do. Well, sir, I will not speak with you. And neither will I speak with that wild animal Topcliffe. Despite what he says, I have told him nothing.'

He slumped against the wall.

'Trust me, Mr Woode. In Christ's name – your Christ and mine – I swear I am here to bring you succour, not to harm you. Please trust me. It is our only hope . . .'

Topcliffe's servant, a thick-set boy with slicked hair and the beginnings of a wispy beard, arrived with a jug of ale, some bread and a candle-holder. He slid the candle to Shakespeare, ceremoniously spat into the ale, then put it on the floor, slopping out a fair part in the process. He dropped the bread and kicked it as it landed.

'Hope it kills you,' the boy said, with studied sullenness.

'Thank you, boy. Now go.'

'I'm leaving this dung-heap. And I'm Nicholas Jones. I ain't no one's boy.'

Shakespeare closed the door and gave Woode a long draught of ale. In the candlelight, he examined the prisoner, who yelped when touched but otherwise put up no resistance. He could scarcely move. His arms hung limp at his sides. There were marks from the manacles, red rings of broken skin round the wrists, but those were the only outward sign of torture. His eyes remained open, alert and bright.

'How long did he hang you on the wall?'

'It felt like hours. Perhaps just minutes. I have no idea. There is more torment against that wall than I had ever thought possible. I do not think I can suffer it again without dying.'

Shakespeare drew closer and spoke quietly in the prisoner's ear. 'I bring you solace, Mr Woode.' He then moved away. 'Catherine has been talking with your lawyer Cornelius Bligh. He is trying to have you brought to court, but Topcliffe has been doing his utmost to block it.'

Woode sighed heavily. Those words – 'I bring you solace, Mr Woode' – were the very words Father Cotton had used when first they met. Only one other person would have known that: Catherine. 'It will be too late. I will be dead before I leave this black hole.'

'Don't say that. Try to remain strong.'

'He won't give up with me. Neither will he let me come to trial, for he has no evidence. He will never let me out of here alive. My only hope is a quick death. Will you grant me that boon?'

'I will not kill you, Mr Woode. Neither is it in my gift to set you free. I had to obtain a warrant to see you here. You belong to Topcliffe.'

'But you and he are the same creature. Between you, and with the patronage of Walsingham, Leicester and Burghley, you will squeeze and choke all those who cling to the old religion until they are no more. Only then will you be content.'

Shakespeare held the jug to his lips once more and he drank deeply.

'Well, Mr Shakespeare, you do not deny it. You come to me as a friend, but it is false. Whose side are you on?'

'The side of truth. If you are guilty of treason, I will do nothing for you and you must suffer a traitor's death.'

'I am no traitor.'

'But you sail precious close to the wind. I discount these tales of stolen timbers, but you consort with Jesuits. They are seditious liars. They sow discord and some do not balk at regicide. But let us cease this talk. We do not have long. Mistress Marvell asked me to tell you that the children are well, as is she. She said you were not to worry about them. She hoped you would help me . . .'

Woode looked ten years older than when Shakespeare had last seen him. His eyes shone, but there was resignation in them. 'My children. Who will look after them? Will *you* care for Catherine and my children, Mr Shakespeare?'

'Have you relatives? Some brother or sister to care for them while you are here?'

He shook his head slowly but said nothing.

'They will be cared for.'

'Swear this in Christ.'

'In God's name, I do swear it.'

'Then I must help you and trust in God that you will not betray my trust.' His weak voice became even quieter. 'You showed me paper with some print on it . . .'

'Indeed. And you recognised it.'

Woode winced at the pain that invaded every part of his body when he tried to move. 'I fear I am a poor liar. I know the press on which it was printed for it was once mine. I no longer needed it, so I gave it to certain priests who wished to publish religious tracts. There was to be nothing seditious or libellous. Things more innocent and pure than you would find in any St Paul's bookseller.'

'That was not the paper I found. There was nothing innocent or pure or even religious about it. It was a seditious libel against Her Majesty and others. It has been burnt as it deserved.'

'Then I am at a loss. That is not the work of my old friend Ptolomeus.'

'Ptolomeus?'

'An old Marian priest. He lives the life of a beggar in an ancient mill in the village of Rymesford, by the Thames upstream of Windsor. He makes his own paper, which is why it was such poor quality, and does some printing for the fathers who come to England from France and Rome. He is a harmless, spiritual soul, Mr Shakespeare. He would never allow anything seditious to be published. I must plead with you: do not harm him . . .'

Woode's rattling gasps were becoming weaker and Shakespeare realised that any other questioning would be pointless. He touched his face, one human to another. Holding up the candle, he saw that the prisoner's eyes were closed now and his lips fixed in a rictus of pain. Shakespeare rose to go, away from this wicked place. Before he opened the door, he looked back at the huddled heap of a once-strong man. 'I pledge that whatever happens, Mr Woode, Mistress Marvell and the children will be under my protection.'

The words from the slumped figure were faint, lower than a whisper, but Shakespeare heard them well enough as he went out: 'I know. You love her.'

Richard Topcliffe moved away from the thin section of wall where he had listened to every word of the conversation between Woode and Shakespeare. He lit a pipe of sotweed and sucked it, churning out plumes of rich, aromatic smoke. He laughed to himself. Where the rack and manacles had failed to produce results, man's green stupidity always filled in the gaps.

Chapter 32

CATHERINE MARVELL BROUGHT the children that evening, with bags of clothes and other belongings. When Shakespeare had told her it was Woode's wish, she happily agreed to it. The house in Seething Lane was not large, with just one spare room that she was to share with Andrew and Grace. Jane was pleased to have extra mouths to feed and the children took to her. That evening Catherine and Shakespeare talked until nine and drank wine together. He told her of his meeting with Woode, sparing her the worst details. Yet he knew she was well aware of the severity of her master's situation.

'He fears his children will be orphans?'

There was nothing to say to that. 'We will do what we can. That is all.'

'In the morning I will keep my side of our bargain.'

Shakespeare barely slept. He lay awake thinking of the dark-haired woman who slept so near, in a room not ten yards from his. He thought of her warm body, naked beneath her night-gown. He could not know that she hardly slept either.

They breakfasted at dawn, the children racing round the table, then set off on foot, leaving Andrew and Grace with Jane.

'Where are we going, mistress?'

'You will discover soon enough. One thing I ask: look about you as we go. We must not be followed.'

It was a cold, misty morning. Eddies of fog blew up from the river and at times it was like walking in cloud as they set off northwards, along Seething Lane.

'Where are you from, Mr Shakespeare? Your voice is not that of a Londoner.'

'Warwickshire. A town named Stratford. I left to follow the law but was waylaid by Mr Secretary and pressed into his service.' Shakespeare laughed. 'I think the law might have been a more comfortable life.'

'And a more honourable one?'

Shakespeare bridled. 'I believe the defence of the realm is an honourable calling, mistress. In fact, I can think of none more honourable.'

'And yet you find yourself a bedfellow to Topcliffe.'

'Topcliffe is a man apart. He is a stain. We share some aims but we do not work together. He is beyond the law. I work for Mr Secretary, who is answerable to the Queen and the Council and operates within the law. No system of human governance is perfect. Consider Rome and Madrid. How many Topcliffes do they employ in their foul Inquisition? How many rackmasters do they have? Topcliffe learnt his art from the Spanish. And the fact that a dog such as Topcliffe is employed in the struggle against these forces does not make England any the less worth fighting for.'

They turned left from Seething Lane into Hart Street. There was silence between them for a few moments and then Catherine spoke, and it was as if the floodgates had opened. 'No, Mr Shakespeare, you are the Queen's dog. It is you who gives her an aura of honour and decency. It is you who cleans the filth of Burghley, Walsingham, Leicester and Topcliffe. They conduct themselves like feral beasts, tearing men's limbs from their bodies and tossing their severed parts into cauldrons, like the bones of chickens, for daring to worship God in the way their conscience dictates. And you, you in your reasonableness and innocence, wash the blood from the hands of those who do these things.'

Shakespeare stopped in his tracks. 'Do you think it wise to speak to me like this, mistress, when you have called on me for assistance?'

Catherine stopped too. Her blood was up. 'Forgive me if I have offended you, sir, but I cannot contain my anger. Even now, that wild animal is destroying the body and mind of a good man. For all we know, Topcliffe may have killed him already. How many of his prisoners never reach the scaffold? One racking can kill a man or break his health for ever. I must say these things because they are true. I know you are a good man. It is why I have come to you. Yet I hate to see your goodness used and abused by others less worthy . . .'

Shakespeare held up his hand, palm facing her. 'I will not listen to this, mistress. I am no one's dog. I serve my Queen and my country in the face of an implacable enemy. And I will defend the honour of my sovereign lady. She has made it plain that she does not wish to make a window to men's souls. Yet we know that these Jesuits come here to subvert the state, not just to bring comfort to their flock. You know it yourself, for you have told me so.'

For a moment it seemed they could go no further. The air between them was a wall of ice and fire; there was no way through. Then Catherine nodded slowly. 'I have spoken out of turn, Mr Shakespeare. It was unpardonable. I had meant to say how highly I esteemed you for your honesty and decency and for going to see Mr Woode. Forgive me.'

Shakespeare still stood on his dignity. Yet how could he not forgive her? 'I am sorry, too, mistress, not for anything I have done, but because you and those you love are suffering in this way.'

'Will you not call me by my given name?'

'I would be honoured to do so. And perhaps you would call me John.'

They walked on through the mist, turning right into Mark Lane. Catherine touched his arm. 'Let us stay a while to see that we are not followed.' They stood under the eaves of a tailor's shop, watching the street. When they were certain they were not observed, they moved on once more, walking faster now through the tangle of streets westward to East Cheap. Despite the early hour, the streets around the meat market were abuzz with life and movement. Here was the bloody stench of the slaughterhouses, the lowing of the great beasts come for their throats to be cut to provide fresh meat for the city, the roads thick with new sawdust to soak up the gore. 'Keep close to me,' she said. 'We must move quickly now.'

She slipped into a side alley, barely wide enough for a man to pass without turning his shoulders sideways. They ran down it, then turned into another lane beside some cattle stalls and waited. When no one followed, they moved on into the laby-rinth of lanes, with overhanging jetties from the houses. Finally, at the end of a woodframe, they came to a brick wall with a wooden gate set into it. Looking both ways to make sure that no one else was about, she knocked on the gate. It was quickly opened from the inside. She and Shakespeare went through and found themselves in a small knot garden, divided by beds of box into geometric patterns where herbs would bloom in summer, filling the air with the heady scents of lavender and thyme. To Shakespeare, it looked like a little maze in which a hedgepig might lose itself.

The door to the garden closed and there stood a man, within arm's length of Shakespeare. He was shorter by perhaps five or six inches, a slight figure who seemed in want of a good meal. His golden beard was straggly, as if it had not been trimmed for weeks. His eyes were blue-grey and shone. Shakespeare knew instantly that he was Southwell and judged that this man was no killer of women, no assassin sent against Drake.

'Mr Shakespeare,' said Catherine, 'this is the man of whom I told you. I will not give you his name for fear of compromising you.'

The men shook hands. 'Good day to you,' Shakespeare said.

'And to you, Mr Shakespeare. I am sure you have a good idea as to my identity but, please, let it not be a matter of concern between us. We have a common purpose: the release of Mr Woode in exchange for the imprisonment of a man who, I believe, should not be at large. Come, sit with me.' The priest indicated a bench at the side of the garden.

It was important to Shakespeare that the standing between them should be clear from the start. 'Father, I will talk with you here today and I will leave you unmolested. But I must tell you that the hunt for you will continue after this, and if you are caught, the full process of the law will descend upon you. I will not intervene on your behalf or shy away from my duty.'

'I understand that, Mr Shakespeare, and I thank you for your forbearance in meeting me under these circumstances. But my life is not important. As in all things, God's will be done.'

Catherine stood away from them, her back against the arched wooden door that had given them access to this garden. She watched the two men, but this was no longer her business.

'I will give you no more information than is necessary, Mr Shakespeare, for I do not want to bring down misery on those who have helped me. I will just tell you that there is a supposed member of the Society of Jesus in London whose motives I distrust. Every tree has its rotten fruit: at first I tried to ignore the possibility that this man was that worm-eaten apple. But now I have to speak plain. I knew Lady Blanche Howard. She had come into the fold and was a much-loved daughter of the Church. This other priest, though I am reluctant to honour him with the title 'priest', seemed to want to become close to her. At times, I would say, he took too great an interest in her. She was a lovely young woman, physically as well as spiritually. I saw the way he looked at her and touched her and I did not like it. She seemed unaware of any impropriety. She was talking, at that time, of travelling abroad to join a convent. But then she realised she was in love . . .'

'With Robin Johnson, the Lord Admiral's steward?'

The priest nodded. 'I would not admit his name to you if I had not heard that he had said as much to you himself. He is safely out of the country now and will soon be enrolling in one of the English colleges. Lady Blanche spent more and more time with him and pushed the priest away. It was as if she found him repellent. Something had happened, something she did not like. And my feelings were the same. It seemed to me he was sent here for another purpose than to save souls. This man could be charming, but intimidating too.' He looked at Catherine. 'Lady Blanche was not alone in growing afraid of him: other women in our flock shied away from him. But what could I do? In the Society of Jesus, one learns obedience. It was my duty to help him.'

'What made you change your mind?'

'The murder of Lady Blanche. This man would disappear for nights and never saw fit to explain his movements to me. The house in which Lady Blanche's body was found in Hog Lane was a safe-house for us, which this man used a great deal for various purposes, though I was never sure what. We rented it under an alias so that none should molest us there. I had never thought it to be used for such infamy.'

'Why do you think he did this thing?'

'I think he feared she knew too much. I think he had taken her into his confidence, and when she moved apart from him, he felt it was no longer safe to leave her alive.'

'And the printing?'

'I know nothing of that, but I read the broadsheets, and I saw that a man called Gilbert Cogg had been murdered at his property in Cow Lane. I was given the name of this Cogg and, under orders from my superiors, I passed the name to the other priest. I confess I had my doubts about doing so, grave doubts, and now I believe those doubts have been confirmed, for I think he killed Cogg, though I have no idea why.'

'And have you a name or description for this priest?'

He laughed. 'I am not sure a name would be of much use to you. We do not use our real names, Mr Shakespeare. However, while he was with me he was known as Herrick.'

'Did he ever use the name van Leiden?'

'Not to my knowledge, but that means nothing.'

'Describe his likeness.'

'He is a Fleming, a tall man, perhaps six foot or more, clean-shaven, short hair. He always dressed modestly, like a Presbyterian, almost. And though he spoke perfect English, he had a Low Countries accent.'

'Thank you. He sounds very much like the man I seek. Where can I find him?'

'We have another safe-house. I have reason to believe he may have gone there. It is a small tenement over the river, on the west side of Horsley Down. The house is old, from the time of John of Gaunt, I believe. It is not in good condition and should probably be razed to the ground, but it serves our purposes. At least, it has done so until now. It is apart from other buildings within a copse on the edge of the common land. It will not be difficult for you to find.'

'Will anyone else be there?'

'No. And that is the last question I will answer, Mr Shakespeare. I will, however, tell you one more thing. On the day I last saw Herrick, as I then called him, he said something that made my blood turn to ice.'

'Yes?'

'He said, "Your weakness, Father, is that you are merely willing to die for God. You are not willing to kill for Him."'

Chapter 33

THE MAN STARED at his reflection in the small looking-glass. He liked what he saw. With practised ease, he cupped his hand round his beard and brushed it down repeatedly until its point was sharp. If he had doubts about the course of action upon which he was set, his reflection did not reveal them. He looked as confident and potent as ever.

Adjusting his ruff, he turned the glass to the wall – an old superstition of his – then picked up his belt with the attached scabbard from the bed, fitted it round his waist and stepped out of the chamber.

He wrapped himself in a fur cloak, donned his favourite beaver hat and walked out into the street. He had a meeting with Herrick and the prospect set his nerves on edge. Until now he had avoided him, dealing with him always through intermediaries at the French embassy, but now that the attempt on Drake's life had failed, he had no choice. Until now, he had been firmly in control of events: he had arranged for the required weapon through Cogg and he had sent messages to Herrick, informing him of where Drake would disembark and from which ship. They were unlikely to get such a chance again before the Vice-Admiral sailed.

Drake had received orders from the Queen and they were due to weigh anchor any day. The plan was for Drake and his young wife, Elizabeth Sydenham, to ride for Dover, then take the wind along the Channel to Plymouth. The ships now in the Thames – four royal galleons and a group of fighting merchantmen – would be sailed westward by others. After that, who could tell? The best guess was that they would make for Panama to plunder Spanish shipping. But whatever the plan, the Spanish King and his ministers wanted Drake stopped. They wanted him dead.

They must act, and soon. Both he and Herrick were equally set on their course, but their motives were different. For him, it came down to the filthy stink of tallow candles. His family had suffered intolerable insult and financial hardship through disagreements with the Crown. At the lowest point, when his father had lost his head to the axe, they had been reduced to lighting their poor cottage with tallow made from sheep fat. He could recall the bitter tears of his mother as it belched its acrid smoke when once she had lit her great hall with beeswax. If Drake died, he would get the seventy thousand ducats promised by King Philip, enough to restore his family's fortune and standing.

He did not use his real name. He was a Percy, a younger, forgotten cousin of the proud Catholic Percy family from the borders. The family that had once sired the great warrior Hotspur had suffered grievous hardship through the putting down of their abortive uprising in 1569: many had died by rope or axe, among them the head of the clan, Thomas Percy, who was attainted and executed. The loss of lands, wealth and reputation had been devastating. And it had not ended there: the family had been persecuted without mercy ever since. Henry, the eighth earl, had died in the Tower not two years since, accused of complicity in the Throckmorton plot to place Mary, Queen of Scots, on the throne of England. How could the family not harbour a grudge? And yet this Percy was not made of martyr stock. Enough Percys had died for the cause of Rome; he wanted others – their enemies – to die instead.

It had been hard keeping up the pretence all these years. The early years had been the worst, learning to dissemble, to become a loyal servant of the Crown in fighting the Spaniard, but the deception had been vital to his long-term goal. Eventually, through the offices of Mendoza, Spain's former ambassador in London and now in Paris – he had persuaded King Philip that he could perform this task for the right price. Seventy thousand ducats was that price. All he needed was a professional assassin and he, the forgotten Percy, would find an opportunity to do for Drake. His own hands had to be clean of blood, at least until the armada landed. Herrick would be his weapon: he was the stuff of martyrdom and did not fear death. The first attempt had been a miserable failure, thanks to the accursed coxswain putting his body between Drake and the musketball.

Now Percy and Herrick were to meet. This entailed high risk, for to be seen with such a man was tantamount to treason, and Percy did not relish a traitor's death.

Herrick was waiting in a corner booth at The Bull, sitting alone, eating a platter of beef and pork as though he had not supped for a week. Percy watched him for a few minutes, to be sure he had the right man. When he was certain it was not a trap, he approached. Herrick was raising a tankard to his lips, quaffing fresh water. He never touched wine except at mass. But that was the Blood of Christ: just as the wafer became Christ's Body on entering the mouth of a communicant, so the wine became His Blood; every Roman Catholic knew that to be true and every Protestant declared it false.

'You take your life into your hands drinking water,' Percy said, by way of greeting. 'Get some beer down your gullet.'

Herrick looked at him sourly. 'Your countrymen take too

much strong liquor. There is nothing wrong with the pure water God provides.'

'Well, if you die before your day is run, blame no one but yourself, Herrick. Or whatever name you are using today . . .'

'Herrick will do.'

Percy raised his head in signal to a serving wench. 'How did you miss?' he asked Herrick.

'You know what happened.'

Percy shook his head in practised dismay. 'I do indeed. You bungled, Herrick, and it must be put right.'

'Where can I find Drake next? How can I get close to him? I no longer have the long-range weapon. I believed I had no further use for it.'

'It will be more difficult now. He has his commission. He will be sailing west, to Plymouth, to gather his fleet within a day, no more. He will have four royal ships of war, with ten other vessels at the least. With surprise, they can do much harm.'

Suddenly Herrick was angry. He beat his hands on the oak table so that the trencher of food jumped in the air. The movement caused a sharp pain in his side where the ball had scored him and he winced. 'Then you must play your part. You will surely be with him. You must do that which you have avoided for so long.'

The wench had returned. She was startled by their angry words, though she had no idea what concerned them. She was a comely girl, breasts spilling out of the front of her dress in most generous measure. Percy smiled at her and preened his whiskers. 'Ah, girl, I will have a pint of your strongest ale and a trencher of meat. Spare no expense, for my friend will pay.'

As she left, Herrick grasped Percy's wrist. 'Do you hear me?' he whispered urgently. 'You are in deep, sir, deeper than the raging western sea. I know how you have tried to work this, but that will no longer suffice. Will you be aboard ship with Drake on his way to Plymouth?'

Percy tried to wrench free, but he could not dislodge himself from Herrick's iron grip.

'Do you hear me?'

'Yes! I hear you. And, yes, I will be with Drake. But I am the whetstone, Herrick. I do not cut the barley. I sharpen the blade that will do it.'

'God's blood, that is not enough. You will be there. Throw him overboard. Or whatever it is you pirates do by way of expedient killings.'

Slowly, Percy bowed his head forward and back in a rocking motion. 'I will try. I will look for opportunities. But he is more heavily protected than ever now. He has his blackamoor, Diego, and an agent of Walsingham constantly at his side. I can see no way of approaching him to do the deed.'

'Find one.' Herrick's grip tightened, then, of a sudden, broke loose as if his hand had been bitten by a snake. His hand flew back theatrically and hung for a few moments in the air.

Percy sighed. 'If there is a way, I will. I want this as much – more – than you, Herrick. My family and my life depend on it.'

Herrick sneered. 'I despise your cowardice. You and those like you – Southwell or Cotton – say the words but do not accomplish the deeds. Do you think God will thank you for your craven dealings on the Day of Judgement?'

'I am not a cleric, Mr Herrick. I have no wish to take Holy Orders, so do not berate me. Martyrdom is your business, sir, not mine. And I scorn your airs. I noted how you looked at that serving wench and I would wager ten marks to your one that you would unfrock her and fuck her without hesitation. Would you have me cheapen a price on your behalf?'

Herrick swept away his platter. It clattered across the table and on to the floor. 'So, you believe we have missed our chance and you are giving up. Well, I tell you, Percy, I will not. If Drake is going to Plymouth, then so must I. But if you have any thought for your mortal flesh and immortal soul, I suggest you make sure that my journey is in vain. If Drake survives to wreak havoc on the King of Spain's war fleet, I will kill you myself, first plucking off your stones, then forcing them down your throat. And that will be just a beginning. After that, I promise you, things will become most unpleasant.'

Shakespeare gathered together a force of twenty pursuivants and rode for Horsley Down.

It was dark when they arrived a quarter of a mile from the house. He reined in his grey mare and raised his hand to halt, then signalled them all to dismount. The men tethered their horses within a clump of trees. There was no moon, but they had their pitch torches. He ordered all but two snuffed.

He had Newall, sneering as ever. It had been unavoidable: Shakespeare did not have his own squadron and Walsingham had insisted he go. At a short meeting not two hours since in Seething Lane, he had commissioned the raid and had also informed Shakespeare of Drake's next move. 'Soon he will be safe at sea. Then the Spaniard shall feel the heat of his fire. But keep him alive until then, John. Keep him alive until his fleet is afloat.'

Shakespeare looked with cold eyes at Newall. He would take no insubordination from him, even though Newall was chief pursuivant. 'Mr Newall, you will take four men to the back of the house. And be wary: he is a hired killer and will not hesitate to attack with whatever is to hand. And he is wounded. Like an injured animal, he may feel he has nothing to lose in attempting to fight his way out.'

Newall grunted. He knew he must to take orders from this

squeamish, book-hugging official, however much he despised him. If it were up to him, he would simply torch the house and all in it; save the cost of a trial and an execution.

Shakespeare waited sixty seconds while Newall and his men moved through thickets to the back of the house. There were no lights from inside. He ordered the other group to the front door with the battering tree, and when they were positioned, he brought down his sword as the signal. With a mighty swing, they wielded the heavy oak log at the door, splintering it on impact. The front men charged in shouting, while those at the rear lit their torches and moved forward to block all exits through windows or roof lights. Shakespeare followed the vanguard, ducking into the low-ceilinged hall. It had the feel of a neglected old farmhouse with dirt floors and ragged walls where the lime plaster had broken away to reveal the wattles.

'Upstairs. Do not give him time to hide!'

The men at the front raced up the rickety steps, shouting and banging as they went. Within seconds they had scoured every room. The house was empty.

'Keep moving,' Shakespeare told the sergeant. 'Spread out. Take the ground-floor rooms first. Search every cupboard, every cranny, break open wainscoting, turn over beds. If he is here, find him.'

Within three hours it became clear they would not find Herrick. But in the main bedchamber they discovered a blood-stained rag, which, it seemed to Shakespeare, Herrick had probably used to staunch the wound from Boltfoot's shot. More importantly, he spotted a small piece of rolled linen, discarded casually beneath the bed. He picked it up and unfurled it. There, poorly painted but easily recognisable, was a portrait of Sir Francis Drake, one of many such pictures sold throughout England and the rest of Europe since the Vice-Admiral's daring circumnavigation of the globe. 'So Herrick has been here,' he said, under his breath, 'and we have missed him. God in heaven, we have missed him.'

Shakespeare left late in the evening, cursing his ill-fortune and leaving a guard of three men.

Across the road, in the shadows, Herrick watched the activity for a short while. He had arrived at the house barely a minute after the onset of the raid. Shakespeare could not have known how close he had come to trapping his quarry.

Quietly, Herrick slipped away down the alleys to Southwark. He would find an inn tonight, then take horse on the morrow. The question that haunted him, though, was how the pursuivants had found the house. Had the locals become suspicious – or had someone informed on him? His only hope now was to follow Drake before he gathered his fleet and set sail from Plymouth. It was time to kill . . . and time was running out.

Starling Day was enjoying life. She had everything she needed: treasure, a beautiful new house and business in the heart of Southwark, the best food money could buy and clothes that would not have looked out of place on a court lady. But behind the happiness, there was a worry – one shared by Parsimony Field: they had heard from a girl they had brought from the Bel Savage that Richard Topcliffe was looking for them and they feared it was only a matter of time before he found them.

They had changed their names. Starling was now known as Little Bird and Parsimony was Queenie. Their establishment was called Queens and it had one of the best positions of all the Southwark stews. Prices were high, as befitted a bawdy-house with good-looking young girls and comfortable rooms, but it was well frequented. Men of money from across the river came there, as did foreigners whose wives were left far away in France and beyond, ships' officers and seamen happy to spend a year's wages and plunder on a night or two of bliss.

Parsimony was in her element. She could indulge her passion for the arts of love with whoever she pleased. Starling, meanwhile, decided she had had enough of such things and had retired from the game, restricting her role to greeting the gentlemen visitors.

They even had their own strong-arm guard, Jack Butler, to look after them, and cooks to provide sweetmeats and drink for the guests. But they were flying too high. Someone would recognise them and go to Topcliffe.

'Perhaps we should go to Bristol or Norwich,' Starling said. They had talked about it, but kept putting off a decision. And the longer they did so, the more business boomed and the more settled they became.

Tonight Starling was dealing cards for some gentlemen. The house, as always, was winning handsomely, but none of the men seemed to care.

'I'll be in The Clink before you're done with me, Little Bird. Up to my ears in debt!' said the eldest son of a northern bishop, who seemed intent on disposing of his inheritance before he had inherited it. He laughed.

'Never mind, Eddie. I'll tell one of my wenches to bring you broth and a kindly hand every now and then.'

'The devil with it! Deal on, Little Bird, deal on.'

Parsimony was upstairs and unhappy. She liked swiving as much as the next girl – rather more than the next girl, if truth be told – but she didn't like this.

She stood with her back to the wall, dressed only in a light kirtle, lash in her right hand, and gazed down at the man on the bed. He was a strange one. He'd come into Queens pissing money, like a conduit of gold, then demanded a room and a girl for the night. He had taken one look at Parsimony and said, 'You will do, mistress. I like the look of you.' Parsimony was in the mood and the man presentable, so she had readily agreed. But then he had wanted her to scourge him. And do it properly so it hurt. Funny thing was, he was already injured: a nasty oozing wound on his side. She had offered to dress it for him but he just wanted his lashing. So here they were.

'Do it, mistress, do it.'

'Look, I don't mind a few light strokes, but I'm not doing it any harder.'

'How much do you want?'

'I don't need your money, sir. I run a respectable business here and I don't want no dead bodies on my hands.'

'Then get another girl who will do it.'

Parsimony shrugged her shoulders. This was a difficult one. 'Wait here, sweeting.'

She left him on the bed and traipsed downstairs. Starling would know what to do. In some ways she was the cleverer of the two.

Parsimony touched her arm at the card table. 'A word if I may, Little Bird.'

They went off to a private room. 'Got a cove upstairs wants me to beat him raw, like a Bridewell penitent. He's got good money. Shame to turn him away.'

'Then give him what he wants.'

'I don't like to, Starling.'

'Well, I'll happily thrash any man. All I'd have to do is close my eyes and think of my husband.'

'Would you do this one for me?'

'Of course. You take over dealing. And the bishop's son, let him win a little. It's bad for business to flay customers into the gutter.'

Chapter 34

EVERY MUSCLE WAS taut like a drawn-back longbow string. How close had he come to Herrick? He had been there. He had definitely been at the house by Horsley Down – and recently. Now he was gone, lost in the sea of people of all shades that inhabited this infernal town.

Shakespeare sipped his wine by the fire. On the morrow, he would ride to Windsor and find Ptolomeus. But he lacked enthusiasm for the task. What purpose could such an outing serve? How could an old, decrepit priest help him find the murderer of Lady Blanche Howard or prevent the murder of Sir Francis Drake?

It was good that Drake would soon be travelling to Plymouth by sea. Reason told Shakespeare that he would soon be out of harm's way, yet anxiety gnawed in the pit of his stomach. Something was terribly wrong. For the first time, Shakespeare began to fear he was going to lose this battle.

And then it struck him. He knew, for certain, the identity of the man sent to kill Drake, though he did not know his present name, but the killer had not worked alone in Delft: why should he be working alone now? Who was the other man in the conspiracy? Cold foreboding descended. He recalled the story of Balthasar Gerard, the man who had fired the shots that killed William the Silent. Gerard had spent weeks, months even, inveigling himself into a position of trust inside the Prince's household. Was Herrick's accomplice doing the same in England? Dread crept through his soul like tentacles of ice: '. . . a man called Death is on his way . . .'

'You are lost in thought, John.'

Catherine was gazing at him with concern in her eyes. Like him, she held a goblet of claret. She was sitting on the settle close to his wooden chair. The children were in bed, asleep, as was Jane. Without thinking, he reached out and touched her dark hair.

She had stayed awake until he returned from the Horsley Down raid and had welcomed him in. There had been something natural about the way she opened the door, almost as if she were more to him than a house guest under his protection. A disturbing vision of Mother Davis and her whore, Isabella Clermont, came to mind; the older woman's head was half flesh, half bone, and she was urging on Isabella, naked astride him and riding him like a horse of the apocalypse. He put the vision aside. He would have naught to do with hexes and spells. Such things were not for Christians of any denomination.

Catherine did not shy away from his touch. Instead her hand went to his and held it to her face, warmed by the fire. His fingers curled through hers and tangled in her hair. Without premeditation, they moved towards each other and kissed. Shakespeare sank on to the settle beside her. His right hand caressed her hair and face, the left moved down the slender length of her body and she did not resist, though she had never been touched like that before.

Their kisses became urgent. Of a sudden he had her in his arms, pulling her down on the settle, devouring her. She pushed him away. 'We can't stay here,' she said. 'The children might wake. Jane might come down.'

'Will you come to my room?'

She smiled and kissed his lips quickly. 'I will.'

As they stood, he held her in his arms again and kissed her with ferocity, at once hard and gentle. For a minute they stood, fused together, scarce able to consider the possibility of not touching for a few seconds.

They broke apart and went silently to their rooms. Shakespeare lit candles and stood beside the dresser in his shirt and breeches, not knowing what to do. Would she come to him? Or was he to be left like a dying man offered water only to have it snatched away?

The door opened and she stood before him, her skin golden in the candlelight, her hair as lustrous as fine black satin. He went to her and, with unpractised fingers, tried to negotiate the ties and stays that held her clothes in place. She laughed and helped him until her underskirts fell away and she stood before him, naked and unashamed.

His hunger for her was almost unbearable. She moved towards him, to help him disrobe. The closeness of her bare skin brought him to the hardness of oak. She whispered in his ear, 'You seem quite lost for words, sir.'

He kissed her, long and deep, then ripped the clothes from his body and pulled her to the bed, entering her in a hurry born of longing. She cried out at the sharp pain of her torn maidenhead and he froze. 'Don't stop,' she murmured. 'Please, don't stop.'

The joints of the old wooden bed creaked with their movements. He had not used the bed for this purpose before. She kissed the palm of his hand. He kissed the bud of her breast. They kissed each other's mouth with lips and tongues. He moved between her legs as in his dreams. She felt filled as never before. The light of candles flickered their shadows on the ceiling and walls of his plain room. The only sounds were of wood on wood and their breathing.

He arched away from her so that he could see her. Her eyes were closed, her long lashes sweeping like crescent moons beneath. His hands reached down to the inside of her thighs, the tender flesh that draws men in. He caressed and traced patterns across the soft, dark down and up to her belly, holding her pinioned with the whole palm of his hand, pushing himself in, withdrawing, pushing in.

She felt no guilt, just abandonment to her senses. If this made her a sinner she would face up to it at another time. Not now. Now she was lost in the moment and she would reach that ecstasy of which she had heard from friends when she was a girl and which she had practised on herself in the long nights alone.

He became more urgent. She pushed up immodestly to meet the quickening pulse of his movements. They were so lost in each other now, so frantic in their passion that pleasure and pain dissolved into one entity. She would part her legs wider and wider still, until they engulfed him and took him into her the more. He would go deeper into her, deeper.

She cried out and he gasped and shuddered and collapsed upon her breasts.

They lay like this, not wishing to move, saying nothing, nowhere near sleep until, soon, their desire awoke again simultaneously and they began once more. This time it was slower, more gentle, and instinctively they found new positions on the small bed. In the candlelight he spotted blood on the white sheets and wondered vaguely what Jane would make of it when she took the sheets for laundering. She would know, of course. How could she not? But he did not care. Not now, anyway.

Starling Day and Parsimony Field talked a long while about the man upstairs. When Starling first saw him on the bed she did not recognise him. He was lying face down, waiting for her, for anyone, to flagellate him as he required. So she beat him, harder and harder, imagining all the time that he was her husband, Edward, getting what he deserved for all the pain he had administered to her. When she had finished, when he called, 'Enough!' he turned painfully on the bed, sitting on the edge. Even then she could see only the back of his head.

Slowly he faced her and bowed his head graciously. Starling fell back two steps, shocked. It was a face carved into her memory like an epitaph on stone, the face of the man who had plunged a thin poniard dagger into the eyes of Gilbert Cogg, straight through into his brain. The sound of his scream and the sight of the spurting gore haunted her still.

'I must have gone red as a smacked arse when I saw who it was, Parsey. But, of course, he had no idea why. He never knew that anyone saw him doing for Cogg.'

'So what are we going to do?'

'Nothing. I didn't let on that I recognised him and he gave me two pounds in gold, like money meant nothing to him. I say we let him sleep, feed him and send him on his way as if nothing has happened.'

'We must be able to get something out of this. I liked Cogg. He looked after me.'

'But there's Topcliffe. He's after us. Cogg and him were close and he reckons we did for him and took the treasure. Don't stir up a hornet's nest, Parsey.'

Parsimony finished her brandy and spread rich butter on two-day-old bread. She was hungry. It was late at night, but the night would go on longer yet. Cogg deserved justice. But, more to the point, this knowledge might help them protect themselves against Topcliffe. They would have to act fast, though: the killer would be gone within a few hours. It was an opportunity not to be missed. 'I've an idea, Little Bird,' she said, her mouth full. 'An old friend of mine called Harry Slide works for

Walsingham sometimes. Harry will know what to do, how to make the best of it. I'll send for him.'

'I don't know, Parsey.'

'I'll send for him now. It's got to be tonight because our man says he leaves in the morning. I know where Harry lodges. I'll send Jack Butler for him on the mare. Trust me, Little Bird. Harry'll know what to do.'

Shakespeare was asleep when Catherine left his room before dawn and returned silently to the chamber she shared with the children. Before she left, she kissed his face.

When they were sated from love-making they had talked. Shakespeare's childhood in Warwickshire, blue skies and dreams, friends and relatives with their peculiarities and eccentricities, Catherine's strange accent, unlike any he had heard before. He teased her gently, mimicking her short vowels, and she jabbed him with her elbow, a little harder than she had intended. He retaliated by tickling her, which made her squirm and ended in them making love yet again, though they scarcely had energy left for it.

Catherine Marvell told him she had come to London from Yorkshire, where her father James was a schoolteacher. 'Thomas Woode's eldest sister, Agnes, was married to a York squire. She died in November last. Her husband knew my family because Father taught her three sons at the grammar school. When Mr Woode's wife died of consumption, Agnes asked me whether I might consider going to London to become governess to Andrew and Grace. She knew me to be a Roman Catholic. And so, aged eighteen, I made the long journey south by palfrey, accompanied by one of Agnes's retainers. In truth it was a welcome relief to me. I had grown to hate the smallness of my home town. London offered a wide world.'

'And how does it seem now?'

She laughed. 'It has its good points, sir.' She recalled her first meeting with Thomas Woode and the children. It had been a household of impenetrable gloom. Grace was being cared for by a wet-nurse. 'She smiled ingratiatingly whenever the master was about but I did not trust her. One day I caught her beating the little girl, even though she was an infant. When I told Mr Woode about it, she was dismissed. But the boy was also unhappy and sat in a corner the day long, pining for his mother. Mr Woode himself was lost in melancholy and would spend days alone in his study, planning the building of this house. His plans seemed always to remain as ink drawings on parchment. I encouraged him to start building. It is a wondrous modern construction, John, of finest timbers and brickwork. By day there are views across the steelyard and the river to the bridge.'

She was silent a while, thinking of Mr Woode and the torments he was enduring. She did not tell Shakespeare more; not her feelings for Thomas Woode which had grown fonder day by day while she had lived with him, for she had no wish to engender jealousy in his breast. Neither did she mention the decision to allow Jesuit priests to lodge in their home.

Such things had no place in this bed. Not once did they talk of Woode's plight, the threat from Topcliffe, the death of Lady Blanche, the looming Spanish invasion or the severing of Mary Stuart's head. They took care to avoid all the subjects that divided them and concentrated on what they shared.

It was well after dawn when Shakespeare woke. He was alone and panicked when he found she was not on the pillow beside him. But he could still smell her earthy scent on the sheets and see the tell-tale sign of her lost virginity.

Jane was already downstairs making breakfast and the children were running around, but there was no sign of Catherine. If Jane suspected anything of the night's events she did not signify it by look or word. But she had news. 'Harry Slide called at about four of the clock. He woke me with his hammering on the door and was so insistent that I had to go down and see who it was.'

'What did he want?'

'To leave a message for you. Said he had found Starling and Parsimony. Gave an address in Southwark. He was going there and might have important news for you later.'

Chapter 35

Shakespeare did not wait for breakfast. He threw his bear cloak over his shoulders and rode for Southwark. The wind was howling off the river, billowing his cloak like demonic wings. He reined in his mare beneath a sign that swung vigorously in the gale tunnelling through the narrow street. It was fresh-painted in black and white, with a picture of two women in coronets and the word 'Queens'. A bawdy-house, and a pleasantly appointed one at that. He dismounted and knocked at the great door. Almost immediately it was opened by a man of forty or so years who towered over Shakespeare by at least six inches. He looked discontented, and a little intimidating too.

Shakespeare came straight to the point. 'I am here on Queen's business. Where is your master?'

'I have no master.'

'Then this is your stew? Who are you?'

'I am Jack Butler, sir. This house is not mine. I have no master but for a while, anyway, I have two mistresses.'

'Take me to them.'

Parsimony and Starling had not slept. They had been chasing round the house gathering their things into any bags or boxes they could find. The treasure had mostly gone, sold cheaply to pay off the lease on the stew and its furnishings. Now, as Shakespeare entered, they were in the parlour, arguing feverishly. They had drunk too much and were befuddled. What seemed clear to them, though, was that they must say nothing and leave for one of the great cities, such as Bristol or Norwich, with the remnants of their treasure.

Butler threw open the door and stood back to let Shakespeare through, then followed him in.

Parsimony looked with venom at Shakespeare, then at Butler. 'Who's this, Jack? We don't want any visitors. Get rid of him.'

Butler raised an eyebrow insolently. 'He can speak for himself.'

'You'll be out of a job if you don't watch your tongue, Jack Butler.'

'You can stuff your job up your pox-rotten cunnies. I don't want no more of you. I heard you and your plans. Bristol! Norwich! Filthy, cautelous whores. You are drawn foxes and will hang for it.'

Shakespeare stepped forward. The women were backing away. 'I am John Shakespeare, here on behalf of Sir Francis Walsingham. Queen's business.'

'We've nothing to say to you,' Parsimony spat.

'Ask them what happened upstairs, Mr Shakespeare,' said Butler. 'That's why they got plans to fetch off from Southwark.'

Shakespeare had no idea what he was talking about. The two women must be Starling Day and Parsimony Field, but where was Harry? 'You will go nowhere. One of my men, Harry Slide, was here. Where is he now?'

Parsimony and Starling looked at each other with something akin to panic. They rose at the same time and tried to get to the door but, awash with strong drink, they stumbled. Shakespeare and Butler restrained them easily.

'I was sent to bring Mr Slide here, sir,' Butler said, 'and these two purveyors of the French pox have stabbed him through the gulf, by the look of him, poor sod. Blood all over the place. I was going for the constable when you arrived. Fine gentleman he was, sir.'

'Harry – dead?' Shakespeare said. 'Harry Slide?'

'We didn't kill him!' Parsimony shouted. 'He was a friend. That's why I called him here. My fine-dressed Harry. The flagellant done for him, not us.'

'What flagellant?'

'The one murdered Gilbert Cogg. Now he's knifed Harry in the neck and run.'

'Where is Harry? Take me to him.'

Butler raised his chin towards the stairs. 'He's up in one of the whores' chambers. I'll show you.' He pushed Parsimony and Starling towards the staircase, Shakespeare following.

The scene in the bedroom was horrible to behold. Shakespeare went down on one knee beside Slide's body. It was obvious he was dead, an hour or two maybe: his body was cold.

A gash, no wider than an inch, had opened up the right side of his throat. Blood had poured out in a flood, spraying across a wide area of the floor at the foot of the bed. Shakespeare touched Slide's face and pulled back from the coolness of his skin. His eyes were wide in horror, his beautiful clothes splattered.

Shakespeare was aghast. How had poor Harry come to this? He put his hands together to pray for Slide's soul, but it did nothing to ease the pain and anger. He turned furiously to the women. 'Tell me again who did this to him.'

Parsimony looked at Starling. 'We should tell him every-thing.'

Starling nodded and Parsimony turned to Shakespeare. 'But you must protect us from Topcliffe. He won't listen to reason and we'll be gibbeted at Tyburn tree before he gives us a hearing.'

'I promise nothing, but if you do not tell me the truth it will be the worse for you. In the meantime, you,' he nodded to Butler, 'consider yourself my deputy. Go now and fetch the constable, then arrange for Mr Slide's body to be consigned to the coroner.' He turned back to the women. 'Who else is in this house?'

'Whores,' said Butler. 'They'll be swiving or sleeping.'

'They're good girls,' Starling put in. 'They don't know anything about this.'

'Very well. You tell me everything.'

They went downstairs, away from the body. Jack Butler went to fetch the constable, while Starling told Shakespeare her story.

'The killer. Tell me about the killer,' Shakespeare was insistent.

She described Herrick in great detail. She told Shakespeare that he had taken a bag with an implement from Cogg, after bundling his body into the barrel. She told, too, of the nature of his wound – as well as the new weals he had received from her beating. 'His back was red with scars. I reckon he must be one of them religious madpikes. His hair was short and he didn't have a beard – I think he couldn't grow one. No sign of stubble. And he was scornful,' she went on. 'He paid good money, but he looked at me like I was dog turd. He was tall and well muscled, too. Didn't laugh or smile. Didn't say nothing good, but then again, he didn't say nothing bad neither.'

'Did he have any religious symbols? Crosses, beads, that kind of thing?'

'If he did, I didn't see them.'

'And what did he talk about?'

Starling was getting bored. She was also sobering. 'This and that. He asked me questions.'

'Like what?'

'Like where I came from. I told him Strelley, a pit village full of men like my husband. He asked me if I knew Devonshire and Plymouth. Now, why would I know fucking Plymouth?'

'Might he have been going there?'

'Well, what do you think? You're the cunning man here. He kept asking about post horses and suchlike.'

'And what did you tell him?'

'I don't know nothing about post horses. Why should I? I've never been on a nag in my life. I walked to London.'

So Herrick was making for Plymouth. And sooner rather than later. But would he get there by horse or try Drake's own route, by horse to Dover and take ship from there? The Dover route might be quicker but would depend on the winds. If the weather was inclement, he might be holed up in Dover for days. Shakespeare reckoned he would have taken the more certain overland route. Whichever way he went, the highways were likely to be bogs at this time of year, but Shakespeare decided to follow him, riding fast across country. He had to leave immediately; there was no time to go home. Herrick had probably had two or three hours' start on him, but with good fortune, he might be caught.

Jack Butler appeared with the constable, a lumbering oaf with the dead eyes of a cod.

'I want this place closed,' Shakespeare said. 'The two women will be held while I decide what to do with them. Keep them in The Clink, but tell no one they are there. No one. You will answer to Mr Secretary Walsingham himself and suffer for it if a single word of this gets out. And when you remove Mr Slide's body to the coroner, you will treat it with honour. Do you understand? You, Mr Butler, find me a quill, ink and some paper for I must write urgent messages that you will deliver in person. The first to Mr Secretary at his home in Seething Lane, the other to my own house in the same street. There is to be no delay.'

Chapter 36

D RAKE WAS IN ebullient mood as his small party took the barge from Greenwich Palace to Gravesend early in the morning. The Queen had wished him God speed during a short private meeting in the presence chamber. Now, with a salty cry as if he were weighing anchor for the Indies, he waved his hat and urged the rowers forward, like a knight spurring his destrier at the tilt.

At Gravesend they took horse and settled into a goodly trot on the well-trodden road that would take them south and east through Kent towards the Channel port of Dover. Diego took the lead on his bay, followed by a band comprising Drake, his wife Elizabeth – side-saddle on a beautiful grey palfrey – her maidservant May Willow, Captain Harper Stanley, his moustaches bristling, two servants of Drake and the deputy lieutenant of Devon, Sir William Courtenay, returning home to Powderham Castle. The group was accompanied by two of Drake's most trusted mariners, men known to be handy with wheel-lock and sword. The rearguard was taken by Boltfoot Cooper, his caliver primed and his hand ever close to the hilt of his cutlass.

Drake settled in the middle of the group, between his wife on the right and Courtenay, whom he knew to be a Roman Catholic, on his left. 'Well, sir,' Drake said, 'have you confessed today your manifold sins?'

Courtenay laughed wearily. He was used to jibes at the expense of his religion. 'I am afraid, Sir Francis, they are too many for the priest to reckon with at one sitting. I have a seven-week rotation: lust one week, gluttony the next, then greed, sloth, wrath, envy and pride in that order.'

'And which is it this week? Lust?'

'Of course, Sir Francis. I could not possibly travel without a goodly helping of lust to boost my spirits.' Courtenay was a dark-haired man in his mid-thirties, of exceptional good looks, fit and strong. While he made mockery of his sins, he had a reputation as one of the court's most ardent ladies' men. He was said to have got two serving girls with child before he was fourteen and had scattered several other bastards around Devon since then.

'Hah! What do you make of it, my lady? Will Sir William go to heaven or hell?'

Elizabeth looked at Courtenay and smiled at him, sweet and demure, her face glowing beneath a fashionable French hood of black velvet that controlled her hair in the mighty wind that assailed them. 'Possibly hell, and most certainly Devon. I would not hazard gold on heaven, though.'

'By God's faith, Sir William, I shall have to look out for my wife in your company. I fear she does hold a little piece of her heart for you.'

'Indeed, Sir Francis. But how will you keep me from her when you are at sea? And tell me, a land-shanks, how you sailors care for your requirements in the middle of the ocean, sans ladies, sans whores, sans pleasure itself.'

Drake scowled. He glanced at his wife irritably, then at Courtenay. 'There are other pleasures, sir, putting Catholics to the sword foremost among them. And oft they deserve it for their base cruelty. Your list of sins, Sir William, where does cruelty fit into it? Or does your church not require you to confess it? Perhaps it is considered a virtue by the apostolic anti-Christ. For certain, you do belong to the cruellest religion in the world.'

The banter, half jest, half stern intent, continued along the miles into Kent. At times Drake fell back to talk with Captain Stanley about provisioning and naval strategy; then he watched in silence as his wife engaged Courtenay in conversation.

Boltfoot's eyes were constantly moving, watching Drake one second, scouring the countryside for dangers the next. This road was known for its banditry, though he could not imagine anyone would dare to attack a group so well armed. Hunger, however, made men resort to desperate things.

They had taken an early meal at Gravesend and did not stop again until they came to a halt soon before six of the clock at a post inn close to Rochester. Boltfoot stayed with Sir Francis and Lady Drake while the servants stabled the horses. Captain Stanley and Diego ordered supper and wine for all in a private room.

They ate well and Drake regaled the company with tales of his adventures when he had lived as a child within two or three miles of this inn. The family had come here from Devon, he said, because his father, a Protestant preacher, had been persecuted during the burnings of Queen Mary's reign. The Drakes had ended up living poverty-stricken in a rotting hulk stranded on a Medway mudbank. 'I foraged for oysters and blackberries to stay alive. And look at me now, as rich as a Mussulman potentate, with the world and its seas at my feet! And all thanks to gold supplied by that same King Philip who shared the bed of murdering Mary.'

Boltfoot Cooper snorted. He didn't believe a word of the story of religious persecution of Drake's father any more than had anyone else in their home town of Tavistock. The word there was that Drake's father, Edmund, had left in haste having been convicted of horse theft, assault and robbery on the highway.

'Something wrong with your nose, Mr Cooper? Will someone lend him a kerchief?' Drake clapped his hands, then smacked them with a thud on the table. 'And now, let us drink our fill that God give health and long life to our sovereign majesty Elizabeth. Long live the Queen!'

They ate and drank too much as travellers will. As the serving wenches cleared away the last of the dishes and brought more flagons of wine, Drake picked up a book that was on the table at his side. 'Charge your cups, for I shall read to you, as I have read to my officers and gentlemen aboard ship on many a long night in the great Pacific Ocean, which is the worst-named sea that ever mariner sailed. There was nothing pacific or tranquil about her or her depths when we did enter her. We were wracked by tempests for weeks without end. But all waters are stormy and I would have it no other way. Soon we shall be at sea again and I shall have the salt spray in my face and beneath my feet six hundred tons of English oak and blazing cannon.'

He tapped the book and continued: 'It seems apt, then, that I should read *The Shipman's Tale* of Geoffrey Chaucer, for we do go the pilgrims' way through Canterbury, then to the sea. And in the instance that any of you do not understand, I shall first explain it to you, for the well-loved Mr Chaucer did not write English as now we know it. I commend this tale to my good lady wife Elizabeth, for her pleasure and nothing more, for I know her to be nothing in the way of the faithless goodwife of Mr Chaucer's tale. And I trust that none here present shall think her otherwise than a chaste companion to me.'

Drake raised his golden-pointed chin to his wife.

She smiled at him guilelessly. 'Why, sir, I cannot think you need to defend me so. For certain, none here could think me other than a loyal and loving bride.'

'Quite so, by God's faith. But perhaps Sir William Courtenay might see himself in this sorry tale. It is the story of an adulterous wife and a cunning monk who pretends friendship of her husband – then beds his lady. Do you see anyone you know in there, Sir William?'

Boltfoot Cooper was not listening. His eyes were fastened on the face of Sir William Courtenay, which was a mask of rage.

'But enough!' Drake continued. 'It is but a story. I cannot believe any man would betray another like that, for they would surely be gelded and run through the heart for such foul dealing. That is nothing less than any husband would do, would you not agree, Sir William? You are a married man, I believe.'

Courtenay hesitated. His eyes strayed to Elizabeth, then back to Drake. 'You must know it, Sir Francis.' There was not an ounce of humour in his voice.

'You would not allow any man to make a cuckold of you, would you, sir?'

Suddenly Courtenay rose from the table, his sword already half drawn. 'Of what do you accuse me?' He lunged forward, scattering goblets and flagons, knocking the large table to one side. 'You insult my religion, sir, and now you insult me.'

The room was in uproar. The armed mariners leapt forward but were slow off the mark. Boltfoot, from one side, and Diego, from the other, were upon Courtenay in an instant. Boltfoot had his cutlass at Courtenay's throat. Diego had the point of his dagger beneath his ribcage, ready to thrust upwards into his heart. Courtenay looked wildly around those present.

'Will no one take my part? I have suffered calumny here.' He looked again at Elizabeth Drake. 'Madam, will you not call your husband to order? He does accuse us of some liaison of which I know nothing.'

Elizabeth laughed lightly. 'Oh, Sir William, it is just his way. Pay him no heed. He likes to make merry with men's sensibilities. It helps to pass the long days and nights at sea when the breeze has dropped and the sails will not billow.'

Diego and Boltfoot took Courtenay by the arms and pushed him back into his chair.

'More drink for Sir William Courtenay!' Drake roared. He had not retreated an inch in the face of the onslaught and his broad chest was puffed up like a fighting cock's. 'God's faith, make the man mellow before he slaughters us all.' He reached into his doublet pocket and took out a piece of blue velvet. 'Madam,' he said, presenting it to his wife with a flourish. 'A necklace of gold, pearl and ruby, each gem harvested from the great continents and oceans of the world. Do me the honour of accepting this humble offering as a mark of my respect for your fidelity and loving goodness.'

Elizabeth put her hand to her mouth in mock-surprise, as if she had not already received a hundred such trinkets from her besotted husband.

'Well that's one way to keep her from going off with any carnal monk,' Diego muttered into Boltfoot's ear.

Boltfoot smiled grimly. There was something that interested him rather more: he had noted which men among the assembled company had leapt to the defence of Drake and which had not.

From the outset Shakespeare's ride west was dogged by ill-chance. Riding along a highway rutted with holes that a man could fall into, with mud deep enough to drown in, his grey mare went lame ten miles into the county of Surrey. He left her with a peasant, promising him sixpence if he took good care of her, then walked on towards the nearest village to find another mount. He had come in the clothes he wore that morning: bearskin cloak, doublet, breeches, hose and a fur hat. He had no baggage or panniers, just a purse with more than enough coin for the journey. Trudging alone, he knew he was vulnerable to attack by highway thieves. Even spattered with mud, his clothes were clearly of a fine cut. With so much hunger in the land, bands of vagabonds and robbers roamed everywhere.

The walk to the village took two hours. His boots became clogged and the damp soaked through to his skin. The wind howled around him and every now and then he was forced to clamber over fallen trees across the road. By the time he arrived at a ford, just to the east of the village, he was hungry, weary, short-tempered and aware that he was losing time in the pursuit of his quarry.

The ferry was little more than a sturdy raft of aged oak, pulled over the river with thick hemp cables attached to deeply embedded posts on both sides. It had room for a heavy dray, half a dozen farm horses and some cattle. Now there were just Shakespeare and the ferryman, who gave him some of his mutton stew. As they made the short crossing, Shakespeare ate with relish. He had had nothing all day. When he had finished he thanked the man and asked whether any single horsemen had crossed the river in the past few hours.

'Indeed, sir. A rider came here five hours since. He rode tall in the saddle and I noted he was unbearded. He did not utter above three words to me, though, so I learnt nothing of him. I believe he had a change of horse at my brother Ben's livery, so perchance he said something to him. Ask him, sir.'

'I will. I think you have met the man who would do for Sir Francis Drake. I have not a moment to lose.'

Chapter 37

B Y THE TIME Drake and his band reached Dover, the wind
was easing. The quay was solid with ships come in for shel-
ter from the Channel storms, their masts and rigging a tangle
of sticks that would make a fine bonfire for a Spaniard with a
tinder-box.

If Boltfoot was tired after the long ride, he did not show it.
His eyes were ever vigilant; a seasoned mariner never allowed
fatigue to interfere with his watch. The group came to a halt
on the cobbled quayside. Waves crashed over the shingle beach
below. In the distance, the Channel across to France was white-
flecked. No boats could make the crossing in such turbulence.

Captain Stanley slapped the steaming flank of his mount and
leant towards Drake. 'Shall I find an inn, sir?' he asked, fishing
for a feather bed.

Drake gazed at him as if he was a madman or worse. 'No, by
God! Are you gone soft that you seek a bed in a tavern when
there are ship's cabins and hammocks to be inhabited? Get
yourself aboard ship, sir, and clear the captain's cabin for my
lady. You will arrange garlands and see to it that she is served
dainties on fine dishes. There will be music as we dine tonight.
Viols will suit us well.' He glanced at Sir William Courtenay,
who had ridden twenty yards behind him in a sulk and had
not looked on him except with hatred all day. 'Are you a music

man, Sir William? Or is that, too, a venal sin in your religion? Come, sir, sup with us this evening and you may confess your wickedness to the cardinal bishop afterwards.'

'I would rather starve than sup with you, Drake. I will stay at an inn tonight, as Captain Stanley suggests.'

Drake bristled. 'Aboard my ship, Courtenay, I am king and answerable only to God. If you wish to travel with me, and if you are a gentleman, you will sup with me. Otherwise you may stay here in Dover and await your chances with a tin carrier returning westward to the Stannaries.'

Courtenay was trapped. 'You know I cannot wait. If those are your terms, I must accept them. But I will repay you in kind one day. One day, what is yours will be mine.'

Drake laughed easily. 'If I were buttermilk hued and listened to Papist threats, Sir William, I would never have stirred from my bed.'

Suddenly Courtenay pulled the head of his horse sharp sideways and barged into Drake's mount. 'I am a patriot, sir, loyal to the Crown. My faith does not preclude my love of England and the Queen!' he roared, his face close to Drake's.

Boltfoot and Diego moved instantly alongside, but Drake was laughing. 'So whose side will you be on when the invasion begins, Sir William? Whose side will you be on when the Pope orders you to rise against our Queen? Has he not excommunicated her and declared it no sin – indeed, God's work – to murder her? Whose command will you obey: your Pope's or your sovereign's?'

'Damn you to hell. Now I know why so many mutiny against you or refuse berths upon your ships.'

Richard Topcliffe rinsed his hands in a horse trough at the side of the road. Newall, the chief pursuivant, watched him respectfully. The magistrate Richard Young lolled nonchalantly nearby, his elbow on the wooden post of a picket built to keep the crowds at bay. The large, noisy throng was dispersing to go about their daily tasks, for the dance of death they had come to watch was now at an end. The body of the condemned man hung limp from the St Giles gibbet, swaying and twisting gently in the wind.

'A good morning's work,' Topcliffe said, drying his hands on the butcher's apron as he untied it from about his waist. He never covered his face at executions but he liked to wear an apron to protect himself from the puke, blood and excrement of the condemned. The hangman had had little to do, for Topcliffe had orchestrated the proceedings as a player-manager directs his drama. He harangued the condemned man, demanding he recant his Papist heresy and treachery. When the man who was about to die asked for a priest, Topcliffe called to the crowd, 'Is there a priest among you? Come forward so that I may hang you, too!' And then he laughed and kicked away the ladder from under the condemned man's feet and left him swinging in the air, his legs kicking like a puppet's as the rope choked the life out of him. The crowd roared with laughter and Topcliffe bowed.

'One Popish priest less to concern us,' Topcliffe said now to Young. 'Ugly brute, wasn't he? His pestilent soul burst through into his poxed face. The world is well rid of him.' He grunted with satisfaction. 'There is yet more work, Dick. The monstrous Papists never cease their wormish burrowing into the body of England so we cannot afford to sleep. There is one we must take today, late of Dowgate, now lodged in John Shakespeare's den of corruption in Seething Lane. A young she-devil by the name of Catherine Marvell. She has the face of an angel, but do not be deceived. She is diseased with wickedness and the putrefaction of sin. For certain she is occupied by demons. An incubus has taken residence within her and nightly fills her with the cold slurry of his loins. We must take her, Dick, for fair England's sake.'

'Seething Lane, Richard? Shakespeare's home? A little close to Mr Secretary's for comfort, do you not think?'

Topcliffe called to the hangman, who was about to cut the dead man down. 'Leave him up there a week, Mr Picket. Pin a notice to his front.' He turned back to Young. 'What should it say, Dick? Something to warn them, eh?'

'For treason and aiding foreign enemies?' suggested Young.

'That's it. "For treason and aiding foreign enemies". Now to the she-devil. You are right about Seething Lane, Dick. We cannot go there in force with a squadron of pursuivants. Mr Secretary would be discomfited. We must take her quietly.'

'How will you do that? If she is under Shakespeare's protection, he will raise such an uproar that you will never have her.'

Topcliffe's mouth turned down. He put a hand into his breeches and adjusted himself. 'Shakespeare's gone after a Fleming to try to save Drake. She's there alone with a traitor's spawn. We'll bring her to my Westminster hostelry and the children can do their schooling in Bridewell. I shall show her laid out on my rack to Mr Woode. That will loosen his tongue. And you are the man to bring her in, Dick Young. As London magistrate you have the full force of Her Majesty's law behind you. You've the authority, Dick. You're the man to do it.'

As they spoke, a well-dressed man watched them from the crowd. Without drawing attention to himself, he had tried to get close enough to hear what Topcliffe and Young were saying. He had come to say goodbye to the condemned priest, Piggott, not because he liked or loved him but because he professed the same faith and had done nothing to warrant hanging. Cotton had spoken the last rites, mouthing them so that Piggott could see, and had made the sign of the cross within his cloak. Then the ladder had been kicked away.

Although he had drawn near to the fence that held back the crowd, he still could not hear what Topcliffe and Young were saying. He cursed his luck and melted into the crowd. Yet he was strengthened in his faith by the day's events rather than weakened by them. The execution of a fellow priest made his desire for martyrdom burn brighter in his heart. He knew, with utter certainty, that one day he would be the man on the scaffold.

Shakespeare could go no further. The sun was long vanished over the horizon and a dense winter fog had settled over the bleak landscape of ploughed fields and thick woodland. The road was so poor he was no longer even sure that he was on the highway that led west to Devon.

His spirits rose when he chanced upon an inn, though it did not amount to much. Barely more than a farmer's house with the sign of a white dog swinging outside, it was a low building of thatch and daub. There was, however, a cheery light from within, that of a warm fire and tallow. A bank of sharpened scythes and plough implements leaning against an outhouse door showed that the usual customers were men who worked the fields.

Shakespeare was cold to the marrow of his bones. Cold, hungry and thirsty. His body cried out for a pint of English ale. He dismounted from the strong black mare the ferryman's brother had provided and tethered her to an iron ring set into the wall.

Seven or eight men stopped talking as he entered the low-ceilinged room. He nodded to them and strode to the long bar under their watchful gaze. Shakespeare did not care that the locals stiffened at his entry; it was only to be expected. He might have been filthy, but it was still plain that his clothes were costly, of such stuff as these farmhands would never have seen before. This was not a wayside inn, merely a village tavern.

The heat of the fire was welcoming. It crackled and gave off a delicious aroma of woodsmoke. The landlady was welcoming, too. Shakespeare said he would have some beef and bread, and asked for small beer. He did not want anything stronger because he had to be up early. The landlady drew him a pint of ale from the cask that stood at his side. Shakespeare took it and downed it in a matter of seconds, then let out a gasp of satisfaction.

'Have you travelled far, sir?'

'From London.'

Shakespeare held out his mug for it to be refilled. 'Have you a room for the night, and some stabling and feed for my mount tethered outside?'

'I will ask my son to see to the horse, sir. We do not have a room, sir, but I will prepare a bed for you in the parlour.'

'Thank you. Before you do so, has another traveller passed this way today? A tall, beardless man?'

The landlady swept sawdust from the great oak bar with a countrywoman's stubby, pink-palmed hands. 'I have most certainly seen such a one. He supped here but rode off maybe three hours since. I warned him there would be a thick mist tonight but he said God would look after him for he was about God's work. Do you know him, sir?'

'Indeed, mistress, I do, and I would speak with him.'

'Well, you will not catch up with him tonight. And now, sir, I will fetch your food.'

Shakespeare was exhausted. The ride had been hard and he was saddle-sore and aching in the lower back. Yet he wondered whether he should go on: if Herrick could risk the fog and dark, why not him, too? No, it must be better to rest and refresh himself. Herrick might get lost in the mist. With luck, perchance he might drown in a bog or be killed by roving bands and never heard of again. Whatever happened tonight, this journey could not be made in less than two days in such poor conditions, so there would still be time to catch his quarry. Herrick would have to sleep sooner or later. Better for Shakespeare that *he* sleep now and get an early start.

He ate heartily. The beef was good, sliced thin with a well-seasoned gravy, roasted parsnips, peas and a thick wedge of black bread. When he had finished, he asked for his bed. As he stepped out of the room with the landlady, he was aware that several pairs of eyes were fastened on the back of his head, but he cared not a jot. He was so tired he could have fallen to the ground and slept in the sawdust.

The room was, as the landlady had said, nothing more than the parlour, but a straw mattress and coarse blankets had been laid out for him on the floor. He asked to be woken before first light, and climbed, fully dressed, beneath the blankets. Within a minute or two he was asleep. A sleep so profound that when the latch was lifted half an hour later, he heard not a thing and slept on, dreaming of the one he had left at home.

Chapter 38

DRAKE'S SHIP SAILED with the tide at four in the morning. The wind had abated but was still stiff and would carry them quickly westward along the widening strait.

When dawn came, Boltfoot peered through the small portage outside Drake's cabin in the stern. He had been awake all night, with only the light of a candle and years of wakeful watching to support him. The Sussex shoreline, misty and blue-grey, raced past on the starboard side. A bracing breeze whitened the tops of the coal-grey Channel waves. The great ship lay over sharply and, pushed by the blustering weight of full sail, fair flew along. They would be at Plymouth, he reckoned, in a day or a little more.

He looked down at Diego, asleep on the deck close by. They had braved many adventures together and here they were again, aboard ship, where Boltfoot had vowed never more to set foot. He laughed to himself. The truth was, he was enjoying it. One could never escape the sea, and one could never be free of Sir Francis Drake. Once under his spell, a sailor was the Vice-Admiral's man for ever. And Diego was a good one to share time with. He had a ready laugh at all the vicissitudes the world could throw at him, and there had been many. He had lost so much: his home somewhere in Africa, his family and friends, his freedom. Yet he had adjusted to this extraordinary new life in the manner of one born to it, for he told the stories of his past without a hint of rancour.

Captain Stanley appeared, fully dressed and ready for the day. 'Mr Cooper, get yourself to the galley for some breakfast. I will sit out the rest of your watch here.'

'I will eat when Diego awakes.'

'Come, Mr Cooper, you have been diligent enough. We are safely at sea now. What possible threat could there be to the Vice-Admiral?'

'My orders are clear, sir. I am to guard Sir Francis at all times.'

'As you wish, but Sir Francis will not thank you for your nursery maid care. He will damn you for it and call you a poltroon.'

'He has called me worse many times, Captain. It is like water off the shrouds.'

Stanley nodded briskly. 'Good day, then, Mr Cooper.' He turned on his heel and was gone along a gangway and up the companion ladder to the quarterdeck.

Diego was stirring as the door to Drake's cabin opened an inch or two. Elizabeth poked her face out. She was still in her nightgown. She smiled winningly. 'Boltfoot, Diego, would one of you fetch me some food? The sea air has brought on an appetite. And for my husband, too, for I am sure he will wake soon.'

'Of course, my lady.'

Inside the cabin, Elizabeth returned to her narrow cot. Her husband was in a hammock stretched between the larboard and stern bulwarks. It swung with the graceful rise and pitch of the ship as she hit wave after wave on her easy passage westward. Drake snored like a man at peace with himself. Elizabeth's bed was warm and she curled into it, looking up at him. He was twice her age. He had circled the world yet there was so much he didn't know. In particular, he seemed to know nothing about women, and he had no children, either with her or by his late first wife, Mary. Elizabeth was beginning to doubt that he would ever get her with child. She listened to the aching creak of the English timbers. Sometimes she wondered whether it might be the women at home that kept him so long at sea.

Richard Young, magistrate of London, knocked softly at the door of John Shakespeare's timber-frame dwelling in Seething Lane. He feared that a heavy pummelling would drive those inside into hiding, which he did not want. He could not afford to tear this place apart, as they had done to Lady Tanahill's property. Topcliffe had overstepped the mark on that occasion and angered the Queen. It could not be repeated, and certainly not at the home of one of Walsingham's officers.

It was early evening, just after dusk. The street was quiet and dark. That was as he had planned it. No fuss. Simply pick up the woman with Thomas Woode's children and cart them away. Mr Secretary, in his great mansion a mere thirty yards down the lane, would be none the wiser and neither would anyone else. Until Mr Topcliffe was ready to bring the matter of the woman's treason to court.

Jane answered the door. She was in her nightgown, ready for bed. It had been a long day of worry since she had been woken by Harry Slide early in the morning, followed by the arrival of the message from Mr Shakespeare to Mistress Marvell saying he was riding west and did not know when he would return. Jane looked at Young and his companion in dismay. Everyone in London knew Richard Young. It was said Topcliffe had learnt every manner of wickedness he could from him, then added his own. These men were devilish devices cast from the same dark foundry.

Without awaiting invitation, Young and his assistant pushed past her and strode into the hall of the house. They looked about them. 'Who are you?' Young demanded. 'Are you Catherine Marvell?'

Jane shook her head. She was trembling but could not control it. 'I am Jane Cawston, sir. I am Mr Shakespeare's maidservant.'

'I am Justice Young and I have a warrant. Bring me Catherine Marvell. At once, Mistress Cawston.'

Jane could scarcely think. All she could find to say was, 'I cannot, sir.'

'Cannot? What do you mean you cannot?' Young was raising his voice now. Jane prayed that Catherine would hear it from her room and find some sort of hiding-place.

'She is not here, sir. She was here but she has gone home to York, whence she came and where her family still resides.'

'You lie, mistress.'

'No, sir. Look about you at your will.'

Young glanced at the pursuivant accompanying him. He was short, with a distended belly. The man's face was a mask of bland unpleasantness. Young looked back at Jane. 'What of the children?'

'They are asleep, sir. They have been entrusted to my care.'

'Well, fetch them. They must come with us. They are a danger to the commonwealth and must be kept under close restraint.'

Jane's mouth fell open in horror. She moved directly in front of Young. What fear she had was gone like smoke. She was still trembling, but with rage, not fear. 'They are but four and six years old. They are a danger to no one and you will not take them.'

Young stepped forward and tried to brush her out of the way. 'Stand aside, woman. I will take them. The Lord Treasurer himself, Lord Burghley, does approve of taking Papist spawn for proper education, to save them from the contamination of wicked priests.'

Jane was healthy and strong from hard work and she pushed herself back in front of Young. She raised her own voice now. She had always been able to make herself heard. Now, she knew, she had to make as much disturbance as she could: anything to delay Young and alert Catherine. 'You will have to kill me first. How will that appear when Mr Secretary and the Queen hear of it? Or will you fabricate treason against me, too? Maybe you will even hang, draw and quarter a boy of six years for high treason. Show me your warrant!'

Agitated, the magistrate drew his sword. He was a man in his late forties, much lined by weather and cruelty, but without the raw physical strength that his confederate Topcliffe possessed. He was a spindly man with a stoop. It was easy for him to inflict torment on men – or women – when they were presented to him in chains. This was another matter. He was painfully aware of the need for subtlety in this arrest and he lacked Topcliffe's confidence. This serving wench was making things difficult, if not impossible. He looked again at the pursuivant for some kind of support, but there was none. The man would do as he was told, but would not engender any course of action and might well balk at the thought of carrying off screaming children.

'Mistress Cawston, you will produce the children now or I will return in force and remove not only the children but you as well. I have the power not only of arrest but of arraignment, and you will be consigned to hard labour in Bridewell. I will see to it.'

'Well, sir, take me if you can. But you will not take the children while I draw breath.'

Justice Young rose to his full beanpole height. Jane could see that he was shaking with anger, just as she was. But she knew now that he could not kill her. Not here, not this day. This was political and he was afraid of the consequences of the arrest not proceeding smoothly. He was afraid, perhaps, of Mr Shakespeare or Mr Secretary.

He stood there, quivering with rage. 'Damn you to hell!' he exclaimed. 'I shall see that you suffer for this.'

'And I shall ensure that Mr Secretary, our neighbour, knows what you are about, sir.' Even as she said it, she knew it was an idle threat: she could not possibly call on the Queen's Principal Secretary and lay this tale before him; but Justice Young did not know that.

Young marched to the door, swinging his sword, slashing a tapestry, knocking a vase to the floor. At the doorstep he swivelled his head and stared at Jane with eyes full of menace. Without a word, he buried his sword in its scabbard and went off into the night, his assistant trailing in his wake.

Shakespeare woke in the night, suffused with dread. He felt sure he was not alone. The night was dark and the window was draped. He might as well have been blind. Jumping up from the mattress, he tried to gauge his bearings. Recalling vaguely where the door was, he stumbled towards it and pushed it open. Light trickled into the room from a glimmering wall sconce in the hall beyond.

He looked back into the parlour. Nothing. Just the mattress on which he had been sleeping and some items of furniture, all pushed to one side to make way for him. He shivered and wrapped his arms round his body. Leaving the door open, he went back to the mattress and climbed under the blankets. He unsheathed the poniard at his belt and clutched it by the hilt in his right hand. It gave him a sense of security. On the floor beside the mattress lay his sword belt. Something did not seem right, or was he imagining it?

Lying in the flickering gloom, he could not get back to sleep though his body cried out for it. His thoughts whirled, with visions of Catherine Marvell and Isabella Clermont. Their faces melded into one and the scent of lust hung over him. He could not wait to see Catherine again, take her again into the sheets of his bed, yet neither could he dismiss the events surrounding the Davis witch and her French whore. Why take an eyebrow? What sort of spell might a witch cast with the short, wiry hairs of a man's brow?

He must have slept again, for he woke with the landlady's hand on his shoulder.

'Mr Shakespeare, it will be daybreak soon. Will you take breakfast?'

Shakespeare felt a moment of panic. In his dream he had been at home in Stratford with his mother as she made raspberry tarts, a long way from all this. And then he recalled where he was. The landlady opened the window drapes and the first whisper of daylight etched the glass. He got up and stretched his arms above his head. 'I will take some warm milk, if it please you, mistress. And I would be grateful if you could prepare some bread and cold meats to go with me, so that I can be on my way.'

Within ten minutes, Shakespeare was ready to settle up with the landlady and ride on. Through the windows he could see that it was thick with fog outside. He could not wait for it to lift. Herrick might be well ahead of him by now. He reached for his purse at his belt. It was not there. His hand scrabbled for it. So that was what had disturbed him in the night. An intruder had cut away his purse while he slept. All his coin had been taken. He looked in dismay at the landlady.

She deduced immediately what had happened. 'You have been robbed.'

'All my gold and silver.'

Her brow creased. Seemingly, she was as dismayed as he. 'Are you sure?'

'Unless it came away while I slept. It would be in the blankets.'

They went back into the parlour and searched in vain. 'I am afraid I cannot pay you, mistress,' he said at last. He was quickly seeing the extent of his predicament. Would she demand something in place of money? His cloak or sword, perchance? Would she call the constable? Any delay might be critical.

But her face was scarlet with mortification. 'Sir, do not think of the reckoning. That such a thing should happen under my roof . . .'

'Do you know who might have taken it?'

'Only my son, Jake, and I live here. I would swear on the Holy Bible it was not Jake. He is a fine boy. It must have been one of my customers. Shall I call the constable?'

'I cannot afford to wait. Time is not on my side. But if you will let me go, I will settle with you as soon as I can. This I swear. I will pass this way again and you will be recompensed.'

The landlady smiled and shook her head. 'I will not hear of it, Mr Shakespeare. Take your food and some money – what little I can afford – and God speed you.'

Chapter 39

HARPER STANLEY LAY on his bed, alone in his cabin, in an agony of indecision. Herrick had let him down. If he was to kill Drake he had to do it now, on this ship, before she docked at Plymouth. There might never be another chance, for when the fleet sailed he would be assigned a command of his own, away from Drake's flagship. Here, on this vessel, he could strike while the Vice-Admiral slept. But Boltfoot Cooper and Diego would have to die first. A sword to the heart of the one on watch and a blade to the throat of the one who slept. Inside the cabin, he would cut Drake's throat and then he would put Lady Drake to the dagger. He could not be squeamish about killing a woman, even one as beautiful as her. Seventy thousand ducats beckoned.

But could he bring himself to do it? If he were discovered, it would be the end of everything. If only Herrick had not missed. Mendoza, the Spanish ambassador in Paris, had assured Stanley that Herrick was the best. Well, he had failed.

The night was cold, but Stanley was wet with sweat. His cabin was close to Drake's. That was crucial, for he would be drenched in blood and would be found out unless he could clean himself before the deed was discovered. Neither could he allow his clothes to be bloodied: he would have to go naked to the murder.

He clenched his teeth. He had not come this far to draw back now. His father, his mother, every forsaken member of the Percy family, living and dead, cried out to him for this act of vengeance and restitution. Quickly, he stripped off his clothes. He had a pail of water ready to wash himself after the deed was done. It could be done. It *had* to be done. And there must be a culprit, one of the mariners first on the scene, quickly put to death so that his protestations of innocence should die with him.

It was midnight. On the main decks, the watch scoured the horizon for the lights of other shipping. But here, below, almost all were asleep, many having had their fill of brandy. He had his play worked out.

Naked, his body hunched forward and hairy like an ape's, he stepped into the companionway. Ahead, he saw the black, familiar face of Diego, lit by candles outside the door to the great cabin where Drake and his wife slept. Diego was awake, staring straight at him. That was good: it meant Boltfoot was asleep. Stanley smiled at him and, with his left hand, patted his ample belly and scratched his stones, like any man stepping from his chamber at dead of night. He mouthed, 'Piss,' to Diego and strode towards him, his sword and dagger held close to the back of his thigh in his right hand, just out of sight.

Diego was squatting on his haunches with his back to the cabin door. He rose to his feet with a wide smile as Stanley approached. 'Captain Stanley,' he said, in a low voice.

Stanley was just three steps from his prey. His hand tightened round the hilts of sword and dagger. 'How goes the night, Diego? I needed a piss and had no pot.'

Diego laughed. As he did so, Stanley pulled back his right elbow. The blades glinted in the candlelight. Diego's eyes seemed to widen and his hands went out in front of him, trying to defend himself. Stanley lunged forward, thrusting the razor-honed blades towards Diego's chest and heart. Diego slid aside easily, laughing as he did so. The sword stabbed into the hard oak of the cabin door, the dagger clattered to the ground and Diego's hand clutched Stanley by the nape and pulled his head forward, taking the wind from him as he pushed him hard into the hilt of his own sword.

Boltfoot was behind Stanley, tripping him, pushing him into a heap, curling his arm round from behind and slipping his poniard into Stanley's fleshy abdomen, as he had once killed the sea monster on the banks of the Thames. Only this was easier. He had felt a kinship with the beast; he had none with this traitor, and his death would bring no regrets.

Harper Stanley grunted and exhaled a long gasp. Boltfoot held the blade in place, deep inside Stanley's body, its tip piercing his heart, just as Stanley had intended to do to all of them.

'Well, sir, Captain Stanley,' Boltfoot whispered into his ear, 'it seems you were wrong. The ocean wave was not so safe and the Vice-Admiral *was* in need of protection.'

Stanley was already dead. A trickle of blood seeped from the small wound to the abdomen where the blade still held him impaled. There was no rush of gore for Boltfoot to contend with. It was a clean kill.

'What now, Boltfoot? Do we wake Sir Francis?'

'I do not think the Vice-Admiral would wish his lady to be disturbed, Diego. Let us send Captain Stanley to a mariner's watery grave. The world shall think he killed himself. It is a common enough occurrence. Stepped overboard in a panic, frighted by the Spaniard, no doubt. If anyone is interested, which I think unlikely.'

Boltfoot slid the blade from the dead body and wiped the blood on his kerchief. 'Come, Diego, look lively. Grasp his legs. I'll take the arms.'

He was heavy but they were strong and hauled him without

difficulty to the deck. Diego dropped his end of the body with a dull thud on the timber and peered about in the gloom. The watch was some way distant. He signalled to Boltfoot, then picked up Stanley's legs. Quickly, they hoisted him up and over the stern bulwark. With a final push, they sent him into the waves like a stone. They scarcely heard a splash.

'Fish food, Boltfoot.'

'I fear he may stick in their craw, Diego. I could not eat traitor pie with relish.'

The fog was dense, slowing John Shakespeare's progress to a crawl, yet he went on, feeling his way along what he took to be the highway. Only when the fog swirled away briefly could he break into a trot. Occasionally he passed a cart or a horseman going eastwards towards London and was encouraged to discover he was still on the right road. Yet no one could give him any news of a lone rider answering Herrick's description. The trail had gone cold.

From the milestones he encountered, he estimated he was halfway to Plymouth by midday. His back caused him pain and his thighs were rubbed to soreness from the saddle, but he would take no break. He had to make up for lost time. Somehow his quarry was slipping through his fingers, like a wraith or will-o'-the-wisp.

On he rode. At nightfall he was determined to continue, but couldn't. It was impossible to make out the road. Better to replenish his body, then move on. He had passed a large post tavern and found his way back to it. The building was well lit and welcoming to a weary traveller. The money the landlady of The White Dog had lent him was just enough for one night.

After a good supper of roast fowl and vegetables, he locked himself into his small first-floor room, prayed, then closed his eyes and slept until dawn.

When he opened his eyes he saw that the fog had lifted. It was a clear day with a few white clouds. By nightfall, he reckoned, he could be at Plymouth. God willing, he would be in time.

Thomas Woode had resigned himself to death. In the quiet moments between sessions of torture, he made his peace with God and prayed for his children.

Topcliffe had learnt nothing from him. Woode had always believed he had not the stuff of martyrs in his veins, yet he had not been broken by the rack or manacles. What could he tell them, anyway? That a Jesuit priest called Cotton and another called Herrick had stayed at his home in Dowgate? He could give them no more, for he no longer knew where they were. The tortures were pointless now and driven by malice alone. When Topcliffe or his apprentice, Jones, taunted him or threatened him with death, he greeted the prospect with equanimity bordering on joy. Anything to end the agony would be welcome.

He had always imagined the rack to be the worst torment devised by man, but in truth he found it easier to abide than the manacles. It seemed to him that the pain he suffered hanging against the wall must have been almost of the magnitude endured by Christ, then chided himself for such unworthy thoughts: who was he to place his own suffering alongside that of the Son of God?

He would die here and that did not concern him. It was Grace and Andrew who made him fearful. How would they survive without him? His will contained instructions for them to be put in the guardianship of Catherine Marvell, but what if his estate were to be attainted – made forfeit to the state – and fall into the hands of such as Topcliffe? For this alone he had to remain silent. He must not sign any confession, whatever the pain.

The stench of the cell no longer caused him concern. He lay

in the filthy straw unable to move. He could not lift his arms to feed himself, so he hardly ate or drank. Nor could he move his legs, which meant he had to defecate where he lay.

One day Margaret came to him as if in a dream. He knew not whether it was light or dark outside for nothing of the world came into the cramped cell in Topcliffe's house of death. She was with him, burning bright in a haze of gossamer, as light as mayfly wings. She dipped a cloth into cool water and mopped his brow. She kissed his lips and, though no sound came from her, she seemed to say, only endure, and all will be well. Sleep, Thomas, sleep, and all will be well. We will be together soon.

Topcliffe was pacing. He had just come from the Queen's privy chamber and she had asked him, casually, about the Jesuits. 'I had thought to see them in the Tower before now, Mr Topcliffe, especially Lord Burghley's cousin Southwell. You did tell me a month since, and I recall it well, that he was as good as taken.'

The key, he knew, was the woman Catherine Marvell and the children of Woode. If Woode saw them threatened with torment or death, he would gabble like a goodwife outside church on Sunday. Woode was Southwell's familiar; he would lead the way to the Popish nest of hornets.

'Tell me again, Dick, do you really believe she was not there, that she has gone to York?'

Richard Young sat at a window-seat in Topcliffe's hall. The room was full of the fug from Topcliffe's pipe of sotweed. 'I believed it then. Now I am not sure. The maidservant may have been lying.'

'Should we bring her in?'

'On what charge? There is no evidence that she is even a Papist. She is well known in the parish as a faithful servant of our church.'

Topcliffe drew deeply on his pipe and strode back and forth, back and forth. The Queen had spoken half in jest, but the other half was what counted, the half that implied: I am deeply disappointed in your failure in this matter, Mr Topcliffe. My patience is running dry.

'Is the house watched?'

Young nodded. 'I left my sergeant there and sent another as relief. It is a small house, easily observed, and would not be difficult to search. If the Marvell woman should venture out, she will be apprehended on the instant.'

'Good.' Topcliffe had to find the Jesuit. Therefore he had to make Thomas Woode talk. Catherine Marvell, stretched on the rack, her face suffused with fear, her joints cracking, would make him tell all he knew. The information would flood out. 'A thousand deaths to the Pope and all his acolyte demons, Dick, we must go back there. In force and with speed. If the woman is there – and I believe she is – we must take her before the alarm can be raised and before Walsingham or any other can intervene. It is the only way. Once she is in our hands, no power on earth will prise her loose before we have what we want, I promise you that. We must do it, Dick, and we must do it before Shakespeare returns. Walsingham will doubtless be angry. He will see it as crossing a line, Dick, shitting on his doorstep. But I would rather cross him than the Golden Virgin. Gather a squadron of pursuivants, our ten best men. We go in before dawn.'

Chapter 40

AFTER EXETER THE countryside changed rapidly. Soon Shakespeare found himself on uncompromising moorland. Everywhere he looked, he saw bogs and bleak outcrops of rock. Wild horses roamed free. He passed a gypsy camp where a fire burnt with a cauldron perched over it.

He was certain now he was travelling in the right direction. He knew this to be the south-eastern edge of Dartmoor and the beaten track was easy to follow without woodland in which to get lost. At the southern tip of the moor the land became more lush and he found himself descending into a wooded valley. He had a choice to make: go directly to Plymouth or first to Buckland Abbey, in case the Vice-Admiral had made straight for there.

Where would Drake be most vulnerable? Buckland Abbey might have a large permanent staff of servants who would spot a stranger straightway, but it would be impossible to provide total protection night and day. Herrick could watch from a distance, choose his time and place to attack.

On the other hand, Plymouth was where Drake would spend most of his time. He had a house there, too, in Looe Street, and he would need to be close at hand to oversee the final provisioning and preparation of his war fleet. If Drake was to be at sea within two or three days, Herrick would have no time to lose.

Shakespeare decided to head for the old abbey first and alert the servants to the danger, then make for Plymouth where he could join forces with Boltfoot.

On talking with a parson whom he found striding out beside a river, he got his bearings and turned north-west towards Buckland Abbey, the fine and ancient home Drake had bought from his fellow admiral Sir Richard Grenville with the immense plunder taken from the Spanish carrack *Cacafuego* in the Pacific. Elizabeth Drake was in her solar sewing a tapestry when Shakespeare arrived and sent for him immediately. When he entered he was struck by her pale beauty; she was bathed in light angling between the stone mullions of a high, arched window.

She smiled in greeting. 'Mr Shakespeare, what a delight to see you. But why, pray, are you in Devon?'

Shakespeare was exhausted, and knew he looked shabby. His clothes were torn and coated with mud like a pigman's. His leather boots were clogged with soil and soaked through. 'Lady Drake, I seek Sir Francis. I must warn him. The killer sent by Spain has followed him here. There is great danger.' He spoke breathlessly, panting with the exertion of the day's long ride.

'We shall send a messenger to him, but in the meantime we must not have you catching your death of the sweating sickness. Please, sit by the fire and warm yourself. Have you a change of clothes? If not, we must fit you out with some.'

Shakespeare ate and drank quickly, for he wanted to be at Plymouth before nightfall. As he devoured the food, Elizabeth told him of Captain Harper Stanley's death on the voyage from Dover. 'It is thought he must have jumped to his death, taken by the melancholy, Mr Shakespeare. No one believes he could have fallen accidentally. Such a tragedy.'

Shakespeare was shocked and disturbed by the news. He had liked Stanley and could not have imagined he would take his own life. 'It is, indeed, a great sadness, my lady. I knew him well.' Could there have been more to his death than that, though? Shakespeare needed to speak with Boltfoot urgently.

'But life goes on, Mr Shakespeare. Weather and winds permitting, Sir Francis is resolved to set sail with the tide tomorrow. He says he must go before the Queen changes her mind, which she is certain to do as she always does. Tonight the town is throwing a banquet in his honour, which you must attend if you are recovered.'

'A banquet? Tonight?'

'Why, indeed. Feasting, music, dancing. Is that such a surprise? The men set sail to do battle with the Spanish tomorrow.'

The thought of such an entertainment filled Shakespeare with dread. Anyone could slip into the hall. And in the milling throng, Drake would be in grave danger.

'If I may ask, my lady, who will be there?'

'All the great families of Devon. The Grenvilles, all the Drakes – and there are many – the Hawkins family, my own cousins the Sydenhams, Raleghs, Carews, Gilberts, Sir William Courtenay and his kin. And then there will be the captains, masters and gentleman officers of the fleet, the corporation of Plymouth, of course, and the shipwrights and chandlers.'

'So everyone will know each other?'

'Most certainly. And we have another young guest, a charming Huguenot gentleman from La Rochelle who intends to join us. He burns with desire to give the King of Spain a bloody nose.'

Shakespeare felt a sudden chill. 'What Huguenot is this, my lady?'

'Now, Mr Shakespeare, I know you fear for my husband's life, but he is capable of looking after himself, as he has proved on many occasions in these past twenty years. This young man is called Pascal, Henri Pascal, and I believe him to be exactly what he says he is: a Huguenot fugitive from France who wishes to fight for the Protestant cause. What is more, he is a mariner, so he will serve us very well. I told him to come to the Guildhall this evening for the banquet, where I shall introduce him to Sir Francis, so that he may sail with him on the morrow. I am sure you can find no fault in that. I must tell you he had letters of introduction from Lord Howard of Effingham. Surely there could be no better recommendation.'

'May I see these letters?'

'I am afraid I do not have them. He took them away.'

'What shape of a man is this? Is he beardless, tall?'

Elizabeth Drake looked puzzled. 'Why, yes, he is.'

'And his accent? Is it strongly French?'

'Well, no, he speaks exceptionally good English. A slightly clipped accent, perchance, but that is all.'

'My lady, I must ride for Plymouth immediately. I fear you have entertained the man who would kill your husband.'

Drake had not believed for a moment that Harper Stanley had taken his own life. 'Come, Diego, the truth.'

The Vice-Admiral was in his cabin with Diego and Boltfoot, aboard the *Elizabeth Bonaventure*, at anchor in Plymouth Sound, one of Europe's most sheltered deep-water harbours. In the distance they could see Plymouth, a town of squat mariners' dwellings and bustling dockyards, which seemed to be burgeoning day by day as England's maritime ventures grew ever bolder. Drake had been conferring with his captains and had now sent them back to their vessels to prepare for the next day's departure for the Iberian peninsula. 'Not an hour is to be lost, gentlemen,' he said. 'Even now a messenger might be riding from Greenwich Palace with orders from the Queen countermanding our commission. Her Majesty has changed her mind four times in five days. We must be at sea to avoid that happening again.'

It was only with his wife safely out of earshot at Buckland Abbey that Drake felt easy talking of Harper Stanley's fate; he did not want to worry her more than necessary.

'He was coming to kill you, Sir Francis. In fact, he was coming to kill all of us. He was naked so that our blood would not drench his clothes. But we knew he was coming.' Diego glanced at Boltfoot, who stepped forward.

'I had suspected him for a while. When Sir William Courtenay lunged at you with the blade on the way to Dover, I saw something in Stanley's eyes. He held back, but it was more than that. I could see he wished you dead, sir. I think he was never what he seemed.'

'Well, I have no idea why he should wish me dead. I always promoted him and gave him great opportunity for plunder and glory. Was he a Papist, do you think? Perchance we will never know. But he was a good seafarer. I would have liked him at my side on this venture.' Drake glowered at Boltfoot. 'Still, I am sure we will find a replacement. Do you think you could captain a ship, Mr Cooper?'

'Perhaps, Sir Francis, but I would rather be flayed than do so.'

'Hah! Still the same mongrel cur, eh? And don't go about boasting that you saved my life. If Harper Stanley had somehow got into my cabin with his sword, I would have cut him down in my sleep. No one bests Drake, and certainly not a beplumed peacock like Stanley. Now, then, I would like your thoughts, Diego. Look at this chart.' Drake jabbed his finger three times at the coasts of Portugal and Spain. 'We will attack the anti-Christ's ships here, here and here.'

There was a knock at the cabin door and the ship's master

opened it. Drake looked up, irritated by the interruption. 'What is it?'

'Mr John Shakespeare to see you, Vice-Admiral,' the master announced.

Surprised, Drake glanced at the entranceway. 'Shakespeare, by God's faith, what are you doing here?'

Shakespeare bowed, then rose, still stiff from his ride, to his full height. He was a good six inches taller than Drake. 'Sir Francis, the killer has followed you to Plymouth.'

Drake looked at Diego and Boltfoot, then turned back to Shakespeare and laughed. 'You are too late, Shakespeare! Your man Boltfoot and my friend Diego have already done for him. He lies at the bottom of the Channel even now, with eels swimming into the hole that Boltfoot put in his belly.'

'You have killed Herrick? How so?'

'They have not killed anyone called Herrick. They have despatched Captain Harper Stanley, Mr Shakespeare. He came for me in the middle of the night, naked, like a thief. Diego and Mr Cooper saved me the trouble of killing him by impaling him on their blades, then dropping him overboard. The world has been allowed to believe he took his own life. Amusing, do you not think?'

Shakespeare was aghast. 'Stanley intended to kill you?'

'It is a certainty.'

'That is a worrying turn of events, Sir Francis, but he was not the one I seek. There is another man, far more dangerous, sent by the Escorial for the price on your head. He is utterly without fear or mercy and has already killed one of my best men, Harry Slide. It was he who shot at you at Deptford. Stanley could not possibly have done that for he was aboard ship, not ashore.'

'Then we have two traitors to contend with. Or should I say "had"? For now there is just the one, which sounds like no danger at all as we are to sail tomorrow.'

Shakespeare sighed. 'And what of tonight, Sir Francis? What of the banquet? I have to tell you that this Herrick will be there. It would be best if you were not.'

'What? Miss my own banquet? You jest, sir! The Spaniard would laugh at me and I would die of shame. No, sir, bring on this assassin and I will happily deal with him. But pray tell me, sir, what the devil has happened to your eyebrow? You look most curious without it.'

The tension in Seething Lane was almost palpable. Jane shuttered the windows as soon as darkness fell and they spoke in low voices in case anyone listened at the door. They felt besieged.

The confrontation with Richard Young had shaken Jane to the core. 'I can't work, Catherine, but there is cheese to be made, linen to be repaired, hose to be darned, preserves to be bottled and stored—'

'Jane, be quiet.'

'If only Mr Shakespeare were here. I won't sleep tonight for worrying. What if the magistrate comes again? What if he brings Topcliffe?'

Catherine took Jane by the shoulders and made her sit on a bench at the table. 'They *will* come, Jane, and that is why you must stop this. We must think.'

Jane breathed deeply. It did not help. She was worried less for herself than for Catherine and the children. 'You, Grace and Andrew must leave.'

'They will come back in force tonight and they are utterly without pity. I must tell you, Jane, they are so soaked in blood that they will think nothing of killing us all. Mr Woode may be dead by now. But even that would not make them falter. They are relentless. Their thirst for vengeance will not be slaked even by his death. They will take his children and break them on the Bridewell treadmill as a warning to others.'

'How can you get out, then? I am sure we are being watched. There is no secret way. If you try, they will take you straightway in the street and you will be done for.'

'Well, we can't sit here and wait. There is no hiding-place, you say?'

'None that they would not easily discover.'

The two women were in the small kitchen. Jane had been making candles and the debris of her work, wax and wicks, lay on the table before them. A helpless silence descended. Upstairs the children slept, unaware of the fate that awaited them.

'I suppose I could try to talk to Mr Secretary.'

'What would his reaction be? Does he not back Topcliffe to the hilt? Would he not turn us over to him?'

They had been over this ground before. Catherine felt sick with dread. This should have been the happiest time of her life, days of honey with the man she loved, but he was gone and there was no way of knowing when – or if – he would return. The message delivered from him to Jane had merely said he was to go west immediately and that he would be a few days. Inside the message was another, hastily written on a small scrap of paper, folded and addressed to Catherine. It said: 'Would that I had poetic words in me. All I can say is that you are my love. Hold firm until I return.' It had made the small hairs on her neck stand and a shiver of warmth spread through her breasts. She had folded the paper again and put it within her bodice.

Jane raised her head suddenly, as if struck by a thought. 'I have an idea.'

Chapter 41

THE GUILDHALL WAS lit by a thousand candles. Guests would soon begin to arrive. Shakespeare paced the main hall. He had examined the building in detail, seeking out every entrance, every staircase, every window through which a shot or crossbow bolt might be fired. He and Boltfoot had interviewed and searched the footmen, the cooks, the master of ceremonies, the musicians, and he had put them on alert in case they should see anything out of the usual.

He had left Drake under the protection of Diego; they would, of course, be the last to arrive. Boltfoot, meanwhile, had come ahead, trudging through the cold, blustery streets by the docks, his heavy left foot dragging behind his squat body. He was now positioned by the grand doorway where the guests would enter in their finery. Shakespeare had questioned Boltfoot yet again about his confrontation with Herrick in the aftermath of the shot from the chandler's attic in Deptford. He picked at his brain, trying to find more clues about the assassin and his appearance. 'Most of all, Boltfoot, would you recognise him again?'

'I don't know, Mr Shakespeare. I did not get close to him.'

'But you must have some kind of impression. Use your instinct, Boltfoot. Take no chances. Look at the men's faces carefully. We know Herrick is clean-shaven and that he is tall.

Study any such men closely. Perhaps he has stuck a false beard to his face or disguised his height by walking with a stoop. If you have any doubt about someone, however small, take no chances. Stop them and search them. This Herrick will come. It is his last chance.'

Shakespeare had borrowed a suit of clothes from the steward at Buckland Abbey. It enabled him to move at ease among the throng as people arrived; as a mere serving man he would attract no comment.

The hall was high-ceilinged with fine pargeting and great coloured windows, but it was not big and the guests would quickly pack it out. As the evening wore on, and the claret and malmsey flowed, it would become increasingly difficult to spot who was coming in or going out, who was bearing arms or advancing on Drake. A poniard, even a wheel-lock pistol, might be concealed in such a crush.

They began to arrive at seven of the clock, just as the church bells chimed nearby. Shakespeare took a deep breath. 'Boltfoot, we know he will be here and that he has no fear. The way he walked into Buckland Abbey proved that. If only Lady Drake could stay by the door with you, for she must recognise him better than anyone. She has taken wine with him in her own house. But her thoughts and attention will most certainly be occupied elsewhere.'

Boltfoot looked unimpressed. He was convinced that Drake was immortal, that he had signed some pact with the devil. He had seen him exchange fire with the finest soldiers of Spain, brave arrows and spears flung at him by native peoples the globe over, walk tall and strong when others were falling down with sickness in mid-ocean. Whatever happened, he never shed his glow of invincibility; he was untouchable. Could a mere mercenary, a mortal with a wheel-lock sent by Philip of Spain, do him harm? Boltfoot thought not.

The guests wore glittering clothes, studded with dazzling gems. This was not the royal court with its plethora of exquisitely cut gowns, but the accoutrements were costly nonetheless. Plymouth was a wealthy town. After London, it was the hub of England's trade with the world. Here lived hard, unsentimental men – Hawkins, Drake and their extensive families, all cousins to one another – who plundered Spanish treasure, stole men and women from their beds in western Africa and sold them as slaves in the Indies, found spices and cloth and jewels from the earth's most far-flung shores to sell in the capitals of Europe. Their wealth, however ill-gotten, shone as gaudily as the night sky in this hall. Shakespeare doubted that there was a single gemstone in the hall paid for other than in blood.

The tables, formed in a great U, were bedecked with candles and silver plate. The guests thronged in the centre of the hall where, after feasting, there would be dancing. In a corner, the musicians played the songs of old England, passed down through Devon's generations for hundreds of years. This was not a time for mournful ballads.

Drake and his lady arrived last, to thunderous applause. He wore a saffron yellow doublet, with an enormous ruff of fine lace and a cape at his shoulder. He bowed with a sweep of the cape and Lady Drake, in her finest blue velvet and cloth-of-gold gown, curtsied with a modest smile. They were accompanied by Diego. Drake caught sight of Shakespeare in his steward's livery. 'Fetch me a cup of brandy, my man,' he said, laughing. Then he and his wife walked sedately to their seats at the head of the main table, acknowledging the applause and cheering of the guests every inch of the way. He then vaulted on to the table with the agility of a man half his forty-six years, puffed out his broad chest and clapped his hands.

The crowd fell silent. Drake stood, legs apart, hands on hips, as if he were on the deck of a royal galleon with a fierce north-easterly in his grey-red hair. His eyes shone. He had his audience, his people, where he wanted them: in the very palm of his hand.

'Welcome, welcome, one and all. Eat, drink and be merry, for tomorrow our fleet sets sail into the teeth of the Spaniard's jaws, where we shall blow out his brains and tear his heart from his cowering chest. Let Philip and Santa Cruz tremble with fear, for I will discover them, mewling in their lair, and turn their towering ships to matchwood. But first let me tell you a little of the ways of this craven prince: he has sent a Fleming to kill me, a man of dishonour who would kill by stealth for he is frit to stand in open combat. I am told he will be here tonight. Well, Mr Fleming, here I am! Draw your pistol, take aim and fire.' Drake beat his hand against his chest. 'Here is my heart. Shoot it to death, by God's faith.'

He stood back and looked round the room. The silence was absolute. All eyes were on the Vice-Admiral. He cupped his ear with a hand. 'Hark, do I hear a pistol cocked? Mind you come closer. We don't want you to miss now, as you did once before.'

An explosion tore the silence. The guests ducked as one, an instinctive reaction to the force of the blast. All eyes turned slowly to the back of the hall, where a man stood holding a smoking wheel-lock. Drake stood where he had before, hands on hips even more aggressively, chest pushed out until it might seem he would burst his doublet, face creased in a scornful grin.

Shakespeare was pushing his way through the throng towards the gunman. He was about to leap on him when he stopped in his tracks. The gunman was also grinning, his red hair and shoulders covered with the plaster that had fallen from the ceiling, where he had loosed the ball from his pistol. He looked back at Drake who was laughing loudly.

''Tis my little brother Thomas, Mr Shakespeare. He has let off his pop-pop into the ceiling. Would you take him away and lock him up in Plymouth gaol?'

Shakespeare shook his head in dismay. By now the whole room was laughing with gusto until the walls echoed.

Drake clapped his hands again. 'Forgive me, Mr Shakespeare. It was a jest we could not resist. Now let us say grace and give thanks to the Lord for the fare we are about to receive.' He clambered down from the table and called on the Bishop to lead them in prayer.

The banquet proceeded in disorderly fashion. The din of laughter and conversation was as loud as a score of anvils being hammered. Shakespeare was worried. He offered to taste Drake's food for poison, but Drake would have none of it. Worse, if the killer had been anywhere in the vicinity when Thomas Drake had shot his pistol, he might have found his way into the hall under cover of the confusion; all the plans to search and examine those coming in would have gone up in smoke.

As the evening grew ever more wild, weapons were produced and mock sword-fights staged along the centre of the tables, with drunken guests kicking food, silver and candles about, like so many pirates. Drake clapped his hands intermittently when he felt it was time to tell another story. At one stage he called for silence and demanded prayers for his cousin John, a fellow sea captain, captured by natives and then by the Spanish in the river Plate. 'Remember, while we eat and drink, he moulders in some Spanish hole in Peru. If he could hear me now, I would say, "Keep strong, John, keep the faith and spit on their saints and relics!"'

The dancing began. Riotous voltas and galliards; not for these revellers the sedate elegance of the pavane. The men threw their ladies high into the air and occasionally dropped them, sprawling in a drunken heap.

Shakespeare was horrified.

Diego came up and slapped him on the back. 'Forgive Sir Francis's little jest, John. He insisted on it.'

'Diego, Drake jests, but this man, this Fleming, will come tonight. He may be waiting in the shadows outside; he may be already inside. But I tell you, I know he has ridden here and he believes this to be his last chance. I think he is without fear for his own life.'

A drunken couple staggered into Shakespeare. The man wore the mayor's chain of office and his hand clasped the woman's breast, his mouth at her neck; her hand was held firm at the front of his breeches. As they barged into him, Shakespeare lurched backwards but Diego held him up.

Shakespeare pushed the amorous couple on their way, stumbling round the room in their curious impression of a dance. 'I fear Mr Secretary would not approve of this.'

'He would not. But he does not stand on the deck of a warship driving it straight into the guns of the enemy,' Diego said. 'They are enjoying life while it lasts, John. Tomorrow we set sail. This may be the last time you see any of us.'

The banquet was descending into a free-for-all. Beautifully prepared food was flung across the tables, ale was drunk from pitchers so that it ran from the mouths of men and women down their jowls on to their fine clothes. Shakespeare watched in despair. All he could do now was stay close to Drake and scour the room for anything untoward while Diego and Boltfoot watched the doors. Yet men and women were slipping in and out all the time.

Drake broke off from a heated conversation with young Richard Hawkins, son of his old friend John. 'Mr Shakespeare, your brow seems uncommon furrowed tonight.' He turned to his wife. 'What say you, my lady?'

'I would say, Sir Francis, that you should be thankful for the care that Mr Shakespeare is taking to preserve your life. You owe him better manners, sir!'

'Hah! Roundly scolded. I would rather be cut at by a Spaniard's halberd than feel the edge of a woman's tongue.'

Someone shouted, 'Fire!'

It was a word to drive fear into the hearts of stout men. Even those who could barely move from an excess of wine stopped and held still.

'Fire! There is fire!' another voice shouted.

A roar went up and guests scrambled for the great doors at the front of the hall.

Shakespeare did not hesitate. He took Drake's arm and pressed his hand into his wife's back. 'Come with me. I know a better way out. This fire will have been laid by the killer. He will make his attempt in the confusion . . .'

A rush of flame took hold of a gold and red French tapestry that hung from a side wall. Fire leapt from it into the drapes and up to the beams. Black smoke billowed in the narrow confines of the hall. The scramble of bodies towards the door turned to panic. Women and men coughed and screamed, pushed and trampled.

Drake thrust Shakespeare's hand away from his arm. He grabbed a silver salver from the table and banged it hard repeatedly. 'Hear me! Hear me!' he shouted. 'Gentlemen, stand aside and let the ladies go first. We will all get out safely with some order!'

Suddenly the undisciplined charge for the doorway halted. Even in the most intense heat of fire, men obeyed Sir Francis Drake. Most stood aside and those few who didn't were hauled back by others. The women then proceeded to leave at a brisk pace.

The fire was growing fast. Cooks and serving maids were running in with pails of water. Shakespeare realised that such action would not be enough. This was going to be a difficult blaze to bring under control. Boltfoot and Diego had emerged from the crush and were now with Shakespeare and the Drakes.

'We must go, Sir Francis.'

'Mr Shakespeare, we are in your hands. Kindly take us your secret way.'

They moved forward. Suddenly Shakespeare saw that the path he had intended, through the kitchens, was blocked by fire. He turned to the west side of the building, to the corporation's council chamber. There had to be a way through there. The smoke was thickening; coughing and choking filled the hall. As soon as they were in the chamber, Shakespeare closed the door behind them to keep out the flames and the worst of the fumes. They stood a moment, catching their breath. The faces of eminent Plymouth burghers looked down at them from portraits round the walls.

'How do you fare, my lady?' Drake asked his wife, touching her arm tenderly.

'It is a great excitement, Sir Francis. I begin to understand why you men are so quick to go to war.'

'You have a fine spirit! Think how brave our sons will be.'

'And our daughters, sir.'

Shakespeare pushed open the door into the council antechamber and stepped through in front of Drake and his wife. At the far end of the room, he could see the side entrance to the building. A group of men was standing at the doorway; serving men and ostlers. 'Is the way clear?' Shakespeare called.

'Aye, sir,' came a reply. 'Come through. We're setting up a pail chain here.'

If I were a killer, thought Shakespeare, this is where I would make my move. This is where I would expect Drake to make his exit and I would attack now. He drew his sword and signalled to Drake to do the same. 'Come, sir, beware.

He will be hereabouts. Boltfoot, have your caliver primed and ready.'

Drake strode ahead, disdainful of Shakespeare's caution. 'Home, Lady Drake, to bed. I have had my fill of this nonsense of Walsingham. I love him as a friend, but I will not be wet-nursed by his nannies.'

They marched out into the street. Shakespeare could see now that flames were licking the sky. A great crowd had gathered outside the Guildhall, all agog at the fire. It seemed the whole town had risen from their beds to watch the spectacle or help with the pail chains. Drake ignored them. 'You will see better fireworks when I put flame to Philip's galleons,' he said, to no one in particular, striding through the chill night air.

The walk to Looe Street, where Drake had his town-house, took little more than five minutes. Two roistering mariners, who had consumed too much brandy on their last night ashore, whistled and called at them, 'Here, sweets, leave them dodderers and come with us. We'll fill yer cunny with honey!' Then they spotted their Vice-Admiral and dashed down a side-street.

'I recognise that voice,' Drake said. 'He's bosun on the *Dreadnought*. I'll have him flogged on the morrow for lewdness!'

Chapter 42

Drake's house in Looe Street, at the top of a sharp incline, was surprisingly modest compared to his majestic mansions and estates in other parts of Devon and in London. It was a tall structure, built of stone to withstand sea-borne gales. Above the ground floor, jettied chambers overhung the narrow street. Clearly, the crucial thing for the Vice-Admiral was its convenience, so close to the mouth of the Plym and to the dockyards where he had to spend so much time repairing and provisioning his ships.

Drake stood at the steps to the house. 'Well, Mr Shakespeare, you have brought us safe home. I think you can tell Mr Secretary that you have accomplished your task like a true and faithful servant. Goodnight to you, sir.' He was about to push open the front door when Shakespeare moved in front of him. He addressed Elizabeth: 'Might I ask you, my lady, did you tell the Huguenot, Pascal, of this house?'

Elizabeth Drake looked flustered. 'It is . . . possible. I might have mentioned it. I cannot recall.'

Shakespeare lifted the latch to the door. 'If it please you, Sir Francis, I will go first. Boltfoot, come with me.'

Suddenly, Drake's good humour turned. He thrust Shakespeare angrily out of the way. 'No one but the Queen commands me, Shakespeare. Remove yourself from my path.

My lady, let us go inside.' He opened the door for his wife. She hesitated, but knew her husband's moods well enough to realise this was no time to try disagreeing with him. Smiling sweetly at Shakespeare, and mouthing a silent 'Thank you, Mr Shakespeare,' she stepped forward into the house.

Drake followed her and was surprised to find the hallway empty and in darkness.

'I think the servants will be out watching the fire, Sir Francis,' she said. 'Perhaps we might ask our companions to set some lights about the house for us.'

'By God's faith, what sort of staff is it that leaves its post to watch a little bonfire, madam? You must look to our domestic arrangements before I am next home.'

Shakespeare and Boltfoot took her cue. Boltfoot produced a tinder-box and began to light some candles. Shakespeare pushed on into the house. He had been convinced Herrick would strike at the banquet. And now? If there had been a Huguenot called Henri Pascal who just happened to turn up at Buckland Abbey, why had he not been at the banquet to intro- duce himself to Drake?

The blow was struck as Shakespeare entered the Drakes' private chamber on the first floor. It came out of the darkness, a crack to the back of the head that felled him. He slumped awkwardly to the floor, his head hitting the foot of the bed. He felt himself losing consciousness but fought the sensation and thrashed out wildly, still clutching his sword. Dimly, he heard a sound like a grunt or cry. He rolled sideways across the room and felt the reverberation of a heavy blade stabbing into the boards where, seconds earlier, he had been sprawled.

Shakespeare scrambled further from his assailant, clawing his way to the other side of a large oaken bed. In the gloom he saw a flickering light, a candle flame, and heard a gasp. Elizabeth had stepped into the chamber. In the dim, shadowy light he saw a face: Herrick. It had to be Herrick. In horror, he saw the man grab Elizabeth, his muscular arm encircling her neck and forcing her back into the corner of the room. The candle fell from her grasp and the room was plunged back into darkness.

Shakespeare jumped to his feet. His clubbed head felt as if gunpowder had exploded within it. He felt blood trickle down the inside of his ruff. He still had his sword, his grasp firm on the hilt.

Another light appeared at the door. Drake. 'What is this?' And then he saw his wife, her neck twisted back, the point of a thin poniard at her throat, pressing into her flesh, blood dripping on to her velvet gown. 'My lady?'

Shakespeare was at Drake's side now.

'Out,' Herrick said quietly, to Shakespeare. He stood scarcely five feet from Drake. 'Out, or she will die. Not you, Drake, you will stay. But the other one, leave now or you will see such a gush of blood from this woman's throat as will sink all your galleons.'

Drake nodded to Shakespeare. 'Leave now, Mr Shakespeare.'

Shakespeare stood his ground. 'I go nowhere. My order is to protect you.'

In one lightning motion, Herrick flung Elizabeth across the room. In the same movement, he lunged at Drake, poniard raised, with all the force of a bull in the ring. As he thrust forward and down with the blade he hissed, 'So die all heretics!'

Drake did not retreat. Herrick's blow descended hard, slicing through flesh and glancing off bone, but it was Shakespeare's left forearm that had taken it, not Drake's body. Shakespeare's right arm came down behind Herrick's neck, the hilt of his sword cracking into the base of his skull and forcing him to the ground at Drake's feet. Shakespeare stamped on the nape of Herrick's neck. He raised his sword, now greasy with his own blood, with his uninjured right arm and held it suspended as if to drive it through the would-be killer's back.

'No, Mr Shakespeare,' Drake said. 'Save that pleasure for the headsman.'

The ships of Drake's fleet sailed with the tide. He was aboard the *Elizabeth Bonaventure*, accompanied by three more royal galleons – *Golden Lion*, *Dreadnought*, *Rainbow* – and twenty other vessels of varying degree. They were manned by three thousand sailors and soldiers, heavily armed and angry, with many tons of cannon and ball. Before weighing anchor, Drake found it in him to say a grudging word of thanks to Shakespeare for his 'diligence', then scribbled a final message for Walsingham and handed it to Shakespeare to carry to him: 'The wind commands us away. Our ship is under sail. God grant we may live in His fear as the enemy may have cause to say that God does fight for Her Majesty as well abroad as at home.'

There was new urgency about the mission. The latest intelligence gathered by Walsingham had revealed that the Spanish admiral, Santa Cruz, planned to have his armada ready to sail this spring or early summer. Drake's task was to destroy the enemy in her ports or at sea and to intercept and capture the Spanish treasure fleet from the Indies.

Shakespeare stood on the shore with Elizabeth Drake, Boltfoot and thousands of townsfolk, all cheering and throwing their caps in the air as the brave pennants of the fleet stretched out in the stiff breeze. Lady Drake touched his face. 'I am sure my husband has not thanked you adequately, Mr Shakespeare, but you have my sincere gratitude. You saved our lives last night.'

He had thought about it at length. Despite exhaustion, he had hardly been able to sleep, so fast did his heart beat and so great the pain in his wounded arm. He could have killed Herrick there and then, helpless on the floor, with one foot on the back of his neck. Like every child, he had killed injured birds and hunted squirrels with bows and arrows for their red fur, yet he had never had cause to kill a man and often wondered whether he would have the stomach for it. Well, now he knew.

His left arm was heavily bandaged and supported across his chest in a sling. It hurt, but the cut had been clean and there was no reason to believe it would not heal. A physician had dressed it with herbal tinctures to prevent gangrene and told him to drink brandy to counter the loss of blood. The ride back to London would be uncomfortable, but manageable.

Herrick had been bound, before being hauled off in a hand-cart to be arraigned before magistrates. Since then he had been left to ponder his fate in Plymouth gaol until his trial, which would be a matter of two or three days; execution would follow swiftly. Shakespeare felt that this was a matter best dealt with locally: Mr Secretary would not wish another Papist martyr to be paraded through the streets so soon after the execution of Mary Stuart. Anyway, Plymouth butchers could bowel and quarter Herrick as efficiently as the London headsmen.

Shakespeare had spent a few hours with him, trying to persuade him to talk. He got little, neither confessions nor denials. Only when Shakespeare mentioned the murder of Lady Blanche Howard did Herrick break his silence. He laughed humourlessly. 'You do not think that was me, Mr Shakespeare? Look to your own . . . look to your own.'

Shakespeare pressed him, but all he would say was, 'My fate is certain. Why should I waste what little breath I have left in talking with you?' Then he turned his back on his interrogator and dragged his heavy shackles and manacles into a marginally more comfortable position. For a moment, Shakespeare wondered whether to bring torture to bear; Mr Secretary would undoubtedly approve. But torture repelled him, as it did most Englishmen.

After Drake's fleet had sailed, Shakespeare and Boltfoot took horse for London. On the way, they stopped at the White Dog inn to repay the landlady who had helped Shakespeare when his purse was stolen. He had been handed coin by Drake. 'It is a loan, Mr Shakespeare, to get you home. Not a gift.' Boltfoot had chuckled.

The days were growing longer. In just forty-eight hours the mist had given way to spring sunshine and crisp, clear nights. All the way, Shakespeare thought of Catherine; every mile they rode brought him closer to her. He clung to their one night together and prayed to God that it had meant as much to her as it had to him. He would ask her to wed him, of course. Yet he had, too, some nagging fear. Walsingham would not be best pleased that one of his senior officials intended to marry a Roman Catholic; perhaps he would even dismiss Shakespeare from his employment. Well, so be it. His love for Catherine was paramount.

The riders made good progress and Shakespeare decided on a short diversion to the Thames near Windsor, where he asked the way to the village of Rymesford.

He found the monk Thomas Woode had told him about huddled in the remains of one of the drying rooms in the old mill. It was a ramshackle, dilapidated place of ancient, rotted timbers and it looked as though it might soon collapse into the river and be carried downstream. Hundreds of birds had made their nests in its beams and rafters and their noise was a cacophony. The old monk was scarce in better condition than the building. His skin was like yellowed parchment, his eyes hollow sockets without light. His old habit, which looked as though he might have been wearing it at the time of the dissolution of the monasteries fifty years since, was little more than rags, hanging from his gaunt shoulders and tied at the waist with frayed strands of rope.

'Are you Ptolomeus?'

The blind monk shied away at the voice like a beaten dog.

A sheet of paper caught in the breeze that blew through the gaping holes where once windows had been and fluttered past the old man. Shakespeare caught it. It was blank, but of identical quality to the papers he had found scattered around Lady Blanche Howard's mutilated body in Hog Lane, Shoreditch.

'Ptolomeus, I have no wish to harm you. I am come to talk with you.'

The old man's beard was long and pepper grey, as was his hair. He was encrusted with grime. He sat on his haunches on the floorboards at the side of the central space beside a worn, cast-away grindstone and a wooden trencher with a few crumbs.

'Boltfoot, give him some food.'

Boltfoot limped back to his horse, which was tethered outside the mill, and took some bread and meat from the saddle-bags. He brought it back and touched the sightless monk's shoulder. 'Here,' he said, less gruffly than usual. 'Food. Take it.'

The monk stretched out his arms from the folds of his habit and held them together like a tray. He had no hands. Both had been severed at the wrist, and not long ago for the scars were fresh. Boltfoot laid the food on the stumps. 'I will bring you ale, too,' he said.

'What happened to you, Ptolomeus?'

'The law, sir, the law.' His voice was old, yet surprisingly firm.

'What crime did you commit?'

'Libel, sedition, illegal printing, unlicensed paper-making. What does it matter? My life is done. All that is left me is birdsong and the scraps the villagers bring me. At least they do not judge me. I am content to be judged by God.'

'I am right in thinking that you have made this paper?'

'I cannot see it, sir. My eyes have been put out. But if you have found it here, I would hazard a guess that it is my work, poor though that is, as anyone who knows about these things will tell you. It is the water here, you see. Too muddy. That, and the sad quality of the rags. The rag men know their worth, sir.' He laughed drily.

Shakespeare stood quietly a moment and regarded the devastation around him. This man sat in the middle of it still, like the silent heart of a storm. When you have lost everything and there is nothing left to lose but your life, what is there to fear? Ptolomeus ate some of the food Boltfoot had given him, hunching his shoulders as he pushed his stumps together round the bread and meat and held it to his mouth. It was obvious that the pain of amputation had not yet dulled, for his body tensed with each movement and his face was set in a grimace.

Much of the panoply of paper-making was still here. The main shaft of the milling machine was attached by levers to mallets for mashing the sodden rags to pulp. Nearby, there were wooden frames with fine sieve-like bases from which the water would drain, leaving a thin layer of pulp that, when dried out, would become raw paper. There was a press, too, to help squeeze the water from the sheets, but no printing press. Where, wondered Shakespeare, had it gone?

'Thomas Woode told me he gave you an old press so that you could print Romish tracts for seminary priests. Where is it?'

'Gone with my hands, sir.'

'Mr Woode told me you would never have printed anything seditious.'

'That, too, is true enough. Or so I thought. Others disagreed and said that whatever I printed was illicit; the Star Chamber has ruled it against the law to print anything without explicit licence.'

'Then tell me who did this to you? Was it the town magistrate?'

Boltfoot put a cup of ale to the old man's lips. He drank thirstily, then wiped his mouth on his grubby sleeve. 'That is good, sir. Thank you. No, it was not the magistrate, but one of whom you may have heard. He is named Topcliffe and I do believe him to be Satan incarnate.'

'Topcliffe?'

'He killed my fellow monk, Brother Humphrey. Topcliffe cut him into pieces before my eyes and threw his remains into the river. Then he took my eyes and, last, my hands. He put my arms together against a log and removed my hands with one blow of an axe. He left me to bleed to death, but God, in His mercy, has let me live a little longer.'

Shakespeare looked at Boltfoot and saw his own horror reflected. Very little could move Boltfoot, yet the cold brutality of the old man's tale had shocked him.

'You are silent, sir? Are you surprised, then, by this demon's handiwork?'

'No . . . No, not surprised.'

'A goodwife from Rymesford tended my wounds and brought sustenance. She still helps me, as do others. Burghley and his like cannot kill our faith so easily, you know.'

Shakespeare touched the monk's shoulder. Ptolomeus did not flinch. 'We will leave you money,' Shakespeare said, 'but you must tell us what happened to your printing press.'

'The money would be a kindness, sir. As for the press, Mr Richard Topcliffe took that. He said he had some use for it. I did hear him laugh as he carried it off on the back of my cart.'

Chapter 43

JOHN SHAKESPEARE AND Boltfoot Cooper rode in silence. They had passed by the great castle of Windsor and were close to London now. The villages that serviced the city with vegetables, livestock, timbers and ironwork were becoming more numerous and prosperous. It seemed to Shakespeare that London was the centre of a great wheel and that these roads in, with their increasing numbers of hamlets and towns, were its spokes. You could hardly turn a corner without spying another church spire against the skyline.

The fields were different, too: better cared for and enclosed than those he had encountered travelling west. They passed through part of Surrey, and Shakespeare collected his grey mare, which had gone lame on the way to Plymouth; she was hale and in good spirits, and he paid the peasant who had cared for her half a crown for his efforts. It seemed fairer than the sixpence he had promised.

The silence between Shakespeare and Boltfoot reflected their thoughts. Each knew what the other was thinking. Shakespeare broke the spell. 'It can mean but one thing, Boltfoot,' he said at last.

Boltfoot nodded.

'It can mean only that Topcliffe himself printed that tract in Hog Lane. But why would he do that?'

'Justification, Mr Shakespeare. To show the Catholics as treacherous.'

'Would he go to such lengths?' But Shakespeare knew the answer: to what lengths wouldn't Topcliffe go in his mission to destroy every Roman Catholic priest and adherent of the old faith? Surely a man who could commission a rack and torture room for his own home would be capable of printing a tract to justify more arrests? 'Yes,' Shakespeare went on, 'he would go to such lengths. The tract was naught but a poor copy of Leicester's *Commonwealth*. It was without meaning and could have had only one purpose. It was a diversion.'

They rode on a little way in silence again. Then Shakespeare turned once more to Boltfoot. 'And that leads us to another certainty . . .'

'He killed Lady Blanche.'

Shakespeare winced at the sound of the words, then said them, more quietly, himself: 'Topcliffe killed Lady Blanche Howard.'

Boltfoot issued a low noise like a farmyard animal.

'But why?' asked Shakespeare. 'Why murder a Howard with all the complications that could bring? She may have been a Catholic convert, but even Her Majesty would not brook the murder of her cousin.'

'I think he killed her by mistake, sir, then tried to cover his tracks. I think he tortured her for information, but she died. The relic and crucifix were added later, as were the cuts to her throat and belly.'

Shakespeare shook his head. 'It was no mistake. He planned to kill her. He knew he could not allow her to live as soon as he had subjected her to torture: if he had set her free the wrath of the Howards would have destroyed him. He planned to kill her and lay the blame on the Catholics by befouling her body with the relic and crucifix, to make it seem like some debauched

Popish rite. That fits with the Searcher of the Dead's findings. He said she had been dead three days and that she was killed elsewhere. The wounds that were supposed to have killed her had not produced enough blood, he said.'

And the marks on her wrists, he thought. They might as easily have been caused by manacles as rope. He had seen similar injuries on Thomas Woode after his sessions against Topcliffe's wall. But what sort of information would Topcliffe have been trying to prise from her?

The answer was plain: he had wanted the same information from Blanche that he was now trying to extract from Woode – the whereabouts of Robert Southwell. He must have heard of some link between her and the Jesuits; perhaps a servant in Howard of Effingham's household had passed on information, or an informant within the Catholic network. Topcliffe was a man possessed when it came to finding the Jesuit priest. He wanted Southwell, and he did not care who he had to ruin or slaughter to get to him. Shakespeare spurred his horse. He had been away from Catherine too long.

Topcliffe, Young, Newall and a force of their ten most hardened pursuivants came to Shakespeare's house in Seething Lane in the darkness half an hour before dawn.

They tethered their horses a street away, then trod softly towards the ancient house so that none should wake and alert Walsingham. There was to be no alarm, no uproar. This was to be done with precision and silence, so that Mr Secretary should wake at dawn or after and be none the wiser of what had happened at his close neighbour's home.

The plan was to go in at lightning speed. Flatten the door with one blow from the battering tree, then advance without shouting or mayhem, each member of the force to take one room so that no occupants of the house should escape. Topcliffe looked about him. The street was empty. 'Where, Dick, is your watchman? Who is guarding this house?' His voice was a gruff, urgent whisper.

Young glanced around. 'The idle fool must have gone home. I'll have strong words with him for this.'

'God's blood, Dick, you'll flog him raw. Let's go in.'

Six men held the heavy tree-trunk and swung back and forward once, then back again and brought it forward halfway up the door, close to the lock, crashing it down with one blow.

Topcliffe went in first, closely followed by Young. Then they stopped where they stood, mouths agape at the scene that confronted them.

The hallway was lit by torches and candles and the room was filled with men, twenty or so. Some stood, leaning on swords or holding bows. Others lay back against the walls. One or two puffed at pipes. They wore martial clothes, thick leather doublets like the pursuivants, and they gazed at Topcliffe and Young with nonchalant disdain.

It was an eerie sight in the flickering light. It seemed that two platoons had come face to face, both armed and ready to fight, yet one of the armies, the one already there, could scarcely bother to stand up for the battle. Topcliffe at last found his voice. 'Who are you?' he bellowed.

One of the men rose to his feet and sauntered forward until he was face to face with Topcliffe. He was a young man, perhaps in his early twenties, with a short, neatly trimmed beard and dark hair swept back about his ears. 'No, sir, who are you? And what are you doing in my brother's house?'

Topcliffe spluttered. 'You are Shakespeare's brother? What do you do here? I had not expected you!'

'My friends and I are lodging here, thanks to the kindness of my brother. We have been levied from Warwickshire to train with the London militias. We will soon be garrisoned at Tilbury for the defence of the realm, not that it is any of your business. And what, pray, is your business? It seems you are trespassing and have caused some criminal damage to my brother's door. Are you housebreakers? If so I shall see you hang for it. It would behove you well to think on this: my brother is a senior officer with Sir Francis Walsingham.'

A vein pulsed in Topcliffe's forehead. He stared at the young man with undisguised rage, then at Richard Young, who seemed nonplussed. 'God in heaven, Dick! Why did your man not bring us word of this?'

Young threw up his hands in red-faced bewilderment, 'I do not know. Perhaps he was afraid of these soldiers.'

Topcliffe took in the room. He was outnumbered almost two to one. There was no hope of taking on a band of heavily armed and trained fighters. This was some trick of Shakespeare's, some stratagem to defeat him. 'I know not how this has come about, but I promise you, Shakespeare – you and your brother – I will be back and you will both pay. I will bring down the wrath of God and Her Majesty on your head. And I will get that which I seek.'

Shakespeare's brother was a steadfast man with bright eyes and a wide forehead, shorter but more powerfully built than John. His mouth curled into a slight smile. 'I think, sir, you rise above your station in invoking the deity and our glorious sovereign lady. I suggest you crawl back into your festering hole and take your brother maggots with you before you are all squashed.'

Topcliffe's rage nearly got the better of him. He drew back his hand to strike the impertinent pup's face, then thought again. Churning inside with fury, he swung on his heel and strode to the gaping doorway. 'Let us go, Dick,' he said. 'Let us pluck your so-called watchman from his wife's sweaty thighs and give him a beating he will not readily forget.'

One of Shakespeare's men rose to his feet and dragged up a cowering fellow by the scruff of his neck. He kicked his breeches and sent him flying towards Topcliffe. 'Is this your watchman? Take him.'

Chapter 44

ON ARRIVAL IN London, Shakespeare rode with Boltfoot to Seething Lane, but instead of going into his house, he went straightway to Walsingham's office to report on the two failed attempts on Drake's life and, finally, his successful departure for the coastal waters of Spain.

Walsingham's dark brow lightened a shade. He nodded repeatedly. 'That is good. You say he is well and that he has definitely left these shores with the fleet?'

'Yes, Mr Secretary. All is as it should be.'

Walsingham chuckled. 'She sent a messenger after him, you know, with orders not to proceed with the mission. You are sure he did not receive them in time?'

'Well, if he did, he did not act upon them. And he sent you this letter.'

Walsingham undid the seal carefully with a knife and read the brief missive. He folded it and put it on the table. 'This is good, John. This is exactly what I wanted. Thank the Lord the Queen's rider did not arrive in time. You have done well, you and Mr Cooper between you.'

Shakespeare allowed the warm glow of praise to wash over him. It did not last long.

'However, things are not so happy for you in other regards. A complaint has been laid against you, with certain serious allegations made.' Mr Secretary looked at his chief intelligencer with accusing eyes.

Shakespeare felt the blood rising to his face. An image of Mother Davis and Isabella Clermont, then of Catherine Marvell flashed through his mind.

'Allegations of lewdness, John, and of witchcraft. There is talk of a charge being laid.'

Shakespeare frowned, as if in bewilderment. 'What are these accusations you speak of, Mr Secretary? And who has made them?'

'Are you sure you do not know?'

'I can think only Topcliffe.'

Walsingham nodded gravely. He paced to the window and looked out on the street. He could just see Shakespeare's modest home further up the way. It was quiet now, but he had heard rumours of a disturbance there. He turned back to Shakespeare. 'Of course. Topcliffe. I warned you, John, not to allow your personal disputes to disrupt our common cause. I even gave you a warrant to enter Topcliffe's home to interview a witness, did I not?'

'You did.'

'And he allowed you to do so?'

'He did. I would say he revelled in showing me his instruments of torture. He seemed proud of breaking Thomas Woode's body. A man not found guilty of any crime, nor even shown in court.'

Walsingham never raged. He did not need to. His whisper was more intimidating than the bear's growl or the wildcat's roar. 'John, this is not the time to debate such things. There are matters of more immediate import to concern us. Topcliffe lays this charge against you: that you did go to the sorceress and whoremonger Mother Davis. That you gave of your face hair and your seed to procure a love potion for a spell to ensnare a young woman named Catherine Marvell, a notorious Papist. These are serious charges, and Topcliffe says he has possession of the items used for the potion.' His eyes lifted to Shakespeare's forehead and the missing brow. 'If none of this is true, how will you explain the loss of an eyebrow and the discovery of identical hair in the possession of Mother Davis and now in the keeping of Topcliffe? The seed cannot be proved as yours, but alongside your brow, a court would accept it as most compelling evidence. You must know the penalty for witchcraft. As the Book of Exodus tells us: 'Thou shalt not suffer a witch to live . . .'"

For a moment, Shakespeare was speechless. Then he erupted like a pot left too long to heat. 'This is madness, Mr Secretary. This is all Topcliffe's doing. I did speak with Mother Davis, but only as part of my investigations. Under duress, Walstan Glebe, the broadsheet publisher, informed me that Mother Davis knew details of the killing and that she would contact me. This she did, so I went to see her. I was met by a French whore and taken to the woman's presence. She gave me drink, but plainly it contained some witch's potion, for the next I knew I was being used most lewdly by the French whore. And yet I could not move. My arms and legs were fixed motionless, dead as though I had imbibed hemlock. Mother Davis showed me a vial with what she said was my seed and told me I was now hers, that I could never escape her. I fell into unconsciousness and when I next awoke my arms and legs were moving once more. The house was empty and in darkness. I discovered my eyebrow was missing, but I have no recollection of it being removed. That is all I know. Except this: Topcliffe was privy to it, because he boasted of it at his house in Westminster. I fear he and Mother Davis are confederates, Mr Secretary. I would go further and say that I know it to be so. The charade was designed to ensnare me. The French whore claimed she was attacked by Southwell but it cannot be true. Her injuries were superficial. It was part of Topcliffe's plan to save his own neck and blame the Jesuit.'

Walsingham watched Shakespeare's face intently as he spoke. Finally he sighed. 'This is grave news, John. You have been a fool, however righteous the cause. But, on your behalf, I would say that your story is so preposterous it has the ring of verity.'

'There is more,' Shakespeare said. 'Much more. The culprit we look for, the killer of Lady Blanche Howard, is none other than Topcliffe himself.'

Walsingham rolled back on his heels. 'Topcliffe killed Blanche Howard?'

'It is certain, Mr Secretary.'

Walsingham shook his head. 'No, John, you cannot say such a thing. Be careful, very, very careful. You have made him an enemy already. I am trying to have the charges against you dropped but if you make wild allegations against him, he will most assuredly proceed against you for witchcraft and lewdness. And I will be hard pressed to defend you for he will produce witnesses and take you before Justice Young. Of that you can be certain.'

'So I am to be damned by the words of whores and murderers while a most cruel killer walks free – is that right? Is that the England you fight for, Sir Francis?' Even as he spoke the words, he realised he had made a mistake. Walsingham's loyalty to Queen and country was beyond question. He could not insult him so and emerge unscathed.

Yet Walsingham did not turn him out. Neither did he react badly. Instead he rang a bell to summon a servant. Then, his voice softer, he said, 'Bring us brandy.' When the serving man had bowed and departed, Walsingham indicated to Shakespeare that he should sit at the table, then took a chair close by himself. 'Come, John,' he said. 'You are overheated and tired after your long journey and you have already rendered your country and

Queen a great service. I will forget what you have just said and I will listen to you. If you have proof against Topcliffe, then tell me. But afterwards you must listen quietly to what I have to say.'

Shakespeare told him everything: the detail of the crucifix and relic found in the body of Lady Blanche, and reported on, however obliquely, by Walstan Glebe in *The London Informer* broadsheet; the full squalid details of his visit to the house occupied by Mother Davis and her whores; the story of the blind monk Ptolomeus and the removal of his printing press by Topcliffe; the certainty that the seditious tract found at the burnt-out house in Hog Lane was printed on this press using paper from Rymesford Mill. 'And, last, there is the motive, Mr Secretary. Topcliffe is possessed with the desire of a Bedlam madman to capture the Jesuit Robert Southwell. He will do anything to find him and bring him to his death. I contend that he believed Lady Blanche, a new-converted Papist, had knowledge of the priest's whereabouts. He knows only one way to extract information: torture. But he went too far and killed her, then had to cover up his crime. If you have doubts, Mr Secretary, then speak with the Searcher of the Dead. Everything I have described fits with Joshua Peace's findings.'

Silence. Walsingham stroked his dark beard. His face hung as heavy as a hunting dog's with a scent. Finally he spoke. 'John, you must listen to me now. You have had your say, and I must tell you that you have too little evidence. Consider, Richard Topcliffe is the Queen's favourite. He has control over the interrogations carried out in the Tower. He is so trusted in his fervour that he has a rack in his home, licensed by the Privy Council. He is the Member of Parliament for Old Sarum, and he is fighting in his own way for England. This is all fact. On your side, you have the word of a blind, decrepit monk and your own surmise. You have nothing.'

'But—'

'I said, listen. You have nothing, John, and that should be the end of the matter. However, you have done an immense work for me and England these past days. You have saved Drake to set sail against the Spanish. I will ignore this sordid gossip about you and some Popish woman named Marvell, for I am sure you would not be so foolish as to embroil yourself with such a person. But I will allow you leeway. You may take your information to Topcliffe and use it against him to secure your own future. Some might call it blackmail. I would call it a trade. You let him know that if he does not drop all charges against you, then you will proceed to tell all you know to Lord Howard of Effingham. That will give Topcliffe pause for thought. He knows that Howard, in his turn, will take your allegations direct to Her Majesty, and that is the last thing he wants.'

'Why can I not go straight to Howard?'

Walsingham's voice rose, not a great deal but noticeably to one who knew him well. 'Because, John, you will dance at Tyburn and Topcliffe will retire wounded to his estate. And that would suit neither me nor you. I need you, John. And I need Topcliffe.'

In the hall of his home, John Shakespeare came face to face with his brother. He looked around the hall in astonishment. 'William! Why are you here? And who, pray, are these soldiers?'

'They are company players, the Queen's Men, and I have joined them, for they were short a man. We are soon to play at the Theatre in Shoreditch but we have already given a fine performance.'

'You will have to explain more clearly.' Distracted, Shakespeare could think of little save his talk with Walsingham and how to act upon it.

'We have been playing the soldier, John. Do we not look the part?'

'Indeed you do.' Shakespeare smiled weakly and at last embraced his brother with his good arm. He stood back and looked him full in the face. They had not seen each other in two years.

William clapped his hands and, as if waiting for the signal, Jane and Catherine descended the stairway, each holding the hand of one of Thomas Woode's children. Jane and the children were smiling, but not Catherine.

'Topcliffe was coming for them, John,' his brother said. 'Jane went out, apparently to market, and found me at the Theatre. I came with my friends dressed as soldiers. Topcliffe battered down the door to take Mistress Marvell and the children, but was confronted with us. We had been rehearsing for a history with battle scenes and were able to raid the costume box for this attire and the prop box for our weapons. Luckily, we did not need them for the swords are as blunt as sheep's teeth. Had Topcliffe known we were but players rather than fighting men, he might not have been turned away so readily. As it was, we had a merry time and sent him and his cohort away. I fear, though, that we are out of pocket. The play should have been staged by now.'

Shakespeare was not listening. He had eyes only for Catherine and approached her slowly, as in a dream, across the hall. He wanted to take her in his arms but he was conscious of the people around him. She let slip the hand of little Grace and touched his. She saw the sling that held his injured arm, but said nothing. She was pale, stiff with tension and distraught.

'Catherine, I have longed to see you.'

'And I you, John, but I can think of nothing but Mr Woode. What has become of him?'

Thomas Woode was at the heart of this outrage. Yet how could that be righted with all that Shakespeare knew of him? The gift of an illicit press to a renegade priest, the harbouring of Jesuits. There was enough to hang him twice and Shakespeare could bear witness against him. But he would not, for Catherine would be implicated, too. And perhaps for another reason: because it would be wrong for Woode to suffer more after all he had been through in Topcliffe's strong room. 'I am going to Topcliffe this day. I will do what I can.' Even as he spoke the words he knew he risked giving her vain hope. There was every chance that Woode was already dead. He moved forward, but she flinched and held back. This was not the time, nor the proper company.

His brother broke into his sombre thoughts. 'We must away, brother. We have a play to perform for the *paying* public. But before we go, we have a matter that concerns you.'

'What matter?'

'The matter of four members of our company who are sorely missed. They arrived here in London ahead of us to ready the Theatre for our coming. After much investigating, we discovered they were taken by you while sleeping in a barn.'

Shakespeare was puzzled. He knew nothing of any players. 'What manner of men are these, pray?'

'You deemed them worthless vagabonds and sent them to Bridewell. They had been near the scene of an infamous murder, I am told, and you considered them possible witnesses. And now they have disappeared.'

Shakespeare felt a stab of shame. 'God in heaven! Of course I remember them. They were removed from my custody by Topcliffe's men. I tried to find them but could not. I had not understood they were players.'

'And does that make a difference in this brave England, John? Are you not thought worthy of protection under the law if you are a mere beggar? Does a player have more justice than a vagabond, or is a knight of the realm better served by jury than a glover's son?'

'William, I am sorry. I will do what I can.'

Chapter 45

THE MEETING STARTED badly. They stood facing each other at the forbidding entrance to Topcliffe's home in Westminster: Shakespeare and Boltfoot outside, Topcliffe and his boy Jones within the doorway, standing four-square like bulldogs guarding their territory.

When Topcliffe spoke, it was in a growl. 'Mr Secretary told me you might arrive here, Shakespeare. How fares your Catholic whore? Does she know you have been a jack-sauce with the beguiling Mademoiselle Clermont? It is my bounden duty to inform her, I think.'

Shakespeare's hand went to his sword, but Boltfoot, whose caliver hung loosely in his arms, restrained him.

'Hah, Cooper! That won't save your master's life. He is at my mercy and I will see him hang before the week is out.'

'No, Topcliffe,' Shakespeare said. '*You* will hang. I know what you have done and I have witnesses. You took Lady Blanche Howard and tortured her because you thought she could lead you to Robert Southwell, the Jesuit. You killed her.'

Nicholas Jones, the apprentice, sniggered.

Topcliffe lashed out and caught Jones full in the face. He reeled backwards, blood gushing from his nose. 'Stow you, Nick.' Jones wiped his filthy sleeve across his face to staunch the blood. He seemed to shrink into his shoulders, like a whipped dog.

'I have all the evidence I need, Topcliffe,' said Shakespeare. 'Only you could have printed those tracts found at Hog Lane because you were the one in possession of the press.'

'That isn't evidence! Who will listen to a dead monk?'

'Ptolomeus is very much alive.'

Topcliffe laughed and now clapped an arm round Jones's shoulders. 'Is he, now? What do you say, Nicholas?'

Jones managed to snigger again, spraying blood. He drew a finger slowly across his throat, then flicked it up theatrically towards the ear. 'Squealed like a piglet. I would never have thought a Popish devil would have so much blood in him, master.' He dabbed at his nose with his sleeve again, wiping away more blood.

Shakespeare felt a sense of overwhelming guilt. He should not have left the old monk to such a fate. But how could he have known that Topcliffe would return? And, in the circumstances, what could he have done? The only comfort was that Ptolomeus had clearly been longing for death; the sadness was the cruel manner of its coming. 'I have enough without Ptolomeus. And I will take it to one who will listen. Howard of Effingham.'

The smile froze on Topcliffe's lips. He raised a hand and made an indecisive chopping motion, as if he was about to make a point but had suddenly lost what it should be. Shakespeare saw that he had hit home, that Topcliffe had realised instantly that such a course of action would make things not just difficult for him but impossible. The Queen might feign ignorance of what he did in her name, but she would not ignore her cousin Charles Howard, particularly in relation to the death of Lady Blanche.

'I see you are lost for words, Topcliffe. Who now has the other at his mercy, pray?'

'I could kill you at this very moment.'

'You could try, but I doubt that you would succeed.

Mr Cooper is handy with cutlass and caliver, as you must know.'

Topcliffe stood a moment, disdain writ across his face. When he spoke, his voice dripped scorn. 'Your problem, Shakespeare, is that you are young. You do not have the stench of burning Protestant flesh in your nostrils. You were not there in the fifties when Bloody Mary and her Spanish droop were burning good Englishmen and women in the name of the anti-Christ. All they know is brutality. It is all they respect, so if they poke out your eye you must poke out both theirs, and their mother's and child's.'

'So, what you do is better?'

'It is God's will, Shakespeare. That is all. God's and Her Majesty's. Enough. What do you want? Why are you here?'

What Shakespeare wanted and what Mr Secretary would allow him were two very different things. He wanted Topcliffe taken off the streets, hanged preferably or, at the very least, locked away where he could never harm anyone again. But he had to settle for less. The words stuck in his craw, but he took a deep breath and laid out his terms. 'You will return what is mine, taken from me most foully by your witch familiar Davis. You will never venture to my house again. Neither will you molest nor interfere with Mistress Marvell, nor the children in her care, nor my maidservant. You will release Mr Woode this day, and you will tell me where you have brought the four vagabonds from Hog Lane so that they may be given their freedom. In return, I will not reveal your murderous cruelty towards Lady Blanche Howard to her family. I have, however, left a deposition with a certain lawyer, who will take it to Lord Howard of Effingham should any accident befall me. Do you understand?'

'Curse you, Shakespeare, you Rome-squealing little clerk. It seems you have me strapped over a cask.'

'It seems that way, does it not?'

Suddenly Topcliffe barked a laugh. 'What think you, Nicholas?' he said to his apprentice. 'Do you think I can be frighted so easy?' Then he turned back to Shakespeare. 'And what would you want with the four Irish clapperdudgeon vagabonds? Perchance you fancy playing girl-boys with one. Now you have acquired a taste for Papism and bitchery . . .'

'They are Crown witnesses and you have cloyed them away illegally.'

Topcliffe shook his head slowly. 'Nothing illegal about it. I had the mittimus from Mr Justice Young, magistrate of London. They languish in one of London's most stinking holes. If you can find them, you can have them. As for the traitor Woode, there isn't much left of him to hand over, so I'll hold him a little longer. As I recall, the warrant from Mr Justice Young allows me yet seven days before I must bring him to court.'

'Then you leave me no option. I will go straightway to Deptford to consult with the Admiral, Lord Howard of Effingham.'

'Do so, Shakespeare! You have no evidence against me, not a shred, and you will find yourself charged with lewdness and sorcery before ever I face a court. I will piss on you while you swing.'

The door slammed. Shakespeare stood in the street, shaking. Above him the majesty of Westminster Abbey soared. There had seemed to be hope in the air, yet on the cobbled stones there was none. A killer would be free to stalk London, taking and torturing at will, while he, Shakespeare, faced an uncertain future.

Boltfoot Cooper slung his caliver back over his shoulder. 'It is time to meet fire with fire, master.'

His words knocked Shakespeare from his dark trance. 'What is that, Boltfoot?'

'I will hunt down the vagabonds. If need be, I will visit every one of London's fourteen gaols and break down the gates to find them. And you must find the Davis witch and her whore.'

'Thank you, Boltfoot. It is good that one of us thinks clearly this day.'

As they moved away in the bright spring sunshine, Shakespeare noticed a young woman, fair of face and light-haired, walking towards Topcliffe's door. She was carrying a bundle that he took to be a baby.

Shakespeare hired a tiltboat from Westminster stairs downstream to St Mary Overy stairs, then walked a half-mile to the street where he had been lured by Mother Davis and Isabella Clermont. He was aware he was being followed by Topcliffe's apprentice, Jones, and another man, more powerfully built. Shakespeare knew he had little time: Topcliffe would have the magistrate, Young, issue an arrest warrant in very short order. Languishing in Newgate, Shakespeare would be helpless to do anything for Catherine or Thomas Woode.

The house in which he had encountered Mother Davis and her whore stood dark and empty, its windows shuttered and its doors locked. A poster was pasted on the bolted doorway announcing that the building was available to let. As Shakespeare looked up at the blank windows, Jones and his companion jeered and barracked him. 'Looking for a wench, Shakespeare? How about a juicy blackamoor? Or you can have my sister for half a crown. She'll spur you on.'

A warehouseman passed, pushing a small handcart, top-heavy with bulging jute sacks. Shakespeare stopped him. He handed him a penny. 'Whose building is this?'

The man was grateful to put down the handles of the cart, and glanced at Jones and the other man. 'Friends?'

'Anything but.'

'Good. I've seen the snivelling little one round here before and I don't like the look of him. This fine building belonged to a Spanish gentry-cove, sir. Imported wines from Portugal and beyond. I sometimes helped him when a ship came in. But he was discovered helping Romish priests, sir, and flung out of the country, back where he belongs.'

'And now?'

'And now it does stand empty, sir, awaiting another occupant.'

'Is it ever used?'

'Not to my knowledge, sir. It was declared forfeit by the court.'

'Who has the keys?'

'That would be the new owner, sir. One Richard Topcliffe of Westminster, a famous priest-hunter, who has made himself exceeding rich, people say, by drawing the innards from young Papists.' The warehouseman laughed.

It was a dead end. Topcliffe had given Mother Davis the key to the building to set her trap for Shakespeare. He had just one more hope. Walking quickly westwards along the bank of the Thames, still followed, he made his way to The Clink, a long, two-storey stone building one street back from the river and close to the London residence of the Bishop of Winchester.

Street traders with baskets of pies, cakes, bread and roasted fowls were bargaining with the prisoners, who clustered on the other side of the iron-barred windows, stretching their hands through the narrow gaps with coins to pay for the food. There was a lot of shouting. Shakespeare banged on the heavy door. The turnkey, a small man with cadaverous cheeks and a tongue that continually licked his lips, like a serpent's, regarded Shakespeare suspiciously. He demanded to see Starling Day and Parsimony Field on Queen's business.

The turnkey leered at him. 'They are here, young gentleman,

but it'll cost you two shillings to consort with them. They can charge what they likes, but I want my two shillings first.'

'Did you not hear me, gaoler? I said I am on Queen's business.'

'And if you will pay me two shillings you can join them in lust and it will be worth every last groat to you.' Angrily, Shakespeare handed over the coins. Jones was right behind him in the street and he wanted to escape him. The other pursuer had gone, probably to take word to Topcliffe and Young. 'You do understand, gaoler, that you might lose your licence for demanding money and turning this gaol into a bawdy-house? I am like to report you to the Liberty of Clink for your dealings.'

'As you please, sir. And do you think they will do anything that might come between them and their own garnish?' He looked over Shakespeare's shoulder at Jones. 'Will you be bringing your young friend, too? Give me another shilling and he can have admittance as well.'

Shakespeare handed the gaoler two shillings more. 'This is to not give him admittance, turnkey. Keep him locked out at all costs.'

'As you wish, master.' The gaoler grasped Shakespeare by the arm of his doublet and yanked him in, pulling the four-inch-thick fortified door closed just as Jones thrust his lower right leg into the gap. He yelled with pain as the heavy wood cracked on the side of his knee.

Shakespeare found Starling and Parsimony living like merchants' wives in the best cells in The Clink, two large rooms, next to each other, with feather beds and a goodly supply of wine and food.

'Ah, Mr Shakespeare, sir,' Starling said, 'what is your pleasure this fine day? You will see we are well settled in here, happy as two bees in honey.'

Shakespeare looked about her cell with some amazement. She had set it up as well as any room to be found in a luxurious trugging-house or inn. There were wax candles burning all about and fine linen on the bed. Starling was well fed and rosy-cheeked. 'I can see you are well provided for here, mistress, but I have come to set you free – on one condition: that you tell me the whereabouts of a whore called Isabella Clermont and her procuress Mother Davis.'

'I ain't never heard of them. Try Parsey. She knows all the game girls.'

Parsimony's door was shut. She was just finishing off with a customer. Two minutes later the door opened and a red-faced, well-fed man emerged. He wore expensive courtier's clothes, which he was busy adjusting. He briefly caught Shakespeare's eye and hurriedly looked away. Parsimony held the door open. 'Come in, Mr Shakespeare. This is a fine vaulting-house you sent us to. A wondrous place full of gentlemen of high birth.'

The room was every bit as well appointed as Starling's. 'I have come to offer you an exchange that will lead to your freedom, Mistress Field.'

She laughed. 'I am well set up, sir. And I have forgiven you for sending us here. I suppose we met in dark times. It was a sad day that Harry Slide was done for, God rest his soul. He knew how to make a girl happy. Attended to our pleasures as well as his own, which is uncommon in a man of any breeding. He was a good friend.'

Starling noted Shakespeare's impatience. 'He's looking for a couple of Winchester geese, Parsey, and he's in a hurry.'

'I need to find Mother Davis and Isabella Clermont. Do you know of them?'

Parsimony turned pale. 'Know of them? I know of Mother Witch, Mr Shakespeare. Don't go near her. That woman consorts with demons and Satan himself. She is succubus and incubus, and every worm with sharpened teeth and poisoned talons in hell.'

'You have had dealings with her?'

'Oh, yes. She snatched two of our best girls when I was with Gilbert Cogg. Took them in broad daylight and settled them with her own lice-crawling doxies. By the time we found out where they were they both had the pox, their paps had shrunk from lack of food, they had rat bites on their legs and arms. Looked as appetising to a man as a bag of foul-smelling bones. They were worthless to us, sir.'

'I must find her.'

'And what do I get in return?'

'Your freedom . . . and vengeance on Davis.'

'And the lease back on our house of entertainment?'

'If at all possible. I can give you no money.'

'Just vouch for us, Mr Shakespeare.'

Shakespeare felt uneasy. But what choice did he have? 'Very well,' he said. 'If you lead me to her, I'll do what I can.'

Parsimony smiled. She had nice white teeth. 'That witch is like smoke,' she said. 'But I will give you a place to try, sir . . .'

Chapter 46

THERE WAS A door at the back of the gaol into a yard, then more doors through outhouses. The gaoler unlocked them and showed Shakespeare the way into a long, muddy garden, where a pair of pigs were rutting energetically.

At the end of the garden was an eight-foot-high wall. The gaoler thrust an apple-tree ladder into Shakespeare's arms.

Shakespeare scaled the wall easily. There was no sign of Jones. He began to lope through the streets away from The Clink, eastwards. He was heading for London Bridge to get north of the river. As he ran on to the bridge, he felt the deathly gaze of the traitors' heads bearing down on him from their pikes atop the gatehouse.

Parsimony had mentioned a house in Billiter Lane, not far from his own home in Seething Lane. It was not the sort of place you would expect to find a sorceress and her whores, for it was in the heart of the city, an expensive street where traders and their fur-clad wives resided. But perhaps that was the attraction of the area for Mother Davis: she could affect the ways of the wealthy and gain anonymity.

Past Fen Church, he trotted along the broad sweep of Blanch Appleton. His heart pounded, his lungs dragged harshly at the air. To his left he noticed the huge works that were being carried out on Ironmongers' Hall. Enormous cranes of oak and elm with dangling ropes and pulleys towered over the skeletal structure.

He turned left into Billiter Lane and stopped in his tracks. Ahead of him, like a wall of steel and black leather, stood twenty pursuivants, swords drawn, wheel-locks armed and pointed along the street towards him.

For a moment he stood, scarcely comprehending what he saw. He turned to run the other way, but his face met the fist of the chief pursuivant Newall full on. Shakespeare's legs buckled and he fell into the muddy ditch in the centre of the street. Then he was hit by another blow, from a silver-topped blackthorn, about the left temple, and darkness fell.

He awoke into gloom. His head hurt in a way it never had before, a heavy, insistent throbbing that made death seem preferable to life. He tried to move and found his feet were fettered in cramp-rings, fixed solidly to the ground. He was in a cell, lit by a tallow candle in a black iron wall sconce. Nicholas Jones, Topcliffe's apprentice, was smirking at him. 'Thought you could get away from me, did you?' He had a pipe in his mouth and belched fumes as he spoke. 'We've got some merriment in store for you, John Shakespeare. You wait there while I tell Mr Topcliffe you've come round. No strolling off now . . .' He took the pipe from his mouth and tapped the burning sotweed and ashes over Shakespeare's head.

He wanted to shake his head to rid himself of the hot embers, but he did not have the strength. His vision came in drifts like snow in the wind. And then he collapsed once more into nothingness.

When he woke again, Shakespeare thought he was in a dream. Above him were the warm oak beams of his bedroom ceiling. Sunshine flooded in through the window across the bed in which he lay. He turned his head. At his side, on a three-legged stool, sat Jane, his maidservant.

'Mr Shakespeare?'

'Jane? Is that really you?'

'You are awake at last.'

He closed his eyes. Immense fatigue enveloped him. Had he dreamt the time in the cell with Jones? Some strange nightmare? An incursion by demons?

'How long have I been here, Jane?'

'Three days and three nights, master. Thank the Lord you are with us. We feared you might never wake. The blow to your head . . .'

'How did I come here?'

Jane took his hand. 'You were brought here on a cart by Mr Secretary Walsingham's men. Don't talk now. Let me bring you some meat and drink.'

Gradually he became aware of his body: various parts throbbed with a dull ache – his arm where it had been cut by Herrick's blade, his beaten face, his head. 'Walsingham's men brought me here? I believed I was in a cell, held by Richard Topcliffe.'

Jane stood from the stool and fussed round him, smoothing his bedclothes and plumping his bolster beneath his head. 'Sir, you have not eaten for three days or more. The physician said you must keep still when you woke and take food and drink slowly.'

Shakespeare raised himself on his elbows. 'Jane, I am not an infant to be coddled. Tell me what I need to know.'

'You were held by Topcliffe, master. We feared the worst. But Boltfoot went to Mr Secretary Walsingham and straightway he sent his men with a warrant to free you. When you were brought here, you were no better than a corpse, sir, covered with blood and filth. Your breathing was so faint I could scarce detect it.'

Shakespeare tried to collect his thoughts. He recalled his dash from The Clink to Billiter Lane, coming face to face with the pursuivants, the brutish blow to the face and the crack on the head. Then nothing, except lightning glimpses of Topcliffe's strong-room and of Nicholas Jones, his infernal boy.

'Is Catherine here?'

Jane busied herself opening the casement window. 'Not at the moment, master.'

'Where, then, is she?'

Jane's eyes were still averted. She looked out over the little garden at the rear of the house. Birdsong filtered in through the open window. 'She is at her master's home in Dowgate, sir. She has left a letter for you.' She handed it to Shakespeare, then made hurriedly for the door.

'Jane, wait.'

Shakespeare carefully opened the seal with the knife that always lay on the table beside his bed. The letter, in a fair hand, was not long but it seemed to take him an age to read it.

John,

If you are reading this letter, I know that you are recovered, for which I give thanks to God that our prayers have been answered. Yet there is no happy ending to this story. I do not have words adequately to explain how it sorrows me to write you this letter. My master, Thomas Woode, is now at home in Dowgate and I must go to him with the children. He is broken. He cannot walk, nor can he raise his arms and hands even to feed himself. He has been close to death and will never be whole again. I must be nurse to him, as well as mother and governess to Andrew and Grace. It is my Christian duty so to do.

You know my love for you, John. You can have no doubt of it. For a few short hours we were as one, and I shall, at least, always have memories of that night. But I cannot be yours for their need is greater than ours. Do not be angry with me, or come after me to Dowgate. I could not bear the pain of saying goodbye to you again.

John, your efforts have brought about the release of my master, for which I thank you. I regret many of the things I said to you and know you to be a good man. I must also thank Jane, your brother and his company, and I will write to them all, for they undoubtedly saved me and the children from a terrible fate. Forgive me, John.

Yours, in the love of Christ, Catherine.

After a while, Shakespeare looked up. He breathed deeply. 'Do you know what is in this letter, Jane?'

'Yes, master.' Her voice was choked and she would still not look at him. She wiped a tear from her cheek.

'Do you think there is any hope that she might change her mind?'

Jane shook her head. Tears flowed and she could not speak.

'None?'

She shook her head once more.

'Thank you, Jane. You may go.'

She ran from his chamber. He heard her howling like a wounded animal as she ran down the stairs. He crumpled the letter into a tight ball and threw it to the floor. Moments later, he slipped tentatively from between the sheets. He felt unsteady, but he was able to walk across the room and pick up the crushed paper. He took it to the window, where he smoothed it out and read it again.

Chapter 47

'WHAT WORD FROM Drake?' Walsingham demanded.
'There is nothing as yet, neither good nor bad,' John
Hawkins replied. 'That is how we would wish it.'

Walsingham seemed unconvinced. 'That is not how *I* would
wish it, Mr Hawkins. I would wish to hear that he has sailed
your ships into Lisbon and set fire to this Spanish fleet before it
can leave port, for assuredly we are not ready to repel it.'

The room was silent. All those sitting at the long table in the
library of his house in Seething Lane knew the truth of what he
had said. England's defences were woefully inadequate. Should
Spain's battle-hardened troops ever land in Sussex or Kent or
Essex, they would sweep past the Queen's new-formed militias
and descend on London like lions. There would be blood-
letting in the fields and towns of England on a scale not known
in five hundred years.

Around the table sat Hawkins, architect of the new navy,
Walsingham himself, his secretaries Arthur Gregory and Francis
Mills, codebreaker Thomas Phelippes and John Shakespeare.

'Well, at least we have got him to sea,' Walsingham said
at last, breaking the silence, 'for which we must thank Mr
Shakespeare.'

All those at the table nodded in Shakespeare's direction. Mills
put his hands together, as if applauding at the playhouse.

'But, Mr Mills, I worry more than somewhat about your intelligence gathering.'

Mills reddened. 'Mr Secretary?'

'Indeed. When last this group was convened – sans Mr Hawkins – you gave a report on the events surrounding the murder of William the Silent at Delft. In the main, it was helpful and accurate, but there was one detail that I now know to have been dangerously inaccurate. In truth, I would go so far as to call it false and misleading. I sincerely hope not deliberately so. You said that the assassin Balthasar Gerard had an associate and you gave intelligence, purportedly from Holland, that this unnamed man was known for his beating of whores and that he battered one to death, mutilating her body with religious symbols. Pray, where did you find this information?'

Mills spluttered, seemingly lost for words. His sharp little eyes widened in something like panic as the gaze of the others in the room lighted on him. 'Why, my contacts in the Dutch network, Mr Secretary.'

Walsingham shook his head slowly. 'I have taken the liberty of contacting the authorities in Delft and Rotterdam. They do not support your information. Yes, they were certain Balthasar Gerard had a confederate, but there was no suggestion of a link with the murdered woman. What they did find was that this confederate of Gerard was a flagellant and that he employed prostitutes to scourge him. At no time was he known to return the favour. Nor were there religious symbols carved into the body of the woman who died.'

'I – I do not understand. That was my information.'

'Are you certain, Mr Mills, that you did not receive that information closer to home? From Mr Topcliffe or his associates, perchance?'

Mills was cornered. Shakespeare watched him. It held the same brutal fascination as a bear-baiting when one of the great bears, Sackerson or Hunks, had a dog in its grip, breaking its back with the immense power of its paws. Mills conceded defeat. He nodded. 'He told me he had contacts in Holland who had told him this, master. I confess I should have made certain.'

'You should, Mr Mills, also have wondered why Mr Topcliffe sought you out to bring you this information. It is scarce within his remit.' Walsingham turned to Shakespeare. 'Do you not agree, John? I think your job might have been a little easier without this false trail laid.'

'Forgive me,' Mills said. He stood up. 'Mr Topcliffe told me he had certain information on this matter from a priest he had interrogated, but he said I must not divulge that he was the source. I should not have passed on this intelligence without checking or at least explaining its provenance. Please accept my resignation, Mr Secretary. I have failed you and must accept your derision.'

'No, Mr Mills, I will not accept your resignation. But I will accept your apologies and I trust Mr Shakespeare will, too. Let us all learn from this. The accuracy of our intelligence is paramount. We must question every scrap of information and examine the motives of those from whom it comes. And you must always divulge your sources to me. I leave it to all of you to draw your own conclusions as to Mr Topcliffe's motives in this case. Now then, let us consider other related matters. First, the question of John Doughty, the brother of Thomas Doughty who was executed by Drake on that far-off shore all those years ago. We know John Doughty had his own plot against Drake a few years ago, that he wanted revenge for his brother's death, not to mention a twenty thousand ducats' reward from Philip of Spain. John Doughty was caught and sent to the Marshalsea. But no one seemed to know what happened to him next and I believe Mr Shakespeare wondered whether he might somehow be at large and involved in this most recent plot. Well, we can now put everyone's mind to rest on this matter. Mr Gregory, if you will . . .'

Arthur Gregory stood as Mills sat down, glad to have the eyes of those present focused elsewhere. Gregory smiled and spoke slowly, trying to cover his stammer as best he could. 'I made further inquiries. It s-s-seems John Doughty was taken from the Marsh-sh-shalsea to Newgate to await execution s-s-some four years past. This sh-should, of course, have been registered in the Marshalsea's black book, but it was not. Doughty cheated the hangman by dying of the bloody flux. A mundane end to a sm-sm-small, resentful man. It s-seems fitting that no one knew, or cared, what had happened to him. The one thing we do know is that he played no part in this most recent affair.'

Walsingham took over. 'So we are left with two men: a Fleming going by a variety of names, including Herrick, and a treacherous sea-captain named Harper Stanley. The first of these, Herrick, certainly fits the description of Balthasar Gerard's associate from Delft. I am convinced he was the 'dragon slayer' sent here by Mendoza and Philip to murder the Vice-Admiral, and he came close to succeeding on at least two occasions. I suspect that we will never know more about him, but that does not worry me. I do not wish to make a martyr of him, which is why I believe Mr Shakespeare was correct to leave him in Plymouth for trial and execution. As far as I am concerned the fewer people who learn of this attempt on Drake's life the better. We want our vice-admiral to be invincible and heroic in the minds of the people. His strength gives us strength.'

'What of Captain Stanley?' Shakespeare put in. 'Do we know aught of him?'

Walsingham looked to his codebreaker. 'I took the liberty

of asking Mr Phelippes to make a few inquiries while you were recovering, Mr Shakespeare.'

Phelippes breathed on his glasses, then wiped them clean on the sleeve of his shirt. The glass was scratched and almost opaque from endless buffings. He did not stand to speak. 'Indeed I did. He changed his name to Stanley from Percy. We should have spotted him a long time ago. I talked to some of his brother officers and discovered he was an habitué of the French embassy. He told friends that there was a French gentlewoman there with whom he was intimately acquainted. He came and went at will. I then recalled some intercepted letters from the embassy to Mendoza, detailing ship movements. We could never work out who sent them. They were exceeding damaging to England, giving away positions and strengths of our fleet. When Drake or Mr Hawkins was at sea, Mendoza would know within days. I have now compared the hand used in these missives with Captain Stanley's in his papers. They are identical. We believe he sold these secrets for the money and out of resentment for the punishments and disgrace inflicted on his family after the Northern Rebellion eighteen years past. I also believe there is a probability he was linked to the man we call Herrick. My theory – and it is no more than such – is that he told the Spanish four or five months since that if Mendoza sent a hired killer, he would provide him with assistance in weapons and access to the Vice-Admiral. In the end, when it seemed the plot would fail, he took matters into his own hands. Fortunately Drake's companion Diego and Mr Boltfoot Cooper stood between him and success.'

Walsingham cleared his throat. 'So, there we have it. Drake has been saved. For the moment. But keep vigilant and work hard to discover conspiracies in the dunghills of London. This will not be the last of Mendoza's plots on behalf of his prince. Say your prayers, gentlemen, every morning and every evening and oft times in between, for truly it is in God's gift now whether England live or die.' As the assembled rose to leave Walsingham raised his index finger to Shakespeare. 'You will stay, Mr Shakespeare.'

When they were alone, Walsingham offered Shakespeare refreshment, then began to walk the room, his hands clasped behind his back. Shakespeare watched him in silence. At last Mr Secretary spoke.

'There is one final matter, John, of which I thought it best to speak with you alone. The matter of Robert Southwell, the Jesuit priest. You have not found him yet . . . have you?'

'No, Sir Francis,' Shakespeare said instantly. He had rehearsed this moment in his mind. Perhaps he had met Southwell, but he could never be sure, for the priest had not admitted his name.

'Topcliffe believes you did meet him. He believes he was harboured by Thomas Woode and his governess, Catherine Marvell, and that you colluded with them.'

'That is not so. I have colluded with no one.'

'Yet if you did find him, you would tell me, would you not?'

'Indeed I would, Mr Secretary.'

'And if you thought that Woode or Mistress Marvell was harbouring Jesuit priests, you would tell me that too?'

'I am sure they are not harbouring Jesuit priests, Mr Secretary.'

Walsingham raised a dark eyebrow. 'Interesting phrasing, John. The present tense. Surely you are not learning the Romish art of equivocation.'

'Mr Secretary?'

Walsingham picked up a paper from the table. 'I will let it pass. This time. But you must not deal lightly with these Jesuits, John. This Southwell is our enemy.' He showed the paper to Shakespeare. 'You see there is a verse here. It is by Southwell.

Read it, John, though it turn your stomach. You see he calls Mary of Scots a saint, a martyr and a rose. This is the woman who worked for the death of our beloved sovereign.'

Shakespeare read the verse. Was this the man he had met in the knot garden? How had he composed such a thing? Surely even Roman Catholics must know her for a scheming murderess.

Walsingham took the paper from him. 'Enough. I will just tell you that Thomas Woode is known to my intelligencers in Rome, where he has been a generous benefactor of the English College. Let us now speak of other things. Tell me, John, I believe there is a fondness between you and Mistress Marvell. Is that correct?'

Shakespeare breathed deeply. He nodded until the words would form properly. 'There was a fondness, sir.'

'It is finished?'

Shakespeare nodded again. He could not speak.

Walsingham's voice softened. 'I am sorry. I understand your sorrow, John, but it is for the best. Trust me on this; such attachments cannot survive in the present climate, not while you do such vital work, not while suspicion and sedition lurk in the shadows . . .'

Shakespeare wanted to shout that it was not for the best, that his heart was broken. He wanted to shout that he would rather be a schoolteacher and married to Catherine than do this job and be without her. But no words would form in his throat.

Walsingham saw his distress and poured wine. 'We will speak no more of it. You must have a few days away from your toil, John. I believe your brother has arrived. Spend some time with him, if you wish. You have suffered injuries; make yourself whole. But before you take your well-earned rest – your ride to Plymouth and all that ensued was, indeed, magnificent and much admired by Her Majesty – I have one more task for you.

I want you to go to Lord Howard of Effingham and tell him you have solved the murder of his daughter. You are to tell him that the killer was a man named Herrick, who is now executed for that murder and for the attempted murder of Sir Francis Drake.'

At last Shakespeare found his voice. 'You are asking me to say something that we both know to be a lie, Mr Secretary. We know who killed Lady Blanche Howard.'

Walsingham's face tightened. 'Do this for me, John. I have gone up against a man beloved of our Queen to save you from the weight of the law. We must do unpleasant things sometimes to protect ourselves from an infinitely greater evil. Which of us would be spared by the Inquisition should the Spanish prevail? None. We seek only those who sow discord. So you will do this thing for me and I promise you that Mr Thomas Woode and Mistress Marvell will never be threatened or molested by Richard Topcliffe again. Do you understand?'

Shakespeare nodded.

'Then do it today, John. And God go with you.'

Chapter 48

BOLTFOOT COOPER LOOKED uncommonly awkward. He held his cap between gnarled hands and twisted it as if he was wringing the neck of a fowl.

Shakespeare gazed at him quizzically. 'Tell me, Boltfoot, what happened with your inquiries into the whereabouts of the four vagabonds from Hog Lane?'

'I have discovered them and set them free.'

'Really? That is wonderful news. Pray, where were they?'

'Still in Bridewell, master.'

'In Bridewell!'

'They were in none of the other prisons, so I went back there. As I questioned the turnkey he seemed uncomfortable, guilty, even. In the end I threatened him with the might of Mr Secretary – and yourself, of course. He broke down, afraid, and confessed they were still there. Newall had ordered him to say they had gone. I think it probable there was some garnish involved in the transaction, though he denies this.'

'What? I shall have that cheating, dissembling gaoler up before the aldermen for this. He insisted to me that they had been taken to another prison. But what of the four men? What is their condition?'

'Poor, master. They had been flogged, set to work stripping oakum and were half starved. But all are alive and will recover from their tribulations. I have returned them, well fed, to their company.'

'And did you question them about what they witnessed on the night of the fire?'

'I did, and they saw nothing but the fire itself. The chief among the four told me that when they saw it they rushed to help. They carried pails for two hours until it was doused. Then, exhausted, they fell asleep in the stables. They said it was warmer there than at the Theatre.'

'So they did not see a body taken to the house in Hog Lane?'

'No, master.'

'And they knew nothing of Lady Blanche?'

Boltfoot shook his head. 'Nor did they see anything suspicious.'

Shakespeare mulled over this information. Of course, Topcliffe could not have been sure whether or not the four men had seen anything, but when he discovered they had slept close by, he had thought it safest to keep them where Shakespeare could not question them. Where better than right under his nose? 'Well done, Boltfoot. You have been a diligent servant.'

'Thank you, master,' Boltfoot said, pleased, yet making no effort to leave. He was twisting his cap even harder. Any rooster or capon locked by the neck between his powerful hands would have been long dead by now. 'Mr Shakespeare,' he said, averting his gaze, 'I would ask you a favour, sir, a boon, if you will.'

Shakespeare sighed. 'Come to the point. I know very well that you want my permission to court and woo Jane. Yes?'

Boltfoot nodded sheepishly. 'Yes, master.'

'Now, why would a pretty young maiden like Jane Cawston wish to be wooed by a truculent, grizzled, stumpy old man of thirty or more like you, Boltfoot?'

Boltfoot's face fell. He looked genuinely hurt. 'I am sorry, master. You are right, of course.'

Shakespeare clapped his arm round Boltfoot's shoulders. 'You ass, Boltfoot. I jest! Of course you may woo Jane. I am delighted for you both. You're a lucky man and she is a fortunate young woman. Step out together with my blessing. I will pray that your children look more like her than you!'

Boltfoot grinned. 'I will pray for that, too, Mr Shakespeare. And thank you.'

Shakespeare smiled back at him. Boltfoot's joy threw his own sadness into stark relief, but he could not fail to be glad for such a man. No one could deserve happiness more than Boltfoot. Life had dealt him a poor hand and he deserved a change of fortune. 'Come, Boltfoot, let us call in Jane and share a glass of sweet wine to celebrate. I have been short of good cheer these past few days . . .'

The interview with Lord Howard of Effingham was stiff from the start. Howard was not pleased to see Shakespeare and betrayed no emotion as he listened to the news that the supposed killer of his adoptive daughter had been apprehended and executed. He nodded briskly. They stood in the entrance hallway to his house in Deptford. Shakespeare was not invited further in.

'So, that is the word being put about, is it, Mr Shakespeare?'

'My lord, the murderer, a Fleming called Herrick, was executed at Plymouth. He had been attempting to kill Vice-Admiral Drake. It is possible he thought he could get to Drake through you. I fear that is why he tried, at first, to become friendly with your daughter. Perhaps she found out too much about him and he wished to silence her.'

'Yes, yes. I have heard all this. I believe you did good work, Shakespeare, but I am not stupid, sir, and I have my own beliefs about the murder of Blanche as, I am sure, do you. However, we are all subjects of Her Majesty and it is our duty to accept certain things.'

'Yes, my lord.'

'So I will bid you good day.' He spoke curtly and held open the door, leaving Shakespeare no alternative but to leave.

As he stepped out on to the quayside, he felt as though he had betrayed Howard. A killer left to walk the streets and murder at will. Howard knew it, too. It was a solution of convenience, nothing more, and a stain on the country. Both men would have to swallow the bitter taste of bile.

Thomas Woode felt the cool linen sheets on his body. It was as if he was floating. If he lay still, there was no pain, but the slightest movement sent tremors of agony through him.

Catherine stood at the side of his bed. Gently she mopped his brow with a muslin cloth dipped in water.

'Thank you,' he said, barely moving his lips.

He had been at home two weeks now. Improvement was slow. They could not know whether he would ever walk again or even use his arms, so badly was he injured. His face was haggard and his hair had turned white, yet there was light in his eyes.

'I had resigned myself to death,' he said, then grimaced with the pain of saying so much.

'You are safe now. We are all safe.'

He closed his eyes and Margaret's face came to him again. Yes, he was safe now. Nothing could hurt him. And yet he knew that something was not right about this. Too many lives had been sacrificed already. It was important that no more should be given up . . .

'Is that it, then, Rose? Is that your baby?'

Rose Downie held him in her arms. He was so much bigger

now, but she knew instantly that it was William Edmund, her Mund. His blue eyes looked up at her without recognition. For two months now he had been held by another mother, the woman who had stolen him from the marketplace when Rose had put him down for a minute to argue with the stallholder.

'He is healthy and fine, is he not, Rose?'

The tears rolled down her cheeks. 'He is, Mr Topcliffe. I had forgot how blue were his eyes. And he is fatter now, much fatter.'

'Good. And I can tell you that the other baby, if such a monstrous creature merits the word, is now with its true mother. But, Rose, you must remember that you have still not delivered me up the foul priest Southwell.'

'I am sorry, Mr Topcliffe, but he was there. I implore you to believe me, sir.'

'I do, Rose, but that is not enough. You must stay in that house of traitors until he returns and then you must get word to me on the instant. For he will be back. Do you understand?'

Rose could not lift her eyes from Mund's face. She kissed his soft pink cheeks and the lids of his eyes. He was blurred by her tears. 'Yes, sir, but Lady Tanahill does not trust me. Nor do the other servants. They know, I think, that I did come to you with intelligence of the priest.'

'And have there been any visitors since last we spoke?'

Rose shook her head, all the while sobbing and smiling at the baby. 'No, sir.'

Topcliffe came to her and clasped her breasts. 'You are milking well, little cow. I can tell that your paps are full and heavy with creamy milk. Your baby will feed well.'

'Yes, sir.'

'Keep looking for priests, Rose. Should I hear of anything you have not told me it will be the worse for you. As I have restored your child, so can I remove it. Remember, Rose, you are my creature now. Never try to escape me.'

Topcliffe took his hands away from her breasts. Rose held the baby tighter. 'I will always tell you everything I know, Mr Topcliffe. I do swear it by all that is holy.'

'Good. And are you not interested to know where your child has been?'

'I am, sir, but he looks well cared-for, thank the Lord.'

'He was with the lady wife of a city merchant. Well-moneyed people, a knight of the realm. I will not disclose their name. The wife was distraught at the birth of her monster and was turned mad with grief. She did not know you. She happened to see you with your baby and followed you. When you put the baby down it gave her the chance she needed and a simple exchange was effected. Unfortunately for her, a wet-nurse noticed the difference in the children and gossiped, and when people gossip, I hear it all. You were wise to come to me as you did, Rose. Topcliffe is your man.' He reached his hand under her skirts and ran his hand along the inside of her thighs. She did not move away from him. He could do whatever he wanted because nothing else mattered now. She had her baby.

'Thank you for everything you have done, Mr Topcliffe. I will tell the world how kind you are, sir.' Yet somewhere at the back of her mind she thought of the child she had cared for these past weeks and felt a pang. She prayed it would be looked after well.

'Do that, Rose.'

Chapter 49

JOHN SHAKESPEARE REINED in his mare at the northern end of Seething Lane and slid from the saddle. He had spent a few days in Stratford and his thighs and back ached from the long ride home to London. But at least his physical wounds were healing well. He could use his left arm again and the bruises had left his face. He walked the grey mare into the cobbled courtyard of the mews and handed the reins to the ostler. He gave her a pat and rubbed her ear, then ordered the man to bring his saddle-bags and walked the twenty yards to his front door.

Jane opened it almost as soon as he touched it. 'Oh, master, thank the Lord you're home safe.'

Shakespeare smiled, but there was concern in his eyes. 'Whatever is the matter, Jane?'

'Nothing, Mr Shakespeare. But so much has happened since you have been away, I do not know where to begin.'

'Well, you could start by helping me pull off my boots. I fear they may be glued to my calves. And some ale would go down well.'

Jane's face broke into a smile and then she burst into tears, gathered up her skirts and ran into another room. Shakespeare watched her in bemusement, then took off his hat and sat on a three-cornered stool in the hallway to attempt the removal of his boots alone.

He had wrenched off the right one, after much tugging, and was working the left one loose when he heard the door open and looked up. Their eyes met and held.

'Catherine,' he said. It was little more than a whisper.

She stood in the doorway. 'Hello, John.' She held out a paper. 'I bring you an invitation. From Little Bird and Queenie. It says they are opening an establishment of unimaginable luxury and would be honoured to entertain you as a guest.'

Shakespeare tore his eyes from hers and tugged impatiently at his boot. He did not know what to say. 'They helped me with my investigation, pointed me towards Plymouth,' he muttered.

'Well, you must certainly accept their invitation.' She noticed his fumblings. 'Do you need assistance?'

He laughed and tears pricked his eyes. 'Indeed I do.'

She knelt before him and pulled his boot loose, then held it aloft. 'Perhaps you should dismiss that useless maidservant of yours and take me on instead.'

'Catherine?'

'Indeed it is I.'

'Thank God you're here.'

'Or you would never have loosened your left boot.'

She rose from her knees. She had never looked lovelier. Her dark hair shone and he could not stop himself reaching out to touch it.

'You may kiss me if you wish, John.'

He took her in his arms and their mouths met. She let his boot slip to the floor, then slid her hands round him and held him to her. 'I have caught you now, Mr Shakespeare.'

'Did I fight so hard to escape you, mistress?'

She moved her head this way and that. 'Perchance not, but I have caught you anyway.'

'And I you, I hope. Will you marry me, mistress?'

'I will insist upon it, sir, for I believe you have already stolen my maidenhead and such a theft cannot go unpunished.'

'As I recall, you colluded in the misdemeanour.'

'Then we are confederates and must suffer our punishment together. Marriage it must be.'

'And all for a maidenhead.' He held her closer. They kissed again.

At last she stood back. 'Well, sir, I see you are as forward as ever. I offered you a kiss, not a feasting.'

He laughed. 'Catherine, how has this come about? I thought your duty to Mr Woode had precluded our match. Has he recovered sufficiently?'

Of a sudden she became serious. 'No.' She shook her head. 'He will never fully recover, but we have a plan. Mr Woode insisted on it and I can see no barrier to it. Though you may have objections, John.'

'What plan?'

'This news should not come from me but from Boltfoot and Jane. They will be seeking your permission to marry. Jane's father has already blessed their union.'

'Well, of course I will permit them to marry. But how does that affect us?'

'Mr Woode is crippled and needs more help than I can give him alone. He is a big man and I am not strong enough to lift him and attend to all his wants. Jane suggested she and Boltfoot might go to him. She does get on exceeding well with the children.'

Shakespeare laughed. It was all so improbable. 'So we are to do an exchange. Jane and Boltfoot go to Thomas Woode and I receive you in return.'

'Not a very good exchange, is it, John? Lose two, gain one.'

'Well, no, put like that it is not at all a good trade. And most like I will have to turn to schoolmastering, for I will of a certain fall foul of Mr Secretary.'

'We will both be teachers, then, for I will still go to Dowgate to tutor the children. I am, after all, their governess.'

'Two and a half to Mr Woode, then, and only half to me.'

'Do we have a trade, then, sir?'

'Oh, yes, Catherine, we have a trade. But Boltfoot still works for me as and when he is needed.'

'Let us shake on it like merchants, then.'

'No,' said Shakespeare, reaching for her again, 'let us seal it with a kiss instead.'

Father Robert Southwell, also known as Cotton, walked the dark early-morning streets from his new lodging in Holborn towards the bridge. He was on his way to the Marshalsea once more, to bring mass and comfort to the faithful there. As he approached the river, a grey fog rose, swirling, from the water.

The stooped, cowled figure of a woman hurried past him along New Fish Street. Southwell did not break his stride, but watched her bustle ahead of him. She was bent over as if she would shrink herself to the size of an ant and not be seen. She walked on to London Bridge and her pace faltered. She trod slowly along the central walkway through the grand houses that lined most of the crossing. Southwell held back, observing her. She was more than halfway across, just before the Drawbridge Gate, when she stopped. She went to the edge of the bridge and looked down from the parapet on the eastern side. Below her the Thames surged and raced and beckoned.

In her arms, beneath her long cloak, she held the baby with the strange cry and the curious, monstrous eyes. All its body apart from its head was wrapped in sacking. For a brief moment she looked at it. Then she slipped a large stone into the sack with the baby. She pulled the sacking over the baby's head and tied it with string. The baby screamed from within like a cat.

Southwell froze. It was a sound he had heard before in another place. He moved towards the woman, but she was already holding the sack with the baby and the stone over the parapet. Without hesitation, she let it drop into the fast-flowing waters below. For a moment it seemed it might float; the sackcloth billowed over the swell of the water, but then it filled and sank. Tears streamed down the woman's face. She turned, saw the face of the man approaching her and brushed past him. Without looking round, she hurried back over the bridge, back to her large house, her tapestries, her clothes of gold and silver threads, her many servants and her rich merchant husband.

BLESSED VICTORY FOR BOLD SIR FRANCIS

✣ ✣ ✣ ✣

Forgive us, dear reader, for the recent absence of this your best-favoured broadsheet, but we have lately sustained an enforced absence. That episode is happily at an end thanks to the gracious offices of that most loyal and upright servant of the Crown Mr Richard Topcliffe, the Member of Parliament for Old Sarum. We are now at liberty to do our pleasant duty as London's foremost harbinger of news and report on a fortunate event. Let us ring the church bells with joy and set bonfires in the streets.

A pinnace from the fleet of Sir Francis Drake has this week sailed into Plymouth harbour, bearing news that the beloved admiral has gained a victory worthy of being writ in the annals of English history alongside Agincourt, Crécy and Poitiers. Drake, our greatest English mariner and sometime hero of the circumnavigation, has saved England from attack with a masterly display of daring and seamanship. We have learnt that on the evening of 29 April last, the Admiral led a bold attack on Cadiz harbour, where he fearlessly engaged the King of Spain's vaunted galleons, destroying thirty-one vessels and carrying off six, for the loss of no English ships. The cowardly Spanish put up little resistance. In the most part, they did attempt to flee the man they call the Dragon, so much did they fear him, but to little avail.

Not a whit afraid, Sir Francis remained in the bay for three days, gathering plunder and putting Señor Felipe's ships to the torch. All the while, ashore, the King's soldiers looked on in wonder and durst not counter-attack.

Sir Francis's fleet is now believed to be stationed off the coast of Portugal, awaiting the Spanish King's treasure ships and preparing to do yet more harm to his ports and shipping. It is now the great pleasure of *The London Informer* hereby to predict with confidence that Drake has rung the death knell for Philip's armada and his so-called Enterprise of England. It will not happen, my lords, ladies and gentlemen. The armada will never sail for England. Yet again, Sir Francis Drake has pre-empted the enemy so that we may all sleep abed without concern for the safekeeping of our sovereign or her people. God Save the Queen.

Walstan Glebe, publisher

Acknowledgements

I AM INDEBTED TO the writings of many superb historians, but a few books merit special mention for the assistance they have given me in understanding the late-Elizabethan period.

Most importantly, I would like to pay tribute to *The Life of Robert Southwell* by Christopher Devlin, a vivid biography and history that was first published in 1956 and makes one feel as if the events described happened last week. Other books I would particularly recommend include: *The Defeat of the Spanish Armada* by Garrett Mattingly; *The Confident Hope of a Miracle* by Neil Hanson; *Elizabeth's Spy Master* by Robert Hutchinson; *God's Secret Agents* by Alice Hogge; *The Awful End of Prince William the Silent* by Lisa Jardine; *The Secret Voyage of Sir Francis Drake* by Samuel Bawlf; *A Brief History of the Tudor Age* by Jasper Ridley; *The Reckoning* by Charles Nicholl; *The Elizabethan Underworld* by Gamini Salgado; *The A to Z of Elizabethan London*, compiled by Adrian Prockter and Robert Taylor; *Elizabeth's London* by Liza Picard; *Shakespeare* by Bill Bryson; *The Master Mariner* by Nicholas Monsarrat; *The Coming of the Book* by Lucien Febvre and Henri-Jean Martin; *The Englishman's Food* by J. C. Drummond and Anne Wilbraham; *Invisible Power* by Alan Haynes; *Palaces & Progresses of Elizabeth I* by Ian Dunlop; *Entertaining Elizabeth I* by June Osborne.

I would also like to thank my wife, Naomi, my brother, Brian, and the Reverend Selwyn Tillett for their invaluable help.

Background Notes

Pursuivants: state-employed officers with the power to execute warrants of search and arrest. They were a rag-tag bunch of armed mercenaries, often hastily assembled from local people, court hangers-on, legal officials and even convicts, all made legitimate by wearing the Queen's escutcheon. They were particularly used in hunting Roman Catholic priests and those who harboured them. Christopher Devlin in *The Life of Robert Southwell* describes them as 'hounds to whom harrying women was cheaper and more sensational than stag-hunting'.

Priest holes: hiding places built deep within the fabric of Catholic houses. The greatest exponent of the craft was Nicholas Owen, a diminutive carpenter and lay Jesuit brother from Oxford, who built many priest holes before being starved out of one himself and dying under torture in the Tower in 1606, staying silent to the end. Owen, who was known as 'Little John', was canonised and beatified in the twentieth century. One of the finest remaining examples of his work, which visitors can enter, is at the National Trust property Oxburgh Hall, Norfolk.

Intelligencers: spies reporting to the Principal Secretary Sir Francis Walsingham, who is seen as the father of the modern secret service. His network of agents and correspondents encompassed Europe and the Middle East, yet he was expected to fund the operation himself and was so impoverished at his death in 1590 that he was buried privately at night, to avoid the cost of the splendid funeral so immense a figure might have warranted.

Jesuits: members of the Society of Jesus, a highly disciplined religious order founded in 1534 by the Spaniard Ignatius Loyola with the aim of converting heathens to Christianity. They took vows of poverty, chastity and pilgrimage to Jerusalem (though this was, at that time, impossible). They were known for their unflinching obedience to the Pope and for their care of the sick and destitute. Jesuits soon became the 'shock troops of the Counter-Reformation' (well, that's the way the Protestants saw them), sending the likes of Robert Southwell and Edmund Campion to martyrdom in England. Elizabeth I and her ministers regarded Jesuits as traitors ready to resort to assassination to restore the Pope's authority. In 1606, the Jesuit Fr Henry Garnet (who had arrived in England with Southwell in 1586) was hanged, drawn and quartered, having been implicated in the Gunpowder Plot.

Weapons: firearms were rapidly replacing the medieval crossbow and longbow. The most frightening innovation for monarchs was the wheel-lock pistol, which was replacing the matchlock. Wheel-locks had a mechanism which span a serrated steel edge against a piece of iron pyrite, sending sparks into the gunpowder, which exploded and discharged the ball or bullet. Previously, with matchlock weapons (including the cumbersome old arquebus, familiarly known as hagbut or hackbut), the gunpowder had to be ignited by a pre-lighted taper, or match. The big advantage of wheel-locks was that they could be held in one hand, be primed and loaded in advance and be small enough to be concealed under a cloak or in a sleeve. Ornate wheel-locks became the must-have accessory for men of substance and whole cavalry squadrons carried them into battle, each man carrying two or more primed weapons in his hands and belts. Men commonly armed themselves with swords and daggers (a poniard is a small dagger). Guards carried pole weapons – pikes and halberds. The pike was little more than a pole with a spearhead, while the halberd had a three-edged head: axe, pike and hook.

Whores: it is curious that the seamier side of life flourished so well at a time of great religious fervour. Southwark was famous for its brothels, which the London authorities could do nothing to control, being outside the City walls. Prostitution was illegal but bribery of constables was commonplace. Whores were often called 'Winchester Geese', as much of Southwark came under the control of the Bishop of Winchester. Other slang names included: bawdy basket, callet, drab, punk, hobby horse, stale, strange woman, strumpet, trug. A brothel madam was known as 'Mistress of the Game', and her clients were called 'commiters' or 'hobby horse men'. Sexually transmitted disease – the 'French Welcome' – was rife and, in the days before antibiotics, virtually untreatable (though that didn't prevent early quacks devising and selling so-called cures).

Army and Navy: Unlike the professional Spanish troops, England did not have a standing army. In times of trouble, such as the impending Armada invasion, militias were raised by the nobility from among their tenants and by the great craft guilds. Nor was the Navy a permanent fixture, but thanks to the enthusiasm for privateering of Drake, Hawkins and others, the English had become great sea warriors. Their ships were designed to be leaner and faster than the towering Spanish galleons which had an advantage in close combat, but were easily harried and outgunned by the English at longer range.

The Privy Council: the rough equivalent of a modern-day Cabinet of ministers. During Elizabeth's reign it varied in numbers from ten to twenty. The Queen did not attend meetings, but the proceedings were reported to her assiduously and she had the final say over matters of policy. Generally, she expected her ministers to get on with the day-to-day business of running the country. As well as executive powers, the Council also acted as a court when it sat in Star Chamber (the old council chamber at Westminster). Lord Burghley and Sir Francis Walsingham were the dominant Privy Council men for much of the reign.

Prison: there were fourteen jails in London. A wide variety of offences could land someone there, ranging from vagrancy, debt or fortune-telling to the most severe of crimes. The conditions prisoners had to endure depended largely on how much garnish (bribe money) they could afford to give the keeper. They were surprisingly open, however, enabling Robert Southwell and other priests to visit prisoners and say mass. The Marshalsea and the Clink in Southwark were seen as softer options than the City jails such as Newgate, Bridewell, Wood Street Counter and the Fleet. Southwell's companion, Fr Henry Garnet, wrote of feeling 'safe from danger' while visiting prison.

Tobacco: tobacco was *not* introduced to England by Sir Walter Ralegh. Though he sponsored ventures to Virginia in the